WHAT LIES WITHIN

Scott Stokes

Inspiring Publishers
P.O. Box 159, Calwell, ACT Australia 2905
Email: publishaspg@gmail.com
http://www.inspiringpublishers.com

 A catalogue record for this book is available from the National Library of Australia

National Library of Australia The Prepublication Data Service

Author: Scott Stokes
Title: What Lies Within
Genre: Science-Fiction, Police Drama, Action

Paperback ISBN: 978-1-923449-42-8

Acknowledgements

I would like to express my deepest gratitude to everyone who helped bring this novel to life. Storytelling is something I enjoy, but reading and writing have never come naturally to me. Coupled with mental health challenges, the process has often been difficult. Fortunately, the support of modern technologies—and, more importantly, the incredible encouragement from friends and family—helped me persevere.

First, thank you to my beautiful wife, Helen, for her honesty and support, even when it wasn't easy given the complexities of my mental health.

Second, but no less important, thank you to my family and friends who generously offered feedback—some even on earlier stories that have yet to move forward.

My goal is to create stories that readers will find worth their time and, if I'm lucky, maybe even enjoyable.

1

In the fading light of late afternoon, Sam Caldwell blended effortlessly into the crowd, his unremarkable appearance and calm demeanour making him virtually invisible. Today, his latest job had brought him to a large rally downtown. The crowd was a sea of passionate faces, waving signs and chanting slogans demanding the defunding and greater transparency of the CIA. The energy was electric, a mix of frustration, hope, and determination. Sam moved with the flow of the marchers, keeping a safe distance from his target while ensuring he didn't stand out.

Sam was a ghost, seamlessly merging with the crowd. At thirty-three, with brown hair cut in a no-nonsense short back-and-sides style and an average, unthreatening build, he was perfect for his line of work. Wearing a plain grey jacket and khaki pants, his attire as ordinary as his face, he was an everyman—and that was his greatest asset as a private investigator specialising in surveillance. Sam preferred the quiet art of observation, finding satisfaction in piecing together a puzzle without ever being noticed.

His target, a middle-aged man with a shock of silver hair, was in the thick of the action, his voice rising above the others as he joined in the chants. Sam observed him, snapping occasional photos with his phone, making quick verbal notes into the recorder. He didn't need to be close; years of experience had taught him how to capture the necessary details from a distance.

The rally snaked through the city streets, the protesters' voices echoing off the tall buildings. Sam kept a steady pace, eyes never straying far from his target. He had no interest in the political message of the rally; his job was strictly professional. Whether the protesters were right or wrong, or what the CIA had done, didn't matter to him. All that mattered was the man he was following and the evidence he needed to gather.

Lost in his thoughts, Sam didn't notice the tension building in the crowd at first. But then, like a shockwave, it hit him. A ripple of unease spread through the marchers, and Sam's instincts immediately kicked in. He heard a loud, commanding voice cut through the chanting, a man's voice, sharp and urgent.

"Stop! Stop or I'll shoot!"

The words sliced through the air. Sam's heart rate spiked, and his senses went on high alert. He turned just in time to see a flash of movement—a woman sprinting through the crowd, her face pale and terrified, her white coat trailing behind her like a cape.

The gunshot rang out, loud and jarring. Chaos erupted as people scattered in every direction. Before Sam could react, the woman collided with him, knocking him off balance. He reached out instinctively, steadying her, feeling warm, sticky blood seep onto his hands. She had been shot.

They spun together, the force of the collision turning Sam so his back was to the woman's pursuers. She clung to him, her breath ragged and desperate. Up close, her eyes were wide with pain, but there was a fierce determination in them.

"Teddy, do the right thing," she whispered, her voice barely audible over the roar of the crowd. "No one can have it. Expose it, then destroy it." Her words were urgent, as if she knew her time was running out.

With one last, pained glance, she pulled away, raising a gun to her face—a black nine-millimetre Smith & Wesson. Before Sam could react, she pressed it under her chin and pulled the trigger. The sound was deafening. She collapsed to the ground, lifeless, like a ragdoll with its strings cut.

Sam stood frozen, disbelief washing over him. The world seemed to move in slow motion as the crowd around him erupted into full-blown panic. He barely registered the heavy footsteps approaching until it was too late.

A sharp pain exploded in his neck and shoulder, as he was knocked to the ground. A man, built like a bouncer and covered in menacing tattoos, loomed over him. The man's eyes were cold, calculating. He pointed a gun directly at Sam's face.

"Don't move," he growled, his voice low and menacing.

For a moment, time stood still. Sam's mind raced, trying to piece together what was happening. He could see another man kneeling over the woman's body, being jostled by panicked protesters.

"Does she have it!" the bouncer called out, momentarily turning his head to look at his colleague.

The momentary distraction gave Sam just enough time to act. With a burst of adrenaline, he rolled to the side, kicking out at the bouncer's knees. The man buckled and fell, hitting his head on the ground, his grip on the gun faltering. Sam took his chance, scrambling to his feet and weaving into the panicked crowd.

Breathless, he ducked into an alleyway, pressing his back against the cold, damp brick wall. His mind was racing, replaying the woman's final words. Who was Teddy? And what was it that no one could have?

In the distance Sam could hear the wail of sirens. He knew one thing for sure: he needed to get out, fast. When they realised the woman was dead, Sam suspected those chasing her wouldn't be far behind—and they'd probably be looking for him. Pushing off the wall, he straightened his jacket and slipped into the shadows. His target was long gone, but now, his priority was getting home safe. It wasn't going to be easy; he still had to make it back to his car without getting followed.

2

Sam pushed open the door to his apartment, the weight of this afternoon's events pressing down on him, replaying in his mind like a broken record. His girlfriend, Emily, looked up from the couch, her face lighting up as she saw him.

"Hey, you're home," she said, her smile a beacon of warmth in the dimly lit room.

Sam forced a smile, hoping it didn't look as strained as it felt.

"Yeah, long day," he replied, dropping his keys into a bowl that sat on the small end table just inside the door.

"I'm going to have a shower." The image of the woman's lifeless body and the sound of the gun shot echoing in his mind. Her white coat, stained deep red.

"You look beat," Emily said, her eyes filled with concern.

Sam nodded, choosing his words carefully.

"Today was a little unusual, but still, the usual surveillance stuff, nonetheless."

He hoped the half-truth would suffice. The last thing he wanted was for Emily to worry about the grimmer aspects of his job.

As he began to undress, he couldn't shake the image of the woman's eyes—desperate, pleading, resigned, and distant. He took off his jacket, noticing the blood stains, suddenly thankful for its dark colour. He looked down at his pants, black chinos. They too had blood on them. He would need to undress in the attached bathroom, so he did not get any blood on the carpet.

He dropped his coat on the tiled bathroom floor. His fingers trembled slightly as he reached for his belt, unbuckling it with mechanical precision. He kicked off his shoes and unbuttoned his pants, adding them to the growing pile of bloody clothes on the floor.

He paused, looking down at the ruined clothes. Blood smeared the white tiles, a grim reminder of the day's violence, and the blood-stained white coat the woman was wearing. It was then he realised something was off. He reached for the gun he carried in his shoulder holster, his hand grasping at empty air. Panic flared briefly before he forced himself to think. The woman. She must have taken it during the chaos. His blood turned to ice.

His mind was flooded with the repercussions of what happened. He knew he would have to report his gun missing. It was registered to him. The police would absolutely have his gun. The investigation of her death would inevitably lead them to track down the gun owner; him. He had nothing to hide, but it would look suspicious if he did not report it missing. There was no avoiding it.

Sam ran a hand through his hair and sighed. Tomorrow. He'd go to the station tomorrow. All he wanted to do now was get clean and sit on the couch with Emily, wrapped in her warmth, letting it ease his mind.

Sam walked back into the living room, the day's events still weighing on his shoulders, but less so now, having finished his shower. Emily was still on the couch, her eyes glued to the television screen. The news anchor's solemn voice filled the room, reporting on the chaos that had erupted at the CIA reform protest rally. Sam's heart sank as he heard about the shooting, a woman suspected of having shot herself.

"The reasons for her actions were still unknown," the news anchor was saying.

"Can we watch something else?" Sam asked, trying to keep his voice steady.

Emily turned to him. He did his best to put on a neutral expression, but he could see in Emily's own expression that he was not doing a very good job of it.

"Are you okay? You look kinda worried?" Emily asked, concern now etched on her face.

"Oh, I'm fine. The person I was following was at that rally," Sam said, not wanting to lie to Emily, but also not wanting to tell everything that happened. That would just make her worry.

"Oh, my God!" she said, starting to get up. "Did you see anything?"

"Oh, no, I didn't see anything, but the crowd certainly became chaotic. I lost the person I was following, so I'm a little frustrated," Sam replied—half-truths again.

Emily reached for the remote, switching the channel to a sitcom. He sank onto the couch beside her, grateful for the distraction.

Sam found solace in the comfort of his couch, the presence of Emily offering a gentle reprieve. They decided to watch a movie, something light and humorous to contrast the darkness he had encountered earlier.

As the screen lit up with scenes designed to provoke laughter, he felt the weight of the day begin to lift, albeit slowly. Emily nestled closer, her warmth a reminder of the life and love that still thrived despite the shadows that loomed over his profession.

As a private detective, he had become accustomed to the darker facets of human existence, regularly encountering scenes that most people would find unimaginable. However, familiarity did not render him immune to the emotional toll. Each incident left a mark, a subtle scar on his psyche that he carried with him.

The memory of the woman's despair haunted him, a reminder of the fragility of life and the burdens people often bear in silence.

Sam could tell Emily sensed his tension. She knew something was troubling him, a shadow that clung to his usually resilient spirit. Yet, when she asked, he brushed it off with a reassuring smile, insisting it was nothing.

Sam didn't want to burden her with the weight of the day's horrors, believing that shielding her from the darker aspects of his job was a way to protect their shared peace.

Despite his efforts to appear unaffected, he knew Emily could see through him.

As the movie progressed, bursts of laughter filled the room—each instance providing an emotional band aid to the sorrow of the day.

Sam glanced at Emily, grateful for her presence and the sense of normalcy she provided. Her laughter was contagious, and he found himself smiling, the heaviness in his chest beginning to ease.

While the image of the woman's final moments lingered at the edges of his mind, the warmth of being with Emily reminded him of the importance of these small joys.

It was in these moments, wrapped in the simplicity of her love and laughter, that he remembered how much he loved her.

3

The next morning, Sam awoke with a sense of dread. Today was not going to be a good day—he had to tell the police the woman who shot herself yesterday did it with his gun. He dressed quickly, quietly picked up the plastic bag filled with clothes, then headed to the door.

Emily was already in the kitchen. She got up early every morning to exercise. Normally, this worked out great for Sam; by the time he dragged himself out of bed and into the kitchen, Emily would already have a pot of coffee brewing. Sharing a morning coffee with her was one of life's little pleasures he loved. Today, however, he hoped to slip out of the house unnoticed. He didn't want to explain what was in the bag.

"Sorry, babe, I have to head out. I'll see you tonight," Sam said. That sounded terrible to him—far too fake—but he couldn't do anything about it now.

As he moved towards the door, Emily appeared, her eyes narrowing with curiosity. "You were going to leave without even a goodbye kiss!" she said. Then she noticed the plastic bag.

"What's in the bag?" she asked, her tone light but probing.

Sam forced a casual smile, trying to mask his unease. "Just some clothes for the dry cleaner," he replied, waving a hand dismissively.

Her gaze lingered on him, suspicion and concern evident in her eyes.

"I think I have some clothes that need dry cleaning. Can I add to the bag?" she said, turning slightly to head into the bedroom.

Sam shook his head quickly, adjusting his grip on the bag. "No, sorry. I have to go. I have to get to the office early," he lied, his words causing Emily to stop mid-step. "I'm meeting with a new client and was hoping to drop this off on the way," he added, nodding towards the bag. "I promise I will make it up to you," he assured her, hoping she wouldn't press further.

Before she could react, he stepped in and kissed her—a quick peck that said the conversation was over. He turned and opened the door, feeling the weight of his unspoken truth between them.

The streets were eerily quiet, the early hour meaning most people were still asleep or just getting their first cup of coffee. He knew the dry cleaner would be open. Mr. Kim was an early riser— he had previously told Sam that the early mornings helped him get more done.

The dry cleaner was a small, unassuming shop tucked between a bakery and a bookstore. Sam had been coming here for years, and over time, he had built a warm rapport with Mr. Kim. The jovial owner always greeted him with a wide smile and a friendly chat. As Sam pushed open the door, the familiar scent of freshly cleaned clothes wafted over him. Mr. Kim looked up from behind the counter, his face lighting up with recognition.

"Sam, my friend! What brings you in so early today?" he called out, the genuine camaraderie in his voice offering a momentary comfort amidst the turmoil swirling in Sam's mind.

Sam put the bag of clothes on the counter, "I have an early meeting," he lied, doubling down on what he said to Emily. The bag knocked against a small box of personal knickknacks, the impact closing its open lid.

"Oh, sorry, Mr. Kim," Sam said, moving the box slightly and lifting the lid again. Inside were various personal items customers had left in their clothes—everyone who came here knew to check the box while they waited. Mr Kim would take the box home with him every day to keep the things safe. There was nothing in there for him.

Mr. Kim opened the bag and pulled out the bloodstained clothes. "Is blood something that can be removed?" Sam asked.

"Looks like you had a rough night," Mr. Kim said.

"You could say that," Sam replied, trying to keep his tone light. "Had a bit of an accident."

Mr. Kim nodded, eyeing the bloodstains with a knowing look. "No problem. I'll take care of it."

"Thank you, Mr. Kim. I really don't know how you get things this clean, but I appreciate it. Say hi to Mrs. Kim," Sam said as he left the store.

With that taken care of, it was time to face the music at the police station.

Emily walked into her real estate office, still trying to shake the nagging feeling from this morning. She made her way to her desk, her friend Victoria already seated, organising paperwork. Victoria looked up, and Emily tried to smile, but it came out crooked.

"What's up with you this morning?" Victoria asked. She was always one to get straight to the point—sometimes bordering on rude.

"Huh?" Emily said reflexively as she put her bag in a drawer and sat down.

"'Huh'? What the hell is 'huh'? I have never heard you say that word, ever," Victoria said, surprised.

Emily sat her bag down. "Oh, sorry, I was just thinking about something weird Sam did."

"Well now, this sounds like a fun conversation. Come on, spill it."

Emily looked at Victoria, but the smile on Victoria's face caused her to also smile. She took a breath. "Sam got home late last night, and he seemed a bit off."

"Did he say why he was late?" Victoria asked, her tone direct and no-nonsense.

Emily shook her head, frustration evident in her expression. "No, he just said work ran late and didn't give any details. Then, he was unusually affectionate, almost like something was wrong, or he was trying to make up for something. It just didn't feel right."

Victoria's expression grew less happy and more serious as she listened. "That does sound odd. Did anything else happen?"

Emily nodded, her unease growing. "Yes. He was in such a rush to leave this morning, he almost forgot to kiss me goodbye—which he never does. And even stranger, he was taking a bag of dry cleaning with him. When I asked to add to it, he got really protective of the bag and wouldn't let me."

Victoria's eyes narrowed thoughtfully. "That seems shady, Em. He is definitely hiding something. Maybe he hooked up with someone. Or he's having a full-on affair," she said bluntly, an innocent smile tugging at the corner of her mouth.

"Jesus, Vic!" Emily was shocked but could see the beginnings of a smile on her friend's lips. Despite that, her heart did sink a little at the thought. She thought back on the night. The behaviour did fit.

"You think he could be having an affair?" she whispered, the possibility making her feel sick to her stomach.

Victoria laughed, her expression softening slightly, "No," she said. "Well… I hope not." Again, a small smile. "In all seriousness, you should talk to him about it though."

Emily nodded slowly, feeling a mix of dread and determination. "You're right. I need to know what's going on, whatever it is," she said, her voice firm despite the fear gnawing at her.

'Look, Em, whatever it is, I am sure there is a good explanation," Victoria said reassuringly. "Whatever happens, you'll get through it. Just remember—you deserve honesty and respect."

Emily gave her friend a grateful smile, feeling a little more grounded. "Thanks, Vic. I'll talk to him tonight and find out what's really going on."

As she turned to start her workday, Emily felt a renewed sense of resolve. She couldn't let this uncertainty ruin her day.

Sam made his way to the police station. The streets were still empty. Eventually, he arrived, the building looming ahead, its stone facade imposing and unwelcoming. He pulled from the road into the station driveway.

Directly ahead of him was a large gate: a sturdy, imposing barrier of heavy metal, designed to withstand forced entry. Designed to control access to the premises, keep the attending officers safe, while also keeping any incarcerated person in. To set it off, a large police badge emblazoned a symbol of authority and protection.

Sam did not go anywhere near the gate. Instead, he turned left into the public parking area and found a free park. Stepping out of the car, he stood for a moment, looking at the dull concrete building. He did not know exactly what awaited him inside. Surely, as an innocent party, it could not be anything bad, but he was an experienced enough detective to know that wasn't always true. At least, not at first.

"Come on, Sam, get it together," he muttered to himself, trying to steady his racing thoughts. "You're a licensed and experienced private detective. You've faced worse than this." He took a deep breath, attempting to calm the knot of anxiety in his chest. "Losing a gun happens, even to the best. The important thing is to be honest and straightforward with the police. You've built a solid reputation; they're going to understand."

He paused, looking at his reflection in the window.

"You've handled complex cases, solved mysteries, and navigated far trickier situations. This is just another bump in the road. Own up to it, deal with it professionally, and move on."

With one final deep breath, he readied himself for the conversation ahead.

4

The inside of the police station was a flurry of activity and muted conversations. The fluorescent lights cast a harsh, clinical glow over the room, revealing scuffed vinyl floors and walls adorned with bulletin boards filled with wanted posters and public notices. A long, low counter stretched across one side, behind which a few officers were busy with paperwork and phone calls. The air smelled faintly of stale coffee and disinfectant.

To the left, rows of metal benches were occupied by people in various states of distress, waiting their turn to speak with an officer. A wall-mounted LED clock ticked away the seconds with unrelenting precision, marking the time as Sam took a deep breath and approached the front desk.

It took a moment for the officer to look up in response to his approach, something that did not improve Sam's mood. When she finally did look up, her expression was one of practiced indifference. "Can I help you?"

"Yeah," Sam said, trying to sound casual. "I need to report something," he said, his voice just above a whisper.

"Sorry, what was that? You have to speak up."

"I need to report something," Sam repeated, more clearly this time. "It is about a shooting yesterday. A woman committed suicide."

"Name?"

"What?" Sam said, surprised by the question.

The officer's eyes narrowed slightly. "Name?"

"Um... Sam Caldwell."

"And what exactly are you reporting."

Sam gave a wry smile. Was this woman even human? She seemed to operate purely on a programmed script.

"Like I said, there was a shooting yesterday," his voice slightly raised, annoyed by her lack of urgency. "A woman shot herself on the street. I was there. I think she may have shot herself with my gun, which I did not realise she had taken."

The front desk officer looked at Sam, as if trying to process what he had just said.

She typed something into her computer, then looked back up. "You can take a seat. An officer will be out shortly to take your statement." She nodded towards the benches across the room.

A few minutes later a uniformed officer appeared and escorted Sam into the Squad Room. A few sour glances followed from people who had been waiting much longer.

The Squad Room was an open-plan area, filled with desks and cubicles, each with a computer, a phone, and office supplies. At every desk, someone was providing a statement. Other areas were sectioned off behind glass—labs, offices, and a heavy-looking metal door. It was towards this door that Sam was led.

Beyond it was a bland concrete corridor lined with more heavy-set doors. The officer led him through one and into what looked like an interrogation room. Inside were two chairs and a metal table, on which sat a tray.

Sam was told to sit, remove all belongings from his pockets, and place them on the tray—including the watch on his wrist. He did so.

The officer picked up the tray and said, "Someone will be in to see you shortly." Without another word, he turned and left, taking the tray with him.

"What is going on?" Sam called out.

Silence.

Then the door shut behind him with a solid, echoing thud.

The walls, painted institutional grey, seemed to close in, their oppressive blankness amplifying his unease. The cold, plastic chair offered no comfort, and the single, bare table between him and the door felt like a barrier to understanding why he was there. The silence was thick, punctuated only by the distant hum of fluorescent lights overhead.

With no clock in sight, time stretched endlessly. His mind raced through a whirlwind of questions and scenarios, each more daunting than the last. The absence of any explanation from the officer heightened his anxiety, leaving him to grapple with the gnawing fear of the unknown and the foreboding sense that his life was teetering on the edge.

This was why Sam had chosen the simple private detective life of surveillance and reporting. Being a ghost was a skill he could be happy with. Playing the game of psychology to get inside the head of a perpetrator was something else entirely—something he was not emotionally equipped for.

After what seemed like hours, Sam heard the heavy lock open. He sat upright in anticipation, not realising he had been slouching. The door opened and two men in dark suits entered. Their presence was immediately unsettling. One was tall and lean, with sharp features and piercing eyes. The other was broad-shouldered, his burly build reminiscent of a nightclub bouncer.

Sam's heart skipped a beat as he recognised the second man as the one who had knocked him aside the night before.

The tall man was carrying the tray, which Sam could see now contained his gun.

"Mr. Caldwell," the tall one said, his voice clipped and formal. "We're with the CIA. We have a few questions for you." He sat on the chair and put the tray on the table just in front of him.

Sam's mind raced. CIA? What the hell was going on? "About what?" he asked, keeping his voice steady.

The agent smiled, his piercing eyes burning a hole in his soul. "I would find it very hard to believe you do not know what it was about."

"Ok… look… all I know is the woman shot herself, then that night when I got home, I realised my gun was missing. So, I assumed she took my gun out of my holster without me realising it."

"What did you do with your clothes."

"I took them to the dry cleaners, this morning, on my way here."

The tall CIA agent smiled, though it did nothing to relax his gaze. "See, now we are getting somewhere." He leaned back in his chair, spreading his arms wide. "And where is this dry cleaner?"

"Um…in a strip mall on Everly Drive."

A vague unease gnawed at Sam as he replayed the conversation in his mind. He was certain he had inadvertently revealed something crucial, though the specifics eluded him. The sensation of an irretrievable slip lingered, a whisper of lost control he couldn't quite grasp.

"Ok, so you went home, undressed, put your clothes into a bag, then gave them to a dry cleaner, who, I can only assume, pulled the clothes out to look at them…" He paused, seemingly waiting for Sam to finish the rest of the thought. But Sam had nothing to add.

"And…nothing?" the agent prodded.

"And…what?" Sam replied, confused.

Suddenly, the burly agent stepped forward, close to Sam. "Let's cut the crap! We know you have the drive. Where is it?"

Sam shook his head. "What the fuck are you talking about, a drive. I don't know anything about a drive. All I know is a woman likely killed herself with my gun, and I am here to report that."

The first agent leaned back in his chair and crossed his arms, eyes narrowing. "You expect us to believe that? A woman you barely knew kills herself with your gun, and you don't think that's suspicious?"

"Of course it's suspicious! But that doesn't mean I took anything from her," Sam said, trying to make them understand that he hadn't taken anything at all.

"Then where did it go? Things don't just disappear. She had the drive before she ran into you. Then she shoots herself—and miraculously, it's gone."

"How many times do I have to say it? I… don't… have… it!"

The burly agent leaned in again, this time so close that Sam could smell his breath—a rancid mix of cigarettes and coffee. "You better start remembering. Because if someone else gets their hands on that drive before we do, things are not going to go well for you— or your family."

That was the last straw.

All the anxiety Sam had felt was now replaced with frustration.

"Get out of my face," he snapped, meeting the agent's gaze unflinchingly. "I told you—I don't know anything."

The door burst open.

Two police detectives stepped into the room. One was a gruff-looking older man with a permanent scowl; the other, a woman with a calm, steady demeanour.

"That's enough," the female detective said. "Time for you two idiots to leave. You have no right to be here."

The burly agent glared at her, his eyes full of the quiet misogyny that still permeated far too many corners of law enforcement. She held his stare, a slight smile tugging at the corner of her mouth as she looked down at him—she was at least half a foot taller.

"Leave the goodies," the male detective said, backing up his partner.

"If you suddenly have a memory jog, don't hesitate to let us know," the CIA agents told Sam as they left the room.

"He most certainly will not, you arrogant pricks," the male detective added as he closed the door behind them.

"Sorry about that," the female detective apologised. "First, let me introduce myself. I am Detective Lawson. This is Detective Marshall. We are not here to fuck up your shit like those idiots." She jerked her thumb towards the door. "All we want is to find out what's going on."

"Well, that makes three of us. Because I don't know what is going on either," Sam replied. His tone was calmer now.

"We also don't have much time. You see, agents from the FBI are on their way…"

"The FBI?" Sam exclaimed.

Detective Lawson smiled. "I know, right?" she said, matching Sam's surprise. "This is why we are in here. Yesterday, we found out that a woman killed herself on the street, after being chased and shot. Now, the Chief has CIA agents in his station, and FBI agents on their way, eager to talk with you. He has no right to stop the FBI from taking over the case, but he does want to know what is happening in his town, and in his station."

"Well, for starters," Sam said, spitting the words like venom, "it was those two CIA agents who were chasing her. And it was that big, bouncer-looking asshole who shot at her. Well… before she shot herself, that is." His tone trailed off into a whisper at the sombre end.

"Sorry, are you saying those two CIA agents were involved?"

"Did I stutter?" Sam snapped, but then immediately softened. "Sorry. I didn't mean to yell."

The detectives looked at each other in surprise. Something passed between them that told Sam they had no idea what to say next. They were obviously here innocently, so he decided to tell them what happened. His thoughts were interrupted by a rumbling in his stomach, which did not go unnoticed by the detectives.

"Look, I will tell you what I know happened if I can get something to eat, and a cup of coffee.

"Oh, of course…" Detective Lawson started to say before being cut off by her partner.

"I'll go. I don't think we are going to do anything here, especially if the FBI are on their way, and the CIA are also involved. This is bigger than us." He started towards the door, before stopping and turning to look at Sam. "How do you have your coffee, and the food will be a sandwich from the vending machine."

"That is fine with me. Milk, no sugar," Sam said.

When Detective Marshall closed the door, Sam told Detective Lawson everything he could remember. "Honestly," he started, "there is not much to tell. I was on the job tailing someone for a client. I started to hear shouting—someone yelling for someone else to stop. When I turned around, the people in front of me parted and I saw a woman running towards me. She was wearing a white coat. It looked like a lab coat, strangely."

He paused for a moment.

"Anyway, as she got to me, I heard a gunshot. The woman fell into me, which spun us both around, so I was now facing back towards her chasers." Sam stopped for a breath, not knowing whether he should tell her what the woman said to him. The idea that they were probably being filmed popped into his head. He looked up to the corner of the room, and sure enough there was a camera. Not the right time to be completely honest, he thought.

"The woman then stepped back and shot herself. Almost immediately after that, I was knocked to the ground. A man stood over me with his gun pointed at me…to be honest, I thought he might shoot me."

"And that was the burly CIA agent that was just in here?' Lawson asked, cutting in. "What happened next?"

"Well, in the chaos of the crowd, I managed to escape… No—wait—" Sam corrected himself, memory clicking into place. "He got distracted with his partner. That's what allowed me to get away."

"When did you realise your gun was missing."

"It was when I got home. The person I was following was obviously gone, so I decided to just go home for the night. I went to have a shower, which was when I noticed my gun missing. That was when I also realised that the woman had shot herself with my gun. At the time, I noted that she held a gun that looked like mine. But my gun is super common. Lots of people have it, so I did not make the connection at the time."

They were interrupted by Detective Marshall returning with a sandwich and a coffee. "The FBI are here," he said, as he put the food on the table in front of Sam.

"Thank you for that information, Sam. I will let the Chief know."

"No worries," Sam said.

Detective Lawson stood in front of her boss, Chief Brennan, her face pale but determined.

"Chief, I need to tell you something about the CIA agents we had in the station," she said. "The man we just interviewed—Sam Caldwell—told us the woman who killed herself with his gun was being chased by those agents. After she shot herself, one of them knocked him to the ground and pointed a gun at him. He only escaped because of the chaos in the crowd."

Chief Brennan's brow furrowed into a deep scowl. "Are you telling me those CIA agents might be involved in her death? That's a serious accusation, Gloria." His voice was a low growl. "Send those agents into my office right now. We need to get to the bottom of this."

Gloria's eyes flickered with a hint of anxiety as she replied, "Sir, I just saw them walking out of the station when I came in to speak with you."

Chief Brennan's expression darkened.

"I'm sorry, Chief. I realise now, I should have tried to stop them, but I was focused on getting the information to you first."

The Chief let out a sigh. "Damn it, Gloria. We can't afford to let CIA agents run around like cowboys. Get on the radio and alert all units. I want those agents found and brought back here immediately. And next time, use your instincts and keep them from leaving." His voice softened just a fraction as he added, "We need to be on top of this. I'll brief the FBI when they finish."

Now seated in front of two FBI agents, Sam was completely exasperated. The tension simmering beneath the surface of their questioning was different—quieter, colder. The agents, who had introduced themselves as Miller and Thompson, were fixated on the exact same timeline as the CIA agents had been.

But there was something else—a sharp, urgent edge to their questions. Unlike the CIA or the police, these two weren't just trying to figure out what happened.

They were racing the clock.

Sam sat back in his chair, suppressing the sigh that reflected his level of exasperation as he recounted the incident for the third time! Yet, Agents Miller and Thompson seemed unsatisfied, their sceptical expressions unchanging. Sam could feel the frustration bubbling up inside him, his answers becoming terser with each repetition. He knew they suspected him of holding back, but the constant badgering only fuelled his resolve to keep the woman's final cryptic message to himself.

Agent Miller stood up and closed his notebook. "Alright, Mr. Caldwell. We're done here for now. You can go, but don't leave town. We might have more questions later."

Sam rose from his chair, his muscles stiff from sitting so long. He rubbed his temples, "Yeah, I got it. Can I get my stuff back?"

Agent Thompson picked up the tray of Sam's belongings. "You'll need to sign for these. I'll take them to the front desk." Her voice hardened. "Don't forget—we're keeping a close eye on you. If you remember anything else, contact us immediately."

"If I remember anything," Sam said, "you'll be the first to know."

It was a lie.

5

Sam pushed open the door to his apartment, a fresh breeze following him. It had been a long day. All he'd wanted was to report that the woman may have used his gun to shoot herself. He hadn't expected it to spiral into three separate interrogations—by the CIA, the FBI, and local detectives.

The strangest part wasn't that both federal agencies were involved in what seemed like a suicide—tragic as it was—but that their agendas appeared suspiciously aligned. That, more than anything, worried him. Especially the two CIA agents. They felt... unhinged. Years of surveillance work had taught him to trust his gut—and it told him those two weren't done with him yet.

His mind swirled with images of the woman—her desperation, her fear, and the horrifying moment she had turned the gun on herself. He took a deep breath before entering, determined not to let any of it spill into the sanctuary of his home.

Inside, the warmth and familiarity of the apartment did little to ease his exhaustion. As he hung up his coat, he turned to see Emily, looking up from her spot on the couch, a warm smile spreading across her face as he looked at her. The day had been long, but the sight of her smiling at him helped clear his head just a little. He forced a smile and walked over to her.

"You look beat. How was your day?" Emily asked, rising to meet him.

Sam nodded, leaning in to kiss her. "Yeah, just a rough day. Nothing I can't handle. Sorry I got home late. The morning got off to a rough start, so I had some catching up to do."

His voice was steady, measured. He always kept his work separate from their life. She knew what he did for a living—but not the details. That was a promise he had made to protect her from the darker sides of his job. And today? Today was too dark to explain. Better to let it lie.

Emily watched him for a moment longer. He could see in her eyes that she was judging him.

He needed to change the subject. "Forget about me," he said, "how was your day?"

That seemed to break her train of thought.

"Oh! My day. It was good, actually," she said, the words speeding up. "You remember that house Vic and I have been trying to sell? The one with the helipad in the backyard?"

Sam smirked. "Oh yes—the eccentric couple with their own helipad."

"Exactly! Well, we found a buyer. Even though the house is a total dump," she laughed.

"Wow. Wonders never cease."

"Well, I was thinking," she said, her tone casual but with a deliberate lightness, "why don't we go out tonight? It's been a good day, and a while since we've had a date night." She looked into his eyes, gauging his reaction.

Sam hesitated. His body ached to collapse on the couch and shut the world out. But one look into her eyes reminded him how little time they'd spent together lately. He'd been working too many long hours. Maybe tonight wasn't such a bad idea.

"Sure," he said finally, forcing enthusiasm into his voice. "Going out sounds good." He hated lying to her but telling her the truth would only bring danger and chaos into their lives. "Let me go splash some water on my face."

When he returned, he noticed she was already dressed—ready to go out. She looked stunning. She wore jeans and a tight white top. It was a simple outfit, but she wore it effortlessly. Perfectly.

She was beaming. The sight surprised him—because after rinsing his face, he actually felt a little lighter. The idea of going out wasn't so bad after all. Maybe tonight they could forget everything else and just enjoy each other.

"Where should we go?" he asked as they moved towards the door.

"Let's keep it simple," Emily replied. "I was thinking downtown."

Under the cloak of night, the men approached the dry cleaners with the precision of seasoned professionals. They moved silently, their dark clothing blending with the shadows. One of them picked the back door lock with practiced ease—the faint click breaking the stillness.

They slipped inside, careful to close the door quietly behind them. Their flashlights cast only minimal beams, just enough to illuminate the path in front of them. They had a mission.

Find what they were looking for.

Leave no trace.

Get out.

Inside, the dry cleaners was a maze of hanging garments and shelving units. They navigated the space methodically, avoiding disturbing any of the carefully organised clothing. They whispered to each other, coordinating their search to cover more ground without creating any signs of tampering. One of the men checked the cash register and office files, while the other scanned the racks looking for a specific set of clothes. Each movement was deliberate, with an acute awareness of the importance of leaving everything exactly as they had found it.

A beam of one flashlight caught a small box, sitting innocuously on a shelf. One man signalled the other, who carefully removed the box and opened it. It was full of small thimbles—not what they were looking for.

The night was a bust.

They doubled back, ensuring every garment and piece of furniture was returned to its original place. Surfaces were wiped down, and not a thread was left out of place.

They exited as quietly as they had entered, locking the door behind them. As they slipped into the night, the dry cleaners appeared untouched—no sign of the covert search that had just taken place.

6

Sam pushed open the glass door of Kim's Dry Cleaning, the bell above it ringing cheerfully. He didn't notice the sound, his mind still entangled in the chaos of the past few days. The familiar scent of freshly pressed clothes and faint traces of cleaning chemicals pulled him out of his reverie.

Mr. Kim, ever the warm and dependable owner, looked up from behind the counter. His face lit up with recognition.

"Sam! Good to see you," Mr. Kim called out, his eyes crinkling with genuine delight. He turned and walked into the back of the shop and began rifling through the seemingly never-ending rack of hanging clothes. He found what he was looking for, reached up and grabbed it off the rack. "Your clothes are ready. I was able to get all the stains out."

"You are a genius, Mr. Kim," Sam replied with a smile, but his mind was still elsewhere. Despite the last few days, he still had responsibility for his clients. All the different things were competing for his attention. He absently reached for his wallet, ready to pay.

Mr. Kim laid the garment bag across the counter and then pointed towards a box of miscellaneous items.

"That USB drive, sitting on top—that's yours. It was in your jacket pocket," he said with a nod.

Sam frowned, glancing at the drive. "That's not mine," he said, shaking his head.

Mr. Kim's brow furrowed slightly, his smile dropping, replaced with a frown. "Yeah, it was. I found it in your jacket pocket. You sure you didn't forget?"

"I don't own a flash drive that looks like…" Sam trailed off. Then something clicked. His posture straightened. "Wait—you said it was in my jacket pocket?"

"Yes," Mr. Kim replied slowly.

"Which pocket?" Sam asked sharply.

"The inside pocket. That jacket only has one. On the right side."

Sam's mind was suddenly racing. He never used that pocket. Being left-handed, that side was where he holstered his gun. He picked up the garment bag and the drive in one fluid motion.

"Thank you, Mr. Kim," he said quickly, already heading for the door.

"My pleasure, as always, Sam," Mr. Kim called after him, slightly louder, unsure what had just happened.

Sam walked into his apartment, a garment bag slung over his shoulder and an uneasy feeling settling in his gut. The events of the past few days had left him on edge, and the weight of the small flash drive in his pocket only added to his tension. The memory of the woman slamming into him played on repeat in his head. The usual vision of her wild with fear, then resignation just moments before she took his gun and ended her life. This time, it included images of her putting the flash drive into his jacket pocket, before taking the gun out of his holster. The ghost of the drive in his pocket felt like a live wire against his ribs.

"Sam, you're home!" Emily's voice called from the bedroom. "I was starting to wonder if you'd gotten lost."

"Yeah, sorry. I stopped to pick up the dry cleaning I dropped off the other day," he said, raising his voice just enough for Emily to hear. He forced a smile as he walked down the hall.

He stepped into the bedroom. Emily was bustling around, getting ready for dinner with friends, oblivious to the turmoil swirling in his mind. He crossed to the closet, hanging up the freshly cleaned clothes, and then, almost casually, reached into his jacket pocket. His fingers closed around the drive, and he slipped it out, hiding it in his palm. He moved to his side of the bed.

Emily rummaged through her jewellery box, trying to decide on earrings. When she turned to face the mirror, Sam slid the drive into a little dish on his nightstand. He tried to keep his movements natural, but he could feel her eyes on him.

"What was that?" she asked, her tone light but with a hint of curiosity.

Sam's heart skipped a beat. He turned to face her, forcing a nonchalant shrug. "Oh, just something from work," he said, waving it off as if it were nothing. "You know how it is. Always bringing home bits and pieces." He gave her a reassuring smile, hoping to deflect her interest.

Emily narrowed her eyes slightly, clearly reading more into it, but then she nodded and turned back to her jewellery.

Sam exhaled quietly. Too close.

But the sense of danger didn't fade. In fact, it intensified.

That drive had been hidden on him. Hidden for him. And now, whatever information it contained—whatever secrets the woman had died to protect—were in his hands.

He knew keeping it secret was no longer just important.

It was survival.

For him.

And for Emily.

7

The man moved with purpose as he slipped through the backstage doors of the bustling conference hall. The silver case he carried gleamed under the dim lights, its edges sharp and professional. His presence was almost unnoticed among the crowd of workers hustling to prepare for the event. A quick inquiry with a passing stagehand directed him down a corridor where the sound and television crews were setting up their equipment.

He walked steadily down the corridor, the buzz of activity fading slightly as he moved away from the main staging area. Halfway down the hall, he paused at an unlabelled door, glanced around to ensure no one was watching, and then pushed it open. It led to a narrow stairwell, dimly lit and echoing with every step as he climbed. The metallic clank of his boots reverberated, but he wasn't worried—noise was expected in a place like this.

At the top, the man emerged onto a network of scaffolding high above the conference hall. He moved with the ease of someone familiar with such heights, carefully making his way along the narrow walkway. The faint murmur of the crowd below reached his ears, a reminder of the multitude gathered for the event. He continued towards the front of the hall, his eyes scanning the expanse below, ensuring he remained unseen.

Reaching the front of the hall, he finally stopped. He knelt, setting the aluminium case on the walkway beside him. The case made a soft thud as it contacted the metal surface, and he opened it with practiced precision. Inside, intricate components of a strange wide barrelled gun, which looked to be straight out of a science fiction movie, lay nestled in custom foam inserts. His hands moved swiftly, methodically, as he checked each piece, his focus unwavering.

From his vantage point, he had a clear view of the stage. He could see a technician busy setting up a podium, adjusting the microphones and arranging papers. The man above watched intently, ensuring his own position was perfect. Satisfied, he began assembling a device from the case, his actions deliberate and calm. The podium was directly in his line of sight, inside forty yards, the focal point of the upcoming event. His presence there was anything but benign.

Agent Daniel Harlow had dedicated his life to protecting the First Lady, but over the years, his role had evolved from mere duty to a profound admiration and deep-seated respect for her. Every time she stood at the podium, delivering a speech with grace and conviction, he felt a swell of pride. Her words were always thoughtful, her presence commanding, and he had witnessed firsthand how her intelligence and compassion inspired countless people. He loved the way she connected with the audience, her eloquence painting visions of hope and unity, and how she always managed to touch the hearts of those listening.

From the shadowed corners of countless event halls, Daniel had watched her rise, seen her navigate the complexities of public life with an unwavering strength that only deepened his admiration. Her speeches were not just words; they were beacons of light in a world often shrouded in uncertainty. Each address was a testament to her unwavering commitment to the betterment of society. Daniel cherished these moments, not only as a protector but as someone who had come to understand and deeply appreciate the essence of the woman he safeguarded. Her resilience and grace under pressure had a way of reigniting his own dedication.

The First Lady stood tall behind the podium, her presence commanding. She began her speech with a fiery passion that had become her trademark, captivating the audience with her dedication to pressing issues.

"Good evening, everyone. Tonight, we gather not just to raise funds, but to rally behind a cause that affects each, and every, one of us—climate change. Our planet is crying out for help, and it is our duty to respond with urgency and commitment," she declared, her voice resonating through the hall.

Her words painted vivid images of the future, both grim and hopeful. She spoke of the rising sea levels, the increasing frequency of natural disasters, and the impact on agriculture and food security. The First Lady's eyes scanned the crowd, noting their attentive gazes and nods of agreement.

"We cannot afford to ignore the science. We cannot afford to delay action. Every day we wait, the cost of inaction grows. And it's not just an environmental issue—it's a matter of economic justice. The cost of living is soaring as resources become scarcer."

As she transitioned to the topic of the economic impact, her tone grew even more fervent. "Families are struggling to make ends meet. The price of food, housing, and energy is climbing, and the burden falls disproportionately on those who can least afford it. We must address these challenges head-on, with innovative policies and a commitment to sustainability," she asserted, her passion drawing a round of applause from the audience.

The man on the scaffolding watched with detached curiosity as the First Lady began her speech. Her voice was strong and clear, filled with conviction and passion that captivated the audience below. From his high perch, he could see the way she commanded the room, her presence drawing in every eye and ear. It was almost a shame, he thought, what he was about to do to her. But emotions had no place in his line of work. He was paid to complete a task, not to question the morality of it.

As the First Lady's words echoed through the hall, the man reached for the button on the side of the round-barrelled device he had meticulously set up. His fingers brushed against the cold metal, and he pressed it firmly. The gun emitted a soft hiss, a nearly imperceptible sound that marked the completion of its deadly task. He didn't flinch or hesitate; his actions were smooth and practiced, a testament to his experience. Albeit he was used to using regular weapons. This was something altogether different.

The First Lady, abruptly, stopped speaking. She stood like a statue, her arms hanging limply by her sides. A hush fell over the crowd as they watched her in stunned silence. Her eyes darted around the room, a look of bewilderment replacing her earlier determination. It was as if she had suddenly forgotten where she was and what she was doing. The transformation was startling, her once fierce demeanour now replaced with an unsettling insecurity.

She took a hesitant step back from the podium, her gaze still sweeping the room as if searching for something familiar. The audience exchanged nervous glances, whispers of confusion rippling through the crowd. The First Lady's composure had crumbled, leaving her looking lost and vulnerable. The organisers and security personnel on the sidelines watched with growing concern, unsure of how to respond to the sudden shift in her behaviour. None more so than Agent Harlow.

Without a word, she turned, stumbling slightly. Agent Harlow took a hesitant step towards her. The First Lady looked down at her feet. He watched as she tilted her right foot to the side slightly, as if inspecting the heel of her shoe. Then, to his shock, and the shock of everyone in the room, she hiked up her skirt enough to allow her to sit down on the stage, not doing anything to hide her dignity. She then unstrapped her shoes and took them off.

Standing back up to her feet, she again looked around. People were now approaching her, and Agent Harlow didn't like it one bit. He rushed forward, telling everyone to get back. They stopped where they were but did not back away. The First Lady, looking at the people standing around her, shied away. She raised her hands defensively. This was not a good situation.

Agent Harlow stepped forward. "Ma'am, are you okay?" he asked, his voice tender and soothing, trying to gauge her condition. She looked at him blankly, as if they were strangers, her earlier confidence completely evaporated. The transformation unnerved Agent Harlow. Her previously strong and articulate presence was now replaced with a distant and detached demeanour.

She looked at him for a moment before walking through the people gathered around to the side of the stage. The people gave her space, on Agent Harlow's instructions. She walked off the stage, her movements slow and deliberate. Like skittish prey skulking through the bush trying not to be seen and attacked. Agent Harlow followed behind, continuing to tell everyone to stay back.

To everyone present in the hall, the scene was surreal, the First Lady's actions so out of character that it left everyone in a state of shock. People in the audience began to murmur more loudly, some standing in an attempt to get a better view, others pulling out their phones to record the strange event. When the First Lady and Agent Harlow left the hall, backstage, through a door on the side, the crowd was now in full voice. The buzz of conversation filled the room.

The door opened into a small area that led into a hallway. Agent Harlow decided to approach her. "Madam First Lady!?" he said hesitantly. She ignored him, starting to make her way down the hallway. This time Agent Harlow stepped past her and put his hand gently on her arm. "Madam First Lady. Are you okay?" he asked, more sternly this time.

The First Lady stopped and looked at him. The same unrecognising, distant, and detached demeanour looked back at him. What he did not notice was the First Lady slowly hiking up her dress again to a point where it would not hinder her. Then she took off running!

The device, now warm from its recent activity, was swiftly dismantled. The man worked efficiently, placing each component back into its designated spot within the silver case. His movements were almost mechanical, driven by routine. As he closed the case, he allowed himself a final glance at the stage. The First Lady's vibrant presence had shifted to something uncanny, her body language altered as if her consciousness had been stripped away. He smirked knowingly.

From his vantage point, he could see the subtle confusion ripple through the crowd. But there was no time to dwell on the aftermath. He needed to leave, and quickly. He picked up the case and began his retreat, walking back along the scaffolding with the same calculated steps he had taken to arrive. The stairwell was a familiar path, its dimness now a comforting cloak.

At the bottom, he approached the door cautiously. He cracked it open just enough to peer through, ensuring his escape route was clear. To his shock, the First Lady ran past, her face alive with fear and urgency, closely followed by the head of her security detail and a stream of others. Again, he smiled, even letting out an unconscious huff of laughter.

He could no longer leave this way. Thinking quickly, he turned and headed back up the stairs towards the scaffolding. The building was a maze of corridors and back doors, many of which he had memorised during his initial reconnaissance. Each step was taken with heightened awareness, his senses on high alert for any sign of pursuit. He knew he had to vanish before anyone connected him to the chaos unfolding in the hall.

8

Sam and Emily arrived at the house of their friends, Gus and Grace, just as the sun began to set, casting a warm, golden glow over the neighbourhood. Sam carried a six-pack of craft beer in one hand and balanced a box of chocolates in the other, while Emily carried a bottle of wine and a bouquet of fresh flowers.

Gus opened the door with a wide, welcoming smile.

"Hey, you two! Glad you could make it!" he said, his voice booming with genuine excitement. "Come on in. You can throw your drinks in the cooler out on the deck. Everyone's already here, and since it's such a nice night, we figured we'd eat outside."

They followed Gus through the house and out onto the deck, where a lively gathering was already in full swing. The smell of grilling meat wafted through the air, mingling with the laughter and chatter of their friends. Gus gestured to the fridge, and Sam shoved the beer inside, except the one he took for himself, while Emily arranged the flowers in a vase Gus handed her.

String lights twinkled overhead, adding a festive charm to the setting. The atmosphere was warm, relaxed, and full of promise.

At the table, the women greeted Emily with a chorus of cheerful hellos. She placed the wine and flowers on the table, leaning in to exchange hugs and kisses. Victoria, her friend from the office, was there, along with Mia—married to Alexander, Nova—Luke's girlfriend, and Grace, of course. Laughter bubbled up among them as compliments on outfits and updates on life were shared.

Sam stood back slightly, his presence steady and reassuring, smiling as he watched Emily interact so effortlessly with their friends, waiting for his turn for a greeting.

They moved over to the grill area, where the men stood around, beers in hand, discussing the finer points of grilling. Emily gave each of them a warm hug, her genuine affection evident in her easy manner. "Mav," she greeted last, "it's good to see you could come."

"I had nothing better to do," he said, with a straight face. If the group did not know Maverick better, they would have been offended by that. Luckily, they had been friends for a long time. They knew his sense of humour. The same sense of humour that got him kicked out of bars more than once.

Sam kept things simple. Starting off with a smile, a greeting of, "What's up guys?" followed by a shake of hands, and a slap on the back. He finished off with sniffing the air and saying, "Damn, that smells amazing." His casual greeting was met with a chorus of enthusiastic responses, the friendship among the men clear and uncomplicated.

Gus retrieved the tongs from Alexander. "Thank you," he said in acknowledgment of the good work done holding down the fort. The night was off to a great start, filled with the promise of good food, laughter, and the easy company of close friends.

As the night continued, the group of friends settled into their seats around the table, plates filled, glasses clinked, and laughter echoing as they enjoyed each other's company. Amid the relaxed atmosphere, Gus asked, "So, has anyone heard from Natalie or Arthur since they broke up?" glancing around the table. The group fell silent for a moment, everyone shaking their heads or murmuring negative responses.

"I haven't," Grace said, her tone tinged with concern. "I've tried calling Natalie a few times, but she hasn't returned my calls. I imagine she's probably just trying to wrap her head around everything."

Mia nodded. "I sent her a message, but I haven't heard back either. It must be so hard for her right now."

Alexander sighed. "It's such a shame. They seemed so perfect together, but I guess you never really know what's going on behind closed doors."

The conversation naturally shifted to the topic of Arthur's affair, the catalyst for their breakup. "It's crazy to think we didn't see the signs," Vic said, shaking her head. "I mean, looking back, there were so many red flags."

"Yeah," Emily added. "Like how he suddenly started working late all the time. Natalie mentioned it a few times, but we just brushed it off as him being busy with work."

"And he was so distracted when we hung out," Nova said. "I remember that one dinner where he kept checking his phone. At the time, I thought he was just stressed, but now it makes sense."

Luke chimed in, "And all those last-minute cancellations. He'd always have an excuse, like he was stuck at the office, or something came up. It seemed plausible, but now it's obvious what was really going on."

"There were also those moments when he was unusually affectionate," Grace pointed out. "One minute he'd be distant, and the next he'd be showering Natalie with attention. It seemed sweet, but in hindsight, it was probably guilt."

As the conversation continued, Sam found himself drifting into his own thoughts. The image of the woman who had slipped the flash drive into his jacket pocket before shooting herself kept replaying in his mind. He couldn't shake the feeling that he was missing something crucial, and it gnawed at him constantly. He was jolted back to reality when Maverick noticed his silence.

"Sam, you've been quiet. What do you think about all this?"

Sam blinked, trying to catch up. "Oh… uh… yeah. It's surprising, for sure," he said slowly. "But just because someone is working late, it doesn't mean they're having an affair. They could just be busy, or it could be other reasons."

The atmosphere shifted slightly, tension creeping in as the group exchanged glances. Emily touched his arm, her expression puzzled. "I get what you're saying, Sam, but in Arthur's case, it was more than just working late. There were so many signs."

Gus, picking up on the shift, tried to steer the conversation back. "True, but maybe Sam has a point. We shouldn't jump to conclusions about people based on a few behaviours."

Vic, however, seemed less convinced. "But when you put all those behaviours together, it paints a pretty clear picture. Arthur was hiding something, and we all missed it."

Mia added, "It's not about jumping to conclusions, it's about recognising a pattern. If we had paid more attention, maybe we could have confronted Arthur, or helped Natalie sooner."

Alexander frowned, looking at Sam. "It just feels like you're defending him, Sam. We all saw the signs, and now it makes sense."

Sam felt the weight of their scrutiny, his mind racing. "I'm not defending him," he said carefully. "I'm just saying that sometimes things aren't what they seem. We don't always see the full picture. I mean, was it the case that every time he did something, he was with the other woman. Does it now mean that any time any of us do something, we are going to jump to the conclusion that person is having an affair?"

Nova nodded. "That's true, Sam. But in Arthur's case, it wasn't that he was doing one of those things. He was doing all of them. It is just a shame that despite the fact we all noticed something was off, we didn't connect the dots until it was too late."

The conversation grew more intense, the group divided on how to interpret Arthur's behaviour. Sam felt a knot in his stomach, the weight of his own secrets pressing down on him. He glanced at Emily, who looked concerned but supportive. He knew he couldn't afford to let his personal turmoil affect the evening further. Trying to calm the situation, Sam took a deep breath. "I think what we're all saying is that it's important to be aware and supportive of our friends. We might not always see everything, and anything may seem like anyone is acting inappropriately, but we can be there for each other when things go wrong."

Grace nodded, her expression softening. "That's true. We need to stick together and support Natalie through this. She's going to need us more than ever."

"Look, to be honest, I am here for Natalie, but I am also here for Arthur," Sam said. Everyone looked at him. A mix of surprise, anger, and curiosity. "He messed up, big time. That is for sure. And he hurt Natalie with his lies, that is also for sure. But I'm not gonna ghost the guy. I hate what he did, but he was our friend before, and he's still our friend. That doesn't mean I condone what he did."

To his surprise, the group seemed to relax slightly, the mood easing as they focused on what he had said. They all had a shared commitment to helping Natalie. Some would never speak to Arthur again, but Sam could see that others were questioning their own stance. The conversation shifted to how they could be there for Natalie, offering support and understanding in the difficult times ahead.

As the evening wore on, the friends found comfort in their unity, despite the underlying tensions and unspoken secrets. Sam felt a sense of relief as the topic moved away from Arthur's affair, but he knew the weight of his own burdens would remain. For now, he focused on the present, cherishing the support of his friends and the love of Emily, hoping that the darkness lurking in his mind would eventually fade.

9

Sam sat in his office contemplating what to do with the flash drive—the harsh glow of fluorescent tubes overhead casting a sterile light. His store was in a quiet hallway of a strip mall, nestled between a vintage bookstore and a run-down laundromat. It was a small storefront, a square space divided into two rooms by a single wall and a door. Customers entered into a small waiting area furnished with a simple couch and a few decorations. He had got the idea to put a bell over the door from Mr. Kim—the high-pitched chime was an easy but effective way to announce a visitor's arrival.

His office was in the back. The space between his office and the busy strip mall hallway, along with the wall separating him from the waiting area, gave him a decent buffer from the noise. That, combined with the soft hum of jazz playing from a speaker, created a white noise sanctuary where he could sift through cases in peace. The past few days had left him on edge, and he welcomed the familiarity of his routine.

Then the doorbell rang.

Sam didn't bother closing his office door that morning, and so he heard the chime clearly.

Two figures entered.

The same FBI agents from earlier in the week.

Agent Thompson, tall and imposing, with her ironclad expression. Agent Miller, slightly shorter, but with eyes that never missed a detail.

Sam's heart rate spiked. He sat up straighter, willing himself to stay composed. He'd done nothing wrong. He knew the law. He had nothing to fear.

So why did it feel like the walls were closing in?

Agent Thompson didn't waste time. "Mr. Caldwell," she said, her tone crisp and cold, "we need you to come back to the station for further questioning."

Sam felt his stomach knot.

He'd told himself it was over—that he could go back to handling dull cases and staying out of trouble. He should've known better.

Sam took a deep breath, trying to steady his nerves. "Is this really necessary? I've already told you everything I know." His voice wavered slightly, betraying his fear.

Agent Thompson stepped forward, her eyes narrowing as she scrutinised him. "It's necessary, Mr. Caldwell. New evidence has come to light, and we need to clarify a few details." Her tone made it clear there was no room to argue.

Reluctantly, Sam nodded. He grabbed his coat and hat, feeling the weight of the situation pressing down on him. As they walked through the narrow corridors of the shopping complex, the vibrant atmosphere felt at odds with the gravity of his predicament. He couldn't shake the feeling that there was more to the woman's suicide than he had initially thought. The FBI's persistent interest suggested that his involvement, however unintentional, might be significant.

They reached the parking lot, where a sleek black SUV awaited them. Sam glanced back at his office, the sanctuary that now felt like a distant memory. He climbed into the vehicle, the leather seats cold against his skin. The drive to the station was silent, the tension palpable. Sam's mind raced with questions: What new evidence had they found? How could he prove his innocence? And most importantly, why had the woman chosen to end her life in such a dramatic manner?

At the station, Sam was led to an interrogation room, its sterile walls and harsh lighting amplifying his sense of unease. He sat down at the metal table, facing the two agents who seemed determined to uncover some hidden truth. Agent Thompson sat opposite him, while Miller moved to the side of the room and leaned against the wall. Agent Thompson removed a laptop from her bag and placed it on the table.

"Mr. Caldwell," Agent Thompson began again, "we need you to recount the events of that day once more. Every detail matters." Sam swallowed hard, knowing that his words could either implicate him further or help clear his name.

As he started to speak, he couldn't help but feel a sense of dread. The woman's death was a mystery he had yet to solve, and the FBI's relentless questioning only deepened his suspicion that something far more sinister was at play. Sam recounted the events leading up to him escaping in the chaos of the crowd. He left out the flash drive.

Agent Miller cut in from his position. "Mr. Caldwell, did the woman put anything into your pocket when she ran into you before she took your gun?"

Sam's heart raced as he replayed that moment in his mind. Despite this, he replied firmly, "No, she didn't put anything in my pocket."

Without a word, Agent Thompson spun the laptop that was sitting open on the table in front of her around towards Sam. She opened the lid, "Take a look at this footage," she said, pressing the space bar on the computer. The grainy security camera footage from a nearby store showed the woman running into Sam, their brief collision, and the subsequent tragic moment she grabbed his gun.

Sam flinched away, turning his head and closing his eyes. He heard the click of the space bar being pressed again. He turned his head back to look directly at Agent Thompson, "Why did you show me that!" he spat. "Don't you think I am traumatised enough from being there, watching it first-hand, you fucking asshole."

Agent Thompson got up and circled the table, stopping next to him. She moved her finger on the mouse pad before pressing the space bar to start the video again. "Have another look. This time, focus on the moment she takes your gun out. Notice anything just before that?" Agent Thompson said in that same cold unemotional tone.

Sam forced himself to focus on the footage once again. Thankfully, Agent Thompson stopped the footage at that stage, saving him from having to watch the moment again. Knowing exactly what they wanted him to say, he said, "I don't see anything."

"Once again, then," Agent Thompson said. This time she did not seem to care if Sam was watching. At the moment where the woman's hand was about to go inside his jacket, Agent Thompson paused the video with that familiar click of the space bar. "Notice anything?" she asked.

Sam looked at the image on the screen. He could see various shadows around the woman's hand. One of those shadows, Sam knew, was the drive. He was convinced of that now. But nothing that could be definitively proven by the footage. "I don't see anything," he said, trying to keep all emotion out of his tone.

The FBI agents were beginning to mirror the aggressive tactics used by the CIA agents in the initial interrogation. Sam felt a familiar chill as the atmosphere grew more hostile. Despite his growing suspicion that the woman might have slipped something into his pocket, he maintained his stance. "I didn't feel anything," he reiterated, looking up at Agent Thompson, who loomed over him, a scowl evident on her face. "She didn't put anything in my pocket."

"Nothing? Are you saying she put nothing in your pocket?"

"That is what I am telling you," Sam said, staring directly into Agent Thompson's eyes.

The agent walked back to her side of the table and dropped into her seat with a huff. Her frustration was evident. She leaned back, her expression hardening. "We need the truth, Caldwell. This isn't a game."

Sam's irritation flared, but he kept his voice steady. "I am telling the truth. I don't know what you want me to say." The agent's eyes narrowed, a silent challenge hanging in the air, but Sam stood his ground.

As the interrogation dragged on, Sam's initial willingness to cooperate began to erode. He had started the interview with an open mind, hoping to clear his name and move past the ordeal. But the agents' relentless questioning and accusatory tone made it increasingly difficult to trust them. Sam began to respond with short terse answers.

The FBI agents grew visibly frustrated with each denial. They needed information, and their impatience showed. "Think harder," Agent Thompson said, her voice tight with irritation. "This is important."

Sam turned to meet her gaze evenly. "I'm telling you the truth," he said, short, cold, nothing more. The agents exchanged a look, their exasperation clear. "Am I going to be charged today?" Sam said suddenly.

Both agents looked back at him. A knowing expression clearly visible on their faces.

"Well, if I am not being charged with anything, this interview is over. I have a meeting to get to." He stood up. The squeal of the chair legs grinding across the cement floor filled the room. Without another word, he walked out.

10

As Sam walked out of the interrogation room, the questioning weighed heavily on his shoulders. The main bullpen of the police station buzzed with activity. Detectives and police officers sat at their desks, pounding away on keyboards, talking on phones, and sifting through paperwork. The air was thick with the hum of busywork, a stark contrast to the intense silence of the interrogation room.

As he made his way through the room, sandwiched between the two FBI agents, Sam's gaze inadvertently landed on Detective Lawson. She was sitting at her desk, her sharp eyes locked onto him. There was something about her expression that grabbed his attention. It wasn't the usual stern look he had come to expect from law enforcement. Instead, it seemed... interesting, even inviting. For a moment, he thought he saw her subtly motion with her head, suggesting he come over to her.

Sam hesitated, wondering if he was imagining things. Was Detective Lawson really signalling him, or was his mind playing tricks on him after the relentless questioning? He stole another glance in her direction, and there it was again—a slight nod of her head. His curiosity piqued, but his nerves were frayed. Every instinct told him to leave the station and put as much distance as possible between himself and the interrogation he had just endured. He wasn't sure he could handle another round of questions, even from someone who seemed sympathetic.

Blowing off the invitation, Sam continued walking, focusing on the exit. He needed fresh air and space to think, away from the oppressive atmosphere of the station. The FBI agents followed closely behind, their presence a constant reminder of the potential trouble he might be in. As he stepped out into the open air, Sam took a deep breath, trying to clear his mind. He couldn't shake the feeling that there was more to this situation than he understood, and Detective Lawson's enigmatic gesture lingered in his thoughts as he walked away.

Detective Lawson had tried to forget about what she had been witnessing, but catching the CIA interrogating the man, then disappearing, plus the FBI being involved had sparked her curiosity. Giving into it, she had spent the morning looking at news reports and social media trying to find out what she could. She looked at her partner, Detective Marshall, over the small divide that separated their two desks and said, "Can you believe there's nothing in the news or online about that guy and the chick's so-called suicide? Not a single red flag."

Detective Marshall looked up from his paperwork, his usual grizzled expression staring back at her. That expression scared her initially when they had first been partnered up. After years of working with him and knowing him better, and his lovely wife, she now only saw it as the look of a loving husband and father of someone from an older generation. "What...!" he said, with a slight shake of his head, having not really heard what she said.

"That guy we interviewed the other day," she said, stressing the point. "Can you believe there is nothing anywhere that suggests it is anything weird."

Detective Marshall just stared at her for a moment, as if trying to understand what she was talking about. "Gloria, if it looks like a duck, and quacks like a duck, it's a goddamn duck."

She rolled her eyes. "Yeah, well this one might look like a duck, but it sure doesn't quack like one."

"What are we gonna do..."

Detective Lawson did not hear the rest of what her partner may have said. Her mind wandered back to the vision of the man walking through the office, flanked by the FBI agents and looking visibly frustrated. It fuelled her obsession. She had tried to catch his eye, to offer him a chance to speak to her, but he had walked right past. There was something about his demeanour that struck a chord with her. It wasn't just fear or frustration; it was the look of a man who was caught in something far beyond his control. She had always prided herself on her ability to read people, and the guy's body language screamed for help, even if he didn't realise it himself.

"Boss, we need to look into this case more," she said, looking back at Detective Marshall. She had called him "Boss" since being partnered up. Initially, it was her being a young arrogant detective thinking they were the shit, trying to annoy the older guy, which worked. But now, it was a recognition that he still knew more than she did, and she needed to respect that.

"Something doesn't sit right with me," she said, her voice filled with determination.

Detective Marshall just stared at her. His grizzled features showing a mix of weariness and understanding. She had seen that look before, many times.

He knew that when she fixated like this, it was hard to sway her. "The Feds are all over it, Gloria. We should stay clear," he replied.

"But think about it, Vince," she pressed. "A private detective gets caught up in a suicide involving his own gun, and now both the CIA and FBI are involved? That's not just coincidence. There's something big here, and we could be the ones to uncover it. Besides, when was the last time anything this exciting happened around here?" Despite her passionate plea, Vince's expression remained unchanged.

"Listen, Gloria," Vince said, leaning back in his chair. "I've seen things like this before. Cases that are too big for us, cases that pull you in and spit you out. It's not our responsibility, and it can only end badly for us. The Feds have their reasons for being involved, and we need to stay out of it."

Gloria felt a pang of disappointment but knew Vince's experience spoke volumes. Despite her burning curiosity, she would have to find another way to satisfy it. An idea came to her. She grabbed one of her business cards from their little holder and stood up. "Sit tight," she said, like Detective Marshall was going to do anything else.

Sam stood outside the police station just breathing in and out. Having been brought to the station by the FBI agents, they would not drive him back. They had simply just called him a cab. It was late morning and the sun was out. The warmth on his face was doing wonders. He did not know if this was mindfulness, but whatever it was he was feeling better for it. That was before he heard his name called from behind.

"Excuse me," a woman's voice said.

He opened his eyes and turned to look. It was the police detective who gestured to him on his way out of the station. He sighed. "What do you want?" he muttered, deadpan.

"I am sorry to bother you. I am sure I'm the last person you would want to speak with right now."

"You got that right," he said.

"You seem to be caught up in something that you are not happy about. I just want to give you my card." She held out her hand with her business card.

Sam just looked at it but made no movement.

"If you want to talk, detective to detective like, I hope you'll call me. From what you said to us the other day, and what I know, it seems like something is happening outside both our control, and it's not entirely kosher. I think people like us should stick together." She continued to hold out her hand.

It would be good to talk things out, detective to detective, Sam thought. But he wasn't even sure how much he wanted to involve himself. This was not the type of case that he was interested in at all. A lifetime seemed to pass by as he stood staring at the detective's card. He finally reached out and took it. A smile came across her face as he did.

Detective Lawson sat back down on her chair with a satisfied look on her face.

"You either banged the guy, or you've just taken a massively satisfying dump," Detective Marshall said, without any emotion.

Detective Lawson laughed. She pointed to her face, "Well, for reference, I did not fuck the guy, but this is my just-been-fucked face."

"Good, now can we get back to our real work?"

11

Sam sat in a red leather booth at Joe's Diner, a greasy spoon down the street from his office. The neon "Open 24 Hours" sign buzzed faintly in the window, and the smell of coffee and sizzling bacon filled the air as he watched a woman approach his table. She looked anxious, her eyes darting around the diner before settling on him. "Mr. Caldwell?" she asked hesitantly. He nodded and gestured for her to sit down. "I'm Linda," she said, her voice trembling slightly. "We talked on the phone."

Linda explained that she suspected her husband, a businessman, of being involved in something illicit. Her voice grew steadier as she described the strange behaviours he had been exhibiting. Late nights, secretive phone calls, and unexplained absences. "When I confronted him about it," she said, her hands wringing nervously, "he just brushed me off and said it was nothing. But I can't shake the feeling that something is very wrong."

Her worry wasn't just for herself but also for their children. "I'm scared for our safety, and I'm terrified of what might happen to our family if he's caught up in something illegal," she confessed, her eyes welling up with tears. She reached into her bag and pulled out a photograph of her husband, sliding it across the table to Sam. "I need to know what he's up to, for the sake of our children and our future."

Sam listened intently, nodding as he took in the details. He understood the gravity of the situation and the fear that Linda was grappling with. "I can follow him and gather information on his activities," he assured her. "I'll also provide you with my professional opinion on what he might be involved in." Linda's relief was visible as she handed over an envelope of cash, her last hope resting on his shoulders.

As Linda spoke, Sam's attention was momentarily diverted by the television in the corner of the diner. The sound was not up very high, but it was high enough that it could be heard. A breaking news headline flashed across the screen. He raised a hand to signal the waitress, who approached with a friendly smile. "Can you turn the TV up a bit?" he asked. The waitress obliged, increasing the volume just as the news anchor began to speak.

"Breaking news from the Capitol," the anchor announced, her voice tense. "We can now confirm that Madam First Lady has been hospitalised following a bizarre incident during a recent public speech. Witnesses say she suddenly stopped talking, began acting like a child, and even sat down on the stage at one point to take her shoes off. She then ran away from her security detail." Video played to show what the news anchor had just said.

The diner's patrons fell silent, all eyes turning to look at the screen as the anchor continued. "The First Lady is safe and currently under medical care. More details will follow as they become available."

Sam's mind raced as he processed the information. He glanced back at Linda, who looked equally bewildered by the news. "That's something you don't see every day," he murmured, more to himself than to her.

As the report ended and conversation slowly resumed around them, a different voice echoed in his mind:

No one can have it. Expose it, then destroy it.

The woman's final words.

He looked at Linda, who was still watching him.

Then, suddenly, he stood—his focus sharpening.

"Alright, I'll take the job," he said, his tone firm and professional. "I'll start following your husband and report back with what I find. And I'll give you my opinion on what's going on, as you requested." Linda's eyes just blinked at his sudden reaction, followed by relief.

"But right now, I am sorry, but I gotta run," Sam said. He tossed some bills on the table to cover the cost of their order.

Sam stepped out onto the sidewalk. His mind focused on the news report. The First Lady, known for her poised demeanour, had been acting like a child during a speech, her behaviour bizarre and unsettling. He shook off the image of her and focused on the task at hand. Sam's eyes scanned his surroundings, a habit ingrained from years of surveillance work.

He prided himself on his ability to disappear into a crowd. Surveillance was his forte, a skill he had honed over years of practice. He preferred the anonymity of observing from afar, relying on his keen senses and attention to detail. It was the art of going unnoticed that fascinated him, the subtle dance of blending into the background while keeping a watchful eye.

He immediately noticed the black car parked across the street; two people inside trying to act like they were just there waiting for someone. A chill ran down his spine as his gaze shifted to the people on the sidewalk. There was a guy pretending to read *USA Today*, a woman fiddling with her shopping bags, and a couple whose attention was clearly focused on him rather than on each other. Their attempts to blend in were amateurish at best.

Keeping his pace steady, Sam walked down the sidewalk, his mind racing. He knew they were following him, and he knew why. He had been silly to think that he would not be followed. The only question he had was which agency was doing it, the CIA or the FBI…or both?

He smiled despite himself. The idea that both agencies might be tailing him at the same time—without realising it—was almost funny.

As he moved, he devised a plan to shake them off, all the while analysing the situation. For the first time, Sam, the master of surveillance, found himself the target of someone else's watchful eyes.

His instincts kicked in. Using shop window reflections to track his tails, he turned into a courtyard just off the street. A market was in full swing. Seven days a week, open stalls, busy foot traffic. Perfect cover.

He slipped into the crowd.

The narrow walkways and bustling movement made it hard for anyone to follow without revealing themselves. He wove between people with ease, eyes alert to every corner and shadow.

He spotted a service entrance to the mall and slipped inside, moving quickly through the storerooms and out the back door into another alley. Pausing only briefly, he scaled an old iron fire escape and crossed the rooftops, knowing his pursuers would struggle to keep up without revealing themselves. From his vantage point, he saw the unmarked black sedan and the confused individuals as they frantically searched for him below. Satisfied he had lost them, Sam descended into the street on the other side of the block. It was only a short walk back to his office.

Sam sat in his office thinking, and smiling to himself. Despite losing him, he knew they would of course wait outside the shopping complex, or in the mall concourse outside his office. He didn't care if his followers found him again. He just wanted to lead them on a chase, expose their clumsy tactics, show them that he too could play the surveillance game and do it much better than them.

But this incident had clarified something: he wasn't going to be left alone.

This was serious.

The black car. The tails. They were just the tip of the iceberg.

His thoughts turned to the drive the woman had slipped into his jacket.

No one can have it. Expose it, then destroy it.

Whatever was on that drive had powerful people watching him—and they weren't going to stop.

It was time to take this seriously.

12

Sam arrived home in the early evening, the setting sun casting long shadows across the quiet street. Their apartment was a cozy but unremarkable unit in a typical complex, with a parking garage below. There were only sixteen apartments in the complex. Their apartment faced the street. He saw that the lights were already on, which meant Emily was already home. He hoped she would be understanding, but he knew this wasn't going to be an easy conversation.

Stepping inside, straight into the open-concept living room, Emily was in the kitchen making herself a drink. The TV was on, tuned to the news. She turned and smiled at him as he entered. Nerves coursed through his body. He smiled back, but it never reached his eyes.

"A pre-party drink to set the mood," she said. "Would you like me to make you one?"

"Hey, Em. That looks good, but no thank you," he said. He walked over to her and kissed her. She took a drink from her homemade cocktail. Might as well get it over with, he thought to himself. Time to break the bad news. "I can't go tonight."

Her smile faded, replaced by a look of concern. "What do you mean? We've had this planned for weeks. Vic's expecting us."

"I know, and I'm really sorry, but something came up at work that I need to deal with immediately," Sam said, trying to keep his tone gentle.

Emily frowned, frustration creeping into her expression. "Sam, this isn't the first time you've cancelled plans because of work. Can't it wait until tomorrow?"

"No, it can't," Sam replied, feeling a pang of guilt. "This is important, Em. I wouldn't bail on you if it wasn't."

Emily crossed her arms, clearly upset. "What's so important that you can't go to my best friend's birthday party?"

"I can't tell you. It's confidential."

"Confidential? Really? This is ridiculous, Sam. You're always so secretive about your work. It's like you don't trust me," Emily snapped.

"It's not about trust," Sam insisted. "It's about keeping you safe. The less you know, the safer you will be."

Emily's eyes narrowed. "So now you're protecting me by shutting me out? That's not how relationships work, Sam."

"I'm doing this for us, Emily. Please try to understand," he pleaded, but Emily shook her head, her expression hardening.

"No, Sam. I'm tired of this. We have been through this before. I am not second to your job," she said, her voice rising.

"Yes, we have had this conversation, and it was then we agreed that we would keep my work separate from us." Sam said.

"Separate, but not instead of…"

The argument escalated, their voices growing louder and more heated. Sam felt his control slipping, the stress and fatigue of the day taking its toll. He knew he needed to end this argument before it spiralled out of control.

"I'm sorry, Em. I really am. But I have to do this," he said, turning to leave the room.

Emily followed him out of the kitchen, her anger palpable. "Where are you going now?"

"To go to the bathroom," Sam replied, trying to keep his tone calm. It was not entirely true. He was also going into the bedroom to get the drive.

After finishing up, he crossed to his side of the bed and pushed aside a few items in his knick-knack bowl. His fingers closed around the small flash drive. He paused, staring at it.

Was he really doing the right thing?

He didn't know what was on it—but he was sure now that it mattered. That it was dangerous. That it was why people were watching him.

He slipped the drive into his pocket and walked back to the living room.

Emily was standing in front of the TV, drink in hand. He was not sure if she was actually listening to what was on it, but she did not turn around when he approached.

"Em, please say something," he said gently. The drive suddenly felt like a brick in his pocket.

After what seemed like a lifetime, she finally turned to face him, her eyes filled with hurt and anger. "If you've got something better to do, then just go," she said coldly.

Sam could not help but feel regret. He wanted to explain, to make her understand, but he knew he couldn't.

"I'm sorry, Em," he said quietly. "I'll make it up to you, I promise."

As Sam walked to his car, his mind spun with competing thoughts. He had to deal with whatever was on the drive—but he also had to find a way to fix things with Emily.

For now, though, he had to focus. No distractions. No matter how much it hurt.

Emily walked out to the street where her Uber was already waiting. She was determined not to let Sam ruin her night.

The ride was quiet—too quiet—giving her mind space to replay their argument over and over. Sam's infuriating secrecy. His sudden change of plans. The way he always seemed to be keeping her at arm's length.

By the time she arrived at the rooftop bar, her frustration had boiled over into something sharper, colder.

As soon as she stepped into the party, her friends greeted her with cheerful shouts and hugs. Vic, the birthday girl, wrapped her in a tight embrace. "Em, you made it! Where's Sam?"

Emily forced a smile, trying to hide her simmering anger. "He's not coming," she said, her voice betraying her bitterness. "He said that he had something urgent he had to attend to at work, which he could not put off until tomorrow. Or, he's off having an affair… who knows."

Vic's face fell in acknowledgment of the conversation she and Emily had the week before. Emily waved her off, determined to have a good time despite her troubles. "No need for pity, Vic, we are here for you. Let's party!" she said, throwing her hands up in the air.

She threw herself into the festivities, dancing and laughing loudly. Every time someone offered her a drink, she accepted without hesitation, quickly losing track of how many she had consumed. The alcohol dulled her anger and replaced it with a reckless sense of abandon.

The night blurred into a haze of flashing lights, pounding music, and the taste of too many cocktails. Emily found herself dancing with strangers, her movements wild and uninhibited. She barely noticed the worried looks from her friends or their attempts to steer her towards water. She was determined to forget Sam and his cryptic job, even if only for a few hours.

As the party continued, Emily's energy began to wane. It was only ten to eleven when she stumbled towards a couch, collapsing into the cushions with a weary sigh. Her friends gathered around her, their faces a mix of concern and sympathy. Vic sat down beside her, gently placing a hand on her shoulder. "Em, are you okay?"

Emily nodded, though tears prickled at the corners of her eyes. "I will be," she whispered, feeling the weight of the night's events finally catch up with her. "I just need a moment," she said, almost throwing up.

"Ok, let's get you out of here and to bed before you make a mess," Vic said, smiling to her friends.

"We will take her home," Grace said. "We were about to leave anyway. Ironically, work tomorrow."

13

Sam walked into the back office of his shopfront. The light from the mall spilled into the room just enough that he could see the way to his desk. He turned on his desk light and sat down. Once the mall lights turned off, the desk light would be sufficient, but not too light to expose him.

His mind was fully focused on the events of the last week now. He pulled out the drive the woman had given him and plugged it into his computer. The screen flickered to life, and a password prompt appeared. He wasn't sure why, but he had not actually expected that.

He stared at the prompt, his mind scrambling for answers. He decided to take a guess, remembering the woman's dishevelled appearance and the blood-stained lab coat she wore. "LAB COAT," he muttered to himself as he typed it in. The screen flashed red, rejecting his attempt. A message appeared, warning him that he had only two guesses left before the drive would lock him out for 1000 hours. "Ah, fuck," he muttered.

Sam took a deep breath, leaning back in his chair. He thought back to the brief, chaotic encounter with the woman. She had been frantic, desperate, and in pain from the gunshot wound to her back. There was no way Sam could realistically guess a password. If he could not access it, what was the point of giving it to him. And, why tell him to expose it if he couldn't even access it. What had she said, "No one can have it. Expose it, then destroy it."

"Expose it," Sam said, again to no-one. "If I can't access it… wait!" he blurted. "She called me, Teddy." At the time, he had dismissed it as the incoherent ramblings of someone in shock, but now, it seemed like it might have been a clever way to tell him the password.

With a mix of hope and apprehension, he typed: TEDDY.

He hit enter.

The screen paused.

Then: Password accepted.

Sam let out a breath he hadn't realised he was holding, relief washing over him. "Who, or what, is Teddy."

The drive's contents began to load, revealing a trove of files and documents, which also included many picture files. He had made it past the first hurdle, but he knew the real challenge was just beginning. He decided to start with the pictures, hoping they might give him some context.

As he clicked through each image, he noticed a pattern. They all seemed to depict some type of device. The initial images were artist impressions, detailed and precise, showing what looked like a wide-barrelled device mounted on a stand, but extremely futuristic.

The device was unlike anything Sam had seen before. It looked like a weapon, but had no trigger, and its barrel was conspicuously large. Each image provided a different angle or aspect, but they all shared common elements. Most notably, there was a cylindrical canister designed to be inserted into the device. The canister seemed to be a crucial component, as subsequent images showed it being removed and replaced by another.

Sam's curiosity grew as he examined a detailed blueprint of the canister. The document was filled with technical jargon and intricate diagrams, but one phrase caught his eye: "Person's data stored inside the canister for retrieval."

He frowned, trying to make sense of it. What kind of device was this? He couldn't shake the feeling that he was looking at something highly advanced and potentially dangerous.

Moving on from the pictures, Sam delved into the text files. Most of them appeared to be gibberish at first glance, lines of random characters and symbols that meant nothing to him. But as he scrolled through file after file, he noticed that some contained large blocks of computer code. These files were stored as simple text documents, yet they were vast, spanning hundreds and thousands of pages.

Sam's limited knowledge of coding left him struggling to decipher the content, but he could recognise the complexity and volume of the information. This was no ordinary project. The sheer amount of data suggested a sophisticated operation, likely involving multiple experts. He felt a growing sense of unease. Whoever had compiled this drive had gone to great lengths to encode and conceal their work.

Determined to find something he could understand, Sam continued his search. He opened file after file, looking for anything that might provide a clue. Amidst the gibberish and code, he stumbled upon a document that stood out. It was a list of names and a series of alphanumeric codes. The names were unfamiliar, but the format suggested they were linked to the weapon in some way.

Sam's mind raced with possibilities. Were these the names of test subjects? Or perhaps the creators of the device? He felt a chill run down his spine as he considered the implications. If this was a list of test subjects, then the weapon might have been used already, and those people's data could be stored in the canisters he had seen in the pictures. The thought was horrifying.

The more Sam uncovered, the more questions he had. He leaned back in his chair, rubbing his temples as he tried to piece everything together. The artist impressions, the schematics, the cryptic notes about data retrieval—it all pointed to a device designed for something beyond conventional use. Some type of personal data manipulation, but without more information, he couldn't be sure.

Sam leaned back in his chair, a sense of dread settling over him. This wasn't his scene. He was a private detective who specialised in surveillance, tailing unfaithful spouses, and writing detailed reports. The complex, shadowy world of espionage was a far cry from his usual work. He lacked the training, resources, and connections to navigate this. The more he thought about it, the more he realised he was in way over his head. He felt the weight of the decision to keep the drive secret pressing down on him, knowing that any misstep could have dire consequences.

He needed help, someone who could handle this kind of heat, someone who was in a position that if this turned out to be something, they could deal with it. Detective Lawson came to mind. She was keen, a detective in her own right. She would have the resources and expertise to dig deeper into this conspiracy and take the necessary actions to prevent a disaster. The only wrinkle was that he could not know if she would be the right person.

As Sam sat there contemplating his next move, his cell phone rang.

Gus.

Frowning, he picked it up. "Hey Gus, what's up?"

Gus sounded worried. "Sam, where the fuck are you?" he said, his voice sharp.

"I'm at the office," Sam replied, anxiety creeping into his tone. "Why?"

Gus paused, then said, "We brought Emily home from the party. She went a bit too hard…"

Sam sighed, guilt washing over him. "I'm so sorry, Gus," he started, cutting him off. "Emily and I had a fight. I told her that I couldn't make it to the party because something urgent came up at work and… well, you can guess how that went down."

Gus's voice grew urgent. "Well, be that as it may, whatever you are doing, you need to stop and come home. Your apartment has been completely trashed."

Sam's heart dropped. A cold fear gripped him as the words sank in.

14

Sam pulled up to the curb across from his apartment complex. The street was eerily quiet, the night air dense with silence. Gus's frantic call replayed in his mind, overlapping now with the sense of constantly being watched.

Followed.

Every shadow seemed to morph into a lurking figure, every rustle of leaves a potential threat. He scanned the street, his pulse quickening as his headlights revealed only fleeting glimpses of movement that vanished as quickly as they appeared. The normally comforting darkness now felt like an ally to those watching him, hiding their intent and amplifying his fear.

He stepped out of his car, instinctively reaching into his pocket and felt the small, metal drive. The weight of it suddenly seemed heavier, the implications more profound. He knew that whatever chaos had unfolded inside his home, it had been for this drive. What made things worse was the fact he couldn't tell anyone about it—not yet.

Two police officers, their faces stern and professional, were standing inside the door as he approached. One noticed his movements and turned to look at him. "Are you Samuel Caldwell?" he asked.

Sam nodded, his eyes darting towards the chaos inside the apartment. "Yes, call me Sam."

"Mr. Caldwell," the officer continued, ignoring the correction, "it appears your apartment has been broken into. We're currently assessing the situation. We need you to come inside and see if anything valuable is missing."

Inside, it was carnage.

Furniture was knocked over, drawers ripped out and their contents strewn across the floor, and broken glass everywhere. Gus and Grace, were huddled in the kitchen with Emily, who looked pale and shaken. She clung to a glass of water as if it were a lifeline. Gus, ever the protective friend, stood by her side, his face a mask of concern and barely restrained anger.

Sam scanned the room in disbelief. "From the state of things, I'm not sure I could tell you if anything's missing," he said. "The TV's still here… broken, but here. DVD player too. Might be a while before I know for sure. Can I let you know after we've had a chance to clean up?"

The officer hesitated, looking around at the mess. "It looks like no one has been hurt, so sure." He turned to Emily and asked if she was happy with what Sam had said.

Emily didn't respond. Her eyes met Sam's—and he saw nothing but sadness.

Grace answered for her. "We checked upstairs. Some jewellery's missing—we already mentioned it to you. So yeah, I guess that's fine."

Emily looked down, eyes closed, leaning against the counter as Grace kept her steady.

Gus then spoke, his voice calm but with an edge of frustration. "Like we said, we got here and found the place like this. We didn't see anyone around."

"Right then. We've got what we need for now." The officer turned to his partner. "Let's go."

"We brought Emily back from Victoria's party," Grace said. "She had a bit too much to drink."

Emily looked up, her eyes meeting Sam's. There was anger in them now.

"I am so sorry, Em," Sam said, genuine regret filling every word.

Emily's voice was barely above a whisper. "I can't stay here, Sam. I don't feel safe."

Gus put a reassuring hand on her shoulder. "We'll take her to our place." He looked back at Sam. "She can stay with us until this is all sorted out. There is nowhere to sleep here in this mess."

Sam nodded gratefully. "Thank you. I will go and get some clothes."

Sam stepped into the bedroom, the light revealing just how thoroughly it had been ransacked. As he sifted through the scattered clothes, his hand fell on a sweater Em loved, soft and comfortable, providing protection against the cold. A sharp contrast to the coldness of the regret he felt at not accompanying Emily to Vic's party. Maybe if he had gone, he could have protected her from the terror that now gripped their lives.

His gut was telling him that what he found on the drive was not right. He would have dismissed the information he found as something well researched for a novel. But when adding in his interrogations, the woman killing herself, him being followed, and now this break-in, it could not be dismissed as mere fantasy. This was going to change everything, but at what cost?

The need to uncover the truth battled fiercely with his guilt for not being there for Emily. Each piece of clothing he picked up felt heavier with the weight of his choices, torn between the life they had and the dangerous secrets he was now entangled in.

He followed Gus, Grace, and Emily down to the street. Gus had parked just down the block. Sam watched silently as Grace helped Emily into the back seat. Grace gave him a hug, wishing him good luck with the clean-up, and letting him know they would take good care of Emily.

As she hopped into the driver's seat, her door shutting with a solid thud, Gus closed the back door with another. The sounds were loud, firm—protective. The kind of protection Sam couldn't seem to offer.

Gus's expression hardened. His usual easy-going demeanour was gone, replaced with something more serious. Almost accusatory.

"Sam, you know I love you, man," he said. "But you need to get your shit together. People don't just ransack houses for no reason.

Whatever you're doing—whatever you've got going on—you need to work it out."

He didn't say what would happen if Sam didn't. He didn't have to.

Sam let out a breath and ran a hand through his hair. "I know, Gus. And you know that I love you guys. I wish I could tell you what is going on, but I really can't."

He locked eyes with Gus, trying to convey all the sincerity he could. Gus held the stare for a moment, then slapped him on the shoulder—their way of ending heavy conversations.

Left alone, Sam began the slow, gruelling task of cleaning up.

He moved methodically, putting furniture back in place and sweeping up the glass. His mind was a whirlwind of thoughts. Hours passed as the apartment slowly began to resemble its former glory. But the sense of violation lingered, a constant reminder of the unseen threat lurking just out of sight. Sam's resolve hardened. He felt a real urge to uncover the truth, but he needed to do it in a way that would protect Emily, and his friends.

With the apartment somewhat cleaned up but still a mess, he finally sank onto the couch, exhausted. Sam knew that his life had just become infinitely more complicated. But this thing could be dangerous, and it seemed to him that the government wanted it and were willing to kill for it. That made sense, he could get that, but why would a criminal tell him to expose it, then destroy it?

He couldn't trust the Feds.

Not yet.

In the early hours of the morning, exhausted and afraid, Sam made a decision.

He would find out the truth—no matter the cost.

15

Sam's left eye snapped open.

He was lying face down, sprawled out, nose squashed against the mattress of his bed. He lifted his head and looked down at the pool of drool saturating the mattress. The fog of waking up slowly dissipated, allowing him to realise that he had fallen asleep, sprawled out over the unmade bed. He rolled over, which was more of a flop, lying on his back looking up at the ceiling. Today was going to be another tough day of cleaning. He slowly sat up. As if to reiterate the point, the bedroom was still in disarray, clothes and personal items scattered everywhere, a tangible reminder of the chaos that had invaded his life, or that he invited in.

The dim light coming in through the sheer curtain cast eerie shadows that only heightened his sense of unease. The overturned dresser and the broken picture frame on the floor seemed to accuse him, reminding him that this invasion was, in part, his fault.

The flash drive in his jacket pocket felt heavier than ever.

Like a key.

Or a curse.

Sam pushed himself up. His muscles ached. But more than that, his mind screamed for direction.

Coffee. Food. Air.

Then answers.

He needed to get out of the apartment—out of his head.

Heading out, the fresh air was like an adrenalin shot straight into his brain. His thoughts instantly settled on what he needed to do, if he was going to get to the bottom of whatever this was. When he reached the sidewalk outside his building, on the way to his car that was still parked across the street, he stopped for a lady out walking her dogs. He smiled at her, acknowledging the day. She returned the gesture with a smile. Sam had not seen her before. Still smiling, he spotted the small receiver nestled in her ear. He had forgotten about his shadow.

If he was going to dig deeper, he needed to upgrade his tools—and his identity. New equipment. New name. Something that couldn't be traced back to him. Not this him.

Sam slid into his car, the familiar scent of leather and faint traces of his cologne and Emily's perfume offering a surprising level of comfort amidst the turmoil. He knew that lady would not be the only person following him. If the CIA and the FBI both had a stake in this, there would be others around. He smiled despite the situation. The idea that the FBI and the CIA were trying to hide from him, plus each other, while trying to follow him was somewhat amusing.

As he drove through the quiet streets, he caught glimpses of nondescript cars tailing him, always at a respectful distance but never out of sight. His training in surveillance, as well as real-world experience told him they were professionals, but so was he. Keeping his movements steady and deliberate, Sam made sure he drove his car along the same route he always did when driving to the office, his mind already working several steps ahead.

Pulling into the parking lot of the mall, Sam parked his car in its usual spot, making sure to act as though everything was routine. He stepped out, locking the car behind him with an audible beep, and walked towards his office with a casual air. The surrounding shops reflected his sameness, but he felt the weight of unseen eyes on his back. Years of surveillance work had taught him to sense when he was being watched, and today was no different. He kept his pace unhurried, forcing himself to exude an aura of normalcy.

Once inside his office, Sam allowed himself a moment to gather his thoughts. The plan was simple. He would exit out the back door of his office, slipping into the corridors used by staff for deliveries and maintenance that ran behind the mall's stores. They were locked at the ends to keep unauthorised people out, so were rarely monitored. Even if those doors were being watched, walking through the corridors would not be, and he could make his way to the electronics store unnoticed.

He navigated the narrow back corridors. The dimly lit passageways, lined with service doors and maintenance equipment, felt like a hidden world within the familiar one. Each step echoed softly, a reminder of the silent urgency driving him forward. His senses remained on high alert, but he kept his pace measured, ensuring he didn't draw unnecessary attention. The electronic store's rear entrance loomed ahead, a plain metal door blending into the industrial backdrop.

Pushing the door open, Sam stepped into the storeroom of the electronics store. The sudden brightness was a stark contrast to the dim corridors, momentarily disorienting. A young attendant, who couldn't have been more than seventeen, looked up from unpacking boxes, his expression shifting from surprise to curiosity. Sam offered a friendly smile.

"Hey," he said, in greeting as he continued past the kid.

"Just a sec," the kid said, standing up and moving towards him. "Can I help you?" he asked, confused.

"Sorry, I have a store just down the corridor. Decided to avoid the crowds and use the back way in. Hope you don't mind."

The attendant's face lit up with a grin, clearly appreciating the shared insider knowledge. "Love it. So, can I help you with something?"

Sam thought about it for a second. He did not know that much about computer hardware, to be fair. He decided to use the kid. He quickly outlined his needs: a mid-range laptop with some bells and whistles, but only what was necessary to make it work well, and a burner phone.

The kid nodded, a knowing expression on his face. "Trying to keep things secret from the wife, huh," he said.

"Ha," Sam huffed, admiring the cheek of the kid. "I am a private detective. Why do you think I actually used the back corridors."

That gave the kid pause. Sam could see him thinking—trying to decide whether he was being serious or pulling one over him. After a moment, the kid just nodded slowly, apparently deciding to go along with it.

"Got just the thing. Follow me."

Sam followed like a loyal dog, trailing behind as the teen moved efficiently through the store, selecting what he needed with confident ease. The sale was rung up and packed into a shopping bag emblazoned with the store logo.

Sam hesitated. "Do you have a bag without a label?"

The kid frowned, still sizing him up. "Wait here—I might have something out back."

The kid returned quicker than Sam expected with a plain paper bag with a handle. It looked to be a bit used. When Sam frowned at him, the kid smiled and leaned in. "It belongs to that guy over there, Hugh." Sam looked to see a man in his late thirties who was attending to another client. "It's his bag. He is my boss. He's a dick. He was going to go shopping after his shift finished using that bag." The kid laughed.

Sam chuckled. "Thanks, kid."

With a nod, he left the store—out the front this time.

Sam walked towards his own storefront, passing a man sitting nearby, dressed like just another casual shopper. The man turned his head away, pretending not to watch him—but the look of confusion on his face gave him away.

Sam stopped, fished out his keys, and locked the door to his shop. Then, without a word, he walked right past the man.

He didn't look back.

But inside, he smiled.

Sam spent the rest of the day methodically cleaning up his apartment, restoring a semblance of order to the chaos left by the intruders. As he righted furniture and put everything back in its place, his underlying tension was a weight on his back, making things feel heavier than they were. Each item he picked up felt like a reminder of the delicate balance between his normal life and the dangerous secrets he was now entangled in.

By late afternoon, the fatigue began to creep in. He gave himself a brief rest. But even as he reclined on the couch, his mind didn't stop. He pulled out the new laptop and burner phone, unboxed them, and set to work.

Creating fake profiles. Encrypting passwords. Configuring anonymous networks.

He crafted every detail with precision—burner accounts, new email addresses, dummy social media setups. The laptop, clean and untraceable, would be his gateway to analysing the contents of the drive. The burner phone would be his silent line of communication—unlinked to his name, his life, or anyone he knew.

By the time he finished, the sun had long dipped below the horizon. The glow of the screen cast a pale light across the now-tidy room. Sam flicked on a lamp and leaned back in his chair, rubbing his tired eyes.

The apartment was back in order. His digital toolkit was ready.

Now, armed with safeguards and a fresh layer of anonymity, Sam could finally begin what he had been avoiding:

The deep dive into the secrets that had turned his life upside down.

16

Victor Langford stood on the golf tee, waiting his turn to tee off. The morning sun cast long shadows, the tranquillity of the golf course at odds with the weighty topics he and his executives were dissecting. He was not a good golfer, but these meetings were never about golf.

One of the men, Charles—the CEO of DataShield Technologies—meticulously placed his ball on the tee, adjusted his stance, and took a powerful swing, albeit the swing of an older gentleman. The ball disappeared with a resounding crack. The men turned to watch it arc through the clear blue sky before it landed, just to the right of the fairway.

"Nice shot, Charles," James said, as he stepped forward, next in line.

"Quite a mess at the rally," Victor remarked, watching Charles pick up his tee and make his way to the waiting men. "The woman who killed herself—did you hear much about it?"

Charles sighed. "Barely a blip in the news, but it overshadowed the rally."

James placed his ball down, then took a step back to survey the fairway. "Yeah, tragic and disruptive. The media was supposed to focus on our message. Instead, all the coverage we were expecting got buried under that incident. Our campaign took a hit because of it." He stepped up and sent the ball flying.

Victor nodded thoughtfully; his eyes narrowed as he considered their words. "It's a setback, no doubt. But the rally wasn't the only angle. We need to adapt and control the optics through other channels."

The third executive, Robert, took his turn at the tee. His ball, however, ended nowhere near the fairway, careening into the trees to the right.

"Damn it," he cursed, bending down to pick up his tee. "And then there's the First Lady. That public meltdown during her speech was... unexpected. People are already speculating about her mental health. If she continues to unravel, she might become quite the liability."

Robert turned to look at Victor. "I am sorry, Victor. I know how good a friend she is of yours. We all have the same opinion about how valuable she is. But..." he stopped, leaving the sentence hanging.

Victor sighed, rubbing his chin as he reflected on the chaotic developments. He stepped forward. "You're right, Robert. I have been friends with the First Lady since high school. But her instability can serve as a distraction, keeping the public's focus away from the message. Plus, if it becomes too much of a circus, we might lose control of the narrative entirely."

"We need to steer the conversation back to the core issues," Charles added. "Remind the public why the CIA's power needs to be checked. Use the chaos to our advantage, but don't let it drown out our message."

Victor nodded, his expression thoughtful, yet resolute. "I agree. We'll recalibrate our approach. Increase our lobbying efforts, ramp up the PR campaigns, and use our data analytics to subtly influence public opinion. We'll have to be smarter and more strategic."

Suddenly, Victor froze—standing perfectly still, posture rigid, hands by his sides, left hand still clutching his golf club. The others noticed immediately. Their conversation halted as they looked at him with confusion and concern.

Victor's eyes were fixed down the fairway. Then, he seemed to come out of the trance. He looked down at his left hand, which wore a pristine white golf glove. The tip of the club handle poked out the back of his hand, the rest angling down to where the club head rested gently on the grass.

Victor, now registering the object in his hand, let the club drop. He stared at the glove—first examining the back, then twisting his wrist to study the palm. He did it again. And again. Completely oblivious to anyone else around him.

"Victor?" Charles called, uncertain. No response.

Victor continued to stare at his hand, turning it over, inspecting each side. His face was devoid of expression, his eyes wide and unfocused. The other men exchanged worried glances, unsure of what to do.

"Hey, Victor, are you okay?" James stepped closer, his hand hovering near Victor's shoulder but not quite touching him.

Victor began to tug at the glove, his movements growing increasingly frantic as he tried to remove it. The glove wouldn't budge, and Victor's efforts only became more desperate.

"Victor, it's okay. Take a deep breath," James said. "What's going on?"

But Victor didn't seem to hear him. His focus was entirely on his hand, and he was visibly trembling now. His breath came in shallow gasps, and the other executives could see the sheen of sweat forming on his forehead.

Without warning, Victor stopped tugging on his glove and looked down. His pants began to darken as he lost control of his bladder. A confused look came over his face. James recoiled slightly, his concern deepening.

"We need to get him some help," Charles said urgently.

"Something's really wrong," James said.

Robert nodded and pulled out his phone to call for assistance. James and Charles continued to try and get Victor to answer them, but he remained unresponsive, staring at his hand with a mix of confusion and terror.

The man drove his golf utility vehicle across fairways and down cart paths, away from the tee box where Victor's executives were frantically trying to get his attention, a silver box resting harmlessly on the passenger seat. His expression was blank, as if this were just another day at work.

Other workers passed by, focused on raking sand traps or clearing debris. They paid him no attention—and he gave them none in return. He maneuvered the cart with quiet precision, blending into the background.

Minutes later, he arrived at a secluded shed at the edge of the grounds—a maintenance storage facility for golf carts and supplies. He rolled the vehicle inside, parked, and quietly shut the door behind him.

The shed also doubled as a general storage space, cluttered with an array of gardening tools and equipment. Rakes, shovels, and hoes hung neatly on one wall, while bags of fertiliser and seed were stacked in haphazard piles on the floor. A musty smell of earth and grass permeated the air, mingling with the faint scent of gasoline from a lawnmower parked in the corner. Wooden shelves lined the walls, filled with various containers of chemicals and spare parts, their labels faded and peeling. Amidst the organised chaos, a tarp covered some sort of form that lay on the floor—its presence adding a disconcerting element to the otherwise mundane space.

Inside the shed, the man quickly unzipped the green overalls the groundskeeping staff wore. He lifted one corner of the tarp, exposing a man's body, but didn't spare it more than a cursory glance. There were no signs of struggle. He tossed the overalls onto the body, then dropped the corner of the tarp, making sure it covered everything.

He grabbed the case off the seat of the buggy and walked calmly out of the shed. His mission accomplished, he slipped away without a trace of emotion, leaving behind the scenes of his silent, insidious work.

17

Sam walked through the house, his steps echoing slightly in the early morning quiet. He carried his new backpack by the top handle, letting it hang low, his new equipment safely packed away inside, including the flash drive. The living room looked almost normal again, save for the faint traces of yesterday's chaos. He paused at the threshold of the dining room, taking in the scene.

Emily sat at the table, her back to him, staring blankly at her cereal. The tightness in her shoulders a silent testament to the break-in and the strange behaviour he'd exhibited lately, and a reminder of his promise to Gus. He sighed, knowing he needed to ease her mind before heading to work.

"Morning, Em," Sam said gently as he approached the table, trying to sound casual. Emily glanced up at him, her eyes clouded with worry. He pulled out a chair and sat down across from her, reaching out to take her hand.

"I know things have been rough lately," he continued, his voice steady. "But I promise, everything's going to be okay. We'll get through this, and I'll make sure nothing like this happens again."

Emily's gaze softened slightly, but the uncertainty lingered. She squeezed his hand, a small gesture of acknowledgment.

"I just... I don't understand why this is happening, Sam. And you... you've been so distant."

Sam swallowed, feeling the weight of her words. He wished he could explain the secrets he'd been hiding, but for now, all he could offer was reassurance.

"Trust me," he said, forcing a smile. "We'll get through this together. Just hang in there, okay?"

Emily nodded slowly, and for a brief moment, Sam felt a flicker of hope amidst the lingering unease.

He descended the steps into the dimly lit basement parking garage, the faint hum of fluorescent lights echoing off the concrete walls. As he approached his car, he spotted his neighbour, Jake, fiddling with the trunk of his sedan. Jake was in his late twenties, a friendly guy who had always shown an interest in Sam's work as a private detective. Catching sight of Sam, Jake straightened up, a grin spreading across his face.

"Hey, Sam! How's it going? Heard about the break-in. You okay?" Jake asked, his voice tinged with genuine concern. "Does it have anything to do with one of your cases? I mean, should I be worried?"

Sam appreciated Jake's concern and enthusiasm but wanted to keep things as calm as possible. "Hey, Jake. Yeah, it was a bit of a shock, but I'm fine. You don't need to worry; you're safe."

Then an idea sparked—seeing Jake beside his open trunk.

"Full disclosure, I think it might be related to a case I'm working on, but I'm handling it." He knew Jake loved the idea of private detecting. He had a romantic James Bond-type association with it. Of course, the work he did was anything but. He paused, considering his next words carefully.

"Actually, Jake, I could use a bit of help. Some people have been following me, and I need to shake them off. Do you think you could give me a ride out of here? Just to the diner down the road."

Jake's eyes lit up, the prospect of being part of a real detective's escape plan clearly thrilling him. "Seriously? Hell yeah! That sounds awesome. Let's do it!"

He looked back at his car. He looked back at Sam, his smile turning into a cheeky grin. He put his hand on the trunk of his car. "Jump in," he said.

Sam laughed. "Thanks, Jake. But I was thinking more about just lying across your back seat."

"Your choice. Just know my trunk is always available if you need it." Jake walked around to the driver's side of the car.

Sam slid into the back seat of Jake's car, tossing his bag across to the other side. He lay down, his mind thinking about what he planned to do. As they pulled out of Jake's parking space, he could see Jake looking around enthusiastically. He needed Jake to be calm if this was going to work. Jake's enthusiasm was infectious, though. "Listen, Jake, you need to be calm. I can understand the excitement, but for this to work, the people outside the building cannot think you are up to something. They need to see you, then dismiss you straight away. The only way this works is if you act totally normal."

"You got it," Jake said, still excited.

Sam instantly regretted it, as Jake put his music on. Heavy metal, rock, at a decibel level that Sam thought would melt his eardrums. It seemed to work, however. When Sam sat up, after they were clear of the apartment complex, he could not see anyone behind them that looked suspicious.

Jake pulled into the parking lot of the diner, the early morning sun casting long shadows across the sidewalk. Before getting out of the car, Sam reached forward and slapped him on the shoulder.

"Thanks, Jake," Sam said, sincerity colouring his voice. "I really appreciate your help back there. You've made things a lot easier for me."

Jake beamed with pride, nodding enthusiastically. "Hey, no problem at all, Sam! Glad I could help. It's not every day I get to be part of a detective's escape plan! You've made my day!"

With a final smile and a nod of gratitude, Sam exited the car, feeling a sense of relief mingled with cautious optimism as he headed into the diner to continue his urgent task.

As he stepped into the diner, the bell above the door chiming softly. Sam smiled to himself at how universally the simple trick of a bell above the door is used. He'd never been here before, which was exactly why he chose it, a small, cozy establishment with checkered floors and booths lining the walls. He noticed a sign near the entrance advertising wi-fi, along with the password. Perfect, he thought, as he made his way to a booth at the back, hoping for some privacy.

Sliding into the booth, Sam took a moment to scan the room. The morning crowd was sparse, a few solitary diners sipping coffee and reading newspapers. No one who he thought was following him was there. His plan had worked.

A waitress approached, a friendly smile on her face. "What can I get you, hun?" she asked, pulling out a notepad.

"Coffee, please. Plus, some bacon and eggs on wheat toast," Sam replied, returning her smile with a tired one of his own. As the waitress walked away, he set his laptop on the table and opened it, feeling the weight of the situation pressing down on him. He had no time to lose.

Before connecting to the diner's wi-fi, Sam inserted the flash drive into his laptop. His fingers moved quickly, copying the contents onto a new drive he had brought with him. The files transferred steadily, a progress bar creeping across the screen. He glanced up occasionally, keeping an eye on the diner's patrons and the entrance, as well as outside.

The waitress returned. "Here's your coffee. Your food will be ready shortly," she said, placing the cup down on the table and pouring coffee into it. As promised, shortly after that, she returned with his food, setting his breakfast plate down in front of him, with a knife and fork, neatly wrapped in a napkin blanket. Sam nodded, offering a quick thanks before focusing back on his work.

As the new drive finished copying, he began to eat, the savoury taste of bacon and eggs a brief comfort amidst his growing anxiety. With one hand on his fork, he used the other to take a series of screenshots from some of the files, plus saved blocks of computer code as new documents. He knew enough about computer code to know that a picture of a page would do nothing. It needed to be something substantial. Each click of the screenshot tool felt like a step closer to exposing the truth, and a step further into danger. He worked methodically, ensuring he didn't miss anything crucial.

Once satisfied with the screenshots, Sam opened his email client for his fake email address. He hesitated for a moment, glancing around the diner one last time before connecting his laptop to the wi-fi. The signal was strong, and he quickly drafted a series of emails to Detective Lawson, attaching screen shots to each of them.

He couldn't shake the nagging doubt in his mind about Detective Lawson. He hoped he could trust her. Their previous encounter had given him a strong feeling that he could. Despite her probing questions, there was something in her demeanour that hinted at a mutual understanding. With the stakes as high as they were, he needed to start bringing people in. He did not understand enough about what was going on and needed her inside knowledge.

In the first email, Sam included his burner phone number. "Detective Lawson," he typed, "in our last conversation, you asked me if I would like to discuss things with you, detective to detective. Before I can be comfortable doing that, I need you to look at the attached files and give me some advice. I think it is something big." He added the phone number of his burner phone, then hit send, watching the email disappear into the digital ether.

He sent several more emails, each with different attachments and more details about what he had uncovered, but no more words. The waitress returned to refill his coffee, and he thanked her with a distracted nod. The urgency of his task consumed him, the diner around him fading into the background.

Sam leaned back in the booth, sipping his coffee and thinking about the events that had led him here. The break-in, being followed, the information on the drive. It occurred to him that he had no expectation of what he expected after sending the emails. Would he just sit and wait for a response? Another look around the diner; another look outside; still no one. He needed to keep moving. Pay the bill, move on.

18

Gloria sat at her desk, the buzz of the station filling the air around her. She was sipping her stale coffee, trying to muster the energy to tackle the paperwork waiting for her. She loved being a detective but did not like the paperwork. Daily reports of her actions just seemed like control. As she was about to dive in, her computer pinged with the arrival of several new emails. The sender was anonymous, which immediately caught her interest. Her paperwork instantly forgotten, she opened the first email, and her eyes widened as she scrolled through the contents.

"Detective Lawson, in our last conversation, you asked if I would like to discuss things with you, detective to detective. Before I can be comfortable doing that, I need you to look at the attached files and give me some advice. I think it is something big," was the first thing she read. While it was from an anonymous source, she knew who it was: Sam Caldwell.

The email contained several pictures of a strange, sleek device that looked like something out of a science fiction movie. It resembled a futuristic weapon, with a metallic sheen and intricate components that hinted at advanced technology. Her curiosity turned to concern as she opened the attachments, revealing a list of names and what looked like computer code. Gloria knew nothing about coding, but the names and the images of the device were enough to set her mind off with excitement. He can't be a crank. He must be onto something. Why else would the CIA and FBI be interested in him?

She quickly scanned through the subsequent emails, each one containing more pictures and snippets of code. The list of names was extensive, and she couldn't help but wonder what kind of operation she was looking at. Two names jumped out at her—the heads of the CIA and the FBI. She aspired to get into either one of those agencies one day, so was very aware of who headed them. This was a puzzle she didn't have the pieces for and with all the computer code, she definitely was not equipped for it. She needed help.

She glanced across to the adjoining desk, where Vince was hunched over, engrossed in their latest case. Trying to be discreet, she tapped her pen on her desk, hoping to get his attention without drawing too much notice. Vince didn't look up, so she cleared her throat softly and tapped her pen a little louder.

"Boss," she said quietly, trying to keep her voice calm.

He glanced up briefly but then returned to his work. Frustration gnawed at her, but she didn't want to make a scene.

"I need you to look at something. It's important."

He sighed heavily, clearly not in the mood for distractions. "If it's got nothing to do with a case, then I'm not interested."

"Just take a look, please," she insisted. Despite the please, her tone left little room for argument.

Vince finally relented, pushing back from his desk and walking around to her side. He leaned over her shoulder as she pulled up the emails and began showing him the pictures.

"What's this?" he asked, only mildly interested. He leaned in closer, his eyes narrowing as he examined the images. "Is that some kind of weapon?"

"It looks like it," Gloria replied, scrolling through the pictures. "And look at this," she added, opening one of the attachments with the list of names and the computer code. She highlighted the two names she recognised earlier.

"What am I looking at?" he said, about to walk away.

"That's what I am saying—I don't know what any of this means, but it can't be good, right!"

Vince rubbed his chin, frowning, obviously still sceptical. "Good for what, good for who? Where did you get this?" he said.

"Well, technically, an anonymous sender," Gloria said, shaking her head, "but I am convinced it is from that guy, Sam Caldwell. Remember him? The private detective we questioned last week. He seems like he has stumbled onto something, don't you think?"

"Seriously, Gloria. That so-called private detective who didn't even notice his gun was gone 'til he got home. You think he has stumbled onto something to do with some type of futuristic weapon, involving the heads of the CIA and FBI!"

"Well, yeah, it definitely looks that way, doesn't it?" Gloria asked.

Vince took pause, shaking his head. He seemed to be wrestling with the idea it might be true. After a moment, he said, "It looks like fuckin' bullshit to me. But, ok, let's play along. Let's say that it is true. Let's say this crackpot has somehow come across information about a weapon, and it does indeed involve the CIA and the FBI. Firstly, how the hell did he come to have that information? And secondly, what exactly are we supposed to do with it? We're small-time, suburban detectives. We investigate robberies, murders. We don't get involved in conspiracies, especially ones that are at the federal government level," he said. "What we do is report them to the FBI."

"And, if the FBI are involved, what then?" Gloria asked.

"Then we dust our hands off and move on with our lives."

"Fuck that!" Gloria said, emphatically. "You saw yourself how those two CIA agents were treating Sam. Then, just disappeared."

"Do we even know they were CIA?" Vince said.

"Exactly!" Gloria snapped. "We don't. Yet another piece of a puzzle we have no answers to. And you know what, this happened on our turf. I think it is for us to investigate."

Vince lifted his head and let out a long sigh—the kind Gloria's mother used to make when she knew her daughter wasn't going to let something go.

"I tell you what, Boss, let me investigate this. Give me a week. If I haven't been able to find anything worth investigating further, I will pass it onto the FBI and move on. What do you say?" Her voice filled with childish pleading, hoping to tap into Vince's fatherly emotions.

He looked down at her with the exact expression she was hoping for. That of a father about to give into their daughter's hopes to go out for the night with a boy, but not happy about it. Gloria smiled.

"I knew you would understand," she said.

"A week," Vince muttered. "And your other work doesn't get put aside."

"Thanks, Boss," Gloria said, beaming.

She turned back to the pictures, her keen eyes scanning the high-resolution images. Besides the list of names hinting at possible victims, suspects, or collaborators, it was the images of complex computer code that were the most perplexing. Each line of code seemed laden with encrypted secrets, potentially holding the key to a dangerous plot, or a big joke. With the gravity of the situation weighing on her, Gloria knew she had to curb her excitement, and tread carefully. She had been given a rare liberty by Vince. She needed to not step all over it.

Gloria's mind raced with strategies, but one clear course of action emerged. Understanding the computer code was crucial, and for that, she needed expertise beyond her own. Given her expertise extended to being able to manage a spreadsheet, that could well be anyone in the precinct. She decided, however, to take the images to the police station's tech expert, Harper Adams. Harper was clever and had helped them in the past. She had a sharp intellect and a knack for deciphering the most cryptic of codes.

She picked up the phone and called Harper's extension.

Gloria leaned back in her chair in the small meeting room, watching Harper intently as she adjusted her glasses and studied the images. The meeting room was modest in size, with pale grey walls that seemed to absorb the soft light from the overhead fluorescents. The only things in the room were an unused white board hanging on the wall, and a rectangular table, large enough to comfortably seat six people, which dominated the centre of the room. The table's surface was a dark, polished wood, unmarred except for a few faint scratches that hinted at years of use. Around it, six ergonomic chairs with black mesh backs and cushioned seats were neatly arranged, of which she and Harper occupied two.

The first image Harper looked at was of the sleek device, which seemed to hum with latent energy even in the photograph. It was unlike anything Harper had seen before, but her interest grew sharply as she began examining the accompanying pictures of intricate computer code.

She flipped through the files quickly at first, her brow furrowing as she tried to make sense of what the code was doing. She mumbled something under her breath about energy dispersion and electromagnetic fields. Gloria watched as Harper's eyes moved back and forth, the gears turning in her mind as she deciphered each line.

After ten minutes or so, Gloria asked, ""What do you think it is?" Her voice broke the silence. She leaned forward, anticipation evident in her posture.

Harper didn't answer immediately. She was too engrossed in the code, her fingers tapping the table rhythmically as if keeping time with her thoughts. The silence stretched, and Gloria's excitement grew. She knew Harper well enough to recognise that this level of hyperfocus meant what she was reading had caused the rest of the world to disappear. At one moment, Harper's eyes twitched, a serious look on her face.

Finally, Harper looked up, her eyes reflecting both confusion and intrigue. "This is... unusual," she began slowly. "The code—it seems to be designed for data capture. But not just any data. If I am understanding what I am reading, it seems to be referencing human data, whatever that means, in a way that's far more complex than anything I've seen before."

Gloria's heart pounded. "Human data?" she said, as if verbalising her thoughts.

"How to describe it..." Harper said, trying to gather her thoughts into a cohesive way that would make sense. After a couple of failed starts, she finally said, "It's like...no, imagine...wait... yes, imagine a camera taking a photo, you know. It captures the data points of what it is looking at and then recreates that image using the data it captures, but infinitely more complicated," Harper explained, stressing the word "infinitely" with a wave of her hand. "This device, whatever it is, seems capable of capturing detailed information about a person?" she said, finishing the sentence as a question, while screwing up her face, as if she did not even believe or understand what she was saying. "But the code is unfinished, fragmented. Is there any more?"

Gloria smiled, though it did not reach her eyes. "Honestly, I don't know. This is all I was sent."

"Gloria," Harper said, her tone suddenly low and serious, "who sent you this?" The colour draining from her face.

"That I cannot say right now. Why do you ask?"

"Two reasons. When developers write code, they always leave notes inside it. That way, when other developers come along years later, they can understand the reasons behind the logic. It is customary for the developer to leave their name as part of their comments. That is the first thing. The second thing, you would know, is when a document is created, it usually has a footer, or header that is the name of the document."

Gloria nodded in understanding.

Harper pointed to the footer of the document she had open on screen. "This is likely the project name: Forever Person, whatever that means," she said. "But here's what I can tell you for sure. This project is very likely connected to the CIA."

Gloria's eyes widened. "How can you tell that?" she asked, excitedly.

Harper's voice remained steady. "Have you ever heard the term, 'Deus ex machina'?"

Gloria frowned and shook her head. Where was Harper going with this, she thought.

"It is a literary term that describes an improbable and contrived event in a story, describing situations that feel unrealistically convenient or miraculous."

"And that is important why?" Gloria asked, growing impatient.

"Because that seems to be what is happening right now." Harper took a breath. "I have a friend—a genius. And I mean genius. Here's Einstein," she said, raising one hand to mid-level, "and here's my friend," she said, raising the other twice as high. "She lives not far from here. She works for the CIA as a computer scientist. Black ops projects. I have no idea what she actually does. But…"

Harper pointed to a comment line in the code, and to a name beside it.

"That comment was written by my friend, Isabella."

Gloria's eyes opened wide, and she moved her hand up to her mouth. Sadness welled up inside her instantly. "Oh my God, Harper, I am so sorry."

Harper just looked at her confused. "Why?"

"Do you watch the news?" Gloria asked, herself a bit confused.

"No," Harper said. "It's too depressing."

"I hate to tell you this, but I think something might have happened to your Isabella."

"What do you mean?"

"I believe the person who sent me this information got it from your friend." Gloria went on to relay the story of Sam and the woman who shot herself with his gun, and now being sent this information. She told Harper that they did not know the name of the woman who killed herself because she had no ID, but was wearing a white lab coat. She mentioned the CIA and the FBI had been here interrogating the man, but he had not said anything to them, and said that she was the only person he had spoken to.

As Gloria spoke, Harper's expression grew increasingly sorrowful. At the point where Gloria mentioned the white lab coat, Harper's resolve broke, and tears began to stream down her cheeks. She wiped them away but could not control herself. She wept for her friend.

After a while, she said, "I had not heard from Isabella for weeks, which is not normal. Now I know why."

Gloria stayed silent while Harper gathered herself together and managed to calm down.

"How can we get access to the rest of the code?" she said finally, a surprising amount of determination in her voice.

"I can contact the person who sent this stuff to me…"

"Do that," Harper said, cutting Gloria off. "I will dig deeper into the code—see if I can piece together more of it."

"Whatever you need," Gloria said. "I'll get it for you. We must know what we're dealing with…and who, I suppose."

19

CIA Director Chris Barrett sat behind his expansive mahogany desk—a symbol of power and prestige, reflecting his self-assured arrogance. The office, bathed in the muted glow of recessed lighting, was a showcase of opulence and meticulous order. Framed diplomas and commendations adorned the walls, each strategically placed to reinforce the aura of authority that Director Barrett cultivated. Heavy drapes framed the floor-to-ceiling windows, partially concealing the panoramic view of Washington, D.C. His high-backed executive chair was designed to dwarf any visitor who sat across from him.

He leaned back, his eyes wandering over the framed photographs on the credenza behind him. Each one captured a moment of significance in his career—a handshake with a president, a group shot with his team in Kabul, a candid snap from an intelligence summit in Brussels. His gaze shifted to the digital clock on the corner of his desk, its red digits ticking away the seconds.

Punctual as ever, Director Landon Walker, the head of special ops, entered the room. Without knocking first, Director Barrett mused. He was a tall, imposing figure, with close-cropped hair and a demeanour that exuded competence and control. He moved with the precision of a man accustomed to command, closing the door behind him with a quiet click before walking briskly to Director Barrett's desk.

He stood at attention on the opposite side of the desk, his posture erect and unwavering. Barrett didn't miss the stiff, military bearing, despite the civilian suit, observing him with a mix of impatience and scrutiny. Despite the tension, Landon exuded a calm confidence that irked Director Barrett, as though the power dynamics in the room were somehow not as one-sided as they should be.

"Good morning, Landon," Director Barrett began, his tone crisp and direct. "Take a seat," he said, pointing to one of the chairs. It was more a command than a gesture of friendship, or etiquette.

He noticed the brief flicker of annoyance in Landon's eyes as he complied, his movements stiff and controlled. It was clear Landon did not appreciate being ordered to sit, viewing Director Barrett more as a peer than a superior. He understood Landon's perspective but firmly believed in the chain of command—this was his show, and Landon was there to follow his lead.

"What can be salvaged from the site?" he demanded, his voice edged with urgency, barely able to contain his frustration.

Landon exhaled before breaking the bad news. "The whole thing is a total fucking shitshow, Director," he replied, his tone sombre. "Everyone is dead, including Dr. Taylor. The place is completely burned. All the hardware is destroyed, which means all the hard drives of the computers, and consequently, all the software that had been developed. The laboratory was obliterated. And, if that isn't bad enough, as you know, the girl killed herself before we could get to her." Landon's words hung heavily in the air, the weight of the disaster pressing down on both men.

Director Barrett slammed his fist onto his desk, his frustration boiling over. "How the hell did this happen?" he demanded, his voice rising.

Landon shook his head, unable to provide a satisfactory answer. "I don't know, Director," he admitted. "But it's not stopping progress, as you know. The database is complete, so all we need now is the access key."

Director Barrett stared at Landon, the magnitude of their setback sinking in, but also the glimmer of a path forward, however difficult it might be.

"Where are we with that?" Director Barrett began, his voice now back to a more measured blend of irritation and authority.

Landon's gaze remained steady. "We have been unsuccessful in locating it, at this stage," he said, as if speaking with a co-worker. "Our teams are working around the clock, but…"

"Spare me the excuses, Landon," Director Barrett interrupted, eyes narrowing.

"We have reason to believe the drive was slipped into the pocket of a bystander, who happens to be a private detective. And, without giving excuses…" Landon said, lacing his tone with disdain at the accusation, "this detective seems to have quite the talent for evading surveillance. When this is all over, it might be worth approaching him for his service," Landon added, ironically, giving a reason why the drive had not been obtained.

"If you do not have the capacity to obtain the drive, at least tell me the recreation of it is progressing," Director Barrett said in a clipped tone.

"Well, that is also proving to be a challenge," Landon said.

Director Barrett's eyes narrowed. "Explain."

"Before the drive was stolen, all remnants of the code on it were meticulously destroyed to prevent any unauthorised access to the database," Landon explained. "Now we are in a catch-22 situation. If we had access to the database, we could have access to a back-up copy of the code needed to access it. And the only code outside the database we can use to access the database… is on that drive. You see my issue?"

"Okay, stop talking." All Director Barrett could see was an asshole trying to baffle him with bullshit. He lifted his hands in a gesture of impatience.

"We've got PhDs on payroll—why the hell can't we just bring in more?"

Silence passed between the two of them. Landon smiled a knowing smile, his expression unflinching.

"So, the drive is the only key?" Director Barrett asked, barely concealing his frustration.

"At this stage. And the irony of that question is not lost on me. Recreating the logic and the exact sequence of the original coding is proving difficult."

Director Barrett leaned back in his chair, the leather creaking under the shift of his weight. His piercing gaze never left Landon's face. "Complicated? How much longer before we have that drive?"

Landon met his glare with an unyielding calm. "We're doing everything we can. The process is painstaking, but our best teams are on it."

"Painstaking is not good enough," Director Barrett snapped. "Every moment we don't have that drive is a risk to national security. I want this resolved quickly. Do you understand?"

"Perfectly, Director," Landon replied evenly. "We're pulling in every available resource."

Director Barrett stood, the action signalling the end of the meeting, but also an implicit command for urgency. He towered over Landon, trying to impose his will through his presence.

"Then make it happen. Failure is not an option."

Landon inclined his head slightly—a gesture of acknowledgment rather than submission. "Understood, Director. We will find the drive."

As Landon turned to leave, Director Barrett watched him with a mix of frustration and grudging respect. Landon never broke under pressure, and his calm demeanour in the face of his demands was both infuriating and admirable.

"Walker," Director Barrett called just as Landon reached the door.

Landon paused and looked back.

"Don't let me down," Director Barrett said, his tone softer but still carrying the weight of authority.

Landon gave a curt nod. "You have my word."

The door closed behind Landon, and Director Barrett sank back into his chair, staring at the space where the head of special ops had stood. He clenched his jaw, the muscle ticking with suppressed anger.

The drive was the linchpin.

20

Director Barrett sat stiffly in the Oval Office, surrounded by the other heads of the US security agencies. The room radiated authority and history, with its distinctive shape framed by tall, elegant windows that flooded the room with natural light. The walls were lined with portraits of past presidents and defining moments in history, a constant nod to its legacy. The iconic Resolute Desk, a symbol of presidential power and duty, sat at the centre, flanked by comfortable armchairs and sofas arranged for intimate discussions and high-stakes meetings. Rich, deep-coloured carpets and tasteful drapery added to the room's dignified ambiance, while the American flag and presidential seal prominently displayed reaffirmed the gravity and significance of every decision made within these walls.

The perfect room for a high-profile puppet, Director Barrett mused.

President Reynolds was a tall and imposing figure, his sharp, blue eyes reflecting a blend of determination and weariness. His salt-and-pepper hair, perfectly groomed, and the tailored suit he wore with effortless authority, projected an image of seasoned leadership and unwavering resolve. Today, however, his normally composed demeanour was replaced by, frustration, pacing back and forth behind the Resolute Desk.

"Alright," the President began, his voice strained, "I need answers. What happened to the First Lady has now happened to Victor Langford—my friend!"

"Mr. President," Director Barrett began, choosing his words carefully, "we are dealing with an unprecedented situation. From studying the footage of the First Lady, we have discovered that there was some type of shimmer, almost like a distortion, in and about her before she began acting... differently."

The President stopped pacing and turned to face the group, his eyes narrowing. "A shimmer? A fucking shimmer! What does that even mean?"

Director Barrett could feel the weight of the President's glare. "Our experts are still trying to understand the nature of this phenomenon. It's unlike anything we've seen before."

FBI Director Karen Shaw leaned forward, her expression equally grave. "We've ruled out any known chemical or biological agents. There are no signs of physical harm or trauma." She turned her gaze back to Director Barrett.

"Then what are we dealing with?" the President snapped, his frustration boiling over. "A psychological attack? Some new kind of weapon?"

Director Barrett always felt a subtle discomfort in the intense gaze of the FBI head—a lingering unease stemming from unresolved issues in their past that cast a shadow over their interactions. Despite this, he maintained a stoic exterior, his demeanour unwavering and composed, masking the disquiet that simmered beneath the surface. Director Shaw, with her sharp intellect and no-nonsense attitude, often challenged his decisions, adding to the friction between them. Their exchanges, while outwardly civil, were tinged with an unspoken rivalry and strain that neither seemed willing to address openly.

"We're exploring all possibilities, Mr. President," Director Barrett said, trying to maintain his composure. "But without more information, it's difficult to pinpoint the exact cause."

The room fell into a tense silence, the air thick with unspoken fears and doubts.

The President ran a hand through his hair, his frustration evident. "This is unacceptable. My wife and now my friend are... incapacitated, and you have nothing concrete to offer me."

"We're working around the clock, Mr. President," Director Shaw said, "But the lack of evidence and the unprecedented nature of the incidents are slowing us down."

NSA Director Mark Holden spoke up, his tone defensive. "Our cyber teams have found no digital traces that could explain the incidents. No communications, no hacking attempts, no anomalies in the systems."

"Then what the hell is it?" the President exploded, slamming his fist on the desk. "I don't want excuses. I want results. Find out who is behind this and why they are targeting me."

"We need to coordinate our efforts better," Director Shaw said, trying to steer the conversation in a productive direction. She needed to know what all agencies were doing so she could better monitor them. "This infighting isn't helping anyone. We need to pool our resources and expertise."

"Agreed," the President said. "We need a game plan—and we need it now."

Director Barrett nodded. He needed to influence what this unified approach looked like.

"We'll establish a joint task force," Director Shaw said, before Director Barrett had the chance to say anything further. "Combining the best minds from each of our agencies. We'll leave no stone unturned until we find out who or what is behind these attacks."

The President's gaze softened slightly, his anger giving way to a desperate hope. "Do whatever it takes. I don't care about jurisdiction or protocol. Just get it done."

Director Barrett stared at Director Shaw. That goddamn bitch. She had never liked the idea of the CIA. If she had any clue what the CIA really did—what he did—she'd lose her damn mind. There was no way she would be able to handle what needed to be done.

"Yes, Mr. President," Director Barrett said calmly. "We won't let you down."

As the meeting adjourned, Director Barrett lingered for a moment, watching the President's weary figure slump into his chair. This was more than a national security issue—it was personal. And the stakes had never been higher.

Outside the Oval Office, Director Barrett found himself flanked by Directors Shaw and Holden. The tension between them simmered, but there was a grudging understanding that cooperation was something he needed to do for now.

"We need to set aside our differences," Director Shaw said quietly. "The President's right—if we don't solve this, we're all out of a job. And worse, we'll have failed to protect our country."

Director Holden nodded, his expression resolute. "Agreed. Let's get to work."

21

Sam pushed open the heavy glass doors of the bank, the whoosh of air passing him as the outside and inside atmospheres equalised. The lobby was bustling with activity—tellers calling out for the next customer, the hum of conversations. The bank's interior was sleek and professional, with promotional posters about mortgages and investment plans lining the walls. To the right, a series of offices with frosted glass doors lined the wall, each occupied by bank employees in business attire, engrossed in their work.

He made his way across to the enquiries desk, the sound of his footsteps captured within the carpeted floor.

As he approached, a young woman with a friendly smile greeted him. "Good afternoon, sir. How can I assist you today?"

"I am here to add something to my safety deposit box," Sam said, his voice steady but carrying an undertone of urgency. He slid his ID and bank card across the counter.

The woman swiped the card and checked Sam's information on her screen. She turned back to Sam, still smiling. "Of course, Mr. Caldwell. I'll need you to sign in." She handed him a logbook, along with his ID and bank card.

He quickly scribbled his name, feeling a slight tension in his fingers.

The woman picked up the phone and spoke into the receiver. "Hi Joel, I have a customer here who needs to access a safety deposit box," she said, then hung up. "If you could take a seat," she added, pointing to an area of the bank that had some comfortable chairs arranged around a small coffee table.

Sam sank into one of the chairs, his back straight and eyes scanning the room. The plush cushion did little to ease his mind as he pretended to peruse a magazine, his gaze flicking up every few seconds to scan the faces of the people coming and going. His heart pounded—each beat a reminder of the drive stashed away.

He scanned the faces around him for anything suspicious, any lingering glances—but everyone seemed preoccupied with their own business. He felt a measure of relief that no immediate threat was apparent, but he knew better than to let his guard down.

After what felt like hours, but was more like ten minutes, another bank clerk came to get him. He was led through a secure door and down a short corridor. The atmosphere shifted the moment they left the lobby. The hallway was quieter, almost sterile, with beige walls and soft carpeting that further muffled their footsteps.

At the end of the hall, they reached another secured door. The clerk swiped his card and gestured for Sam to follow him inside.

The room was small, about the size of Sam's office, with rows of metal doors lining the walls—each securing a safety deposit box. A table stood in the centre, flanked by a couple of sturdy chairs. The air was cooler here, as if the room were refrigerated to preserve its contents. Sam heard the faint hum of air conditioning and the soft click of the door locking behind them.

Sam was led to his box. The clerk inserted one key and took Sam's key to unlock the second slot. With a swift turn, the door popped open slightly. The clerk pulled it open and stepped back.

"I'll leave you to it. Just press the button when you're done, and someone will escort you out."

Sam nodded, waiting until the clerk left before stepping towards the box. His fingers trembled slightly as he pulled open the drawer, revealing a small, velvet-lined compartment. A few documents sat inside, but his focus was on the computer drive in his pocket.

He pulled it out and placed it in the box. Such an innocuous-looking item, yet it held immense significance. He closed the drawer and locked it, feeling a weight lift off his shoulders, replaced by a different kind of tension. He was now fully committed.

Sliding the box back into the hold, he turned the key to secure it. Then he walked to the exit and pressed the button as instructed.

Within moments, the clerk returned, his polite smile still in place.

"All set, Mr. Caldwell?" he asked.

"Yes, thank you," Sam replied. The clerk retrieved his key, and they began walking down the corridor.

Sam said, "I need to ask you something."

The clerk looked at him but did not stop walking. "Sure, what is it?"

"If anyone comes in asks if I've been here, could you tell them I haven't?"

The clerk's smile faltered for a brief second before he regained his composure. "To divulge information about any of our customers, Mr. Caldwell, would be a breach of privacy."

Sam nodded. "I was hoping you would say something like that. Thank you."

As they returned to the lobby, Sam's mind raced. He replayed the events of the past few days, trying to anticipate what might come next. He knew placing the drive in the safety deposit box was the right move, but he couldn't shake the feeling that he was in over his head.

It was not the detecting part that worried him. His biggest concern was keeping his loved ones safe.

Back in the lobby, the noise and activity seemed louder, more chaotic. Sam glanced around, slipping into surveillance mode, even though he knew it was unlikely someone would have found him. He forced himself to walk calmly to the exit, resisting the urge to look over his shoulder.

Outside, the air enveloped him. He took a deep breath, trying to steady his nerves. The weight of his decision lingered, but he knew there was no turning back now.

As he walked away from the bank, Sam could not help but feel that he had just crossed an invisible line. The safety deposit box, with its cool metal and secure locks, now held a secret that could change everything.

With that, he stepped into the uncertainty of what lay ahead.

22

The next few days were a whirlwind of non-stop activity. The joint task force was established, bringing together the top experts in various fields—psychologists, cyber specialists, forensic scientists, and intelligence analysts. They worked tirelessly, combing through every piece of evidence, every theory, every possible lead.

Despite his true intentions, Director Barrett needed to appear fully engaged in solving the mystery. So he put himself front and centre, overseeing operations—controlling the narrative, both inside and outside the task force.

The scientists were focused on the footage of the First Lady, especially the shimmering effect that occurred moments before her behaviour changed. This was believed to be the clue. He had been told it was as if reality itself had been distorted—leaving no physical trace behind.

Initial psychological evaluations of the First Lady and Victor Langford yielded no answers; they were in perfect physical health but mentally regressed to a childlike state—possibly even pre-childhood—operating purely on instinct.

Late one night, Director Barrett stood in the command centre, staring at the array of monitors displaying data from various sources.

"Director Barrett," one of the analysts called out, snapping him from his reverie. "We've found something."

Director Barrett walked over. "What is it?"

The analyst pointed to a video feed from the night of the First Lady's incident. "Look closely at the shimmer. It appears for just a fraction of a second, but there's a pattern—almost like a digital signature."

Director Barrett leaned in, scrutinising the footage. It was faint, almost imperceptible, but there was indeed a pattern, a flicker that hinted at something more.

"Can you enhance it?"

"That is the enhanced version, but we're working on refining it further," the analyst replied, fingers flying over the keyboard.

As the image sharpened, Director Barrett felt a surge of something he could not put his finger on. Was it worry? Excitement? He could not tell.

"Get this to the cyber team immediately. We need to know what we're dealing with."

The hours that followed were tense, filled with a flurry of activity as the cyber specialists dissected the digital signature. It was unlike anything they had seen—a complex, almost organic pattern that defied conventional understanding.

Director Barrett's phone buzzed, jolting him from his thoughts. Seeing who was calling him, he sighed.

"Chris," the President's voice was weary but hopeful. "Do you have anything for me?"

"We might have found a lead, Mr. President," Director Barrett replied, keeping his voice steady. "A digital signature in the shimmer. We're analysing it now."

"That's something," the President said, a note of relief in his voice. "Keep me updated."

"Yes, sir," Director Barrett said, ending the call.

Over the next few hours, the digital signature was traced back to an article about a sophisticated piece of technology, one that could create a localised disruption in perception—essentially a high-tech illusion. It was the kind of cutting-edge tech that only one organisation in the world had the capability to develop.

"Which company?" Director Barrett asked.

"DataShield Technologies, as far as we know," the analyst said, his voice grim. "Unless I am mistaken, that is Victor Langford's company."

This information and the implications were staggering, exactly what Director Barrett could have hoped for. Sanctioned access to DataShield. He smiled.

"Let's keep digging deeper into DataShield. Find out who had access to this technology and why it was used. Oh, and keep this within this room for the moment. If this leaks, we lose the upper hand," he warned.

His directive was met with solemn nods.

23

Sam stepped into his apartment around seven in the evening, after a long day that had changed everything—for him and Emily. The door closing behind him with a quiet click. The warmth and familiarity of their apartment usually offered a refuge from the world, but tonight it felt different.

He took a deep breath, steeling himself for the evening ahead. The living room was dimly lit, the soft glow of a lamp casting long shadows. Emily was on the couch, her eyes flicking up from the book she was pretending to read as soon as she heard him enter.

"Hey," Sam said, trying to sound casual as he hung his jacket on the hook by the door.

"Hey," Emily replied, her tone cool and sceptical. "How was your day?"

"Busy," Sam replied, moving to the kitchen to pour himself a glass of water. "A lot of following people around, a meeting, and paperwork. The usual."

Emily watched him, her gaze piercing. "A meetings? What kind of meeting?"

Shit, why did he say, "a meeting"?

Sam took a sip of water, trying to buy himself a moment to think. "Just work stuff. You know how it is."

Emily closed her book with a snap, setting it aside. "I got a text today," she said, her voice deceptively calm. "From the bank. They said you put something in the safety deposit box. Mind explaining?"

Sam felt a cold knot form in his stomach. He had forgotten the bank's protocol—how both he and Emily were notified about access. How could he have been that stupid?

"It's nothing important," he said, forcing a smile. "Just some documents a client wanted me to keep safe. Part of a case. Which was what the meeting was about. I know I should have said something to you about it. I'm sorry."

"Documents…for a client…in our safety deposit box?" Emily said, her scepticism growing. "What kind of documents?"

"Just some documents," Sam said, his heart pounding. "Really, it's nothing to worry about."

Emily stood, her frustration evident in the way she moved. "Sam, why are you lying to me? I know when you're not telling me the whole truth. What's going on?"

"I'm not lying," Sam said, trying to keep his voice steady. Well, not entirely. "I just… I can't talk about it right now."

Emily's eyes flashed with anger. "Can't or won't?"

"Emily, please," Sam said, feeling the weight of his secrets pressing down on him. "It's complicated."

"Complicated?" Emily repeated, her voice rising. "You're keeping things from me, Sam! And now you're telling me it's complicated? Do you think I'm stupid?"

"Of course not," Sam said, taking a step towards her. "I just need you to trust me on this."

Emily threw her hands up in exasperation. "Trust you? How can I trust you when you won't even tell me what's going on? What am I supposed to think?"

Before Sam could respond, his phone rang. Not his normal phone, but the burner. The number he had given to Detective Lawson, which Emily did not know about.

His stomach dropped. Fuck! This was terrible timing. He closed his eyes for a moment before pulling the phone out of his pocket, flipping the screen open. Sure enough, it was Detective Lawson.

Emily's eyes widened, her mouth falling open. "What the fuck is that?" she said, her expression hardening.

Sam just looked at her. What could he say? He pushed the button to answer the phone and put it to his ear. "Hello?" he answered, trying to keep his voice steady.

"Sam, this is Detective Lawson. I was hoping you could come to the station. Now. It's important."

Sam watched as Emily stiffened, her ears pricking. It was clear she could hear the sound of Detective Lawson's voice; a woman's voice. "Who is that?" she demanded, pointing at the phone, her arms crossing defensively.

"It's Detective Lawson," Sam said, his mind racing. "She needs me to go down to the station."

"Oh, a female Detective Lawson," Emily said, her voice dripping with suspicion. "Who needs you to, 'go down to the station'," she added, making air quotes with her fingers. "Well, we both know what that might mean."

"I just got home," Sam said into the phone, desperation creeping into his voice. "I can't meet up right now."

"I don't think it can wait. We need to talk about your emails, and what we understand. Bring the drive." Lawson's voice came through the phone, firm and unyielding.

"You are going to meet up with her, aren't you? I can see it in your face," Emily's own face twisted with anger. "Unbelievable," she said, shaking her head. "What the hell is going on, Sam?"

"Fine," Sam said into the phone. He snapped the burner shut, ending the call. "Emily, I'm sorry," he said, his heart aching at the pain in her eyes. "I have to go."

"Yeah, of course you do," she snapped, turning on her heel and storming into the bedroom. "Go do whatever it is you're doing. Clearly, it's more important than being honest with me."

"Emily, please," Sam called after her, but she slammed the bedroom door shut, the sound echoing through the apartment.

Sam stood there for a moment, his heart aching. He hated seeing Emily like this, knowing that his actions and secrets were tearing her apart. He just hoped it wasn't tearing them apart. But he had no choice. There were things he couldn't tell her, not yet.

He took a deep breath, trying to compose himself, then grabbed his jacket and headed for the door.

As he left the apartment, the door closed behind him with a finality that echoed through the empty hallway. Sam's thoughts were a jumble of guilt, fear, and regret. He wanted nothing more than to protect Emily, to shield her from the chaos that was creeping into their lives. As he walked to his car, he couldn't shake the feeling that he might be losing her, one secret at a time.

Emily sat on the edge of her bed, her heart still pounding with anger and confusion. She picked up her phone and dialled Victoria's number, her fingers trembling slightly. The phone rang twice before her friend answered.

"Hey, Em! What's up?" Victoria's cheerful voice was a stark contrast to her turmoil.

"Hey, Vic," she began, her voice shaky.

"Are you okay, Em,?" Victoria asked, her cheerful tone instantly turning into concern.

"I just need someone to talk to."

"Is this about Sam? Is he continuing to be a dick?" Victoria asked bluntly—never one to mince words.

Emily took a deep breath, trying to collect her thoughts. "He came home late again tonight. But that wasn't the main issue. He put something in our safety deposit box without telling me. I got a message on my phone to say there had been access to the box. When I confronted him, he wouldn't tell me anything. And while we were discussing it, he got a call from a detective—a female detective— asking him to go down to the station. He just left, Vic. What am I supposed to think?"

"I will be honest. He could have been telling the truth, but a female detective?" Victoria questioned, her scepticism evident. "That ruins any credibility I might have given him. Are you sure it was a woman?"

"Yeah, I could hear her voice on the phone. He told her he couldn't meet up right now, but then he said he had no choice and left. He wouldn't explain anything to me, and now I'm just... I don't know what to think."

Victoria sighed heavily. "Em, that doesn't sound good. At the very least, he has confirmed now that he's keeping secrets from you, hiding things in the safety deposit box, and then rushing off to meet some woman? You know how bad that looks, right?"

Emily felt tears prick at her eyes. "You think he's cheating on me?"

"Honestly, it sounds like an open and shut case," Victoria said bluntly. "He's probably using this whole 'detective' story as a cover. Who knows what he's really up to."

Emily put her head in one of her hands, feeling the weight of Victoria's words. "But what if it's something else? What if he's really just...I don't know, involved in something he can't talk about?"

"Em, you're my best friend, I love you," Victoria said. "If he's not being honest with you about this, what else is he hiding? You deserve better than to be left in the dark, constantly wondering what he's up to. Maybe you guys need some space to sort this out. That will also allow you space to think clearly."

Emily nodded, even though Victoria couldn't see her. "Maybe you're right. I just don't want to believe he'd do this to me."

"I know, Em," Victoria said softly. "But sometimes we have to face the hard truths. You need to look out for yourself, too."

"What if I am wrong," Emily whispered.

"Then you are wrong, and I am sure he will understand."

There was silence for a while, as Emily felt the weight of the world on her shoulders. The bedroom walls felt like they were closing in. The softness of the bed suddenly felt like stone. She couldn't help but wonder if this was the beginning of the end for her and Sam.

24

Sam arrived at the police station a little after 8 p.m. The familiar station loomed over his car, as it did the first time he was here. He noticed the gate once again, big and imposing, warning him not to do anything that would cause him to be behind it. He mused at the irony of that thought. He pulled into the same parking spot as before, by coincidence or fate.

Across the street, a car idled. It had followed him from his house. Further down the block, a second vehicle waited. He couldn't tell which was CIA and which was FBI. But he knew he was being watched.

Inside the station, the foyer, normally bustling with activity, felt eerily quiet. The fluorescent lights cast a harsh glow on the empty seats. Not all empty, of course. The hum of the air conditioning was the only sound that accompanied his footsteps. He made his way to the single front desk officer. He told the officer who he was there to see, then took a seat.

It was not long before Detective Lawson stepped out from the bullpen.

"Hello Sam," she said, smiling, happy to see him.

"Detective," he replied, a little stiffly.

"Just call me Gloria."

Sam just nodded.

They made their way through the near-deserted corridors to the back entrance, where Harper was waiting. She stood as he approached, her eyes filled with a mix of curiosity and excitement. They exchanged brief greetings before Gloria suggested they move outside to talk. While not too many people were in, outside was best for what they were going to discuss.

They exited through the back door to the station's smoking area, a small spot. The area was nestled at the end of the courtyard, away from the back entrance. Cracked concrete stretched beneath a few scattered metal benches, their surfaces worn and chipped from years of use. Overhead, a corrugated metal awning offered minimal shelter and cast patchy shadows. The air smelled faintly of stale cigarette smoke and nearby dumpsters. A couple of overflowing ashtrays stood in the corners. A single, flickering fluorescent bulb buzzed overhead.

It was uninviting. But tonight, it offered privacy.

"All right, Sam. Do you have the drive?" Detective Lawson said.

Sam shook his head. "No, I didn't bring it," he lied. The drive was nestled in his pocket, a ticking time bomb about to explode. He needed to know more before deciding who he could truly trust. "I need to understand what we're dealing with first."

Harper looked at Detective Lawson, her disappointment obvious. "Sam, we need that drive. What's on it is beyond anything we've ever seen."

"Break it down for me," Sam said, standing firm. "Then I'll decide what to do."

Harper sighed, rubbing her temples. "Okay. The drive contains technology that shouldn't exist. It can copy human data like taking a photograph. But more than that, it can transfer that data to a database, and even extract it back."

"What do you mean, human data? Are you talking about DNA?" Sam asked, totally confused.

Harper looked away for a moment, as if trying to come up with the right words. She looked back to Sam, "No, not like DNA, but yes, like DNA at the same time," she said, clearly aware she wasn't making much sense.

Sam gave her a blank look. What else could he do?

"It's more than that," Harper continued. "It's like copying a person's essence. Something akin to consciousness.

Sam was already confused.

"I use that word because I saw a reference to consciousness in there," Harper explained, seeing the confusion in Sam's face. "But I don't fully understand what is meant by that. I am not even remotely as clever as Isabella." Her voice faltered. "If she were still here, she could explain it."

Sam brow furrowed. "That sounds... impossible."

"I know," Harper replied, her voice tinged with frustration. "But that's what it seems to be."

"Wait," Sam interrupted. "Who's Isabella?"

"One of the developers," Harper said. "She mentioned consciousness in one of her notes in the code, but the code isn't entirely clear on that. There's something more to it, something we're not seeing."

Sam shook his head, which was starting to hurt. He was clearly missing something. "So, who do you think created this? Who's behind it?"

"We think the CIA is developing it," Gloria said.

Sam looked at her, stunned. Then he closed his eyes and muttered, "Of course. That's why they were chasing that woman. She must've been involved somehow. No wonder they were so keen to question me."

Harper nodded. "Yes. The woman you mentioned, the one who committed suicide, she was my friend, Isabella. A brilliant computer scientist." Her bottom lip trembled as she spoke. "She worked for the CIA, right here in this area," Harper continued, her determination evident. "She made comments in the code, so I know she developed part of it."

"Harding!" Gloria suddenly blurted out. Harper and Sam both looked at her. She was looking past them towards the police station.

Sam turned to look. A man—presumably Harding—was approaching. He had already pulled out a cigarette and was lighting it, not bothering to wait until he reached the smoking area. He eyed them curiously as he came closer.

"Didn't know you two smoked," Harding said, exhaling a plume of smoke.

Gloria smiled, her expression casual. "We're not smoking. Just discussing a case. It's quieter out here."

Harding raised an eyebrow, glancing between Gloria and Harper. "Discussing a case, huh? And what about him?" He nodded towards Sam, who was standing a bit further back, trying to blend into the shadows.

"Sam's from another unit, out of town," Gloria said smoothly.

Sam nodded, playing along. "Yeah, just lending some fresh eyes on the case."

Harding took another drag, his curiosity waning. "Well, good luck with that, I guess."

Gloria chuckled. "Thanks, Harding."

The next five minutes were filled with awkward bouts of conversation followed by awkward bouts of silence. Harding finished his cigarette, stubbed it out in the ashtray, and nodded to them. "Catch you later." He walked back inside, leaving the three of them alone once more.

"I am sorry to hear about your friend, Harper," Sam said, honestly, once Harding was safely out of earshot. Harper didn't say anything. She simply nodded, still obviously sad.

"But how would she have known to slip it into my pocket?" Sam said, continuing to rationalise things.

"My guess? She slipped it into your pocket, not because she knew you were a detective, but more because she hoped it would end up here, with me. If someone was to die, around here, she knew the investigation would take place out of this office," Harper said.

Sam felt a little embarrassed. Why would she know who he was.

"Harper thinks we should take this to the FBI," Gloria said.

"No," Sam said firmly straight away. "I am sorry, Harper, this might upset you further, but your friend, she…"

"Isabella," Harper said, cutting Sam off, "her name is Isabella."

Sam nodded. "Isabella said that she wanted me to expose it, then destroy it, before she…well…" Sam paused, not wanting to finish the sentence. "That's what I intend to do."

Harper looked taken aback at first, but then softened. "Exposing it sounds like something Isabella would do if she found something wrong with what she was doing. Destroying something, that is next level. To do what she did…" Harper stopped, feeling her composure slipping.

"We can understand, Harper," Gloria said, putting a hand on her arm.

After composing herself, Harper said, "She might have worked on black ops projects, but she was a good person. Sam. This is bigger than us. We need help."

Sam shook his head. "I do not trust the FBI. I plan to investigate this myself… well, with your help hopefully."

Before Harper could respond, a couple more officers stepped outside, giving the trio more curious glances. "What are you guys doing out here?" one of them asked, when they reached the area, lighting a cigarette.

"We're discussing a case," Lawson replied smoothly.

The officers nodded and moved to the far end of the area, staying out of earshot.

Gloria turned back to Sam, her own voice lower, "So, if we're not going to the FBI… what's the plan?"

As Sam shook his head slowly, Harper interjected, "We could check out the address we found in one of the documents," she said. "It's not that far away."

Sam nodded. "That could be interesting. If it's a CIA site, there's no way we're walking in the front door, but it is worth a look. Would you both be available tomorrow," he asked.

"Well, I was thinking tonight," Harper said. "Like, right now."

Sam and Gloria looked at each other. They shared an unspoken moment, where neither of them could come up with a reason not to go now. They looked back at Harper, who was smiling at them.

Sam hesitated, remembering the two cars waiting for him outside the station. "The station is being watched," he said. Gloria and Harper looked at him. "They have been following me for a few days now. I don't know if it is the FBI or the CIA, or both, but they are there. Obviously, they know I'm here. We need to work out a way to get away from the building unseen."

Gloria raised an eyebrow. "So, what's the plan?"

"To be fair, we only need me to get out unnoticed," Sam said. "They don't know you two. Harper could walk right past them without raising suspicion."

Harper nodded. "They wouldn't know me from a barista on her way home."

She turned to Gloria. "What about you? Think they'd recognise you?"

"No," Sam said, interjecting himself. "None of the people following me are the CIA or FBI agents that were here". He thought for a moment. "I'll do what I did with my neighbour earlier today, which was to lie across the back seat. This time, though, I will get in the trunk."

"You what?" Harper said, incredulous.

"This morning. I lay across the back seat to sneak out. There was no reason to tail my neighbour, so they didn't. Hiding in the trunk tonight could work even better. If they spot your car, they'll just see two cops heading home."

"That's risky," Gloria said. "If they suspect something, they will surely look in the trunk as well."

"But would they?" Sam said. "Think about it. I came here. They have no idea who I was going to see, or even what I am doing here. For them to suspect the two of you, would be to suspect every car that leaves here. Unlikely. I mean, it would be even better if we could go in an actual patrol car," Sam said.

"No chance of that," Gloria said, emphatically.

Another officer stepped out, looking at the group with mild curiosity. "What's going on here?"

"Discussing a case," Gloria repeated, her clipped tone brooking no argument.

He nodded and quickly moved on to join the other two officers.

"We need to move soon," Sam said. "Before more people start asking questions."

"All right, let's do this. We will take my car, with you in the trunk," Harper said.

As they moved towards the parking lot, Sam's mind raced. The weight of the secrets he carried, the tension with Emily, and the uncertainty of what they were about to uncover all pressed down on him. He hoped that whatever they found at the address would bring some clarity, some resolution.

They reached Harper's car, a small hatchback. It had a compact, streamlined design with a sleek metallic finish that glinted in the dull light of the building. Its rounded edges and modest size made it perfect for navigating tight city streets and fitting into cramped parking spaces. It did not make for a very comfortable space for someone to hide in.

"It's a fucking hatchback?" Sam said, staring at Harper's car. "How am I supposed to fit in the back of that?"

"Hey, this is your idea. Besides, it's only until we can confirm we are not being followed," Gloria said.

Gloria tossed three flashlights into the back of the car, before Sam climbed in. While the inside of the car smelled nice, some type of floral scent, and was clean, the space was still quite cold, and claustrophobic. The hatch closed with a heavy thud, sealing him inside. Darkness wrapped around him like a vice. He could feel the car shift slightly as Harper and Gloria got into the front seats. The engine roared to life.

He already wanted it to be over.

As they drove, Sam's thoughts drifted to Emily. He hated keeping her in the dark… he smiled at his own pun. Collecting his thoughts, he also hated the pain it caused her. But he couldn't involve her in this, not until he understood it himself.

Suddenly, the car began to slow, then stop.

"What are you doing?" Sam heard Harper ask Gloria.

"We are being pulled over. An unmarked car," Gloria responded.

"Now what are you doing?" Harper asked.

"Putting your hand in my lap. When this guy sees your hand on my thigh, all he is going to see is a lesbian couple. It will trigger his male brain, making him think of all the porn he's ever watched.

This will distract him when we press him on why he has stopped us, which he should not have." she added.

Sam heard a knock on one of the car windows. His heart was pounding. He concentrated on staying very still, covering his mouth with his hand. He heard the electric window being opened.

"Can I help you?" Gloria asked, letting frustration fill her tone.

"Sorry to bother you… ma'am," Sam heard a strong voice say. He smiled to himself, noticing the pause. "We're performing random stops. There is a fugitive at large."

"Ok," Gloria's voice was calm and noncommittal.

"What are you gals up to tonight?"

Sam was genuinely shocked at the officer's question. Were men really that simple... stupid… predictable?

"Well, my girlfriend's had a long day, so I'm taking her home to turn it into a good night. If you know what I mean?" Gloria said casually.

"Do you have any ID?" Sam heard Harper ask. "I would like to confirm who you are. Two women out at night, stopped by a random person, who is not driving a police car, one can never be too careful, you know?"

Sam smiled. Harper was a natural.

"No need to worry, everything looks good here," Sam heard the man say.

"Hope you find who you're looking for," Gloria added as the window whirred back up.

Moments later, the car lurched forward, and they were on the move again.

25

Sam's muscles ached as he uncurled himself from the cramped trunk of the hatchback. The night air was cool with a light breeze, but it did little to ease the stiffness settling in from the rough ride. He stood up, stretching out his limbs and scanning his surroundings. The area was dimly lit by a few scattered streetlights, with the occasional flicker of a failing neon sign from a distant, run-down storefront.

"I thought we were stopping to let me out," he asked.

"I didn't like the look of those two agents that pulled us over," Gloria said. "I didn't want them to be able to follow us."

Sam did not reply. That was a good enough reason, and to be honest, it didn't really bother him much.

The warehouse stood before him, a hulking, run-down structure that loomed in the shadows. The walls were streaked with soot and char, telltale signs of a fire that had ravaged parts of the building. Several windows were shattered, and the roof sagged ominously in places. The ground was littered with debris, broken glass, rusted metal fragments, and the odd scrap of burned wood. Sam could make out remnants of yellow crime scene tape fluttering in the breeze, some still clinging to the chain-link fence that surrounded the property.

"Are you sure this is the right place?" Sam asked, his voice low and uncertain. He turned to Gloria and Harper, who were standing nearby, both staring at the warehouse with much the same questioning look.

Harper, her sharp eyes scanning the perimeter, nodded. "It is definitely the right address," she said, her tone clipped and confident. She pulled her jacket tighter around her. To Sam's surprise, her silhouette cut a formidable figure against the backdrop of the rundown warehouse.

Gloria nodded in agreement, already moving towards a gap in the fence, ducking through with an ease that suggested she had done this sort of thing countless times before. Harper followed, surprisingly confident for a desk jockey.

Sam hesitated, taking another look at their surroundings. The area was desolate, eerily so. The streets were empty except for a few stray cats slinking through the shadows. Graffiti covered the walls of nearby buildings, a chaotic mix of tags and murals that added to the sense of decay, and Sam's deepening sense of unease.

"Who even knows if this is the right place," Sam muttered, but he followed them through the fence.

As they moved closer, the aftermath of the fire became clearer. The air smelled faintly of rotting charcoal and scorched plastic. Gloria led the way, her steps precise, each movement confident.

But then Sam saw it.

A massive, gaping hole in the side of the building—jagged and blackened, as if something had torn through it. The surrounding ground was scorched, barren of life. No weeds. No trash. Just burnt earth.

It looked less like a fire... and more like something had erupted from inside.

Gloria stopped at the edge, peering into the darkness. She glanced back at the two of them.

Sam shrugged.

Without a word, Gloria stepped inside, disappearing into the shadows.

Sam swallowed hard, his mouth dry. He looked at Harper, who was watching him with a mixture of impatience and encouragement.

"Come on, Sam," she said. "This is why we're here."

Taking a deep breath, he followed her into the warehouse. Something felt off. He couldn't explain it. It wasn't just the hole torn through the side of the building—it was something else. Something unseen. He'd been in situations like this before, while tailing suspects, but this place unnerved him in a way he couldn't shake.

The interior was even more desolate than the exterior, with piles of rubble and twisted metal scattered across the floor. The remnants of the fire were everywhere, and the darkness seemed to press in on him from all sides.

"Just stick close and keep your eyes open," Gloria whispered, her voice barely audible. "We need to find out if this place holds any answers."

Deep inside the warehouse, the trio moved cautiously, their footsteps echoing softly in the vast, hollow space. The scent of burned, decaying materials seemed to still be lingering in the air. The faint light from their flashlights revealed more details as they progressed, until they came to a section that appeared to have had recent human occupation.

This section was completely different to the rest of the warehouse. It looked to be divided into two distinct areas. On one side was a large room filled with rows of computer terminals. The machines were all burned beyond repair, their plastic casings melted and warped, and the screens shattered. Tangled wires and cables lay strewn across the floor, covered in soot and ash. Harper immediately began examining the remains of the computers, her flashlight casting harsh, moving beams of light over the wreckage.

"I will help Harper look through this area. You check out that area," Gloria said, her flashlight pointing to the other side of the room.

Sam was already staring in that direction. That section had clearly once been behind a glass wall—now shattered, with shards crunching underfoot. It looked like what had once been a cleanroom. White tiles covered the floor and walls, many of them cracked or blackened. Metal tables and cabinets were overturned. Lab equipment lay twisted and half-melted from the intense heat.

Sam could do nothing about the sound of his footsteps as they crunched on the broken glass. The sound mixed in with the other sounds coming from Gloria and Harper digging through the wreckage.

Sam stepped gingerly into the former laboratory. The sterile room had an eerie quality, as if it had once been a place of order, now reduced to chaos. He moved carefully, his flashlight playing over the remnants of the lab. Broken glass and twisted metal continued to crunch under his feet as he navigated the debris.

Near the back of the room, partially buried under a pile of rubble, something caught his eye. It was a canister, about the size of a metal drink bottle, slightly scorched but intact. Sam bent down and picked it up, brushing off the soot and ash. His breath caught in his throat as he examined it more closely. He had seen this before.

He turned the canister over in his hands, his heart pounding. There were initials etched into the metal, partially obscured by the scorch marks.

"J.T."

His mind raced, trying to recall the details from the drive. The canister reminded him of a picture he had seen on the drive, the implications of what he might be holding landing heavily on him.

"Gloria, Harper," he called out, a little over a whisper, his voice tight with urgency, "You guys need to see this."

Gloria looked up from the computer area, the beam of light she shone in his direction hitting him directly in the eyes. He flinched away, closing his eyes. "Sorry," Gloria said, moving the beam slightly away from him.

Sam held the canister into the beam of light. Gloria quickly made her way over, with Harper close behind.

"What is it?" Gloria asked, her tone serious.

Sam handed her the canister. "This... matches something I saw in one of the images on the drive..."

"Yes, the canister," Harper said, excitedly, Gloria handing her the canister.

"It has initials on it," Sam continued, "J.T. This has got to be something, doesn't it?"

Harper examined it closely. "Good find, Sam," she said, a note of approval in her voice. "We gotta get this out of here and figure out what the hell we're dealing with."

26

As Sam, Gloria, and Harper prepared to leave with the canister, a sudden burst of light from two flashlights stopped them cold. The beams cut through the darkness—and froze on their faces.

Then came the voice.

A voice Sam knew too well.

"We'll be taking that!"

As their eyes adjusted to the new light source, they saw two men standing at the entrance of the room, guns drawn and aimed directly at them.

The sound of that voice was like a slap in the face for Sam. Obviously, Gloria and Harper's story did not have the effect they thought it did.

He kept that to himself.

It was the burly agent who barked the command, "Step out from the room and hand over the canister, now. Oh, and we'll be having the flash drive also," he said.

"You—" Gloria began, but Sam shot her a look, shutting her up instantly.

Shit. He needed to turn this around quickly. "You know, that is the second time you have pointed a gun at me," Sam said to the agents, trying to give himself time to think of what to do. "Didn't go too well for you last time."

He could see both agents now with their guns pointed at them, and standing close together.

Sam's mind clicked. An idea. Reckless. Dangerous.

But it was the only shot they had.

They had one advantage left.

Surprise.

"Yeah? Well, hate to break it to you, but this time, you won't be walking away," the agent said with an arrogance of someone in his position.

Sam looked around. Gloria glanced at him, her eyes filled with a mixture of fear and defiance. Harper's face was unreadable, but her body was tense, ready to react.

Sam took a deep breath and walked over to Harper, making sure his footsteps were deliberate and loud enough to draw the agents' focus. He reached out and took the canister from Harper, whispering in her ear as he did so, "When I say go, turn your flashlight off and run towards the light from mine."

Harper looked at him confused. He looked at Gloria who could sense something was up, and looked ready for it, whatever it was.

"Now, Mr. Caldwell!" the agent said again, letting Sam know they knew exactly who he was.

Sam turned to face the agents, holding the canister in one hand, his flashlight in the other. As he walked towards them, he kept his movements steady. The agents did not lower their guns, and more importantly, they continued to stand together. He was banking on them staying like that. If he timed this right, it should work. They should fall like dominos.

"Alright, alright. We're coming out."

When he was just a few steps away, Sam lunged.

With every ounce of momentum, he drove his shoulder into the big guy's ribs—just beneath his arm. The agent staggered backward into the other, just as Sam had hoped. Both stumbled over the wreckage, their guns swinging wildly as they hit the floor.

What Sam could not have dreamed was to see the agents drop their flashlights, which skidded across the floor, ending up pointing at nothing but rubble.

"Go!" Sam yelled, hurling his flashlight towards the hole in the wall they'd crawled through. As darkness swallowed the room, he saw Gloria already grabbing Harper's arm and pulling her to the exit.

She'd been ready.

In the chaos, Sam drew his gun from the shoulder holster beneath his jacket and fired two shots into the air. The agents shouted and scrambled, disoriented in the dark.

The room exploded with noise. Yelling. Gunfire. Crashing bodies.

Sam heard Gloria and Harper's footsteps echoing as they ran. He had to move—now.

He sprinted towards the opening, dodging wildly as bullets zipped past him. He fired back, blindly. He didn't need to hit them— he just needed cover.

Then—click.

He was out.

Still clutching the canister, he kept running. He reached the hole in the wall and spotted Gloria and Harper already clearing the fence line.

Sam's lungs burned. His arm stung from a grazing shot, but he pushed through the pain.

He bolted to the car as Gloria and Harper dove inside. He flung open the rear door and hurled himself in just as more bullets sliced through the air.

"Go, go, go!" he shouted.

Gloria slammed on the gas, and the car roared to life, speeding off down the lane. The warehouse and the agents disappeared into the distance, but the sound of gunfire still echoed in Sam's ears. He collapsed against the seat, breathing hard, the canister still held tightly in his grasp.

"Is everyone alright?" Gloria asked, her eyes flicking between the rearview mirror and the road ahead.

"Yeah," Sam panted, sitting up, wincing as he looked at his grazed arm. "We made it."

He turned to Harper, who nodded. But blood streamed down the side of her face.

"Shit! Harper, are you okay?" he asked.

"Oh my God, Harper," Gloria said, only just noticing.

"I'm fine," Harper said through gritted teeth. "Just focus on getting us out of here."

Sam's heart thundered as they tore through the darkened streets of the warehouse district. He glanced behind them—and froze.

Headlights.

"They're on our tail!" he shouted. "Gloria, step on it. This night's not over yet."

"Hang on!" Gloria shouted, her knuckles white as she gripped the steering wheel. The engine roared as she pushed the car to its limits, weaving through the empty streets.

A sudden burst of gunfire shattered the rear window.

Sam ducked instinctively, as he was covered in shattered glass.

"They're right on us!" he yelled, trying to keep his voice steady.

The little hatchback was no match for the high-powered sedan they were driving. Gloria swerved sharply to the left, as the sedan came up beside them, causing the pursuing car to overcorrect and rub against their rear bumper. The screech of metal against metal filled the night. Sam clung to the seat, his heart racing.

"Hold on!" Gloria warned again, this time more urgently.

Sam looked forward. A red light.

Of course.

But Gloria didn't hesitate. She gunned it.

They screamed through the intersection. Gloria and Harper let out shouts of panic. Sam braced himself.

Nothing.

They made it through.

Sam turned to look out the now missing back window. The pursuing agents had dropped back slightly. They weren't so lucky. As they followed, a truck barrelled through the cross street, their green light giving them right of way. The truck clipped the back half of the agents' sedan. The impact, while not actually that great, still caused them to lose control.

With a sickening crunch that echoed through the night, Sam watched as the agents careened off course, skidding and crashing straight into a streetlight. Sam saw the airbag deploy, in a cloud of powder and dust, as the metal front buckled around the post. The back lifted into the air slightly, before settling back down. The sedan was no longer going anywhere.

Sam turned back to face the front. He could see the stunned look on Gloria's face, which matched his own. Gloria kept her foot on the gas, not daring to slow down. Sam exhaled a shaky breath, his grip on the canister tightening. They had escaped, for now, but he knew their troubles were far from over. They knew that he now had both the canister and the drive.

Whatever that meant.

27

Agent Thompson slowly maneuvered her car through the chaos of the intersection. Beside her was Agent Miller. Cars and people were everywhere, with a semi-truck parked halfway across it. Something had happened here. She weaved around the truck to see the CIA's black sedan crashed, head on, into a streetlight. The two agents were sitting on the side of the road, clearly shaken. She continued past. None of that was for her and Agent Miller to deal with.

It had been hard to follow the two cars as they raced through the dark, narrow streets of the warehouse district. The headlights of the vehicles flickering in and out of view, weaving dangerously through the maze of warehouses and abandoned factories.

Miller dialled a number on his phone. "They've left the warehouse," he said, his eyes never leaving the car ahead. "The situation got heated and out of control—there's been gunfire exchanged. The CIA agents pursued them, but somehow whoever was driving the car that Caldwell was in, managed to run them off the road, where they crashed into a light post. We've got a visual."

Thompson glanced at Miller briefly, her expression tense. She could hear the muffled voice of their superior on the other end, issuing rapid instructions. Miller listened intently, nodding occasionally, his face illuminated by the soft glow of the dashboard lights.

"Understood," he replied after a moment. "Should we move in to apprehend them?"

There was a pause as the response came through. Miller's expression shifted slightly as he absorbed the instructions. He ended the call. "Negative on the apprehension," he relayed, his tone professional. "We're to keep an eye on them tonight. Tomorrow, we'll head to the station and talk to the officers involved. Head Office will send us a file of everyone who works there."

Thompson nodded, her focus returning to the road ahead. "Roger that," she muttered, more to herself than anyone else. She eased off the gas slightly, maintaining a safe distance, their orders clear.

"You know, Thompson, I think there is a lot more to this than we have been told," Miller said, suddenly. "I know we haven't been read into this completely, and our job is to do what we are told, but what did we get into the FBI for?" It was as if Miller was thinking out aloud.

"I know what you mean," Thompson replied. "The CIA are obviously conducting business on American soil. Why aren't we arresting those guys?"

"Let's dig up some dirt on our own tomorrow," Miller said, as if he was formulating a plan.

The adrenaline was still coursing through Sam's veins as they sped away from the warehouse district, leaving the chaos of the car chase behind. He glanced at Gloria in the driver's seat, her face set in a furious scowl. Harper sat in the front passenger seat, her expression unreadable. The canister, their unknown but precious prize, was clutched tightly in Sam's hands.

"You fucking lied to us, Sam," Gloria snapped, her anger very present. Her eyes flicked to the rearview mirror to check for any tails. "You said you didn't have the drive, and it was in your pocket the whole time!"

Sam winced. "I know, Gloria. I'm sorry," he said—though not without a trace of defiance. He'd made a calculated decision, and it had paid off. "I thought it was safer that way. Like I told you, I needed to know I could trust you first."

"Trust us? We almost fucking died! Look at Harper's face!" she yelled.

"I am sorry, truly I am. But what happened in that warehouse is not because I told you I didn't have the drive. That would have happened anyway," Sam said, trying to smooth the situation. "In my defence, you know as well as I do they would have shot us had we not done what we did."

Gloria's grip tightened on the steering wheel, but she didn't argue further. She just glared at him through the rear-view mirror. Sam tried to put on a calm face. Gloria knew he was right. She just needed a chance to get it off her chest. After a long time of nobody saying anything, it was Harper who finally broke the silence.

"Now that we have it, what are we going to do with the canister?" she asked, her voice calm.

They all knew the canister was too important to keep with them. After a brief discussion, they decided Harper would take it. She had access to the station's computer room. She would easily be able to store the canister in there, and no one would know. They could not have all their eggs in one basket. Sam would keep the drive with him, but not have the canister as well.

"Only a few people have access to the computer room," Harper explained. "There are many computer-related items in there that people just look past. This canister will just look like another one of those. Plus, no one will be allowed to just rummage around in there."

Sam handed the canister to Harper, feeling a slight pang of anxiety as it left his hands. "Be careful with it," he said. "This might be our only lead."

Harper nodded, putting the canister in her lap. "I will. Let's get some rest and regroup tomorrow. We've got a long day ahead." The tension in the car eased slightly as they settled on their plan, but Sam knew this was just the beginning.

Agent Thompson parked their unmarked car outside the police station. Shortly after, hers and Agent Miller's phones pinged, signalling new messages. Thompson opened the message. It was the files of the employees. She began to scroll through them. When she reached the file of Detective Lawson, she paused. "Detective Lawson," she said, tapping the photo attached to the file. "She was the one driving the car. She was also particularly interested in our case when we had first arrived to question Caldwell, remember? She asked a lot of questions."

Miller nodded, but his focus shifted as he stopped on another file. "Harper Daniels," he said, pointing to the photo of a woman with a steely gaze. "I am sure this was the other woman in the car."

Thompson leaned over to look, her expression hardening. "You're right. That's definitely her." She closed the file and met Miller's gaze. "Now we know exactly who to talk to."

Miller nodded grimly.

The tall CIA agent stood fuming on the side of the road, phone to his ear, glaring at the crumpled remains of their sedan. The crash had been a disaster, and now they were stuck, vulnerable and exposed. His partner was sitting in the gutter.

"Whoever the idiots were who searched the warehouse are fucking blind. They missed a canister," the agent said sharply into his phone, his voice tight with frustration. "Caldwell just found it. He also seems to be working with two other officers now. They all, fucking, got away." He kicked at a stick.

He clenched his fists, barely containing his anger. "What should we do?" the tall agent asked, casting a wary glance down at his partner. The sound of passing cars, police sirens in the distance only heightened his irritation.

He listened intently to the response on the other end of the line, his expression shifting from frustration to resignation. He hung up. "We've been told to cool our heels for the night. They're going to send us further instructions in the morning," he said, looking at the intersection.

The burly agent spat on the ground, his face twisted in anger. "Great, just fucking great," he muttered. "We had them right there, and now we're supposed to just wait?" He shook his head, trying to suppress his rage.

"This isn't over. At some stage, we are going to be allowed to bring them in. And when we do, they are not going to know what hit them. Well, they will know who hit them," the tall agent said.

<h1 style="text-align: center">28</h1>

Emily lay in bed, her eyes wide open, staring at the dark ceiling above her. The soft glow of the streetlights seeped through the sheer curtains, casting faint patterns across the room. Her mind raced. A storm of thoughts and emotions she couldn't silence.

Sam hadn't checked in all night.

No text, no call. Nothing.

He was always good about that. Always considerate. But tonight? Silence.

She glanced at the clock on the nightstand, almost midnight.

She couldn't stop the thoughts running through her head, each one worse than the last. Where was he? Who was he with? The silence of the room was deafening, amplifying her anxiety. She had checked her phone countless times, hoping for a message that never came. Her heart ached with the possibility that Sam might be cheating on her.

The sound of the front door opening broke through her thoughts. Emily tensed, straining to hear. The door closed softly, and she heard footsteps, cautious and deliberate, trying to avoid making any noise. She knew it was Sam. He was always quiet when he came in late, thinking she wouldn't notice. But she always did. Tonight, his attempts at stealth felt like an insult, a betrayal of the trust she had placed in him.

The footsteps grew closer, moving through the hallway and into the bedroom. Emily kept her breathing even, pretending to be asleep. She felt a mixture of anger and a gnawing sadness that made her want to cry out, to confront him then and there. But she held herself still, her body rigid with the effort to contain her emotions. She listened as Sam undressed, each piece of clothing falling to the floor with a soft rustle. He was trying so hard to be quiet, and it only made her more furious. If he cared so much about not waking her, why couldn't he care enough to call or message that he was going to be late?

The odd scent of something she couldn't place mixed with a faint, unfamiliar floral fragrance reached her. It wasn't her perfume. The realisation felt like a dagger to her heart. Sam slid into bed slowly, the mattress shifting slightly under his weight. He lay there for a moment, then gently adjusted himself, trying to find a comfortable position without disturbing her. Emily's heart pounded in her chest. She wanted to scream at him, to demand answers, to let out all the hurt and anger that had been building up inside her. But she couldn't move, couldn't speak. The betrayal felt like a physical weight, pressing down on her, making it hard to breathe.

In the dark, Emily felt the distance between them grow, an invisible wall that separated her from the man she loved. She had always trusted Sam, believed in him, and now that trust was crumbling. She replayed the past few weeks in her mind, looking for signs she might have missed. The late nights, the vague excuses, the way he had been distracted lately. It all seemed so clear now, exactly like they had spoken about at dinner with their friends, and it broke her heart.

Emily lay there, eyes wide open, staring into the darkness, feeling more alone than ever.

29

Director Barrett leaned back in his leather chair, fingers steepled as he watched Landon stride into his office. The room was dim, except for the soft glow of the desk lamp casting long shadows. Tension hung in the air, and the faint hum of the air conditioning was the only sound breaking the silence.

He watched Landon settle into the chair across from him, his face unreadable. As he waited for Landon to report, he couldn't help but reflect on the decision to bring him onto the project. Despite Landon's reputation and skills, he had reservations; their past clashes over methodology and strategy were hard to forget. Yet, with the stakes as high as they were, and the complexity of the operation demanding the best, he had no choice. He needed Landon's expertise, even if it meant enduring the tension that simmered beneath their professional veneer. His jaw tightened as Landon delivered the news.

"Caldwell found the warehouse," Landon reported, his voice steady but with an edge of frustration. "He was confronted by our two operatives, but he managed to evade them."

Director Barrett felt a surge of irritation, mixed with grudging respect for Caldwell's evasive skills. His mind raced, already considering the implications and recalibrating their strategy. Caldwell was becoming a real problem. One they had to handle—fast.

"It's worse than that," Landon added.

Worse. Barrett clenched his jaw. He was beginning to take back his thoughts of Landon being an asset. It was starting to seem like he had no idea what he was doing. While he continued to report, part of his mind began to think about ways he would be able to remove Landon from the project. It would need to be strategic. Landon knew too much.

Landon's expression darkened slightly. "Caldwell seems to now be working with two police detectives. Sniffing around the warehouse, it appears they retrieved a canister from the site."

That was very bad news, and Director Barrett felt a cold knot of anxiety tighten in his gut. His mind raced, evaluating the potential fallout. "Did it contain information?"

"Impossible to say, but it's safe to assume it's something," Landon said. "Caldwell appears to be no slouch."

A rare admission, Director Barrett thought. Landon had no time for civilians. He thought of them as cattle, tools to be used to further the cause. For him to admit something like that was well, something. "Interesting to hear you say that, Landon."

"We have underestimated Caldwell this whole time. When this is all over, I would suggest approaching him to become part of the network," Landon said, as an aside. "That is, if he survives the ordeal. He seems very thorough. It is safe to say now that he does indeed have the drive."

Director Barrett rubbed his chin thoughtfully. "We'll need to keep a close eye on that development. If the canister is linked to our operations, it could complicate things further."

Landon nodded in agreement. "We'll monitor, of course. If there's anything of importance, we'll know about it."

"Good," Director Barrett said, leaning forward again. "Stay on top of it and keep me informed. This is a delicate operation, and we can't afford any missteps. What of the new team and restoring access to the database?" Director Barrett asked, changing the topic.

"No real change on that front, unfortunately," Landon said.

"We've been handed another possible way into DataShield Technologies' top-secret tech."

Landon raised an eyebrow, intrigued. "Another way? Is the drive still our primary objective?" he asked, a clear shift in his mood.

Director Barrett nodded, leaning forward. "It is. But it seems our methods aren't yielding the results we need on that front, as you have reported." He could see from the shift in Landon's posture that comment hit home, as he had hoped. "The drive's importance has diminished slightly in light of recent developments. We need to be flexible."

Landon crossed his arms, his gaze intense. "So, what's this new development?"

Director Barrett leaned back again, eyes narrowing thoughtfully. "We've received intel about a new access point into DataShield's network. It won't get us the information that is on the drive directly, but since the foundations of what is on the drive came from DataShield in the first place, it will provide us with the information we need for the new team to finish the job. And, quicker than they are doing it now, one hopes."

"What is this new way?" Landon asked.

Director Barrett watched Landon's eyes widen in surprise as he relayed the latest development. "The President convening a high-level task force to investigate what happened to the First Lady and Victor Langford, the influential owner of DataShield. This task force has turned its focus onto DataShield as a potential suspect. This is great for us. While ever the task force is trained on DataShield, the longer we have to achieve our objectives."

"I'd heard about the task force… but DataShield as a suspect? That changes things."

"I want you to make one more push for the drive. Turn the heat up on Mr. Caldwell and his new friends," Director Barrett said. "Do whatever it takes. If you come up empty-handed, we switch focus"

There was a brief pause as Landon weighed the options. "Understood. We'll give it everything we've got on the drive, and I will have the team produce some options on a fallback plan. We'll be ready to pivot if necessary."

Landon stood and began walking to the door of the office.

"Oh—one more thing," he said. "What of Dr. Taylor? This would be a lot simpler if we could find him."

His lack of trust in Landon caused a thought to linger in his brain that he might be playing him. The possibilities of this operation were endless. To the victor go the spoils. There was no telling what things were being cooked up in that brain of his. Both Landon and Dr. Taylor were smart, that was for sure, but for Dr. Taylor to just disappear without a trace. That seemed too much.

"No sign of him," Landon said. "We are continuing to search, but we are as yet unable to locate him. It is like he has walked off the face of the earth."

The doctor's disappearance complicated everything, leaving a critical gap in their operation. Director Barrett knew this was no ordinary vanishing act; someone, somewhere, was orchestrating something. The stakes had risen, and the pressure to find the doctor before their adversaries did was mounting.

Director Barrett watched as Landon left the room, the door closing softly behind him. The room felt heavier. The stakes were high, the risks even higher. He knew Landon was the right man for the job—dedicated, resourceful, and unyielding, but Barrett wasn't sure who he trusted less—Caldwell, or the man who'd just walked out his door.

As he turned his attention back to the reports on his desk, Director Barrett felt a glimmer of confidence. They had a plan, and even though it was fraught with challenges, they were prepared to see it through.

30

Gloria shifted uncomfortably in her chair, her eyes darting towards Harper, who sat beside her, a fresh gash marring her otherwise smooth face. The tension in Chief Brennan's office was palpable. The overhead fluorescent lights buzzed faintly, casting a sterile glow over the grim expressions of everyone present. Her partner, Vince, plus Agents Thompson and Miller, stood just inside the door, their faces inscrutable. The office had become quite crowded with everyone in it. Gloria was feeling a little claustrophobic.

Chief Brennan sat forward in his chair behind his desk, his perpetually furrowed brow deepening. His eyes, cold and piercing, bore into Lawson and Harper as he spoke. "What the hell were you two thinking?" he barked, slamming a fist onto his desk. "Going to that warehouse last night—do you have any idea the kind of trouble that has caused?"

Lawson took a deep breath, trying to steady herself. "Chief, we were investigating…"

"I don't give a damn what you were investigating!" Brennan interrupted, his voice rising. "This isn't your case. In fact, this isn't even this police station's case. This is an FBI investigation, and you had no business being there!"

He glanced at the two agents, who remained silent.

Brennan turned his attention to Harper, his gaze softening slightly as he looked at the wound on her face. "And you," he said, his tone a mix of anger and concern. "Look at you. You're a tech expert, Harper, not a field agent. What were you thinking, putting yourself in that kind of danger?"

Harper winced, touching the edge of the bandage lightly. "We were following a lead, Chief. We received information that could not wait to be investigated," she said, doubling down on what Gloria had started to say.

Gloria was spurred on by Harper's words, "That's correct, Chief, we thought…"

"You thought wrong!" Chief Brennan shouted. He ran a hand through his hair, exasperated. "To make matters worse, you took along a civilian."

"He is a private detective, Chief," Gloria said, hoping it may help things. It didn't.

"Are you even listening to me, Gloria. Do you know what they told me?" Chief Brennan said, pointing at the two agents standing along the wall of the office.

Gloria looked over to the agents, who just looked back, impassive.

"They said you two almost blew their operation," Chief Brennan said. "They may have to change their approach because of your little stunt."

Gloria's frustration boiled over. "With all due respect, Chief, this is all happening a result of that woman who killed herself," she said, turning to look at the agents, "whose name is Isabella, by the way." To her surprise, the two agents looked at each other, a knowing look passed between them.

"That happened in our jurisdiction," she said, still looking at them. "We have a right to know what's going on. We can't just sit back and…"

"Yes, you can!" Brennan snapped.

Gloria turned to face him.

"And you will. The FBI is in charge here," he said, pointing back over to the agents. "Thompson, Miller, they're the ones calling the shots. Not you. Not Harper. You need to stay out of their way." Chief Brennan turned to look at Vince. "And you," he said, pointedly, "I am still trying to work out what your role in all this is."

"That makes two of us, Chief," Vince said, honestly, looking at Gloria. "And you can be sure I will find out after we finish here."

Gloria took in Vince's stern face. She had crossed the line with him, as her partner, and she did regret that. She could also see there was warmth in his gaze. He knew that she did not get worked up like this unless she believed in something to her core. She would speak to him later.

Gloria's jaw tightened. She didn't trust the FBI agents as far as she could throw them. There was something about the way they operated, always keeping local law enforcement in the dark, that rubbed her the wrong way. She glanced at Agent Thompson, who met her gaze with a steely, unreadable expression.

"We found something in that warehouse," Gloria said, her voice low but defiant.

Brennan leaned forward, his eyes narrowing. "What did you say?"

Gloria hesitated, exchanging a quick look with Harper. They had agreed not to disclose everything to the Chief, not until they were sure of what they were dealing with. "Well, to be fair, it wasn't much, nothing definitive," she said finally. "And besides, this is as you say, the FBI's case, so it doesn't matter what I think I found, they would already know about it," she said, back-peddling.

"Don't play games with me, Detective Lawson," Brennan warned, using her title instead of her first name. He only ever did that when he really needed her to listen.

"Pay attention." His voice taking on a quieter tone, "you are a good cop, and an even better detective. But you need to step back. And you, Harper, your computer skills around here are invaluable to lose. But I can tell you. If you two pull another stunt like this, I'll have your badge, Gloria, and Harper will be out of a job. Do you both understand what I am telling you?"

Gloria swallowed hard. She hated admitting it, but she understood.

"I understand, Chief," she said quietly.

"Me too," Harper added.

Brennan straightened up, his face still red with anger. "Good. Now get out of my sight. And stay out of the FBI's way."

Gloria and Harper stood, the weight of Brennan's words hanging heavily between them. As Gloria walked past the FBI agents, Agent Thompson leaned in slightly, her voice low. "Despite your intentions, it was a mistake going there, Detective."

Gloria's eyes flashed with anger, but she kept her mouth shut. She didn't need to give them more ammunition. Once outside the office, she let out a frustrated sigh. "I can't believe this," she muttered. "We're just supposed to sit back and let the Feds handle everything?"

Harper shook her head, wincing again as the movement tugged at her wound. "I don't like it any more than you do, Gloria. But it is pretty clear that we are on thin ice here. We have to be careful."

"Careful doesn't always solve cases," Gloria snapped, though she knew Harper was right. "This is our jurisdiction. We can't just let them push us around."

Harper put a hand on Gloria's arm, her eyes serious. "I know. But we need to play it smart. If we're going to keep investigating, we need to be more discreet. And we need to figure out who we can trust."

Gloria nodded reluctantly. "Alright. But I'm not letting this go. Something's not right, and I intend to find out what it is."

They walked towards Gloria's desk in silence, each lost in their own thoughts. For Gloria, the frustration was almost unbearable. She was used to being in control, to following leads wherever they took her. Being told to stand down, especially by the Feds, was like a slap in the face. But she knew one thing for certain: she wasn't going to let anyone, not even the FBI, keep her from doing her job.

As they reached Gloria's desk, she glanced at Harper, her resolve hardening. "We'll find another way," she said quietly. "We'll get to the bottom of this. They can't stop us."

Harper gave a small, determined nod. "Together," she agreed, "for Isabella."

Gloria's hands trembled slightly as she fidgeted with the edge of a piece of paper, her mind racing through the events of the previous night, and the meeting she had just had with the Chief.

The surveillance job had taken a dangerous turn, leaving her more rattled than she cared to admit. As Vince sat down across from her, she forced herself to meet his gaze, her eyes betraying the turmoil beneath her calm facade. Before she could utter a word, Vince leaned in, his voice steady and reassuring.

"Gloria, I don't know what went down last night," he began, his tone gentle but firm. "But I've never seen you this worked up about something. I get the feeling you have found something about the case involving this Caldwell character."

Gloria just nodded, not knowing where Vince might be going with this. She certainly did not need him to give her an "it will be alright" speech.

"I also know you too well to know that you are not going to let this go. So, whatever it is you're about to cook up, I'm in."

Gloria looked at him, her glum expression turning to one of surprise, mixed with a bit of excitement.

"You're my partner. I have gotten to know you, and care about you."

Gloria smiled.

"Shut the fuck up," Vince said, in anticipation of what Gloria may have been about to say. "I will not let you ruin your life, especially if I can help it."

His words hung in the air, a lifeline in the midst of her chaos. Gloria felt a surge of gratitude. Vince's support was exactly what she needed right now. Taking a deep breath, she nodded, trying to calm the storm within her as Vince's presence brought a semblance of stability to her frayed nerves.

Agent Thompson knocked on the window that looked through to the computer room, where she could see Harper sitting at her desk. Harper looked up to see her standing there.

She smiled at Harper, making it the warmest smile she could. She hoped Harper might be more receptive to a calm, reasoned conversation than the intense confrontation Chief Brennan had with Detective Lawson. She mouthed through the glass: Meeting Room 1.

Sitting in the small meeting room waiting, she hoped Harper would join her. The room was only big enough to fit four people comfortably, the chairs arranged around a circular table in the centre. She had asked Agent Miller to give her this time. A conversation one on one would be much better than the two of them being there. Two on one was more like an interrogation. And woman to woman would be better still.

It wasn't long before Harper walked through the door. Agent Thompson smiled at her, and Harper smiled back. That was a good sign.

She knew she would have to start things off slowly, with something personal perhaps. This needed to be a conversation Harper was willing, not ordered, to have. "Thank you for meeting with me, Harper. I can appreciate your mind must be in a whirl," she said, her voice measured and soothing.

Harper did not say anything at first. She just walked to one of the chairs and sat down. Agent Thompson's heart began to beat a little faster. Harper was sitting. That was a good thing, but would she stay? She seized the opportunity before Harper changed her mind. "Would you be willing to tell us what you know about Isabella? Her being the person who killed herself has not been shared with anyone."

Harper's lips pressed into a thin line, but she didn't immediately shut down. Instead, she seemed to be weighing her options. There was also an edge of sadness, Thompson could see.

"Isabella was a friend of mine," she said, finally.

Shock and excitement coursed through Thompson. Harper looked at her, expressionless. It was important for Thompson to not flinch, offering only warmth.

"I'm sorry for your loss," she said sincerely. "I can't imagine how hard this is. And I understand that my questions might be difficult. But I promise—we're on the same side here."

She gave the words room to breathe before continuing.

"I only have a few questions. Three, technically—the first has two parts," she said with a small smile, hoping to coax some humanity into the moment. Harper didn't smile back, but she didn't leave either.

"How did you know where the warehouse was, and why did you go there?"

"We were following a lead," she said cautiously, not giving away too much.

"A lead given to you by Mr. Caldwell?" Agent Thompson asked carefully.

"You wouldn't ask me that if you didn't know that already," Harper said.

"Fair enough. But where did you get the address from? Or do you know where Mr. Caldwell got it?"

"Well, that I would rather not say. Suffice it to say, he is in possession of some pretty… out-there information that needs to be investigated for its authenticity before anything else," Harper said.

Thompson nodded, her demeanour encouraging. "Okay," she said, her mind thinking on whether to press her more along that line of questioning or move onto her second question. She decided to move on.

"And what was it that you found in the warehouse?" she asked.

Harper looked at her, her body stiffening. Her small movement giving away the answer. "Harper," Thompson said, being very careful with her words. "I would really appreciate it if you told me what you found. I am not asking you to hand anything over to me. I just simply want to know what it is you discovered," she said.

Harper hesitated, clearly conflicted. "Someone was working on something in the warehouse. There were two rooms. One had several computer terminals, the other was some type of laboratory," she finally said, her voice steady despite the situation.

Thompson kept her gaze steady, and her expression composed. Her instincts about Harper being more receptive to a calm, reasoned conversation had turned out to be correct. Thompson's voice was measured as she continued, "Harper, I know last night was rough, and I can see you're shaken. I just want to understand what happened."

Agent Thompson's eyes narrowed slightly. From what Harper said, they would have no doubt seen things, like computers and laboratory equipment, but she could sense that was not what

Detective Lawson was talking about when she said they had found something. She kept her tone friendly. "Harper, Detective Lawson made it sound like you had found a thing. Your description was more like you just found workspaces. Did you find something or was it just workspaces?"

When Harper did not say anything for a while, Agent Thompson began to worry that she had overstepped the mark.

"I cannot answer that question," she said finally, sliding her seat back and standing up. "In fact, I think I have already said too much."

"Before you go, Harper," Thompson said, hoping to stop her from leaving without giving her a business card, at least. "I'm not here to make things difficult for you. You have been more than generous in coming and talking to us now. I'm here because we're on the same side. We're working for the good guys in this."

She reached into her pocket and pulled out a business card, sliding it across the desk. "If you remember anything or decide there's something more you can share, please call me. This is a complicated puzzle. We need as many eyes looking at this as we can. That way we might just be able to work out what is going on."

Harper stood at the edge of the table, half-turned, ready to walk away. She sighed before taking up the card.

Agent Thompson gave her a smile. "Thank you, Harper."

Harper returned a tight smile. "No promises," she said, then left the room.

Shortly after Harper left the room, Agent Miller walked in. He was looking at her, an impressed expression on his face. "I got to hand it to you. You got more information out of her than I would have," he said.

"What do you think they found?" Agent Thompson asked.

"Do you think we could actually trust them?" Miller asked, not answering her question.

Agent Thompson looked at him questioningly.

"Think about it. They found the warehouse. No one should have known about the warehouse. She is friends with Isabella, according to her. Is it not out of the realms of possibility that she and Isabella spoke about things? Black ops agents are usually good at keeping secrets, but can we really say for sure…"

"Well, I am sure of one thing. The seed of trust has definitely been planted," Agent Miller said. "Let's just report in, then sit back and see how this plays out."

31

Emily sat inside the restaurant, surrounded by the comforting presence of her friends Victoria, Mia, Nova, and Grace. The brunch spot, nestled in a trendy neighbourhood, was abuzz with energy, a popular gathering place on weekends. The exterior featured large, inviting windows, allowing sunlight to flood in, creating a laid-back and lively vibe. A small patio area with a few tables spilled onto sidewalk seating, packed with people enjoying their meals under cheerful yellow umbrellas.

Exposed brick walls were adorned with local artwork, and wooden beams across the ceiling added a cozy touch. The air was filled with the enticing aromas of freshly brewed coffee, crispy bacon, and fresh pastries. The open kitchen allowed diners to watch the chefs in action, flipping pancakes and garnishing plates with colourful fruits and herbs.

None of this had any effect on Emily, as she stirred her coffee absentmindedly, her thoughts elsewhere. Waitstaff moving swiftly between tables were non-existent, as the events of the previous night weighed heavily on her. "So, Sam was out all night again," Emily began, her voice barely above a whisper.

Her friends looked up from their menus, concern etched on their faces. They had been here before, discussing the problems of their respective worlds, over countless meals. Victoria, always blunt and to the point, was the first to speak.

"Come on, Emily. This is insane. He's clearly up to something. What did he say this time?" Victoria's eyes bore into hers, demanding honesty.

Emily sighed, pushing her hair back. "It was the other day," or was it yesterday? She could not remember. "Sam came in late. He didn't say anything. He smelled like smoke and a floral type of scent. He actually thought he could sneak into bed without waking me up. I was, of course, awake."

Mia reached out and gently squeezed her hand. "Oh, Emily, that sounds so hard. I'm sorry you're going through this. Did you even get to talk to him this morning, or was he already gone?"

Before Emily could respond, she noticed the bubbly server, who matched the energy of the place, walking towards their table. He moved gracefully through the crowded space, balancing a tray laden with their drinks. She scowled at him, in no mood for his vibrancy.

"Got your drinks, ladies," he said, his voice a pleasant, soothing baritone, that was calm and confident to reassure even the most harried diners. He placed the mimosas and lattes on the table with a smile. "Are you ladies ready to order?"

They quickly gave their order. He did not need to write it down. Of course, he didn't, the arrogant prick, Emily thought.

"You need to confront him, Em," Nova said. "You can't keep letting this slide. It's affecting you too much."

Grace, who had been uncharacteristically quiet, suddenly spoke up, her voice tinged with anger. "This is bullshit. We talked about this the other day, remember, at our house? All the signs? The late nights, the vague excuses, cancelling plans, always distracted? Sam is doing every single one of those things."

Emily nodded, her eyes welling up with tears. "I remember. I just—I don't know how to bring it up without it turning into a huge fight."

Vic leaned forward, her expression intense. "You need to be direct. Don't let him wiggle his way out with more excuses. You deserve to know the truth."

Emily took a deep breath. "The thing is, I love him. I want to believe there's a reasonable explanation, but I just can't think of what else it could be."

Mia's eyes were soft with empathy. "It's okay to still love him, Emily. But you also need to love yourself enough to demand honesty and respect. You shouldn't have to live like this, always wondering and worrying."

Nova nodded in agreement. "You need to lay it all out for him. Tell him what you've noticed, how it makes you feel, and what you need from him going forward. If he cares about you, he'll make the effort to be transparent."

Grace's anger seemed to grow with every word. "And if he doesn't? Then you need to think about what's best for you. You can't keep waiting around for him to change while you're suffering."

Emily's mind flashed back to dinner that night, the laughter and camaraderie, and the serious conversation that followed. Her friends had pointed out the red flags then, and now those warnings seemed to be coming true. She had brushed it off at the time, hoping it was just a rough patch. But now, the reality was staring her in the face.

"I just don't know if I'm strong enough to handle it if it's what I think it is," she admitted, her voice trembling.

Victoria's expression softened slightly, though her words remained firm. "You are strong enough. We're here for you, no matter what happens. You can't keep living in this uncertainty."

The server returned with their food, and they paused the conversation as plates of avocado toast, eggs benedict, and pancakes were distributed. Emily took a moment to collect her thoughts, grateful for the brief respite.

As they began to eat, Mia spoke again, her voice gentle but insistent. "Have you considered seeing a therapist together? Sometimes it helps to have a neutral party mediate these conversations."

Nova nodded. "That's a good idea. It could provide a safe space for both of you to express your feelings and work through this."

Grace, still simmering, added, "And if he refuses to go? That's a sign in itself. You deserve someone who's willing to fight for your relationship as much as you are."

Emily felt a swell of gratitude for her friends. Their support was unwavering, each offering a different perspective but all with the same underlying message: she deserved better than this uncertainty and pain.

"I'll talk to him," Emily said finally, her voice gaining strength. "I'll suggest counselling. I will talk to him this weekend at dinner. It's our anniversary. Seems like a good time to find out the truth, no matter how much it hurts."

Victoria raised her glass. "To Emily, finding the strength to demand the love and respect she deserves."

The others followed suit, clinking their glasses. As Emily sipped her mimosa, she felt a renewed sense of determination. She wasn't alone in this. Her friends had her back, and with their support, she could face whatever came next.

32

Harper walked into the small kitchenette of the police station. It was a compact space, designed more for functionality than comfort. The walls were a neutral off-white, and the flooring consisted of scuffed linoleum that had seen better days. The room was well-lit by fluorescent lights that cast a bright, clinical glow over everything.

Against one wall stood a row of cabinets and a countertop cluttered with various appliances: a worn drip coffee maker that was perpetually brewing a fresh pot, a microwave with a few stains from past spills that smelt like burnt popcorn, and a small, slightly dented refrigerator covered in magnets and notes, reminding officers to label their food. The cabinets held a mismatched collection of mugs and plates, evidence of years of use by different shifts.

A bulletin board on one wall was cluttered with various flyers, memos, and schedules, pinned haphazardly. A nearby sink was filled with a few unwashed mugs, and a roll of paper towels hung precariously from a holder that had seen better days. The faint hum of the refrigerator provided a constant background noise.

Gloria was standing at the middle of the bench, preparing her lunch. She did not make any type of movement that would suggest she had heard Harper come in.

"Hey, Gloria," Harper greeted her. Gloria jumped in fright, startled by the sound of her voice.

"Hi," Gloria replied, her eyes bright. She stepped aside slightly, but Harper indicated that she was headed for the coffee machine.

Harper poured herself a cup of coffee. "I need to talk to you," she said, her voice a whisper.

Gloria looked at her. "What's up," she asked, her voice a similar whisper.

"Well, I really want to investigate the drive further, as well as the canister, but not here."

Gloria raised an eyebrow, intrigued. "Go on."

"Think you can get Sam to swing by my place this weekend? We can investigate the contents more thoroughly without the constraints, distractions, and most importantly, prying eyes of the station." Harper sipped her coffee, watching Gloria's face. "Plus, I have some equipment at home that might help us. Can you make it?"

Gloria's jaw tightened. "I'm in. And I'm sure Sam will be on board as well. He's as invested in this as we are."

Relief washed over Harper. "Great. Saturday evening?"

"Sounds good," Gloria said.

As Harper turned to leave, she reached out and briefly touched Gloria's shoulder. A small piece of paper fluttered down, landing on the food she was preparing.

Gloria looked down at the piece of paper on her lunch, its edges slightly crumpled. Harper's neat handwriting stared back at her—an address and a time: 6:30 PM, Saturday. She folded the paper carefully and slipped it into her pocket, her mind already racing with the implications. Harper's house would be the perfect place to dig deeper without prying eyes.

She returned to her desk, glancing around to make sure no one was watching. The station was bustling with the usual midday activity—officers coming and going, phones ringing, and the hum of conversations.

Gloria's mind was now thinking about the weekend. They seemed to have barely scratched the surface of what was on that drive. A deeper dive could reveal way more.

She sat and began to eat, more quickly that she normally would. She was eager to find Sam. As she ate, she stopped to wipe her mouth. Vince, the ever-present figure, sat across their adjoined desks. He was engrossed in a report, but she knew he would help her. "Vince, I need a favour," she said, her voice just loud enough that he should hear her.

He looked up, raising an eyebrow. "What's up?"

"Can you keep the Chief busy while I duck out? I've got to talk to Sam Caldwell, and, well, I can't do that if I am being watched."

Vince's expression shifted from curiosity to concern. "About the drive?"

Gloria nodded. "Yeah. Harper wants us at her place this weekend to investigate further. I need to make sure Sam is on board."

Vince leaned back in his chair, crossing his arms. "Alright, I can run interference. But on one condition—I'm coming with you to Harper's."

Gloria hesitated, weighing her options. "Fine," she said after a moment of contemplation. Vince was her partner. But not just that, he was sharp and having him along could be an asset.

Vince smirked. "You've got it. Now, go do what you need to do. I'll keep the Chief busy. But make it quick."

With a nod, Gloria made her way to the exit, moving with purpose. She slipped out of the station and headed for the parking lot, her mind focused on the conversation she needed to have with Sam.

Gloria walked briskly into Sam's shopfront, her eyes immediately scanning the room. The reception area, as sparse at it looked to be, was a mess. Books and magazines were scattered across the floor, the two chairs overturned, and the couch cushions lay in front of the couch, which was half-turned away from the wall. Sam sat on the uncomfortable couch, his face sullen. It seemed clear to her what had happened.

"Sam," she called out softly, walking over to him. He looked up, his face etched with frustration and exhaustion. "This all doesn't look good," she said, with compassion.

"Yep, full ransack. Take a look," he said, pointing at the entrance to his office, his voice flat.

Gloria peered through the open door, confirming his words. The room was a complete mess. As Gloria stepped into the dimly lit space, her eyes widened at the scene. The air was thick with the scent of dust stirred up from overturned furniture and disturbed surfaces. His desk was a chaotic mess. Drawers hung open haphazardly, their contents strewn across the floor like confetti after a storm. Papers, photographs, and case notes lay scattered, some crumpled underfoot.

The filing cabinets along the walls had not been spared. Several drawers were pulled out, their contents dumped carelessly onto the floor. Folders were ripped open, their contents spilling out, revealing glimpses of confidential documents and evidence from ongoing cases.

Gloria walked back out to where Sam was and sat down beside him. "Looks like they were very thorough," she said. "Did they find what they were looking for?"

"No," Sam said.

"Any idea which agency it was?" Gloria asked.

"There's nothing on the security cameras, so no. They must have come in through the service hallways," Sam said, his voice a low monotone.

"This is bad," she muttered. "But we can't let it derail us. Harper wants us to go to her house on Saturday. Investigate the drive and the canister further there, away from prying eyes."

Sam nodded, but there was little enthusiasm in his expression. "Alright. I'll be there."

Gloria placed a reassuring hand on his shoulder. Seeing how distracted he was by the state of his office, Gloria decided it was best to leave him to it. "Until Saturday," she said. As she stood to leave, she tossed Harper's note into his lap. "Here's the address and time. I'll see you then."

Sam picked up the note, his eyes meeting hers with a brief flash of gratitude. "Thanks, Gloria. I appreciate it."

She gave him a small, encouraging smile before turning and walking out of the shopfront. The mess left behind by the intruders was troubling, but it only strengthened her resolve. They were onto something significant, and no amount of intimidation would stop her from uncovering the truth.

<h1 style="text-align:center">33</h1>

❦

Sam sat in a comfortable chair in Harper's living room. He could tell it was a house that was owned by a computer scientist, living solo. It reflected both her profession and her personal taste in a harmonious blend of functionality and style. The colour scheme was subtle yet elegant, with walls painted in soft shades of grey and white that provided a serene backdrop for the room's furnishings. A plush, low-pile rug in muted tones of blue and grey covered the hardwood floor, adding warmth and texture to the space. Nearby, a sleek, minimalist coffee table made of polished wood and metal sat atop the rug, adorned with a few carefully chosen art books and a small, tasteful succulent plant.

Gloria and Vince sat on a couch to match the chair Sam was sitting on. Upholstered in a durable fabric that hinted at practicality without sacrificing style. Throw pillows in geometric patterns added a pop of colour—subtle greens and blues that complemented the overall colour scheme. Vince shifted in place, obviously not finding the cushions to be a comfortable necessity. Harper sat on the other chair to match his.

Against one wall stood a state-of-the-art entertainment system, complete with a large flat-screen TV mounted on the wall and surrounded by speakers discreetly integrated into the room's architecture. The shelves beneath the TV housed a collection of tech gadgets—smart speakers, gaming consoles neatly arranged with their controllers, and a row of organised DVDs and Blu-rays.

Harper had connected her computer to the TV, so they could all see what she was looking at.

Sam shifted uncomfortably in his chair, his brow furrowed as he glanced at Vince, who had shown up unexpectedly. The presence of an outsider, even one the others knew well, grated on Sam's nerves.

He opened his mouth to voice his concern, but Gloria's steady gaze met his, her eyes conveying reassurance and a silent plea for trust.

"He's on our side, Sam," Gloria said softly, her voice carrying conviction. "We have been partners for a long time now. We have both proven ourselves to each other time and again. I trust him with my life," she said, the conviction in her voice was evident, and left no question.

"Sam, when we first met, things were a lot different. I trust Gloria, and I am here to support her. You can be sure of that." Vince's tone was equally convincing.

Sam hesitated, still wary but slowly relenting under Gloria's steadfast gaze and Vince's reassuring words. With a sigh, he nodded reluctantly, acknowledging the practicality of their situation despite his reservations. Deep down, he knew that in this intricate web of deception and uncertainty, having allies could make a difference.

Harper turned her attention to the computer and began opening files from the drive. The screen filled with dense code, technical diagrams, and an interface none of them—except Harper—understood.

The room went silent except for the quiet taps of Harper's keyboard. She scrolled, paused, read, and continued. To Sam, it felt like hours. Finally, she broke the silence.

"This can't be real," Harper said, as if speaking to herself. "The drive seems to have multiple functions." She split the screen in two, one side showing a picture of the device, with the other side showing a document they had been looking at. "The device seems to fire a pulse of…let's call it light, at its intended target. That beam extracts the 'human data'…"

"What the hell is meant by human data," Vince asked.

"Well, that's the thing," Harper said. "It doesn't explain what that is, it just says human data. But it does say, extract, which is usually not the same as taking a copy, or a picture. Extracting means removing or taking out." She looked at Vince, then turned to look at Sam.

"Before we make too many outlandish claims, what else does the drive do?" Sam said. "You said it does multiple things."

"I am gonna grab a beer," Vince announced, then stood up. "Let's be honest, you might as well carry on. I don't understand any of this. Anyone want anything?" he asked.

"I'll have a beer, considering Harper was good enough to supply them," Sam said.

"I'll have a beer as well," Gloria said.

"I'm good," Harper said. "I'm not a drinker."

"You don't drink," Vince said, surprised. "So, why did you say you would supply the drinks," he asked.

"Because it's the polite thing to do," Harper said, confused by the question.

Sam and Vince exchanged a look and chuckled. Vince shook his head as he walked into the kitchen. A light from a passing car flashed briefly through the window, illuminating the room before disappearing just as quickly. Sam didn't notice—it barely registered in his mind.

He turned back to the screen as the fridge opened and the faint clink of bottles echoed from the next room.

Emily sat in the elegant restaurant, surrounded by warm lighting that cast a soft glow over polished wooden tables adorned with fresh flowers in delicate vases. The ambiance was sophisticated yet inviting, with soft music playing in the background and a faint aroma of culinary delights wafting from the open kitchen. Large windows offered a view of the bustling city street outside, adding a touch of urban charm to the upscale setting.

As she fidgeted with her napkin, Emily glanced at her watch for what felt like the hundredth time. Sam was now twenty minutes late. A knot of nervous anticipation coiled in her stomach. She had chosen a quiet corner table, hoping for privacy but feeling increasingly conspicuous as time ticked by.

A server approached with a warm smile, his demeanour professional yet friendly. He was dressed very neatly, to match the quiet charm of the restaurant. "Good evening, ma'am. Are you expecting anyone else to join you?" he inquired politely.

Emily forced a smile, her nerves betraying her usual calm demeanour. "Yes, I'm waiting for my boyfriend," she replied, trying to sound more assured than she felt.

The server nodded understandingly. "Could I offer you a starter while you wait. Some bread and dip, perhaps," he said, discreetly.

"That would be lovely." She looked down at her wine glass, now empty. She had finished it without realising.

"And another glass of Rosé, please," she said.

"Certainly," the server said with a nod, before turning and walking back to the kitchen.

Emily's thoughts raced. Was there a reasonable explanation for his lateness, or was it a sign of something more troubling? She tried to quell her worries, reminding herself of the times he had been delayed by work or traffic. Yet, the longer she waited, the harder it became to ignore the nagging feeling that something was amiss.

Time had marched on very slowly as Sam tried to keep up with what Harper had been explaining, as she went through the drive.

"Once the data is extracted," Harper started again, "it's stored in the canister. That part doesn't seem to require the drive. The drive is then plugged into the device, whereby a program initiates to transfer the data from the canister to the database. The drive, it seems, acts like a type of key."

"The database?" Gloria asked, before Sam had a chance. "What's the database?"

"Well, commonly, we all understand that a database is where electronic data is stored at scale. And while that is the same thing here, the database being referenced here in this code is more like the ones used for large language models. Like the types of databases that run the AIs that are everywhere, for example. Having said that, however, this database code is as different from the code used for large language models, as they are to traditional databases. But, please, I am obviously not an expert in anything that I am saying. I might be completely wrong."

"Harper, out of any of us, you are most likely to be right. We are having a hard time just keeping up with what you're saying, let alone trying to deduce it in the first place," Gloria said.

Harper turned to look at Gloria, smiling. She turned back to the screen, "Another program on the drive seems to be for loading the human data, into the database."

Harper moved the computer mouse around the screen and clicked on some things, before a new document of code appeared on the screen.

"That is what this program seems to do. It was part of the stuff you sent the other day, Sam," Harper said, but kept looking at the screen.

"But the most exciting—or shocking—thing," Harper continued, "is that there's another program. One that lets someone communicate with the extracted data. Like… actually talk with it. Like you're speaking to the person themself."

"You mentioned that before, Harper. What do you think that actually means?" Sam asked.

This time Harper turned to look at Sam. He could see in her eyes that it meant exactly what she said. "Exactly what I said," she confirmed. Communicate directly with the 'person' data." She made air quotes. "Not a simulation. Not an AI that pretends to be the person. But the actual person's data."

"What I am hearing you say, Harper, is you can communicate with the person," Vince said, as he walked back into the room. He handed Gloria her beer, then Sam his. "Forget the word data— you're communicating with the person?" He continued walking to the large window that looked out onto the street.

"Well, yes. That is what I mean," Harper said.

Another car drove by while Vince was standing at the window. "How busy is your street, Harper?" Vince asked. "I mean, normally.

Obviously, I am not suggesting you pay any type of attention to it, but…" He left the question hanging.

Harper raised her eyebrows at the unexpected question. "I have no idea," Harper said.

Vince just nodded.

"I haven't noticed it being busy. It's not part of a thoroughfare or anything. The only people who use this street are the people who live here—or nearby," Harper said.

With nothing else said, their attention turned back to the task at hand. Sam tried to make sense of Harper's explanation. He exchanged a glance with Gloria, who mirrored his confusion. The implications of what Harper was suggesting were staggering, almost too fantastical to believe.

"You mean to tell us, Harper," Sam began slowly, "that this drive and canister not only store data but interact with individuals whose data has been extracted? Like some kind of… virtual communication?"

Harper nodded, her expression troubled.

"That's what it seems like, but then not," she said. "The software—it's just so ridiculously sophisticated. It's not storing simulated memories. It's not simulating responses. It's engaging with the subject. The person."

Gloria leaned forward, her voice low.

"Are you saying someone could manipulate people through this technology? Control them remotely?"

Harper hesitated, her fingers tracing patterns on the table. "I… I don't… no, I don't think so. That would be something, though, wouldn't it?" she said, her voice gaining an edge of excitement. "But it does talk about 'people' or 'person data', using the words extracted, so I can't say that isn't a possibility. The implications…" Her voice trailed off, overwhelmed by the enormity of what they were discovering.

Another set of headlights drove by as Sam's mind raced, piecing together fragments of information and forming unsettling conclusions. If what Harper suggested was true, it meant they were dealing with technology far beyond their understanding.

"While you are grappling with that possibility, here is the thing that is going to melt your brain," Harper said, ominously. "Not only does it use words like human data, and extraction, but I have also seen references to consciousness," she said.

Harper turned to look at Sam and Gloria, each in turn. Her face showing the same mix of concern and disbelief mirrored in their expressions, as the full weight of what she said settled down on Sam. "Extract... consciousness... load to database... communicate with person. Is that what I am hearing?" Sam asked, embarrassed to have even thought it.

"Yeah, I think that is what I am saying, Sam," Harper said.

"Is that what has happened to the First Lady, then, and that other guy?" Vince asked, as if this all made perfect sense to him.

Sam looked at Vince, shocked. He was right. It all fitted. "Oh fuck," Sam said, eyes wide, a second realisation hitting him. "Harper, when you say human data, are you really talking about the person's fucking consciousness? I can't believe I am even saying those words," he said, putting a hand to his head.

Harper looked at Sam, her eyes wide too. She suddenly stood and walked to the bag that was sitting near the wall. She grabbed the canister from the bag and returned to her seat. She turned the canister so that everyone could see the initials on it: J.T.

"Do you think this holds the data of a person. That is why it has these initials on it."

"If that drive gives you access to the database that holds the people, why don't we plug that canister in and find out?" Vince said, his voice calm, as if nothing mattered.

Emily continued to sit alone at the table, her half-eaten meal in front of her. The once beautiful presentation of the dish was now disrupted, reflecting her own inner turmoil. The warm lighting of the restaurant seemed to mock her solitude, casting shadows that danced on the empty seat across from her. She took another bite, barely tasting the food as her mind remained fixated on Sam's absence. Any hope she had of him walking through the door was dwindling as fast as the minutes were flying by.

The server approached her table again, his expression a mix of concern and professionalism. "Would you like another drink, madam?" he asked gently, noting her near-empty glass.

Emily picked up the glass and downed what was left. "Keep them coming," she replied with a smile that did not reach her eyes, handing him the now-empty glass. He gently took it from her. She watched as he nodded and walked away to fetch her another drink, her thoughts returning to the reality of her situation. She wasn't convinced that her relationship with Sam was over, but the signs were hard to ignore. His absence was deafening, a confirmation of her worst fears.

The server returned shortly after with a new glass. She noticed this one was fuller than the last. She took it from him, and lifted it in the air, acknowledging the sentiment. The server winked at her, before leaving her again, alone.

With each sip of her drink, Emily's resolve to drown her sorrows strengthened. She could feel the alcohol dulling the edges of her pain, offering a temporary reprieve from the heartache that gnawed at her. Tonight, she would allow herself to forget, to numb the betrayal and disappointment. Tomorrow, she would face the fallout.

34

Ideas and theories swirled in Sam's mind—each more unsettling than the last—as they continued to discuss how they thought the canister would work. Sam couldn't shake the chilling thought that they were only scratching the surface of something far more sinister and complex than they had ever imagined.

"Harper, do you own a gun? And do you have homeowners' insurance?" Vince asked.

In an instant, all conversation stopped. Everyone looked at Vince. Sam's heart began to race, more than it was, but this time with a spike of sudden anxiety. Vince's voice cut through the air like a knife.

Harper blinked, taken aback.

"No, I don't own a gun. And, yes, I have insurance, but why—"

"We've run out of time," Vince interrupted. "The cavalry has arrived to spoil our party. A black van just pulled up next door, headlights off. I give it five minutes before they kick the door in."

Panic rippled through the group. Sam felt a cold sweat break out on his forehead as he exchanged a worried glance with Gloria. Thank God for Vince, Sam thought. He was only just now realising that Vince had been standing at that window for a long time, staring out. In fact, ever since that first car drove by. All Vince's questions about traffic were making sense now.

"What do we do?" Harper's voice wavered, her usual calm demeanour slipping.

Vince continued to stand at the window, peering through the curtains, "We need to split up. Sam, Harper, Gloria, you leave through the back door. I will stay here."

"The hell you will," Gloria said firmly, stepping closer to Vince. "We are all leaving," she said defiantly.

"Gloria, listen to me," Vince argued, his voice low and urgent. "We're cops. They won't do anything if we don't resist. You need to go with Sam and Harper. We can't all get caught."

"I'm not leaving you here alone!" Gloria was having none of it.

"He is right, Gloria. We can't all get caught," Sam said. "They will also send people around the back, so if we don't leave, right now, none of us are getting out of here. And they get the drive and the canister."

"Then you two go. You are a surveillance detective, you know how to move in the shadows. Vince is right. We are cops. They will not harm us if we don't resist."

Sam could see that Vince was giving Gloria a look that meant he was not happy with her staying.

"I said no!" Gloria snapped, her eyes blazing with determination. "I'm staying."

Sam could see the resolve in Gloria's eyes and knew there was no changing her mind. He turned to Harper. "Grab your computer, the drive and the canister, and let's go," he said.

Harper nodded, her face pale but resolute. She unplugged things as quickly as she could.

"They are out of the van. You should be gone already," Vince said, his voice urgent.

As Sam and Harper ran to the back door, Sam grabbed a cloth bag that had been slung over a dining chair for Harper to put her stuff in. They moved quickly. Sam's mind was racing. He hoped Harper's back fence was not blocked by bushes. As they reached the back door, Vince's voice called after them, "Good luck. We'll hold them off as long as we can."

Sam and Harper slipped out into the cool night air, the garden illuminated by faint moonlight. Sam immediately looked to the back fence. There were bushes, but there were gaps they could get through. They ran across the yard, both breathing hard from the panic that had now well and truly set in. Sam fought hard to keep his emotions in check. Slow is smooth, smooth is fast, he thought, as the saying goes.

Reaching the fence at the far end, Sam told Harper to quickly put her stuff in the bag, before boosting her up, almost throwing her over. He heard her land on the other side with a thud. She groaned in response. He jumped up onto the fence and quickly climbed over, landing with his own thud. Both ducking down, Sam looked back through a hole in the fence to see if they had been seen.

Three men in tactical gear ran around the side of the house into the backyard, moving swiftly and silently. They took positions by the back door, weapons ready. Sam's heart pounded in his chest as he watched them, his breath shallow and quick. It did not look like they had been seen.

In a sudden burst of activity, the men breached the back door with a loud crash, and moments later, shouting and gunshots erupted from inside the house. Sam's blood ran cold as he heard the chaos unfold. He wanted to run back to help Vince and Gloria, but he knew it would be suicide.

"Come on," Harper whispered urgently, tugging at his sleeve. "We have to keep moving."

Harper was right. Sam forced himself to tear his gaze away from the scene and followed Harper as they ran through the neighbour's yard, trying to put as much distance between themselves and the house as possible. They reached the street, where Sam took the lead.

The sounds of the raid were still audible as they moved quickly, clinging to the shadows of trees and shrubs—like their panic clung to them—urging them onward. Sam tried to block out the images of Vince and Gloria, hoping against hope that they were alright.

Finally, they paused in a narrow alley, leaning against the cold brick wall to catch their breath. Sam's thoughts were a whirlwind of fear and guilt. They were risking themselves to help him and he had left them behind. The uncertainty of their fate gnawed at him.

"Sam," Harper said softly, her voice trembling. "What do we do now?"

He took a deep breath, trying to steady himself. "We need to find a safe place to hide. Somewhere we can regroup and figure out our next move."

Harper nodded, her eyes reflecting the same determination and fear that Sam felt. They couldn't afford to stop now, not with the stakes so high. Together, they pushed onward into the night, their footsteps echoing softly in the empty alleyway.

Stopping once again, Sam asked Harper to check that she still had everything. She checked her bag. She looked up at Sam, horror on her face.

"What is it?"

"I don't have the drive," she said. "I must have dropped it at the fence. We have to go back."

"No, Harper," Sam said, as a matter of fact. "The drive is gone. If we go back there, we get caught." Harper looked like she was about to collapse. "It doesn't matter anyway. I made a copy—so we can use that."

Harper looked at Sam, relief evident in her expression.

35

Agent Thompson sat in the driver's seat of the unmarked sedan, eyes trained on the small, nondescript house in the middle of the quiet suburban street. The air was still, only punctuated by the occasional whisper of a gentle breeze rustling through the leaves of the well-tended trees lining the sidewalks and manicured lawns. Streetlights cast a soft, amber glow, their halos of light creating small islands of visibility amid the darkness. The asphalt of the road, smooth and unblemished, glistened faintly from a recent passing shower, reflecting the light in a subtle, shimmering pattern.

Her partner, Agent Miller, was beside her, flipping through the pages of the case file for the hundredth time since they had started. The clock on the dashboard read 9:13 PM. Time seemed to slow, each moment stretching out in a perfect tableau of peace and stillness, a world away from the hustle and bustle of the day.

The past few hours had been uneventful, other than cars driving by as people came and went, their headlights casting brief shadows that flickered across the walls of the surrounding houses. Agent Thompson's fingers drummed lightly on the steering wheel, her patience wearing thin. Tonight felt like something. The house belonged to Daniels, the police station's tech expert. They knew Sam was inside with Daniels, Detective Lawson, and her partner Detective Marshall.

"Think we're gonna get anything tonight?" she asked, her voice low.

"Hard to say," Miller replied, still looking through the papers.

"Does something feel off to you?" she asked. "You live in the suburbs, how many cars normally travel down a street at night, and not turn into a driveway?"

Just as she finished speaking, a van turned into the street, its headlights off. Agent Thompson's fingers curled tight around the wheel, her heartbeat spiking as the van approached. It wasn't the usual van or SUV; this was a tactical team van. The kind that didn't just show up unannounced.

"What the fuck is this," she said, more as a statement than a question, straightening in her seat. She turned to look at Agent Miller, who was also now looking at the scene in front of them.

"Did you know about this?" Agent Miller whispered, his voice tense.

Agent Thompson shook her head, her eyes fixed on the van. "No. This is news to me."

The van came to a stop at the house next door. There was no movement for a few minutes before heavily armed agents poured out, moving stealthily through the night. Agent Thompson's heart rate quickened as she watched them take positions around the house; two going to the front door, while three went around the back.

"Something ain't right. This is wrong," Agent Miller muttered, echoing her thoughts. "Stay sharp, this could get messy."

They watched as the team made their move, breaching the front door with a resounding crash that echoed through the stillness. This was followed by shouting, then gunfire, two sharp cracks, piercing the night. Screams could be heard, followed by cursing. The people inside the house seemed to be still alive, but they were not happy.

Agent Thompson's mind raced. They had no intel about a raid. No coordination with local law enforcement. This was wrong on so many levels. She and Agent Miller exchanged another look, their concern mirrored in each other's eyes. Then she had a thought. "Something has changed," she said, suddenly. "Something has happened within the CIA, I bet, that has caused this to happen."

She opened the door and got out of the car, making the snap decision to confront the team making the raid. "What are you doing," Agent Miller said, his voice tense. She ignored him.

Agent Thompson marched towards the scene. Her heart pounded in her chest, each step fuelled by a mix of frustration and determination. She approached the nearest officer, his face obscured by the tactical gear. "I'm Agent Thompson, FBI," she said, flashing her badge. "I demand to know what's going on here."

The officer, tall and imposing, barely glanced at her. "This is outside the purview of the FBI, Agent. Step back."

Agent Thompson's jaw tightened. "This is our jurisdiction. We've been on surveillance for hours. Why weren't we informed about this raid?"

The officer's eyes met hers, cold and unyielding. "I'm telling you, Agent, this is none of your business. Get out of the way."

Anger flared in Agent Thompson's chest. "You don't get to shut me out like this. I have a right to know what's happening in my investigation!"

The officer took a step forward, his voice low and firm. "Your investigation is over. Now step back, or I'll have you removed."

Agent Thompson's fists clenched at her sides, her mind racing, unable to comprehend how her investigation could be over without her knowledge. They had been painstakingly tracking Sam, compiling evidence and waiting for the right moment to move on him. Yet, here she was, blindsided by an operation that had seemingly bypassed all standard protocols.

The lack of communication from her superiors gnawed at her, raising questions about the integrity of the raid and the true objectives behind it. How could such a crucial decision be made without a single word to her or Agent Miller? Something was deeply wrong, and Agent Thompson's instincts told her this was far from over.

With no choice but a final, seething glare, she turned and made her way back to the car, frustration boiling within her. "Those motherfuckers are completely off the rails!" she spat, as she got back in.

"What did he say?" Agent Miller asked, trying to keep his voice calm.

Agent Thompson was not calm. "Apparently, our investigation is over, according to that asshole," she said. She tapped the quick dial icon on her phone. "This is Agent Thompson, requesting immediate clarification on a tactical raid at the residence of Harper Daniels. We were not informed of any operation."

She waited for a response. Then, a voice came through, terse but familiar. "Stand by, Agent Thompson. We're looking into it."

Thompson's jaw tightened. "Stand by" wasn't good enough. Not by a long shot. She glanced at Agent Miller, her resolve hardening. They were going to get to the bottom of this, one way or another.

As her mind seethed, she heard a sharp yell from an officer emerging from Harper's house pierce the tense night air.

"Caldwell and Daniels have escaped! Everyone, spread out and find them!"

The command given, the tactical officers started to disperse.

Her heart jumped. She could not tell if things were getting better or worse, by the second. She turned to Agent Miller, who looked ready for action. "We need to get out and search," she said urgently. "We can't let them find them before we do."

Agent Miller nodded, and they both stepped out of the car, blending into the chaotic scene of law enforcement officers spreading out across the suburb. Agent Thompson's mind raced as she moved, trying to piece together the rapidly unfolding situation. How had Caldwell and Daniels managed to escape? If they got caught, all their hard work could be undone in an instant.

Agent Thompson scoured the streets, yards, and alleyways, her flashlight slicing through the darkness. She checked behind bushes, under parked cars, and in every shadowy nook, but there was no sign of them. Her frustration grew with each passing minute. Porch lights flicked on, and a couple of nosy neighbours stepped onto their lawns, trying to figure out what the hell was going on. She told them to go back inside, for their own protection. She could hear echoes of similar commands from elsewhere.

After what felt like an eternity of searching, Agent Thompson found herself on a quiet street, separated from the main group of officers. Her breath was steady, her senses heightened. The faint sound of footsteps caught her attention, and she spun around, only to be met with a blinding light in her eyes.

"Freeze!" a voice commanded.

Agent Thompson's hands instinctively went up. "I'm Agent Thompson, FBI! I'm part of the search team."

The officer didn't lower his weapon, as he crept closer. "Drop the gun and get on the ground, Daniels!"

Her confusion turned to alarm. "I'm not Daniels! I'm…"

The officer didn't wait. He swung his gun, the butt connecting with the side of her head. Pain exploded through her skull, and she fell to the ground, darkness creeping into the edges of her vision.

While in a daze, her hands were cuffed behind her back, and she was made to walk. Panic and anger surged through her. How had things gone so wrong, she thought trying to keep her balance while everything spun around her.

By the time her dizziness had abated, she was back at the house, and taken inside. The atmosphere was tense. Agent Thompson was forced into a chair, the officers around her eyeing her warily. "I'm Agent Thompson," she repeated, her voice weak but determined. "Check my ID."

One of the officers scoffed. "Nice try, Daniels. You're not fooling anyone."

Bouts of pain lanced through her head, causing her vision to blur slightly. "You're making a mistake," she croaked.

The interrogation continued, the officers firing questions about her supposed involvement with Caldwell. Thompson's denials seemed to fall on deaf ears. She was starting to feel the weight of hopelessness when a familiar voice cut through the haze.

"Stop! She's FBI!" Agent Miller burst into the room, his badge held high. "This is Agent Thompson, you fucking morons. You've made a mistake."

The officers exchanged uncertain glances before one of them stepped forward, unlocking her cuffs. Agent Thompson rubbed her wrists, glaring at the officer who had hit her. "Next time, do your damn homework."

Agent Miller helped her to her feet, his eyes filled with concern. "You okay?"

"Been better," she muttered, her head throbbing. "Let's go back to the car. We're done here."

Back in the car, Agent Thompson leaned back in her seat, feeling the lingering ache where the officer had struck her. She pulled out her phone and dialled the same number as before. As the line connected, she took a deep steadying breath.

"Director Shaw," came a familiar voice.

"So, things haven't gone well here, Director," she began, her voice tinged with frustration. "Caldwell and Daniels escaped during the raid. It looks like Detectives Lawson and Marshall have been taken in. Please tell me you know what just happened," she demanded.

There was a brief silence on the other end before Director Shaw responded. "The situation is clearly escalating. The raid was not orchestrated by us, but I don't need to tell you that. What I need you and Miller to do is head to Mr. Caldwell's apartment. If he's there, bring him in. This has become too dangerous, and we need to contain this situation immediately."

Agent Thompson nodded, even though Director Shaw couldn't see her. "We're on it, Director," she replied, then ended the call. She turned to Agent Miller, who was watching her intently. "We're heading to Caldwell's apartment. If he's there, we bring him in. If not, we stake it out till he shows. No more surprises." Agent Miller gave a curt nod and started the car, determination hardening their resolve as they drove into the night, ready to face whatever awaited them.

<h1 style="text-align:center">36</h1>

⸻ ❦ ⸻

Sam sat in the back of the taxi, the city lights blurring as he stared out the window, lost in thought. His chaotic life had just spiralled completely out of control., and he was in serious danger. So would Emily be. He knew he had to find a way to protect her, to keep her safe from the dangers closing in around them. All he could think was to urge her to go to her parents. Sam felt a knot tighten in his stomach as he and Harper approached the apartment.

All was quiet, save for the pounding in his ears. He glanced at Harper, whose eyes were still wide, lost in her own thoughts. Feeling his stare, she looked at him, then looked out the window, only then realising they had stopped.

"Should we even be here," she said, clearly nervous.

"This will not take long. I just need to talk to Emily. Ask her to go to and stay with her parents. Maybe get some clothes for the both of us, if you don't mind wearing other people's clothing, that is." Harper just shrugged. "Would you mind sticking around, leave the meter running. We won't be long," Sam said, turning his attention to the driver.

"As long as the meter's running, I'm happy to do whatever."

Sam approached his apartment, exhaustion weighing him down. He had spent the taxi ride contemplating how to convince Emily to go to her parents, where he believed she would be safer. It was time to come clean.

As they reached the apartment door, expecting it to be quiet with Emily asleep inside, Sam's heart skipped a beat. The sound of

167

music drifted into the hallway. He pushed the door open, his senses alert to any sign of trouble. The fear in his mind was overwhelming; worry for Emily's safety mingled with concern for his own, unsure of what awaited him inside their once peaceful sanctuary.

Sam stood in the doorway, stunned by the scene before him. Emily, clad in nothing but her underwear, danced alone in the middle of the living room. Her movements were unsteady, almost erratic, as if trying to drown out the world with each sway of her hips. A bottle of wine dangled loosely from one hand, its contents visibly diminished. Her hair was dishevelled, her makeup smudged—a stark contrast to the composed woman she normally was. Sam's concern deepened, a pang of guilt and embarrassment knotting in his stomach at the sight of her unravelling in front of him, knowing Harper was standing behind him seeing what he saw. He hesitated, unsure of how to approach her.

As Sam stood there, Emily's piercing gaze locked onto him. Her voice sliced through the tense silence, sharp and filled with hurt.

"So, you finally decided to come home, huh? After standing me up at our anniversary dinner."

She then focused on Harper.

"Oh, and look, you brought the home wrecker whore with you," she said, slurring.

Sam's heart sank, his gut twisting with guilt. He had forgotten about dinner. They had organised it to celebrate their anniversary of being together. What was supposed to be a night of celebration had become a scene straight out of a nightmare. And it was his fault. "Em, I'm so sorry. It's been... it's been a crazy night. I didn't mean to…"

Emily cut him off, her voice rising with each word. "Crazy night? Do you think that excuses what you did? We had plans, Sam. Plans that meant something to me, but obviously nothing for you!" she said, finishing with a yell.

Sam took a step forward, reaching out.

"I know, and I messed up. But let me explain…"

Emily's eyes flashed with anger, pulling away from him as if his touch would burn.

"Explain? What's there to explain? I see you standing here, with her!"

Her voice cracked with emotion as she gestured angrily at Harper.

"And you expect me to believe it's all innocent?"

She swiped her arms through the air, finishing with pointing in the direction of the bedroom, swaying as she steadied herself.

"Go ahead, see if I care. Go fuck her brains out."

Emily then looked at Harper again.

"But I give you this tip for free: he doesn't like a finger in the arse."

She smiled at that, pleased with herself.

Sam's heart was tearing. "Em, it's not what it looks like. Harper's…"

"Just a work colleague, I know. I know all the excuses. And I don't care anymore!" Emily's voice echoed off the walls of the apartment. "All I want is for you and that bitch whore to leave."

Sam felt Harper bristle beside him. That was twice now that Emily had called her a whore. Sam shot Harper a pleading look, hoping she would realise Emily was drunk and there was obviously history behind what she was saying. He turned back to Emily, desperation in his eyes. "Please, just listen to me. Harper's not… it's not like that."

But Emily was beyond reason, her emotions raw and unchecked. "I don't want to hear it, Sam. Just go."

Sam had enough—he had to get through to her. "Em, shut the fuck up!" he yelled. This time it was his voice that reverberated off the walls. Emily stopped, her body going rigid from the power in Sam's words. Her face began to contort, and she began to cry. Sam closed the distance between them, grabbing hold of the top of her arms.

Emily tried to pull away, as if Sam's touch did indeed burn her, but his grip was too strong. "Let me go," she said, trying to twist free.

"Em, look at me."

She did. Her face a mixture of sadness and anger.

"Em, you are in danger," he said, deciding the best thing was to get straight to the point. "I am involved in something that has gotten out of hand."

Emily looked past him, towards Harper.

"No, Em. I don't mean that I am involved with another woman. Whether you want to believe it or not, Harper is honestly just a colleague. What we are involved in actually involves the CIA and the FBI."

Emily looked back at Sam. Her face began to change to a different look. She started laughing. She doubled over, laughter taking control of her. Sam let go, allowing her to steady herself while she laughed. After a while, she began to calm down enough to speak again. "You fucking asshole. I have heard some lies in my time, but that takes the cake. Trying to cover up an affair by saying you are working with the CIA and the FBI. That's a new one. I think you should leave."

Sam's shoulders slumped, his voice pleading. "Em, please…"

She shook her head, her eyes and face glistening with tears. "Leave, Sam. Just go," she said, her voice now low and calm.

Sam glanced at Harper, who nodded silently, understanding the gravity of the situation. With a heavy heart, Sam turned and walked to the door of the apartment. He stopped at the threshold and turned to look back at Emily, only to see her back as she walked into the corridor towards their bedroom, the wine bottle hanging limply from her hand.

Sam left the apartment, each step heavier than the last. He couldn't blame Emily for being upset—he had let her down in the worst possible way. The weight of his mistake settled on him, a crushing burden as he made his way down the hallway and out into the cool night air.

Outside, Sam leaned against the wall of the apartment complex, his mind racing. How had everything gone so wrong? His relationship with Emily had been the one stable thing in his life, and now it felt like it was slipping through his fingers. He replayed their argument in his head, the hurt in Emily's eyes burning into his soul.

Harper gently touched Sam on the arm. He looked at her, his expression grim. "I'm sorry, Sam. I am sorry things went down like that."

Sam shook his head wearily. "It's not your fault, Harper. I should have handled this whole situation better." He sighed, running a hand through his hair. "We should go. I'll come back in the morning. Maybe I can smooth things over then," he said, resignation in his voice.

The cheap motel room was a study in faded simplicity, a caricature of motel rooms seen in any movie. The walls, once painted in a neutral beige, now bore the marks of countless guests and luggage. A single window, overlooking a dingy car park, was adorned with worn curtains that barely blocked out the streetlight glare. The air held a smoky mustiness, a testament to years of inadequate ventilation.

In the centre of the room stood two identical twin beds, each draped with a faded bedspread that had long lost its original colour. The mattresses, though clean, sagged slightly under the weight of past occupants. A small bedside table separated the beds, its surface marred with water rings and scratches. A dim lamp with a frayed shade cast a feeble glow across the worn carpeting that stretched from wall to wall.

Opposite the beds, a modest dresser stood, its drawers sticking slightly when pulled open. On top of it, a cracked plastic clock ticked away quietly, its red digital numbers barely visible in the dim light. A small, outdated television sat on a precarious stand in the corner.

The bathroom, accessible through a narrow doorway, was cramped and functional. The linoleum floor tiles were scuffed and faded; the sink chipped around the edges. The shower curtain, a thin vinyl sheet, hung limply from rusted rings on a flimsy rod.

Not wanting to pay using a bank card, which might alert both agencies to their whereabouts, they had pooled the cash each of them had to pay for the room. Sam made sure he always carried cash on him. He could never be sure when he would be in a situation where he needed to use it—something he had learned the hard way. They found they had more than enough for the room for a couple of days, with some left over for food, and a few taxi rides.

Sam found himself sitting on the edge of his bed, the recent past swirling in his mind like a turbulent storm. Isabella's death haunted him, the drive slipped into his pocket with her final act. It seemed like a cruel twist of fate that this drive, a key to a virtual universe that defied all logic, had landed in his possession.

But amidst the wonder and danger of this newfound discovery, Sam's thoughts inevitably turned to Emily. The woman he loved, who had been pushed to the sidelines as he delved deeper into Isabella's mystery. He had neglected her, missed their anniversary dinner—a moment meant to celebrate their bond, now tainted by misunderstanding and hurt that bordered on betrayal. Emily, who now believed he was cheating on her, a rift widening between them with every passing moment.

Lost in his thoughts, he did not hear the shower turn off. He jumped in fright as Harper walked out of the bathroom. Her wet hair hanging down past her shoulders. She was crushing clumps of hair with the towel, attempting to dry it. She had dressed back into her clothes, which were still stained from their escape.

Harper saw him looking at her. "At least I can feel clean, even if it is under dirty clothes," she said, with a smile.

Sam smiled back.

"Tomorrow, I'm going back to the apartment—see if I can get Emily to go to her parents, that is, if she's calmed down." He paused. "While I'm there, I'll grab the key to the safety deposit box. From there, I can go to the bank and be back around lunchtime."

"Well, I can come with you," Harper suggested.

"I don't think that is a good idea. If we are together and we get caught, then that is the end." Sam continued quickly, seeing Harper wanting to interject. "Only one of us can go out at a time, I think. And, honestly, out of the two of us, that should be me. You understand this shit more than I do, and can explain it much better."

Harper didn't say anything as she continued to dry her hair. Sam could see that he had made a good point, and Harper was contemplating what he had said. Without being able to come up with a good response, she finally just nodded.

"I guess you are right," she said.

37

Gloria and Vince were dragged through a dimly lit hallway, their steps faltering due to the searing pain from the bullets lodged in their legs. One each, in the knee. A rough black bag covered their heads blocking their vision, intensifying their sense of vulnerability. Their captors yanked them along, not caring about their injury that slowed their pace. Their hands zip-tied behind their back.

Vince heard a large metal door open, the sound reverberating through the corridor. He was turned and pushed through the door, while he heard Gloria continuing her staggering journey down the corridor. As Vince entered, the sound of another metal door opening also echoed ominously through the corridor. He felt the temperature drop, the air heavy with dampness and foreboding.

Without a word, Vince's captor shoved him into a chair, unceremoniously strapping him in. The leather bands wrapped tightly around his wrists, ankles, and torso, securing him in place with brutal efficiency. The straps biting into his skin, further immobilising him and exacerbating the agony from his wounded leg. Despite his muffled groans, his captor remained indifferent, their movements mechanical and devoid of empathy. A silent promise of what was to come. Vince's breath quickened, fear coursing through his veins.

The rough bag was ripped from his head. He blinked while taking in the stark room, a concrete box, bare and uninviting. He seemed to be sitting in the middle of it. A table off to the side displayed an array of intimidating utensils—pliers, scalpels, and other sharp, menacing tools, their purpose unmistakable. The overhead light was dim and did not do a lot to scare away the starkness of the room. Shortly after, the sound of another metal door closing could be heard…Gloria.

Standing before him was a burly-looking CIA agent, his face a mask of cold detachment. The agent's eyes bore into him, assessing, calculating, devoid of any trace of compassion. His voice cut through the oppressive silence, low and menacing.

"I'll be the one asking you questions," he began, his tone leaving no room for misunderstanding. "Well, demanding answers, actually."

He paused, letting his words sink in.

"My partner, he's got a thing for women. Likes to make them talk. He'll be servicing your partner."

The agent leaned in, his face inches from Vince's, eyes dark and unforgiving. "

We'll let you settle in for now," he said softly, the sinister tone in his voice sending chills down Vince's spine, although he did his best not to let anything show. "But when we come back, you'd better be ready to talk."

With that, he straightened up, shoved the bag back over his head, then turned and left the room. The heavy door slamming shut with a finality that echoed in Vince's ears.

Alone in the cold, concrete room, Vince's heart pounded against his ribs. The unrelenting pain in his leg was a constant reminder of his helplessness. As he strained against the straps, the realisation of his dire predicament settled over him, a suffocating blanket. He was at the mercy of ruthless men who had no compassion, trapped in a place where time seemed to stand still, the promise of torment looming just ahead.

As a repeat of what Vince experienced, Gloria was also hustled into an equally oppressive room and strapped to the metal chair, which was positioned in the middle of the concrete box that was her cell. She cried out, as the strap tightened around the ankle of her injured leg, the pain searing through her. When her captor finished fastening the strap around her torso, he allowed his hand to slowly draw across her body. She tried to move away, but she was strapped down tight.

"Get your fucking hands off me, you piece of shit!" Gloria said, throwing as much malice into her tone as she could.

The rough bag was ripped from her head. Her hair flying up briefly, before settling back down, with some strands falling in front of her face. Gloria's breath quickened, her heart pounding in her head, as she set eyes on the tall CIA agent standing in front of her. On a table beside her were displayed the same intimidating utensils.

"You are a motherless son of a bitch," Gloria spat. "How dare you treat me like this."

The agent said nothing. He just looked at her with a smile on his face. Then as quick as a whip, he slapped her. The crack of his hand connecting perfectly with the side of Gloria's face echoing within the room. Gloria's head was forced to the side, in response to the contact, that went close to knocking her and the chair over. She turned back to look at the agent, her eyes defiant, despite the searing pain coursing through her.

"Don't talk about my mother like that. She is not the one responsible for me. In fact, I don't even know who she is, and neither do you. So, you do not have a right to judge her," the agent said, his voice low and calm, his piercing eyes boring into her. "The only things that you will speak are the answers to my questions," he added.

All Gloria could do was blink against the pain, her breathing shallow.

"That is not a good way to start our relationship," the agent said. "I will be asking you some questions. You will be giving me answers, and all will go well—for your sake." His tone gained a sharp edge Gloria did not like. "My partner is asking questions of your partner, next door. He likes the tough guys. He likes to see how tough they are."

Gloria's eyes widened.

"Don't you touch him," she said, this time with less conviction. Her face was still smarting from the blow.

"I promise, I won't touch him. I feel like you are not listening to me. This doesn't bode well for the future, I fear."

He leaned forward. Slowly, and deliberately, tucking the pieces of hair behind Gloria's ear, his face inches from hers. "I'll let you settle in," he said softly, the sinister tone in his voice sending chills down Gloria's spine. "But when we come back, you'd better be ready to talk."

He shoved the rough bag back over Gloria's head. She heard him leave the room, the heavy door slamming shut with a finality that echoed in Gloria's ears.

38

Sam stood outside the door of the motel, the cool morning air brushing against his skin. He hadn't slept much, tossing and turning through the night, but the crispness of the dawn seemed to invigorate him. The sky was a pale blue, streaked with the first hint of sunlight, and the sounds of the world waking up around him felt oddly comforting.

He took a deep breath, feeling the tightness in his muscles ease slightly. The motel's neon sign buzzed faintly behind him, casting a flickering glow on the worn asphalt of the parking lot. Despite the exhaustion lingering in his bones, there was a clarity in his mind that hadn't been there the night before.

As he shifted the paper bag in one hand and adjusted the tray of coffees in the other, he couldn't help but feel a surge of determination. The uncertainty and fear that had plagued him seemed a little more manageable in the light of day. They had a plan, and despite the disaster that was the night before, he felt like they were taking control of their situation.

Sam glanced at the motel door, knowing that inside, Harper was waiting. They had been through so much, and they both needed to see this through. With a final deep breath, he pushed the door open with his shoulder and stepped inside, ready to face whatever came next.

The door swung more easily than Sam had anticipated, banging against the doorstop attached to the bottom of the wall. He stepped inside and walked straight to the drawers separating their two beds, placing his packages down. Harper was still asleep. He walked back to door and closed it. The room returned to darkness as he did. He stepped to the only window and swung open the curtain. Light flooded the room. When he turned back around, Harper stirred on the bed, her eyes fluttering open.

Her hair was tousled, strands sticking out at odd angles. She blinked and rubbed her eyes against the sudden light, trying to clear the fog of sleep. She slowly sat up, the blanket slipping off her shoulders to reveal her crumpled T-shirt.

"Morning," Sam said softly, walking back between the beds and sitting down across from her.

"Morning." She looked at the drawers, the smell of the coffee and bagels attracting her attention. "You got breakfast?" she asked, her voice raspy and weak, yet a hint of a smile played on her lips.

"Yeah," Sam replied, reaching in and pulling out the bagels. "Thought we could use a decent start to the day."

Harper reached for one of the coffees. Seeing the possibility of a spill, Sam picked up her coffee and handed it to her. She accepted it graciously, cradling the warm cup in her hands. "Thanks, Sam," she said, taking a slurping sip, sucking in air with the hot liquid to ward off the heat.

"I am sorry to rush things, noting you have just woken up, but I think we need to talk about our plans," Sam said.

Harper lifted a finger, gesturing for Sam to pause for a moment. "Wait," she said, grabbing the side of her bed covers and swinging them off her. "Hold that thought, gotta hit the bathroom first," she said, placing her cup on the drawer, and standing up.

Sam took a couple of bites from his bagel, the warm, chewy texture momentarily distracting him from his swirling thoughts. As he chewed, he found himself running through the possible scenarios of their upcoming conversation. Would she be adamant about going to the FBI, or would she be more hesitant, perhaps second-guessing her own resolve in light of the dangers they faced? He knew he had to be ready for both, to balance his own doubts with her conviction. The weight of their situation pressed on him, and each bite of the bagel felt heavier as he considered the risks and the thin line between caution and action they had to walk.

Harper exited the bathroom, looking more refreshed. It was clear she had splashed water on her face in an attempt to finally rid herself of any residual tiredness. Before Sam could say anything, Harper said, "I think we should go to the FBI, Sam. They can help us."

Having anticipated this, Sam was ready to argue the point. He frowned, shaking his head. "I don't know, Harper. We don't know who we can trust. What if they're in on it?"

Harper sat across from Sam picking up her coffee and taking another sip, before putting it back down and picking up her bagel. "Thank you again for getting something to eat. I am starving," she said, leaning forward and taking a healthy bite.

Sam stayed silent while Harper chewed her mouthful and swallowed. "Oh, that's delicious," she said, picking up a napkin and wiping her mouth. "Sam, we can't do this alone. The FBI is our best chance."

Sam rubbed his temples, feeling the weight of the situation bearing down on him. "I get it, Harper. But what if it's a trap? What if they use us to get the drive and then leave us hanging?"

Harper looked at Sam, as if trying to decide something. "Sam, I think we can trust Agent Thompson. Besides, she already approached me," she said, softly.

"What? When?" Sam asked, clearly shocked.

"The other day, at the station. We had just been chewed out by Chief Brennan. She came to me and told me that she was on our side. Sam," Harper said, stressing his name, hoping to make the next thing she said hit home with him. "I believe her. And more to the point, Agent Thompson believes us. Now that we know what we know, we need to escalate. They have the resources to not only help, but also to protect us."

Harper's words echoed in Sam's mind, striking a chord deep within him. The image of Isabella came flooding back to him. Who had been protecting her? The thought of denying safety and reassurance to Harper gnawed at him. How could he deny her that semblance of security, especially when the stakes were so high? The FBI might be their best chance and refusing to take that step felt like turning his back on her. The realisation left no room for doubt; he had to trust the very institution he had been wary of.

"Sam," Harper started to say, her voice soft and vulnerable. "I am extremely scared. I don't want to be running and hiding. I am not that person," she said.

Sam stared at Harper, his head unconsciously nodding. The silence stretched between them, the remnants of his bagel forgotten on the table as he became lost in thought. He remembered who he was—an observer, not a detective who dived headfirst into action. His comfort zone had always been the shadows, quietly watching and analysing from a distance, compiling detailed reports for others to act upon. He preferred the background, where he could control his environment and minimise risks.

"Sam, we really need to go to the FBI," Harper said, her eyes welling, emotion filling her tone.

"You're right," he said finally. "The FBI would also have the resources to find out what happened to Gloria and Vince." Sam noticed Harper wince at his comment.

"I agree. I am on board. We'll go to the FBI. But first, I think we need to get my copy of the drive. To do that, I need to go to my apartment and get the safety deposit box key. While there, I would also like to talk to Emily. I am hoping she might have calmed down a little, so we can talk about what is going on."

Harper nodded, relief washing over her features. "Okay. We can do that," she said.

Sam shook his head, "Not we. Me."

Harper started to speak, but Sam cut her off as he continued, "We cannot go together," he said. "If we are together and get caught, then it is all over. If I go alone, at least you will still be able to go to the FBI, and…" Sam shrugged his shoulders, leaving the sentence unfinished.

There was a moment of silence, where they both contemplated what Sam had just said.

"I'll go home. Have a quick conversation with Emily, get the key, go to the bank and copy the drive. Then I'll come back here, and we will take the drive and the canister to the FBI," Sam finally said, as if he was ticking off a checklist.

Another moment passed. "Okay," Harper said. "That sounds like a plan."

Sam nodded, feeling a sense of resolve. Now, they just had to execute it. "I will need to take your computer though," Sam said.

39

Emily's head throbbed as she stood over the stove, the smell of sizzling bacon and brewing coffee barely helping to ease her pounding hangover. She had showered, but the dull ache behind her eyes and the lingering fuzziness in her mind made her morning routine feel like wading through molasses. She cracked a couple of eggs into the pan, the sound of their soft hissing joining the rest of the morning sounds in her small kitchen, seemingly designed to exacerbate her aching head. She buttered the toast and set it to the side, reaching for the coffee pot to pour herself a much-needed cup.

As she tipped the eggs onto a plate, the high-pitched sound of the front doorbell rang, piercing through the air and her head like the stab of a knife. Emily instinctively winced, closing her eyes and turning her head slightly, as if any of that was going to help. She sighed, her shoulders slumping. If that was Sam coming back, he was going to regret it, she thought. If her mood lingered on the edge from the hangover, the sound of the doorbell certainly sent it over. She set the plate down and wiped her hands on a towel, her irritation mounting as she made her way to the door.

Peering through the peephole, she saw two people standing there, a woman and a man, both dressed in business attire. The woman looked to be wearing a tailored grey pant suit, with a crisp white blouse. The man was a male version of her. They looked to Emily like door-to-door salesman. She squinted, trying to make out more details, but the throbbing in her head made it hard to focus. "Go away," she said, not interested.

The woman introduced herself, "I'm Agent Thompson, and this is Agent Miller," she said introducing her partner. "We're with the FBI."

Emily's initial reaction was one of disbelief. She rolled her eyes and replied, "I'm not buying whatever you're selling."

"Wait," the woman said. She removed a leather pouch from her jacket pocket and held it up to the peephole. "Emily, we really are with the FBI. This is important. We need to speak to Sam." Thompson's tone was firm but not unkind.

Emily froze. She squinted through the peephole. She had no idea what FBI credentials would look like, but there they were. The mention of Sam's name, however, brought a surge of anger and betrayal that made her stomach churn. She didn't care about their badges. "He's not here. And even if he was, why should I tell you?" Her voice was sharp, laced with the bitterness of their recent arguments and his sudden reappearance with another woman.

Emily saw the woman's expression soften slightly through the tiny fisheye piece of glass. "We believe he's in serious trouble, and he might have a woman with him. Please, we need to talk to him."

Emily hesitated, her mind racing. The anger she felt towards Sam was raw, but there was something in the woman's eyes that made her pause. Reluctantly, she opened the door, "Fine. Come in then," she said, turning and walking back to the kitchen counter, where her breakfast was getting cold.

The agents stepped inside, their presence immediately making the living area feel crowded. After shovelling some food into her mouth, Emily looked at the "agents", her stare, and her stance defiant despite the hangover clinging to her like a heavy fog. "Sam isn't here, but he did come back last night. With a woman. I told them to leave," she said, through her mouthful of food.

Agent Thompson caught the whiff of a suggestion in Emily's words. Something was going on between them that she did not, and could not, know, but she was sure she could guess. She exchanged a glance with Agent Miller, who she could tell understood as well. Agent

Thompson stepped forward. "Emily, I don't pretend to know what is happening between you and Sam, so I am not going to try. Sam, however, we believe might be involved in something much bigger than he, and by extension, you realise. I genuinely apologise for asking this of you but is there any chance you might know where he is?"

Emily looked up from her breakfast completely uncaring where Sam might be, "Rotting in Hell, hopefully." She was already bored with this, and now regretting letting the agents in.

"Please, Emily, whatever Sam has done, I am sure he deserved it, but for now we really need to get hold of him."

Emily couldn't bring herself to care. He wasn't here. That's all she knew and all she cared to know. She just wanted to eat her breakfast in peace, not think about Sam, and definitely not entertain these people any longer. "I don't know, and don't care."

Agent Thompson looked at Agent Miller, who shrugged.

"Why don't we just give it to her with both barrels. I mean, it seems clear she doesn't care where Sam is, but maybe, if she knew the extent of what is at stake, she might be willing to give us something we can work with," Agent Miller said. He turned back to look at Emily.

"Fuck you!" Emily knew exactly what he was trying to do.

"Look, Emily," Agent Thompson cut in. "We believe Sam has uncovered something very serious. If not handled properly, it has the potential to completely destabilise the world as we know it."

Emily looked at Agent Thompson for a moment before starting to laugh. Her laughter quickly died down when she saw neither of the agent's expressions change. A sudden pang of anxiety washed over her.

"Are you about to rob me?" she asked, a small amount of fear creeping into her voice.

Agent Thompson's face turned to confusion and alarm. She put her hands up in a surrendering way.

"Oh, God, no, Emily. No, no, no, no. We are being serious. This is serious. We are really FBI agents, and we really believe Sam has uncovered something that could destabilise the world as we know it. It is something the FBI..." she turned and pointed back and forth from Agent Miller and herself, "…we, have been investigating for some time."

Emily's expression faltered, replaced by confusion and disbelief, which was clear on her face. "What? Sam? My Sam? Part of some… plot that will change the world. That's ridiculous!" She shook her head. Sam wasn't the type to get involved in anything dangerous; he was more comfortable in the shadows, observing and reporting, but doubt began to creep in. "How serious could it actually be that my Sam could be not only involved but have discovered it?" The disbelief was now radiating out of her. Her head ached, and her breakfast was all but forgotten.

"Serious enough to involve the CIA," Agent Miller interjected.

Agent Thompson turned to look at her partner, eyes wide.

"What?" he said innocently. "Oh, come on, I think we have past the point of hiding what the fuck's going on."

Agent Thompson nodded. She turned back to Emily. "I can understand your scepticism, Emily. I know it's hard to believe, but we have reason to think that he's stumbled onto something critical. We're here to help him, and you, if you'll let us."

Emily's thoughts raced, replaying the events of the last weeks. She had been so quick to assume the worst, when he was cancelling plans, coming home late, keeping secrets, then when he returned with another woman while she was there. The evidence was all there, though. What if she had been wrong? What if there was more to the story than she had allowed herself to see?

A pang of regret pierced through her anger. She had thrown Sam and the other woman out without listening, too consumed by her own hurt and betrayal to consider that he might have been trying to protect her. Too consumed with being right, without really listening to him. Her eyes stung with unshed tears as she looked at the agents.

"What the hell have I done?" she whispered, more to herself than to them. The reality of the situation began to sink in, and she felt a wave of guilt for how she had treated Sam.

Agent Thompson stepped closer, her voice gentle. "Emily, it's not too late. We need to find Sam—and the woman—and make sure they're safe. Can you help us?"

"Harper. Sam said the woman's name was Harper," Emily said as she nodded, her anger giving way to a desperate need to make things right.

By this time, Agent Miller had made his way over to the window of the living room. "We may have company," he said, his calm but stern voice cutting through the conversation.

Emily and Agent Thompson moved quickly to the window. The doors of the black sedan opened in unison. The car's tinted windows reflecting the mid-morning sun. The sleek and unmarked car, blending seamlessly into the urban landscape, designed to be inconspicuous yet ready for action at a moment's notice.

Two agents stepped out. The first, a tall man with a chiselled jaw and close-cropped hair, moved with an air of quiet control. He wore a dark suit that fit him perfectly, accentuating his broad shoulders and muscular build. His eyes, hidden behind aviator sunglasses, scanned the surroundings with the sharpness of a hawk. There was an intensity to his movements, a readiness that suggested he was prepared for any eventuality.

Beside him emerged a woman of medium height, her auburn hair pulled back into a tight bun. She wore a similarly tailored suit, her posture erect and confident. Her eyes, piercing and alert, missed nothing as she took in the scene. She moved with a grace that belied her strength, each step measured and deliberate.

The two agents disappeared from view as they closed in on the building. Without saying a word, Agent Miller walked to the front door and opened it, just enough for him to fit in the space. He stood looking out, his posture strong and confident. Emily looked at Agent Thompson, who shrugged.

"Hello, agents," Emily heard him say, after a short time. There was a pause. As the silence wore on, Emily could feel her heartbeat quickening. "We have the place covered. You can go," he said, in a tone that brooked no response. After another short pause, Agent Miller stepped back to allow the door to swing past him. It shut with a resounding thud. Emily smiled at the look on his face.

"I honestly didn't think that would work that well," he said, with a smile.

Emily turned to look out the window. She watched as the two agents walked back to their car and got in. The car did not move.

"They will now be calling their superiors to ask them if other agents had been put on the case. When they are told there haven't been, they will stay," Agent Thompson said.

Emily looked at her. "So, what do we do now?" she asked, as she turned to look out the window.

"Well, maybe if you can tell us more about Sam's movements over the last couple of weeks, we might get a better understanding where he might be," Agent Thompson said.

Emily watched as a taxi drove by the building. With the taxi just out of sight, the agents suddenly started and took off down the road, in the same direction. Emily looked at Agent Thompson, who was also looking out the window.

"Were you expecting Sam to come back this morning?" Agent Thompson asked Emily.

"No, why?"

Thompson took a breath. "Because I think Sam might have been in that taxi," she said. She turned to Agent Miller. "You go after that taxi. I will stay here."

40

Sam sat in the back seat of the cab, his thoughts spinning as he went over what he'd say to Emily. The events of last night weighed heavily on his mind, and now, more than ever, he needed to make things right with her. He fidgeted with the edge of his jacket, his gaze drifting out of the window as the city passed by in a blur.

As the taxi turned into their street, Sam's heart skipped a beat when he saw the two black sedans parked strategically on either side of the road. One was directly in front of his building, its tinted windows betraying nothing of its occupants. The other was positioned slightly further down the street, across from his building. Sam's instincts screamed danger, and a cold sweat broke out on his brow.

"Keep going," Sam instructed the taxi driver, his voice tight with apprehension. He saw the cab driver look back at him through the rearview mirror, a questioning expression on his face. "Yeah, sorry, I just remembered something. Can you keep going, back to the motel," Sam said.

The driver's face continued to be puzzled, but he did what was asked. He kept the car travelling at the same speed, past the two cars and the building. Sam's mind raced with possibilities. Were they watching him? Had they found Emily? The knot of fear tightened in his stomach as he considered the implications of the CIA's presence so close to his home.

Past the cars, Sam's chest did not ease until they had turned a corner and put some distance between themselves and the sedans. He leaned back in his seat, trying to steady his breathing. The urgency of reaching Emily now weighed even heavier on his mind. Whatever was happening, he needed to find a way to contact her that would not compromise her, to warn her, and to explain everything before it was too late.

Sam's relief was short lived. A police siren blared from behind them. Blue and red lights flashed in the rear-view mirror. He quickly looked back to see one of the sedans that had been parked in front of his building directly behind. Sam sat back in the seat and looked at the taxi drive through the rearview mirror. The taxi driver was looking back at the sedan, and the flashing lights. Sam began to feel the car slowing down.

"Don't stop!" Sam said, before he had time to think of anything else to say. The taxi driver just looked at him through the reflection. "Please do not stop. They're not good men. They're trying to haul me in." He could feel his body becoming wracked with panic.

"Look," the driver said flatly, "I'm just a cab driver, not a getaway driver. Whatever you've gotten yourself into, that's your problem. I want nothing to do with it."

The taxi pulled over to the side of the street and stopped.

Before he knew what he was doing, Sam was out of the car and running down the street. He heard a man's voice telling him to stop. He didn't. He then heard a gunshot go off. Instinctively, he ducked his head but did not stop running.

"Mr Caldwell, if you do not stop running, you will be shot!" he heard the voice say again. This time it was much closer.

Sam stopped running and put his hands in the air. With an explosion of pain, he was knocked to the ground. Someone grabbed his arms and dragged them behind his back. He felt the sharp tug of zip ties locking around his wrists. Then he was yanked to his feet and marched back to the black sedan.

He could see now, the agents after him were not the two he had seen before. These two were a man and a woman.

They shoved him into the back seat. He smacked his head on the doorframe going in and ended up sprawled awkwardly across the seat. The door was slammed shut behind him.

He heard one of the agents apologise to the taxi driver for any inconvenience, before they both hopped into the car, and drove off.

Agent Thompson paced around the apartment, her mind racing through the possibilities. When her partner walked through the door, his expression was grim. She turned to him, her eyes narrowing with a mixture of hope and dread. "So, what happened? Was Sam in the taxi?" she asked, her voice tight with anxiety.

"I found the taxi, and yes, Sam was in it. But when I got there, he was gone. The driver told me that he had been captured and thrown into the back of a car." He paused, letting the weight of the information sink in.

"This is bad news," Agent Thompson said, her own voice sombre, her face filled with dread.

"We're dealing with a situation where Sam's safety is in serious jeopardy," Agent Miller said.

Agent Thompson's heart sank as she absorbed the implications. "We need to find out who those agents are and where they took him." Her voice was firm despite the unease gripping her.

"You know that's a waste of time," Miller said—not to dismiss her, but to be realistic. "These guys are part of it. We need to focus on what we can control."

"I guess you are right," Agent Thompson said, her shoulders sagging. Her mind jumped to Harper. She hadn't been in the cab with Sam. She looked at her partner, shoulders lifting. "We need to find out where Harper is. We know they were together," she said. She knew that every second counted, and she was resolute in her mission to bring Sam back safely.

41

Every step felt heavier than the last as Henry approached the entrance of the White House. The grand building loomed before him, its pristine facade a stark contrast to the grit and grime of his everyday life. His heart pounded in his chest, and he could feel sweat starting to trickle down his back despite the cool breeze. The crisp bills in his pocket felt like a burning weight, reminding him of the task at hand.

When the man in the dark suit approached him yesterday, offering ten thousand dollars, cash, to deliver an envelope to the White House, it seemed too good to be true. But the hunger in his belly and the desperation in his soul pushed him to accept. How could he refuse? That money could change everything for him, even if just for a little while.

Henry's appearance was a harsh testament to the years he had spent on the streets. His clothes were tattered and stained, hanging loosely on his gaunt frame. His hair was matted and greasy, a tangled mess that hadn't seen a comb or shampoo in far too long. His beard, thick and unkempt, only added to the haggard look. The smell of sweat, grime, and the faint hint of urine clung to him, a rank smell that he had grown used to but was acutely aware of in the pristine surroundings of the White House, which seemed to mock him.

Standing in line, waiting for his turn to go through the metal detectors, Henry could feel the judgment radiating from the guards and staff as they eyed him with thinly veiled disdain. It infuriated him, the way they looked at him like he was less than human, just because life had dealt him a losing hand. They didn't know him, didn't know the man he used to be or the kindness he still harboured despite everything. Their sneers and whispers stung more than any cold night on the streets, a harsh reminder that in their eyes, he was nothing but scum. He wanted to scream that he wasn't to blame for his situation, that a series of misfortunes had stripped him of his dignity, not his worth. Their judgment was a knife twisting in the wound of his pride, making an already desperate situation almost unbearable. He wanted nothing more than to deliver his package, and leave. Leave the haters to hate.

As he reached the metal detectors, Henry took a deep breath, trying to calm his racing heart. The guards eyed him suspiciously, and he couldn't blame them. He was not the typical tourist.

"Step through, please," one of the guards instructed.

Henry complied, his hands shaking slightly as he moved forward. Being someone who had nothing, he made it through the detector without an issue. Wanting to get his task over and done with as quickly as possible, he reached into the pocket of his tattered coat for the envelope he needed to hand over.

"Whoa!" the security guard said, putting one hand up towards Henry, with the other hand poised above the gun he wore on his hip. "What are you doing?"

Henry lifted his hands to indicate he meant no harm. As he did, the hand that was in his pocket pulled with it, an envelope. It slipped from his trembling fingers and fluttered to the ground like a fallen leaf. His heart sank as the guard immediately drew his weapon, the metallic click echoing loudly in the tense air.

"Freeze! Get down on the ground!" the guard barked, his voice sharp and commanding.

Henry's heart hammered in his chest, a cold sweat breaking out on his forehead. The tourists around him gasped in fear, the previously serene atmosphere of the White House shattered. Those who had already passed through the metal detectors rushed further into the building, seeking safety. Others, still waiting to enter, screamed and bolted for the exits, the scene descending into pandemonium.

"I don't want any trouble," Henry said, his voice barely audible over the din. He slowly lowered himself to the ground, his cheek pressing against the cold marble floor. His body trembled uncontrollably'.

He felt the guard's knee press into his back, the cold steel of handcuffs snapping around his wrists. "Stay down," the guard ordered, his tone brooking no argument.

Henry complied, his face flush with humiliation and fear. He could hear the murmurs of onlookers who had stayed, their voices filled with a mix of fear, curiosity, and judgment. He wanted to explain, to tell them that he was just a desperate man who had taken a chance for a better life. But the words stuck in his throat, choked by the gravity of his situation.

As he lay there, hands cuffed behind his back, Henry's mind raced. The money seemed like a cruel joke now, a fleeting dream that had dissolved into a nightmare. He could only hope that the authorities would realise he was nothing more than a pawn in someone else's game. All he could do was wait, his fate now completely out of his hands.

From Henry's limited field of vision, he could see the envelope laying harmlessly on the floor. The front of the envelope facing up. The word, "President" clearly displayed on it, in what looked to be a child's handwriting. A polished pair of shoes came into view.

"What is that?" the voice of the security guard asked.

Henry swallowed hard, his mouth dry. "It's…it's just a letter, for the President," he stammered. "Someone gave me $10,000 to bring it here," he added, as he saw the guard's hand came down and take up the envelope. "The person told me to tell you that it is a ransom letter, related to the names on the back," he continued. All he could think of was to get his message out as quickly as possible.

Henry was dragged to his feet. "The First Lady, and Victor Langford, that's who is being ransomed," the guard said, not believing him. "You really think I'm buying that? From last I knew, the First Lady had not been kidnapped."

Henry had nothing else to tell the guard, "That is all I was told to say," he said.

The guard stepped forward and patted him down. The guard's hands landed on the bulge from the envelope of money that was now burning a hole in Henry's pocket.

"What's this," the guard said.

"An envelope with ten thousand dollars in it," Henry replied with a patronising smile.

The guard removed the envelope and looked inside. There was indeed a large amount of money in it. "See, I am telling the truth. I have nothing to do with this. Now let me go and give me back my money.

Panic clawed at Henry's chest, and his breathing became shallow. That money was a lifeline, an escape from the cold, unyielding streets. It was more than just cash; it was a promise, a second chance. Now, watching it disappear into the guard's hands, his world began to crumble once again. The familiar weight of hopelessness settled in his gut. All at once, he was thrust back into the harsh reality he had momentarily escaped.

"We will see about that. You're coming with us," the guard said, as they took Henry away.

<h1 style="text-align:center">42</h1>

Gloria's wrists throbbed as she twisted against the leather straps. She could feel the blood that had soaked through her pants and down her leg, her muscles screaming every time she shifted. The room smelled of sweat and iron—her own blood, metallic and sharp.

She heard the heavy clang of the bolt sliding free from the door, followed by the creak of the door opening. Footsteps approached, deliberate and slow, then stopped directly in front of her.

The bag was ripped from her head. The tall CIA agent was standing in front of her. Without a word, he slowly undid the straps around her wrists, his fingers lingering a little too long on the buckles, as though he enjoyed every second of control. "You're going to undo those ankle straps now," he said, stepping back, gun raised lazily at her chest. "And don't even think about doing anything stupid."

Her heart pounded, and she eyed the gun in his hand, calculating the distance between them. She flexed her fingers, feeling the pins and needles flood her hands as circulation returned. Her legs felt weak, the shot wound pulsing with each beat of her heart. But her mind was sharp. There had to be a way out.

She slowly undid the first ankle strap with trembling fingers. Her mind calculating her options. The agent was too confident, too sure of himself, his eyes glinting with amusement. She would not have much time. She would need to act quickly to push the gun aside, then using all her strength, leading with her elbow straight into his jaw. The second strap slid free. She reacted before she could second-guess herself.

Her body screamed in protest, the pain in her leg nearly dropping her before she got to him. But she was still fast—faster than he expected. Her hand was out, aiming for the gun. Her other arm curling in, so the point of her elbow was at his face.

But he was faster.

Her hand managed to touch the gun, but in a blur, she was thrown to the ground with a sickening thud. The wind rushed from her lungs, and her vision blurred as the back of her head slammed into the cement floor.

The agent's knee dug into her stomach, pinning her down. His hand wrapped around her throat, cutting off her air. His face was close now—no amusement left in his expression.

She heard the gun cock next to her head. She hadn't even realised she'd let go of it.

"Don't do that again," he hissed, his grip tightening just enough to make her panic, to make her realise how easily he could crush her windpipe. "Well done on the attempt, though. It shows you have spirit. Next time, things won't end this well for you."

Gloria's vision swam, but she locked eyes with him, her defiance burning bright. Even with his hand around her throat, struggling to breathe, and pain coursing through her body, she would not give him the satisfaction of seeing anything but defiance.

The agent stood up. Gloria gulped for air, her chest heaving, her throat raw. The ache in her leg throbbed with a brutal pulse, a constant reminder of just how deep she was in. This wasn't some petty thug trying to scare her—this was a professional, someone who knew exactly how far to push without breaking her.

"Let me tell you how this is going to go," the agent started. "I don't like cops. You are basically irrelevant. However, you can be cagey sometimes. So, you are going to take your clothes off. Everything, down to your underwear. You can keep a little dignity—I am not a monster. Once you have done that, you are going to sit back down again, and we are going to redo those straps."

Gloria did not move, still recovering from the choking. "If you want to see me naked, you are going to have to take my clothes off yourself." She did not look at him.

She heard the man sighed. "You see that wall over there. The one to your right," he instructed.

Gloria looked at the wall. It was a simple concrete wall. Nothing much to note, save the holes that had been chipped into it. "So?"

"See those holes? Bullet holes. That should tell you I can do whatever the hell I want, and no one's gonna give a damn."

She swallowed hard, the metallic taste of blood still on her tongue. He would keep pushing, and she knew she had to play along, for now. Maybe answer a few questions, give him just enough to think she was caving. But she wasn't broken, not yet. Not by a long shot. There was still a fire inside her, burning low but fierce.

Gloria's whole body trembled as she pushed herself off the cold floor, her muscles burning with every small movement. Her leg screamed in pain, but she gritted her teeth and forced herself upright. Her eyes never left the agent's face, daring him to look away first. He didn't. Instead, he stood there, gun loose in his hand, watching her with that same cold, calculating gaze. Her hands did not move.

"Do it," he said, voice calm, almost casual.

Her hands shook as she reached for the hem of her shirt, pulling it over her head. The air hit her skin, chilling her immediately. She peeled off her undershirt next, tossing it to the floor, left now in just her bra. She could feel his eyes on her, watching her every move, but she didn't flinch. She wasn't about to give him the satisfaction.

She glanced down at her pants. This was going to hurt. Hands still trembling, she fumbled with the button, pulling it free, but when she tried to push the fabric down, her injured leg refused to cooperate. The pain shot up her thigh, sharp and searing, making her gasp despite herself. Her fingers slipped, and she clenched her fists against the pain.

"Go on, take a seat," the agent said, smirking at her struggle like it was a damn game.

Gloria hobbled back to the chair and sank into it. She gritted her teeth as she tugged the pants the rest of the way down, wincing every time the fabric brushed against the gunshot wound. Her heart pounded in her chest, the humiliation bitter in her throat, but she wouldn't let it show. She'd strip down to nothing if it meant getting a chance later. For now, she was left in her underwear, her bare skin prickling with cold and fury.

The agent circled her slowly, taking in the sight, his eyes flicking over her as if evaluating. "Doesn't look like you're hiding anything," he muttered, almost disappointed. "Tie the ankle straps back up," he ordered.

Gloria glared at him but moved her hands to the leather straps. Her fingers moved stiffly, the cold and pain slowing her down, but she tied them. One strap at a time.

He stepped in, grabbed one of her wrists, and secured it. Then, he yanked the other straps, checking they were tight, making sure she was completely locked down again. Gloria didn't wince, didn't flinch. She just stared at him, defiance burning in her eyes, daring him to think this would break her.

Her pulse quickened as the agent walked to the table, where an array of cold, gleaming instruments waited. She had forgotten about the table. She forced herself to keep breathing, steadying the tremble in her chest. Her wrists strained against the straps, her body aching, but none of that compared to the knot forming in her gut. She knew what was coming. Every step he took towards that table tightened the grip of dread around her, but she wouldn't give him the satisfaction of seeing fear in her eyes.

The agent placed his gun on the table before picking up what looked to be a long, thin stick. She braced herself, muscles tensing, her mind racing for any sliver of a plan. Whatever he chose, she would endure it—she had no choice. The shock of what happened next was almost enough to instantly break her.

The agent, without a word, turned to her and whipped her across the shins with the stick. The pain was so shocking and unexpected that she screamed. It was as if her legs had just been cut off. She heard something that sounded like a man's voice coming from somewhere else but could not tell who or where from. The sound of her own scream was deafening in her ears. It took a long time for the pain to subside. All the while, the agent just stood there watching her.

When she had managed to calm herself down, the agent spoke again. "Ok, first question," he said, in a cold emotionless voice. "Where is the drive?"

43

Sam sat stiffly in the cold plastic chair of the interrogation room, his hands restrained with zip ties to an "O" ring screwed into the table. The fluorescent lights above cast a harsh glare, amplifying the tension in the air. It was like any other interrogation room he had been in, or even seen on television, except for the distinct lack of a mirror window. Across the table were the two CIA agents he had become accustomed to seeing. Disconcertingly, their clothes had blood spatters on them. On the table were Sam's two phones, his personal one and the burner phone he bought, and Harper's computer.

"Where are Gloria and Vince," Sam said. "What have you done to them?"

"No," the tall agent with the piercing eyes said, in a tone that told him that they were not open to a discussion. "Where is the drive, Sam?" the agent asked.

"And the canister," the burly agent added, his eyes boring into Sam's.

Sam leaned back, trying to gather his composure. "I want a phone call," he demanded, his voice steadier than he felt.

The tall agent smiled. It was a genuine smile with no sinister element to it. "You really think that is how this works. In here," he said, lifting arms up and looking around the room. He let the moment hang in the air. But then, to Sam's surprise, he leaned forward and picked up Sam's personal phone. "You know, you have been a popular boy. Your phone has rung a lot." He went to hand the phone to Sam, but stopped just out of reach of Sam. "Wait. You can't make a call with your hands tied like that. Tell me your passcode, I will dial the number, then turn the speaker on. That way there will be no secrets.

Sam looked at the agent. Would he really be giving him a phone call? Sam's mind raced through all the options he had. They all came back to one fact: he was stuck here until he could make some type of contact to the outside world. Besides, there was nothing on his phone that they could use. He smiled, before telling him his passcode. The agent typed it into the phone, then smiled when the screen on the phone opened.

As Sam suspected, the agent did not give him his phone, he just began searching through it. "Oh, dear, Sam," the agent said. "I have some bad news. I take it things have not been going too well between you and Emily." He clicked his tongue, "I am afraid it looks like she wants to take a break. She is going to stay with her parents for a while."

The agent turned the phone around to show Sam a text that Emily had sent him. The time on the text showed that she had sent it in the early morning.

Sam's heart plummeted as he read Emily's message. The words cutting through him like a knife: "I can't do this anymore, Sam. The deception, the secrets... it's too much. I need a break. I'm going to stay with my parents for a while."

Her words, stark and final, echoed in his mind, amplifying the guilt and regret that had been gnawing at him for days. He had always feared his double life would push Emily away, but seeing her decision in black and white made the reality inescapable. The thought of losing her, compounded by the perilous situation he was in, weighed heavily on his heart, threatening to crush the last vestiges of his resolve.

"How about now, you give us the passcodes for your other phone and your computer," the agent said, his voice calm.

"No," Sam said firmly. "You know the saying, fool me once, and all that."

The agent's eyes narrowed. "Sam, we know where Emily's parents live."

Sam's heart pounded in his chest, the weight of the situation pressed down on him, chipping away some more off his wavering resolve. He wondered if any of this was worth it, knowing that Emily and her family were now in definite danger because of his actions. The thought of Emily's safety tore at him, making him question everything. But then—what of Gloria and Vince?. He remembered them being captured. What if they were holding out, only for him to mess things up? He decided to stay quiet.

The room fell silent. "I don't have time for this shit," the burly agent said after a long uncomfortable silence. He stood up and left the room.

"I think you might have pissed him off, Sam," the tall agent said.

Another long uncomfortable silence ensued. The tall agent did not take his eyes from Sam's as they sat there. Sam was beginning to feel very uncomfortable, his mind racing, anxiety gnawing at him. Moments later, the burly agent returned. With him were two monitors mounted on wheeled stands. The agent banged and jostled them through the door. He dragged the monitors to Sam without a word, plugged them in, then turned them on, still not speaking.

The images were horrifying.

Gloria and Vince appeared on each screen. They had been strapped to a chair and looked to have been beaten. Their bodies were bruised, cut, and bloodied. They both sat with their heads hanging low. There were small pools of blood beneath them.

"See that? That is what is going to happen to Emily and her parents, and your parents, if you don't start talking," the agent said, frustration evident in his tone.

"This can all stop, Sam," his partner said softly. His tone was the exact opposite to the burly agent. "Just give us the information we need."

Sam's vision blurred with unshed tears as he stared at the screens. Gloria and Vince had risked everything, and now they were paying the price. And that was going to happen to the people he loved.

He knew what the right thing to do was—but seeing them in such a state made it almost unbearable.

"No," he whispered, his voice trembling, a tear running down his face. "I can't tell you anything."

"No worries then, Sam. Hope you enjoy the show," the tall agent said as he stood up. The burly agent followed his partner as they both exited the room.

"Where are you going? What are you going to do?!" Sam called out. No answer. The next thing Sam saw on the monitors was the two agents each walking into the cells that Gloria and Vince were in.

44

Chief Brennan sat at his desk, the shadows from the afternoon sunlight streaming in through the blinds, casting slanted lines across his paperwork. He rubbed his temples, feeling the familiar tension of a busy day. His desk was cluttered with reports and case files, a testament to the station's current workload. He stood up, deciding to close his blinds. After shutting them, he turned and glanced into the main part of the station, where his officers and detectives were.

It took him a moment to realise he could not see Gloria—or Vince.

In fact, he had not seen them at all the whole day.

He looked at his watch: 2:35 PM.

Where the hell were they?

He walked out into the bullpen, scanning the faces of his officers. "Anybody seen Gloria or Vince today?" Brennan barked, frustration creeping into his tone.

Many officers looked up, exchanging puzzled glances. "Not since yesterday, Chief," one of them replied, shrugging. "Maybe they're out following a lead?"

Brennan's frown deepened.

They'd never be gone all day without checking in. As he paced through the station, asking around, it became clear that no one had seen or heard from them. His frustration began to morph into a gnawing worry.

Returning to his office, he sat down heavily in his chair, the concern growing like a knot in his stomach.

He couldn't shake the feeling that something was wrong. His mind wandered back to his last conversation with Gloria. It had not ended well. She had argued passionately, defiance clear in her eyes.

He sighed, the weight of his responsibility pressing down on him.

It was his job to keep his officers safe, to make sure they followed protocol and stayed out of unnecessary danger. Yet, he couldn't help but wonder if he had been wrong to dismiss Gloria's concerns so quickly. What if she had been right? What if there was something more to the case she had been investigating?

Brennan picked up his phone, dialling Gloria's number. It went straight to voicemail. He tried Vince, with the same result. Anxiety twisted in his gut. He knew he needed to act, to find out where they were and what had happened.

His phone rang. He snatched it up. "Brennan here," he barked, trying to keep the hope from his voice, expecting to hear either Gloria or Vince's voice. It was neither.

"Chief Brennan, this is Agent Thompson with the FBI."

His heart sank. He remembered Agent Thompson well, but her call wasn't the one he had hoped for.

"Agent Thompson," he said, forcing a polite tone. "What can I do for you?"

"Have you seen Harper Daniels today?"

Chief Brennan frowned, confused. Not the question he was expecting to be asked. "No," he answered. He remembered the scar on her face. Worry gripped him. "Hold on a minute," Brennan said, putting the phone down before Agent Thompson had a chance to reply.

He went to the door of his office and called out. His voice echoed through the bullpen, filled with urgency and concern. "Has anyone seen Harper?" he called out, his tone cutting through the ambient noise of ringing phones and shuffling papers. The officers exchanged glances, but the response remained the same: silence, broken only by a collective shake of heads.

He returned to his seat, picking up the phone receiver. "No sign of her," he reported, his voice heavy with worry.

Agent Thompson's silence on the other end of the line was telling. "Chief Brennan, I need you to do everything you can to find her. I'll work on things from my end, but we need to move quickly."

"What the hell is going on, Agent Thompson?"

"Honestly, Chief, I don't have time to explain, but I will try and sum it up quickly. It appears two of your detectives, Lawson and Marshall, have been taken captive by the people we have been investigating. That happened last night during a raid at the house of Ms. Daniels. Again, I don't have time to explain. She and Sam Caldwell, we believe, managed to escape. However, Sam has just been captured. This means that Ms. Daniels is the last of them still out there. I don't know exactly what the four of them have, but these people are very keen to get it. We need to find her before they do."

"Who are you talking about? And don't feed me that 'classified' crap," Chief Brennan demanded.

"We believe it is a rogue faction of the CIA, and they are very dangerous. We need to hurry."

As he hung up, Brennan felt an overwhelming sense of failure. It was as if he were a father who had just realised his children were missing, lost in a world full of danger. Gloria, Vince, and Harper were more than just his detectives—they were part of his work family, and it was his duty to protect them.

He stepped out of his office, the concern etched on his face now fully visible to his team. "Listen up, everyone," he called out, his voice filled with a newfound urgency. "We've got a situation. Harper is missing, and we need to find her. I don't care what you are doing. We need eyes everywhere—now."

He heard his phone ring once again. He looked back at his desk, to confirm it was his phone ringing, then back to his officers. "Hold off on that for one second," he said, as he rushed back to his phone.

Harper paced the dimly lit motel room, her mind racing with worry and fear. Something had clearly gone wrong with Sam's attempt to retrieve the drive. The longer she waited, the more anxious she became, the uncertainty gnawing at her resolve. She had considered every possible scenario, trying to figure out the best course of action. Should she stay put and hope for Sam's return, or should she take matters into her own hands? Every minute felt like an eternity, and the weight of the situation pressed down on her.

She paused, looking at the phone on the nightstand. Chief Brennan was someone she could trust. He had always been fair and protective of his officers. Perhaps he would believe her and offer the help she desperately needed. With a deep breath, she picked up the phone and dialled his number, her fingers trembling slightly.

Chief Brennan picked up his phone. "Chief Brennan here."

"Chief, it's Harper. I... I need your help."

"Harper! Where have you been? I've been worried sick about you. No one has seen you all day. Have you seen Gloria or Vince?" Brennan's tone was a mix of relief and concern.

"Chief, it's worse than you think. Gloria and Vince were captured by who I believe to be the CIA last night. I managed to escape with Sam Caldwell. I've been hiding out, waiting for him to come back with some crucial information, but he hasn't returned. I think something's gone wrong."

There was a brief silence as the wheels turned in Brennan's mind. "Harper, you need to come in. I have just gotten off the phone with the FBI. They want you to come to the station for your own protection."

There was a silence on the other end of the phone. He was becoming more worried. Trust was a precious commodity in their line of work, and recent events had made it seem like he was not on her side. He hoped that was not what she was feeling now.

"Okay, Chief," she said finally, her voice firming with determination. "But I have no transportation. I will need to catch a cab."

"Does anyone know where you are?" Chief Brennan asked. He did not like the idea of her being out in public, if it could be helped.

"No. Well, only Sam, but I am worried something has happened to him."

"Then wait there. I will come to you. I don't want you going out into the public for any reason. Not without me."

"I'm at the Northside Motel, room 203. I'll wait for you here," she said, her voice taking on an air of something more serious. "I actually have a plan. For now, I need you to get something from my house. It is a flash drive. It will be outside somewhere near my back fence. I will explain further when you get here."

"I am going to come straight to you. I will send Harding to get the drive."

45

Emily watched Agent Thompson, who sat on the edge of the couch, her posture tense and her eyes scanning the small, cluttered living room of Emily's apartment. Beside her, Agent Miller leaned against the wall, his arms crossed, projecting an air of calm that Emily envied. She sat across from them, wringing her hands, her eyes darting between the two agents. Anxiety filled the room, the air thick with unspoken fears and unanswered questions.

"Emily," Agent Thompson began, her voice brisk, "we need you to think carefully about the last few weeks. Has Sam been acting differently? Anything at all that stands out?"

Emily nodded, her face pale. "Yes, he has. He's been working late, cancelling plans, not telling me where he's going if he's going to be late. It's not like him." It appeared to Emily that was not the answer Agent Thompson wanted, as she seemed to fight to keep her frustration in check.

"That's good to know, but we need specifics. Did you notice anything unusual he might have been handling or anything that seemed out of place?"

Emily's eyes flickered with confusion and worry. "Handling? Like what?"

"Like a computer drive, perhaps," Agent Thompson said, trying to steer the conversation. She leaned forward, Emily sensing the urgency. "Anything at all related to his work that he might have mentioned, or you might have seen?"

Emily thought for a moment, her brow furrowing. "Well, there was something. He dropped something into the bowl that he has next to his bed, where he puts little trinkets in. I asked him what it was, but he just blew it off, as something relating to a case."

Agent Thompson's posture changed, her stare becoming more intense. "Did he tell you anything else about it? Did you see what it was?"

"No," Emily said.

Agent Thompson turned her partner, but he was already on the move. After a little while, he returned. His face was sullen, he was shaking his head. "It's not in there," he said.

"Could he have put it somewhere else? We really need you to think, Emily," Agent Thompson urged, her voice becoming a bit terser.

"Well, he did put something in our safety deposit box a few days ago. But he said it was just some documents that he was keeping safe, as part of a case he was working on, something of a client's that needs to be kept hidden. I can't tell you if it relates to what you are talking about, or another one of Sam's cases," Emily said.

Agent Thompson shared a look with Agent Miller, who raised an eyebrow. She turned back to Emily, her tone softening slightly. "Emily, this is very important. Did Sam mention who the client was or why they needed something hidden?"

Emily's face crumpled slightly as she shook her head again. "No, he didn't. I wish I could tell you more, but he was tight-lipped about it. Also, we have this agreement that he would not tell me about the specifics of a case, for my safety."

Emily felt a wave of embarrassment wash over her as she heard herself explain to Agent Thompson that she and Sam had an agreement. It suddenly sounded naive, even to her own ears. Sam had been doing exactly what they had agreed upon, and yet she had accused him of hiding things from her, letting suspicion and frustration cloud her judgment. The realisation stung, filling her with regret. She wished she had trusted him more and questioned him less, understanding now how much weight and responsibility he must have been carrying.

Agent Thompson exhaled sharply.

"We need to find Sam, and quickly. Emily, I know this is hard, but we need to access that safety deposit box. It could be crucial to finding Sam and figuring out what's going on."

Emily's eyes widened in fear. "Do you really believe he's in that much danger?"

Agent Thompson hesitated, then nodded. "Yes, Emily, we do. But we're going to do everything we can to find him. We just need your help."

Emily's stomach churned as the thought of Sam being captured took root in her mind. The image of him in danger, perhaps hurt or worse, filled her with a profound sense of dread. She felt a cold sweat break out on her forehead, the enormity of the situation pressing down on her. A wave of guilt washed over her, and she couldn't shake the feeling that she was partly responsible. Emily swallowed hard, her hands trembling. "Okay. I'll do whatever I can to help."

Agent Thompson offered her a reassuring smile, though it looked forced. "Thank you. Do you think we could start with taking a look at what he might have put into your safety deposit box? And, when I say take a look, I mean right now?"

Emily nodded.

"We will take our car," Agent Thompson said.

The trio walked across the street in front of the apartment. They all got in, Agent Miller driving, with Agent Thompson beside him, and Emily in the back. Agent Miller turned the key, and the familiar rev of the engine rang out, as the car started up. As he put the car in drive, Agent Thompson's phone rang. She put her hand on Miller's hand, indicating for him to wait while she took the call.

"Agent Thompson," she said.

"Agent Thompson, it's Harper Daniels," came the shaky voice on the other end. Harper was trying to sound composed, but Thompson could hear the underlying fear. "Do you remember speaking with me at the station?

"Of course I do, Harper. I'm so glad you called," Agent Thompson said, a sense of relief washing over her. Harper was crucial for providing the missing piece they desperately needed. Without her insight, they might continue to grope in the dark. She felt a renewed sense of purpose and determination; Harper's decision to reach out vital in saving, not only Sam, but Detectives Lawson and Marshal.

"Agent Thompson, I think something might have happened to Sam Caldwell," she said, worry evident in her voice. "He was supposed to come back hours ago," Harper explained, her voice wavering. "He said he was going to the bank to copy the flash drive, then bring a copy back here, but he hasn't shown up. I've been waiting all day."

Agent Thompson's heart sank. "Harper, Sam has been captured. Two agents showed up at his apartment. We saw him drive by in a taxi, but by the time Agent Miller reached the taxi, Sam was gone. He was taken by the agents."

A sharp intake of breath came through the phone. "Oh my God, I knew it. I knew something was wrong. Agent Thompson, I think the CIA have been working on some impossible technology, and I think they've managed to get it to work. I don't know what their agenda is, but I believe they used it on the First Lady," she blurted out.

Agent Thompson's grip on the phone tightened. "Harper, what makes you think that?" she asked.

"Because, when we were looking through the drive at my house…oh my God, Gloria and Vince…" she left the sentence hanging, not able to finish.

It was Agent Thompson who spoke. "Harper, don't you worry about them for now, the agency is working on finding them," she said, trying to ease Harper's distress, and hopefully move her focus back to what she knew. "Keep going, Harper."

"Well, as much as this is not going to make sense, I believe the CIA have found a way to isolate a person's consciousness, and be able to copy, or even extract it."

"What makes you think it is the CIA, Harper?" Agent Thompson asked.

"The files on the drive have CIA case numbers, plus there was an address in one of the documents which turned out to be a place run by the CIA. Agent Thompson, it gets worse, the drive has list of names on it. It includes the head of the CIA, and the FBI," she said.

The head of the FBI involved in this conspiracy. The thought was almost too much to bear.

If this went all the way to the top, who could she trust?

Agent Thompson's mind raced, grappling with the implications. Could Agent Miller be part of this? She had known him for years. She trusted him—didn't she? She looked at him. He was looking back at her, a confused look on his face.

She had to trust him.

"There's a possibility that Director Shaw might be involved in this mess. We have to be careful about who we trust."

She watched his reaction closely, hoping against hope that she wasn't making a grave mistake.

Agent Miller's eyes went wide, "What?" he said, the disbelief evident.

Agent Thompson felt relieved at his reaction.

"There is so much more, but we can talk about that later. For now, we were right. Powerful people in the CIA have gone completely rogue. But, if the FBI is involved, then we need to expose this, and it might have to be publicly."

Turning her attention back to Harper, on the phone, she asked her again where she was.

"I am at a motel. The Chief is coming to get me," Harper replied, her voice trembling.

"Listen to me carefully, Harper. Do not go with the police. If what you say is correct, we can't trust anyone. Agent Miller will come to get you," Agent Thompson instructed, her tone firm. "We have Emily, Sam's partner in the car with us. We will go to the bank to get the drive. We'll all meet back at the FBI office."

Agent Thompson looked back to Agent Miller, who nodded.

"Agent Thompson, you mention exposing this publicly. I think I know the best way to do that," she said. "But I'll need access to the FBI's network."

"Understood. Agent Miller will be there soon," Agent Thompson said.

"Please hurry," Harper said, after giving them the address of the motel. The call ended.

Thompson exhaled deeply, turning to face Miller and Emily. "Miller, get to Harper's motel and bring her to the FBI office. Emily and I will head to the bank and retrieve the drive. We need to move quickly," she said. "Emily, we will need to take your car."

With that, Thompson and Emily got out of the car and hurried back to the apartment car park.

46

Vince gritted his teeth against the pain as his captor re-tightened the straps that bound him to the cold metal chair. The dimly lit cell offered no solace, only the harsh reality of his situation. He glanced around, trying to maintain his composure despite the throbbing ache in his body from the beatings he had endured. He knew he couldn't afford to break, not now.

"Just need to tighten things up a bit. Things look a bit slippery, what with all the blood and sweat." The burly CIA agent's voice was a dull sound in Vince's throbbing head.

He felt a mess. He could feel the swollen skin around his eyes. One eye even partially closed, puffed up so much that it was almost impossible to see out of. His nose felt misshapen, likely fractured, with dried blood crusted around the nostrils. His lips were split and swollen, dried blood caking the corners of his mouth and fresh blood oozing from the newer cuts. One cheek felt markedly more swollen than the other, where the impact was most severe.

His body wasn't doing any better. He could see red lines streaked his stomach and chest—the remnants of the thin stick used as a whip. Long streaks of blood, coming from his mouth and nose ran down his torso, crossing over the whip lines.

Next door, separated by a thick wall but close enough to hear the faint echoes of anguish, Vince could hear Gloria struggling against her own tormentor. He fought in vain against the leather straps that cut into his wrists and ankles. The pain was excruciating, but nothing compared to the bullet in his leg. But he refused to give them the satisfaction of hearing him scream. The sounds of Gloria's screams were having an effect on his psyche, however.

Time blurred as he endured relentless questioning and physical abuse from the agent, who was absolutely delighting in the event. He was a grizzled old detective, though. If this guy wanted to test his toughness, he would show them his toughness. What he was being asked to endure was unlike anything he had faced before—but he wouldn't crack.

The agent was relentless. The methods—brutal and unyielding.

Vince heard Gloria scream once again, the sound piercing through the silence of his own cell. He clenched his fists, frustration and helplessness washing over him as he listened to her pain. "Gloria," he called out, his voice hoarse from the hours of torment. "Hang in there!"

A crack sounded, as the agent whipped the thin stick he was still holding across Vince's shins. With his body in such a state, and the constant pain that coursed through him, the pain from this whipping, while horrific, simply washed into the ocean of pain he was already feeling.

"You just worry about yourself," the evil voice of his torturer said. "Look, we know your little band of misfits has the drive and the canister. Tell me where they are, and this will all be over," the agent said, his voice steady.

"I will never tell you, even if I knew. Lucky for me, I don't," Vince said, with gritted teeth, through the pain.

"I don't understand the mindset of some people. Why do you give a fuck to keep information to yourself, knowing what is happening right now?" the agent said.

"Because you don't deserve to know. Scumbags don't deserve to know," Vince said.

The agent laughed.

"But scumbags rule the world, Vince. Do you watch the news?" the agent said, moving forward. "How about we try this," he said, shortening his grip on the stick until only a couple of inches hung from under his fingers. He knelt down onto one knee and slowly pushed the short bit of the stick into the bullet hole in Vince's leg.

This time, the pain was too much for Vince. He cried out, thrashing around in his chair. That just made the pain worse. He stopped moving and closed his eyes. He focused all his energy on dealing with the pain. The agent removed the stick. Vince breathed hard, the relief overwhelming.

"Now, why don't we talk about what you found on the drive," the agent said.

Vince stared at the agent now standing again. A realisation coming to him as he looked into his eyes. This guy had no idea what he was even after. No, this guy would not be given that information. The other realisation that came to Vince was the grim clarity of his situation, his body battered and broken. The relentless pain had numbed into a dull, throbbing ache, and with it came the acceptance that he would not escape this place alive, even if he told him everything he knew; especially if he told him everything he knew.

He took a shuddering breath, his resolve hardening. The information he held was too crucial, too dangerous to be given to this guy. As much as he feared the torment that lay ahead, he knew he had a duty to protect the secrets he had uncovered. If that meant sacrificing his own life, then so be it. Vince found a sliver of peace, knowing that his silence might prevent a greater catastrophe. He would endure whatever came next, holding onto the hope that his companions would find a way to continue the fight. And above all that, he would not let Gloria down.

"You still with me there, Chief?" the agent asked, interrupting Vince's thoughts, undisguised arrogance dripping from every pore.

"Fuck you," Vince said. Not his best comeback, but he was not currently at his best.

"To be honest, I am very surprised," the agent said. "You have been around the block; you must have done this before to get answers. You know it can be over quickly."

Vince huffed a laugh. "Over," he said.

The agent smiled, a smug grin, then sighed. "Don't go anywhere," he said, before turning and leaving the room.

Sam sat in an impotent rage, his head bowed, eyes shut, his breath shallow. His hands still bound by the zip ties, which were shackled to the "O" ring. He could feel his hands trembling. A constant reminder of his helplessness. He tried to block out the sounds, but the low hum of the monitors next to him, mixed with cries of pain and anguish were relentless.

Having his eyes closed did nothing to remove the video in his mind of them being tortured. He couldn't bring himself to look anymore. Every scream, every muffled grunt echoed through the speakers, clawing at his nerves. His stomach churned, nausea rising, but he forced himself to keep his head down. He couldn't bear to see them like this. The only thing that kept him from breaking was the determination he could hear from them both.

"Bring her into my cell," he heard a voice say, before the unmistakable screech of a chair being dragged across concrete cut through the room. Sam flinched, his head snapping up in spite of himself. His gaze locked onto the monitors. To his horror, Gloria, still strapped to the chair, was being dragged by the hair towards the door of her cell, her face pale and streaked with blood.

As Sam watched Gloria being dragged out of her room and into Vince's, his chest tightened.

"No..." The word was barely a whisper, his voice weak from fear. He pulled against the restraints, panic surging through him as Gloria disappeared through the door. They were putting them together. Whatever was about to happen, it wasn't going to end well. His heart pounded, a steady, suffocating drumbeat in his ears.

Vince heard the sound of a metal chair being dragged, through the ringing in his ears. Shortly after that, Gloria was dragged into his room, by the hair, and still strapped to her chair. She was dragged in front of Vince and moved around so she faced him. Vince did not know what he looked like, but if Gloria was anything to go by, it was not good.

Gloria looked at him, face covered in blood, smeared with large streaks of tears. Red lines marked her stomach and chest, indicating the agent torturing her had also used a thin stick.

"You say a fucking word, I will never forgive you," Gloria said to Vince.

The tone in Gloria's voice hit Vince like a slap. He had to stay strong. He and Gloria were in this together, and together they would endure it. Vince looked up at the two men standing in front of him, behind Gloria. "Once this is all over, I am going to find both of you, and make you pay. You think what you are doing here is dramatic, you just wait," he said.

Vince watched as the tall agent bent down from behind Gloria. His hand appeared underneath her arms, and slowly cupped under each of her breasts. He moved his head next to Gloria, all the while staring directly at Vince. He looked at Gloria, who was staring at him. Her face a mask of determination, oozing with hate. She would not give this guy the satisfaction of seeing her expression be anything but stoic. She was better than he was, and she would show him that.

"You think what I am doing here is bad… is humiliating. This is nothing. We start with some physical encouragement. Then we move on to psychological encouragement. You have no idea what we have in store for you if you continue to act tough. People always break. It is just a matter of finding the right switch."

He turned his head slightly so his voice would project directly into Gloria's ear. "Tell us where the drive is, and where your two companions are, and this will be over. We could all then go and have a drink and celebrate our success, even have some fun," he said, jiggling Gloria's breasts up and down.

Vince watched Gloria smile. "Ok, fine," she said. "I will tell you."

The agent let go of her and moved to be next to her, enough to see her face fully. Gloria spat a large wad of bloody spit into his face. He recoiled from the attack, only to then punch Gloria on the side of the head. The blow had enough force to knock her out instantly and send the chair she was strapped to toppling over.

Vince winced at the sound of the punch, followed by the sound of Gloria's head hitting the cement floor. The agent turned to him, Gloria's bloody spit sliding down his face. Vince smiled at seeing that. He had underestimated how strong Gloria was. He would never do that again.

"You like that?!" the agent yelled, before stepping forward and punching Vince in the face. The blow was also strong enough to knock Vince over, backwards.

It wasn't enough to knock him out instantly. As he fell, he thought about how the power of the agent's punch was a lot stronger than he had given him credit for. When his head hit the concrete, everything went instantly black.

Both the agents stood over the unconscious bodies. "Well, fuck," the burly agent said. "It looks like it is up to Sam to tell us what we need."

The tall agent looked at his partner and started walking towards the door.

Sam could not stop looking at the monitors, hoping to see some type of movement from either Gloria or Vince, but there was none. He knew the agents were on their way back to him, so it did not come as a surprise when the door to the room opened and they both walked in, their clothes bloodied.

"Do you really want more blood on your hands, Sam?" the tall agent said, his voice soft and calm.

The question hung in the air, heavy with implication. Sam closed his eyes, trying to summon the strength to endure. They had come this far; he couldn't break now. Too much was at stake.

"They're going to die because of you," the agent said, continuing to pile on the guilt. "Is that what you want?"

Sam opened his eyes, meeting the tall agent's gaze with a resolve he barely felt. "I want a lawyer," he said, with no conviction in his voice.

"No lawyers, Sam. Give us the information, and everyone will be let go. No more torment. No more need for questioning," the agent said.

Sam looked at him, then at the two monitors—still no movement—then back at the agent. "You would let us go, all of us, really? You can't expect me to believe that."

"Why not?" the agent asked, genuine curiosity in his voice.

"Because…well…as soon as you do, we will report you," Sam said, not able to comprehend why the agent would be surprised at his questions.

"Of course you would report us. So would I expect Gloria and Vince, too," the agent said matter-of-factly.

Sam said nothing, all he could do was stare at the agent completely confused by what he just said, and the confidence with which he said it.

"Look, Sam, everyone knows what the CIA does," he said, pointing at the monitors. "No one cares. Why do you think we can do what we do? Because no one cares," he repeated. "Under the banner of national security, everything is permissible. Do you really think a government who employed Nazis after World War II to run top-secret operations, like NASA, gives a damn about a couple of local cops getting roughed up? Come on. I think you might have to grow up a little."

Looking at Gloria and Vince lying on the ground, not moving, and the understanding of what the agent was telling him was too much for Sam. He was caught in a spider's web that he could not get out of without the help of the spider. His mind raced to think of what he could do. What could not happen was to end up in one of those cells.

"Okay, I can take you to the drive. I can't take you to the canister, though. I really don't know where that will be. The woman I was with and I went our separate ways. She told me that she would be in touch when she thought it was safe enough," he lied. "That way, if one of us got captured, the other wouldn't know where the other was."

The tall agent looked at him. He took a deep breath. "I don't believe you about not knowing where Harper is, albeit that was a good lie," the agent said, a small amount of admiration bleeding through his otherwise arrogant tone. "But let's deal with the drive first. If you know where it is, you can simply tell us."

"That's the thing. When I said I know where it is, I meant that I know where it might be. You see, I lost it, when I was escaping you."

The agent's eyes bore into Sam. With his resolve all but gone, he did what he could to hold the agent's stare.

"Hmm," the agent huffed, assessing the truth in Sam's words. "That, I believe," he said after a few moments of silence.

"It would be far easier for me to go with you and show you, than it would be for me to relay the information to you, and you trying to relay that same information to someone else."

The tall agent smiled. "You really should be working with us."

He turned to look at his partner, who was still staring at Sam. "It would be easier to take him, then relay information. Then who knows what might happen, right?" he said, his smile becoming a mocking. "What do you think?"

The burly agent took a moment to think. Sam could see the cogs turning in his mind. He shrugged. "Why not? If we don't find it, we can beat the fuck out of him then," the agent said. "…For the information, of course," he added, with a smile of his own.

47

Emily gripped the steering wheel tightly as she parked her car in the small, almost empty parking lot down the street from the bank. Her heart pounded in her chest, and her hands were clammy with sweat. She glanced over at Agent Thompson, who gave her a reassuring nod. The presence of an FBI agent should have made her feel safer, but the gravity of the situation weighed heavily on her. People's lives were in danger, and she couldn't shake the feeling that hers might be too.

As Emily approached the street, her eyes darted nervously in every direction, searching for any sign that they were being followed. Every passing car and lingering pedestrian seemed a potential threat, heightening her anxiety. She hesitated, her heart pounding, fearing that the simple act of crossing the street could expose them to danger.

As they stood at the curb, Agent Thompson noticed Emily's hands trembling and her eyes darting anxiously around. She placed a firm, reassuring hand on her shoulder, grounding her in the moment. "Emily, look at me," Thompson said gently, her voice steady and calm. "I'm here to protect you. No one's going to hurt you while I'm around."

Emily met Thompson's gaze, finding solace in the agent's unwavering confidence. Thompson's presence felt like a shield against the chaos threatening to overwhelm her.

"We've got this," Thompson added with a small, encouraging smile. "Just one step at a time."

Emily took a deep breath, nodding slowly, and allowed Thompson's words to bolster her courage. With Thompson by her side, she felt a spark of hope amidst her fear, ready to cross the street and face whatever lay ahead.

As they crossed the street, despite all that she wanted to believe, Emily's stomach churned with anxiety. She was acutely aware of every step, every passerby, every car that drove by. She believed Thompson would protect her, but she also knew that if they were caught, the consequences could be dire.

As they approached the bank, a new wave of anxiety washed over her. What if the drive wasn't there? What if it had been moved or stolen? What if the drive had nothing to do with their case? What if it belonged to something—or someone—else entirely. The thoughts gnawed at her, making her steps falter. She tried to push the doubts away, but they clung to her mind like stubborn shadows.

The cool, conditioned air inside the bank was a stark contrast to the heat Emily was feeling inside. She walked up to the counter that contained a bank clerk who could direct them to where they needed to go, her legs feeling like they might give out at any moment. She forced a smile as she addressed the bank clerk, a middle-aged woman with kind eyes and a no-nonsense demeanour.

"Good afternoon and welcome to First National Bank," the woman said warmly. "How may I assist you?"

"Hi. I would like to access my safety deposit box, please," Emily said, her voice trembling despite her efforts to sound calm.

"Certainly," the woman said, picking up her desk phone. After a short conversation with someone on the other end, Emily and Thompson were instructed to go into the second office on the left.

Another well-dressed woman met them at the door. "I'm Cora," she said, in a polite welcoming tone.

"Hi, I'm Emily."

Cora directed them to enter the office and sit at one of the two chairs on the opposite side of her desk. The office was small and organised. Designed for efficiency and confidentiality. The only colour in the room was on the wall behind Cora's desk, which had the bank's latest slogan painted. "Here to help protect your assets," the slogan read.

"So, I understand you are here to access your safety deposit box," Cora said, addressing Emily.

"Yes, that's correct." Emily held her hands in her lap, trying to hide her nervousness.

Cora's eyes flicked between Emily and Agent Thompson, who stood just inside the door, a silent sentinel. Her expression flickered ever so slightly to one of concern but returned instantly to the friendly face that greeted them at the door. The flicker was not lost on Emily, as she tried to reflect Cora's friendly smile.

"Is everything okay, here?" Cora asked, her tone gentle but probing.

Emily's mind raced. It seemed she had not done a good job of reflecting Cora's friendly smile. She knew she must look a mess, nervousness written all over her face. "Yes, I'm fine. Just a bit anxious," she managed to say, her voice barely above a whisper. "I just want to get into the box," she said, but then regretted it straight away.

Cora looked at Emily, then to Agent Thompson, who had not moved. She looked back to Emily, beginning to shake her head slowly, "No, I don't think this looks very good," Cora said, gesturing between Emily and Agent Thompson with a sceptical look.

"Oh, no, I promise it is fine. We are just in a bit of a hurry, that's all," Emily said, hoping to God she wasn't making things worse.

Before Cora could speak, Agent Thompson stepped forward, her presence commanding and authoritative. "I'm Agent Thompson with the FBI," she said, producing her credentials. "Emily is assisting us with an ongoing investigation. We're here to retrieve something from her safety deposit box, that is crucial to the case."

Cora's eyes widened slightly, but she nodded, her professional demeanour taking over. "Of course, Agent Thompson," she said. Her gaze turned back to Emily, "I will need you to fill out some paperwork."

As they worked through the necessary paperwork, Emily tried to steady her breathing. She could feel Agent Thompson's eyes on her, a steady, reassuring presence in the midst of her turmoil. The clerk's hands moved efficiently, in stark contrast to Emily's trembling ones, which made her part of the paperwork look less than efficient.

"That's all I need," Cora said, collecting up the paperwork. "Please, take a seat in the waiting area. When we have collected the right key, we will come and get you."

Emily nodded and walked over to the small seating area, her legs feeling like they were made of lead. She sank into a chair, trying to calm the storm of thoughts in her mind. Agent Thompson sat beside her, posture relaxed but eyes sharp, scanning the room for any potential threats.

Emily clasped her hands together, her knuckles white from the pressure. She couldn't help but feel exposed, vulnerable. The bank's sterile, clinical environment only heightened her anxiety. She had closed million-dollar home purchases, but that paled in comparison to how she felt at this point in time. She took a deep breath, trying to remind herself that she wasn't alone, that she had Agent Thompson by her side. But the fear lingered, a constant, gnawing presence.

Minutes felt like hours as they waited. Emily's mind raced with worst-case scenarios, her imagination conjuring up every possible danger. She glanced at Agent Thompson, who gave her a small, encouraging smile. Emily tried to return it, but it felt hollow.

Cora watched the two women out of the corner of her eye as she completed the preliminary paperwork for accessing the safety deposit box. Something about the situation felt off. The woman, Emily, was visibly nervous, almost trembling, while the older woman who introduced herself as Agent Thompson seemed calm but intense. Cora had seen her share of anxious customers, but this felt different. She couldn't shake the feeling that Emily was under duress.

After directing Emily to the waiting area, Cora closed the door softly and took a deep breath, her heart pounding. She returned to her desk and picked up the phone. She dialled the local police station, her fingers trembling slightly.

"Rockford Police, how can I help you?" a calm voice answered.

"This is Cora Nelson at the First National Bank. I need to report a possible robbery—it's not the bank being robbed, but I think a woman here is being coerced into accessing her safety deposit box by another woman pretending to be an FBI agent," Cora explained in a hushed but urgent tone.

The officer on the other end immediately took note of the seriousness in her voice. "Can you stall them while we send a car over? Try to keep them from leaving," he asked.

"Yes, I'll try," Cora replied, her voice faltering slightly. The reality of what she was doing hit her—if she was wrong, she could cause a significant disturbance. But if she was right, one of her customers could be in danger. She couldn't take that risk. "Please hurry."

"I understand, Cora. Please try to stay calm, a car will be there shortly," the police officer reassured her.

Cora hung up and took another deep breath, trying to calm herself. She stepped out of the office and back into the lobby, her eyes scanning the waiting area. Emily and Agent Thompson were seated, the latter speaking in low tones to the former. Emily looked pale and frightened, her hands clasped tightly in her lap. She walked over to them.

"Sorry, Emily," she said, with a forced smile. "There seems to be a small issue with the paperwork. Nothing big."

"What seems to be the problem," Agent Thompson said, her voice cool and authoritative.

"Oh, it is nothing…it's…just that…" Cora stammered, her mind scrambling for a lie, then it hit her, she smiled at the stupidity of it, but also because it has actually happened before. "Well, it is a little embarrassing, but you would be surprised how often it happens; the person who can authorise access is…well…indisposed, if you can understand what I am saying," she lied, hoping Emily and the fake agent would believe it.

Agent Thompson's gaze lingered on Cora for a moment, and Cora felt a chill run down her spine. She tried her best to keep the warm smile on her face.

"Oh, that's fine," Emily said, with a small laugh. Some of her nervous energy escaping.

"As soon as they have finished, I will have them come to you," Cora said, before turning and walking through a door at the back, on the side of the teller's counter, her mind racing. She needed to keep them here without raising too much suspicion.

Time ticked by slowly as Cora stood in the staff area. She occasionally glanced at the clock, willing the police to arrive quickly. Her heart pounded in her chest, each beat echoing her growing fear for Emily's safety. She hoped she had read the situation correctly, that she was doing the right thing.

Josie, the branch manager, came into the room. "Oh, there you are," she said, looking relieved to see her. "There is an FBI agent out there," she gestured with her head to the main part of the bank, "who has been hassling the staff, and is now hassling me. She is threatening to start arresting the staff for obstructing an FBI investigation, starting with me. What's going on?"

"I don't think she's an FBI agent, Josie. I think she is going to rob the woman she is with," Cora said. "I have contacted the police, who are on their way. I was told to stall them as long as I can. I didn't know what to do. I didn't want them to see me going into your office."

"What makes you think she is going to get robbed, Cora?" Josie asked.

"Because the woman, Emily, is scared out of her wits. The other woman was ice-cold. Like this was routine. I just have a bad vibe about it," Cora said, her face pleading for Josie to believe her.

"Right, well, the woman looks like an FBI agent to me, and I do not want to lose my job for obstructing an FBI investigation," Josie said. "But then again, I also don't want to lose my job for letting a woman get robbed, either."

"What should I do then?" Cora asked.

"How long ago since you called the police?"

"Um, I don't know, maybe five minutes," Cora guessed.

"Only five minutes! God that woman is pushy," Josie said. "Ok, I tell you what, let Emily access her safety deposit box. While she is in there, we will call the police again asking when they expect someone to arrive. When she buzzes to let her out, we will bring her into my office and have her wait there until the police get here."

Agents Adcock and Harris were sitting in their black sedan, both bored out of their brains, stuck watching nothing happening inside the apartment. When Adcock's phone buzzed, he answered it, his expression shifting from sleepy to alert within seconds. Harris watched his partner closely, recognising the intensity of the call.

"Understood. We're on our way," Adcock said before hanging up. He turned to Harris, his face set with determination. "We've got a situation at the First National Bank. Caldwell's wife is there retrieving something from a safety deposit box. Our orders are to apprehend her and secure whatever's in that box."

Harris nodded, leaning forward, grabbing the key to the car, already in the ignition. He turned the key, and the car engine roared to life.

"She is with an FBI agent, Thompson," Adcock replied, his tone grim. "Our orders say apprehending Caldwell's wife is the priority. We are free to use any means necessary."

Harris stepped on the accelerator. The car lurched forward, wheel's spinning.

Emily's heart pounded as she followed Cora into the safety deposit box room. Every step felt heavy with anticipation. The room was as stark as she remembered it, a secure space designed for privacy and security, rows of metal safety deposit boxes lining the walls. Handing over her key, she watched Cora unlock her box with a soft click.

"You can take as much time as you would like," Cora said, giving Emily a fleeting, concerned look before leaving the room.

Emily took a deep breath and opened the safety deposit box. Inside, nestled amongst a few personal items, lay a small, unassuming flash drive. She had never seen it before. She assumed it must be what she was after, because she recognised everything else. She reached out to take it, but her hand hesitated as her eyes fell on another item—a small, velvet ring box.

Emily's heart softened as she picked up the ring box, memories flooding back. She remembered the day she bought the engagement ring. It had been a whim, a spontaneous decision spurred on by the sight of the exact ring she had always imagined for herself. It was a delicate band of white gold with a single, brilliant diamond. She had been out shopping with no particular purpose when she spotted it in a jeweller's window. The ring seemed to call to her, a perfect embodiment of her dreams and future hopes. A simple existence, surrounding and supporting a brilliantly colourful life.

She bought it on the spot, surprising even herself. She wasn't ready to get married; her life was too chaotic, and she had always envisioned a proposal from Sam, not the other way around. Yet, the ring felt like a promise to herself—a tangible piece of her future.

Later that evening, she took the ring to Sam. She had been nervous, unsure of how he would react. "I did something today," she had said, her voice shaky but determined. "I don't want you to react straight away. I need you to listen to what I am saying." She smiled at the memory of him smiling, his beautiful eyes glinting with the uncertainty of what was about to happen.

"I bought an engagement ring," she had said. "I know it sounds crazy, but when I saw it, I realised that when I am ready to get married, it's you I want to marry."

Sam had looked at her with such tenderness, his eyes filled with understanding. He took her hands in his, smiling gently. "I get it," he said. "And when the time is right for both of us, I promise I'll propose—without telling you that I am going to—so it can still be a surprise."

Emily smiled at the memory, a warmth spreading through her. Sam had understood her completely, embracing her impulsive decision with love and patience. She returned the ring box, closing the lid gently. The drive was the priority now, but the ring reminded her of what she was fighting for—a future with Sam, a future she wanted to protect.

With a renewed sense of purpose, she took the flash drive and slipped it into her bag. She knew the risks, but she also knew she wasn't alone. Sam's promise and their shared dreams gave her strength. She squared her shoulders and prepared to leave the room, ready to face whatever came next.

48

Director Barrett sat in the Oval Office, the pressure in the room was like nothing he'd felt before. The room was filled with the heads of various security agencies, including the FBI, all summoned by the President for an emergency meeting. The atmosphere was tense, the air thick with unspoken concerns.

The President stood at his desk, holding a letter in his hand, his face grave.

"We have a situation," the President began, his voice steady but with an undercurrent of urgency. "I've received an anonymous ransom letter demanding that we stop the investigation into the CIA's operations," he said, staring directly at Chris. He paused, letting the gravity of his words sink in. "The letter was delivered in by a homeless guy who was paid to deliver it. He's currently in a holding cell downstairs."

His heart skipped a beat, but he kept his expression neutral, his years of experience in the intelligence community serving him well. He had told Landon to turn the heat up on the situation. Was this letter a result of that? If it was, he would not be happy.

He glanced around the room, noting the concern on the faces of his colleagues.

The President continued.

"The letter says that cuts to the CIA and making its operations more transparent might lead to further incidents like the ones involving the First Lady and Victor Langford. If I drop the investigation, both the First Lady and Langford will be returned."

The room erupted in a murmur of shock and disbelief. The President raised his hand for silence. "What the hell does 'returned' mean? Chris, thoughts?"

Director Barrett leaned forward, his face a mask of calm professionalism. "It's hard to say, Mr. President," he started, with a smooth, practiced confidence. "It's clear that whoever is behind this is deeply concerned about the transparency of our operations. I will not lie to you and tell you that I, too, am concerned about opening the CIA's dealings. As you know, our black ops programs deal with some very dangerous individuals and organisations. Making these operations public could annoy the wrong people—people who wouldn't hesitate to use extreme measures to protect their interests."

The President's gaze was unwavering.

"Are you saying this is a threat from someone within our own operations?"

Director Barrett shook his head slightly.

"Not necessarily from within, but potentially from those who are affected by our actions. The task force has already found a link between what happened to the First Lady and DataShield Technologies. I'm well aware of the irony, given Victor Langford's connection with that company," he added. "We're currently investigating this connection."

The President frowned. "How is DataShield involved?"

Director Barrett chose his words carefully. "When we were investigating the moment when the First Lady…well, became affected, an analyst spotted something in the shimmer in front of her. When they looked deeper, they found a type of digital patterning— like a signature of the technology involved. That signature was traced back to DataShield."

Shock rippled through the room, followed by cries asking why the others in the room were not advised of this.

Director Barrett continued. "They're a major player in cybersecurity and have extensive contracts with the security agencies, as you know, including the CIA. We believe there may be elements within DataShield that are involved in some illicit activities, possibly in collaboration with outside threats. Exposing the CIA would expose DataShield. Doing to Langford what they did to the First Lady might have been a way to remove any suspicions."

He scanned the room. Heads were nodding. He had them. He decided to push the envelope, just a little.

"Just to play devil's advocate, Mr. President—dropping the investigation, even temporarily, might not be the worst move. That might give the task force more time to gather some more conclusive evidence. If they think they have won, then they might slip up."

The President rubbed his temples, clearly under immense pressure. "We can't let these people dictate our actions. But at the same time, the safety of the First Lady and Victor is paramount."

Director Barrett nodded, his mind racing with potential strategies. "I suggest we continue the investigation discreetly, ensuring that our efforts aren't compromised. We can also question the homeless man further, who delivered the letter. Ten grand is a lot of money to deliver a note."

"No. Let him go with his money. He isn't part of this," the President ordered. "I want regular updates. And Chris, make sure the task force is fully supported. We can't afford any mistakes."

"Understood, Mr. President," Director Barrett replied, standing up, the meeting clearly over.

Time to deal with Landon.

49

Agent Thompson kept a vigilant eye on the door to the safety deposit box room. Her senses were on high alert, her instincts honed by years in the field. Her attention was momentarily drawn to her left, as she saw the branch manager walk past her. She followed the manager with her gaze as she approached the door and pushed a button, unlocking it with a soft click. Agent Thompson tensed, ready for anything.

Emily emerged, her face pale but determined. She glanced at Agent Thompson and gave a small nod, a silent confirmation that the drive was in the box, and that she had it. Relief washed over her, and she stood up, her eyes never leaving Emily. They were so close to completing their mission.

Emily reached her, and Agent Thompson placed a reassuring hand on her shoulder. "Good job," she said quietly.

Their moment of triumph was cut short when the branch manager spoke. Agent Thompson was so focused on Emily that she didn't realise the manager had followed her.

"I'm sorry, ladies, but I can't let you go," the manager said firmly. "I believe something is not right here. My name is Josie—I am the manager of this branch. The police have been called. Would you mind waiting in my office until they get here?"

Agent Thompson felt a surge of frustration. They couldn't afford to be delayed. Every second counted. "You called the police?

This is a federal matter, and you're interfering with an ongoing investigation," she snapped.

The branch manager remained unrelenting. "What it looks like to me is this lady is being coerced into getting something from her safety deposit box, and you are about to take it from her. So, I don't care what you think it is. I need you to both come to my office until the authorities arrive."

Agent Thompson clenched her jaw, frustration simmering beneath her controlled exterior. They were on the brink of a breakthrough, on the cusp of unravelling a complex web of intrigue, and now this branch manager was obstructing their path. Who did she think she was, meddling in affairs she clearly didn't understand?

She didn't get it. None of them did.

The drive Emily retrieved held answers, critical pieces to a puzzle that threatened to destabilise everything. Agent Thompson's mind raced with plans and contingencies, her irritation fuelling her determination to push forward despite this unexpected setback.

She couldn't hold it in anymore. She snapped. "Get out of my way," she said, with a fire that even had Emily taking a step back. "You have no idea what is at stake here, and how far out of your depth you are."

She looked at Emily, "We're leaving," she said, grabbing Emily's arm and marching her towards the front door. They moved quickly, but a security guard stepped into their path, blocking their way.

"Stand aside," Agent Thompson ordered, giving the guard one chance to get out of her way, but the guard held his ground. She let go of Emily's arm and took the guard down in a few swift, controlled movements. He crumpled to the floor.

Agent Thompson looked back at Emily.

"We cannot linger. If the police have been called, then those who want that drive will also be on their way. We need to get to the FBI office before they find us. Come on," she said softly, grabbing Emily's arm again, pulling her through the front door. They burst outside, only to see a cop car screeching to a halt in front of the bank. Two officers jumped out, guns drawn, aiming at Agent Thompson and Emily.

"Stop right there!" one of the officers yelled, using the door of the car as a shield.

"What's happening?" Emily said, clearly not used to situations like this. This was not new to Agent Thompson, however. Frustrating yes, but not new.

"I'm Agent Thompson with the FBI. My badge number is 2619," Thompson shouted. "I am going to move slowly and reach into my jacket and get my badge," she said, slowly reaching into her jacket.

"Slowly!" one of the cops yelled, ready to act.

Agent Thompson slowly held up her badge. "Call it in!" she stressed, trying to project authority. "Badge number 2619," she repeated.

The officers didn't lower their weapons, their eyes flicking nervously between her and Emily.

At that moment, a black sedan pulled up in front of the police car, its occupants spilling out with guns drawn. One of them, a man in a suit, yelled, "Stand down! We're with the CIA. Those two women are wanted in relation to national security!"

Agent Thompson's instincts screamed danger as she now found herself and Emily the focus of a standoff between the police officers and the newly arrived CIA agents. The guns of the officers pointed unwaveringly at her and Emily, their hesitation evident as they assessed the sudden escalation. Meanwhile, the CIA agents, with their trained and clear intent, posed an immediate threat.

Her mind worked swiftly, calculating the odds in a split second. She knew the police officers wouldn't shoot without confirming her identity, but the CIA agents operated on a different protocol—they were here for the drive, eliminate any threat.

"Stay close!" Agent Thompson hissed to her side, in the direction of Emily. "When I move, you follow. Do not hesitate."

Agent Thompson watched the police officers turn to look at the newcomers, momentarily distracted. She seized the opportunity, and without hesitation, grabbed Emily's wrist, yet again, pulling her towards the cover of the police car, hoping to position it between them and the inevitable gun battle.

As anticipated, a shot rang out. One of the CIA agents had fired at them, the bullet whizzing past Emily's head and embedding itself in the brick wall of the bank. The cops, startled by the gunfire, fired back.

Agent Thompson's thoughts raced: strategy, survival. One wrong move and they were dead.

"Get down!" she yelled, throwing Emily behind the police car for cover. She needed to find a way out of this. Things were now officially out of control. The mission becoming a secondary concern to their immediate survival.

"Emily, listen to me," Thompson said urgently, her voice low but firm. "We're going to make a run for the car. Stay close to me, and don't look back."

"My car!" Emily said, her eyes wide open, flinching every time a bullet hit the police car. "Are you crazy, that is across the street!" Her face had turned pale. The look she gave Agent Thompson showed that she was not going to be able to do that.

"Fine. Give me your key," Agent Thompson said, holding out her hand. "I will get the car and bring it here, for you to jump in."

Emily did not look much happier with this plan, but they had no choice.

As the gun battle raged, Agent Thompson took off across the street. The surprise movement allowed her to make it halfway, before she heard the whizzing of bullets going past her. She didn't stop however, thankful for the trees that took some of the shots.

She reached the car, bullets peppering the bonnet and doors. She ducked into the driver's seat, shoved the key into the ignition, and turned it. The engine roared to life.

Without hesitation, she threw the car into drive and floored the accelerator.

She had seen there was nothing in front of the car, as she ran to it, so driving straight was not an issue. The car bounced and bumped its way out of the parking lot and onto the road. Agent Thompson drove the wrong way down the street towards Emily. Shots continued to strike the car, with two piercing the windshield.

As she approached Emily's position, her car still getting peppered with bullets, she could see her still cowering behind the police car.

One of the officers had joined her. She watched the officer stand up, fire a volley of bullets, then duck down again. From what she could tell, he was the only cop returning fire. The officer was saying something to Emily, but that was of no consequence. She would soon be in the car, and they would be escaping to the office; if all went to plan, that is.

To her anguish, she spotted the other police officer lying on the sidewalk in front of the bank. Her concern was instantly replaced with relief when she saw the officer's foot move; alive for now then.

This had to work. Those agents were not going to take any prisoners.

When she got to the police car, she reefed on the emergency brake, stopping the back wheels from turning instantly. The car began to skid, rear tires screaming. She turned the steering wheel to the side, causing the car to spin, the back colliding with the back side of the police car, creating a shield for Emily.

To her surprise, Emily did exactly what she hoped she might, despite most of the gun fire now being directed at her car. Agent Thompson watched as Emily stood to a crouch, opened the passenger door, and dived in.

What she didn't expect was for the police officer to do the same. After seeing what Emily was doing, he followed suit. She couldn't fault him—his volley of bullets gave them both just enough cover to move without being directly hit.

With both off them in the car, albeit sprawled across the seats, the officer across the back and Emily in the front, her head ending up in Agent Thompson's lap, she slammed on the accelerator once again. The car lurched forward, both passenger doors slamming shut. The car screamed down the street, pursued by more bullets.

They were out. For now.

The only problem was outrunning the CIA agents. And in a beaten-up, bullet-ridden hatchback not designed for performance driving, that wouldn't be easy. Agent Thompson knew the CIA's black sedan would be faster and more durable.

This was going to take every ounce of her driving skill.

There was no other choice—they had to make it.

50

Sam stood in the living room of Harper's house. What was once a harmonious blend of functionality and style now lay in disarray, a tragic shadow of its former elegance. The once-pristine couch, a masterpiece of modern design with its sleek lines and luxurious fabric, was now torn and upended, its cushions scattered across the floor. The matching chairs, once perfectly complementing the couch, were knocked over, one of them missing a leg, another's fabric slashed open, exposing the stuffing within.

The wood-and-metal coffee table, once the centrepiece of the room, was flipped on its side, covered in deep scratches and dents. Papers, books, and miscellaneous items were strewn about, some shredded, others crumpled. The delicate plants, once thriving and adding a touch of nature to the modern decor, were overturned, their pots broken, and soil spilled across the once-immaculate hardwood floor.

The state-of-the-art entertainment system, which had been a testament to modern technology, was not spared from the chaos. The large flat-screen TV that had been mounted on the wall now hung askew, its screen shattered into a web of cracks. The sleek black cabinets that housed the sophisticated sound system, DVD players, game consoles, all kinds of tech, were flung open, their contents either missing or broken beyond repair.

Sam's every movement was being watched by the two CIA agents. The taller of the two, lean and menacing, hovered close, while the other stood with arms crossed. He managed to convince them to bring him there, because he would be able to find the flash drive. That was not his primary concern. Right now, he needed to come up with a way to escape his captors.

"Move faster," the tall agent snapped, his voice cold and impatient.

Sam feigned compliance, sifting through the wreckage. He pretended to be methodical, examining the upended couch, the broken coffee table, and the scattered debris. His mind raced, searching for a way out of this dire situation. He glanced around the room, the devastation offering a grim backdrop to his predicament.

"Place is a mess," Sam muttered, hoping to buy himself some time. "Hard to believe anything of value could survive this. You idiots probably stepped on it in your haste to destroy what was a nice living room."

The tall agent leaned in close to Sam. He drew his gun and pointed it at him. "Call us idiots one more time," he said, his voice a low growl.

Sam may have gone too far with that comment. He held his hands up in surrender.

"Just find the drive," the agent growled.

Sam continued to search, his movements deliberate but his thoughts elsewhere. He needed a plan. As he neared the window, a flash of movement caught his eye. He glanced outside and saw a car pulling up—looking like the standard unmarked police car— no sirens, moving stealthily. His pulse jumped, but his face stayed neutral—years in the intelligence game had taught him how to hide that. The agents hadn't noticed—yet.

He bent down, pretending to examine a pile of broken plant pots, and took a deep breath. "It's gonna take a while," he said, trying to sound convincingly frustrated.

"You're stalling," the tall agent accused, his eyes narrowing.

Sam straightened, brushing dirt from his hands. "I'm not stalling, I'm being thorough," he retorted, injecting just the right amount of irritation into his voice. He needed to keep them distracted just a bit longer.

His mind raced. If the police were here, maybe they were already aware of the situation. He had to find a way to signal them without alerting the agents. He moved over to the entertainment system, now a twisted heap of metal and shattered glass. As he did, he risked another glance at the window. The police car had now parked. The officers inside scanning the area.

"Come on, hurry up," the burly agent barked, stepping forward aggressively.

Sam's pulse quickened. He had to act fast. "Okay, okay, just give me a second," he said, holding up his hands in mock exasperation. He crouched down again, this time near the window, pretending to rummage through a pile of books.

He saw his chance. With a swift, covert motion, he grabbed a small, broken mirror from the debris. If he could find a way to angle it towards the window, it might just catch the sunlight and signal the officers outside. It was a long shot, but it was all he had.

Sam stood up, holding the mirror casually. "Just a bunch of junk here, and broken glass," he said, holding up the broken piece of mirror to show the agent. He made sure the mirrored side was towards the window—and the light. He prayed silently that his signal had been seen. The police were his only hope of getting out of this alive.

"What are you planning to do with that?" the tall agent asked.

Sam looked down at the piece of glass, "hopefully, stick it in your eye," he said truthfully.

The agent just smiled back, almost daring him to try.

He turned around and looked back down at the spot he was just looking through. As he did, he spotted the police officers—plain clothed—now out of the car. One was walking cautiously towards the front door, while the other was walking around the back of the house. It had worked, Sam thought trying not to show his delight on his face. He tossed the glass back on the pile, when the burly agent spoke.

"Look, it's clearly not in this fucking room," the burly agent said, his voice laced with clear frustration. "I am sick of watching you stall for time. Where did you go to escape?" he asked.

"Well, we actually saw you arrive," he started without moving from the spot, prepared to tell them the whole story. "Before the van arrived, we had seen a couple of cars drive by…"

Sam's story was interrupted by the sound of a gun cocking. He turned to the sound, to see the tall agent pointing his gun at him. "I am going to shoot you if you don't get to the point. I will make sure it is in the knee—so it really hurts," he said.

Sam's time was up.

"Well, when we saw the van, we grabbed some stuff and ran to the back of the house. We were hoping to escape over the back fence," he said. He did not move from the spot, however.

The agent waggled his gun at Sam, indicating to him to lead them to the back of the house.

As he did so, he saw that the rest of the house matched the living room. It seemed they were very thorough in their search. If they only knew it was not in the house, he mused.

As he approached the back door, his heart was pounding with nerves. He glanced over his shoulder, making sure they were following closely. "I escaped through here," he explained, pointing at the door. "I made a run for the back fence."

The tall agent eyed him suspiciously, but the burly agent seemed convinced for now. "Fine, but if you try to run, I will shoot you, you know that," the tall agent said, as a matter of fact.

Sam nodded. His mind raced as he opened the door and stepped outside, keeping his composure. He hoped desperately that he had bought enough time for the police officer to circle around to the back of the house.

Sam's heart was beating fast as he walked to the back fence. He made sure not to rush, despite the urging of the burly agent following a step behind. He scanned the bushes, his eyes sweeping over each leaf and twig.

The drive had to be here. It had to be. His fingers brushed against branches, feeling for any sign of the small, elusive device. About to give up on this side of the fence, he spotted it. There it was, a glint of metal nestled in the crook of a small bush. Relief washed over him as he snatched the drive, clutching it tightly in his hand. But his relief was short-lived.

"Hand it over," the burly agent ordered, his hand out.

Sam stood in the flower bed at the back fence, his shoes sinking slightly into the wood chips. The weight of the drive in his hand felt heavier than it should have, like a ticking bomb. The agent stood just a few feet away, his face cold and expressionless, one hand holding the gun, the other stretched out towards him. Sam's heart raced, his every instinct telling him to run, but there was nowhere to go. He was trapped between the agent and the fence, with the house looming behind him.

The air was thick, the scent of wood chips mingling with the metallic tang of fear. Just as Sam was about to hand over the drive, he saw movement out of the corner of his eye. The police officer rounded the corner of the house, his hand resting on his holster.

Sam froze, the drive still in his grip. He could feel the agent's eyes burning into him, but his attention was now divided between the agent and the approaching officer. This was his chance.

In a move that surprised the agent, he tossed the drive past him into the grass.

"Get it yourself!" Sam shouted.

Without waiting for a reaction, Sam leapt to the side, crashing into a thorny bush. Sharp branches scratched at his arms and face as he landed, the impact knocking the breath out of him. The crack of gunfire split the air before he could even process what was happening. A bullet whizzed past him, shattering the fence behind him into splinters. He flinched, pressing himself deeper into the bushes, his heart pounding in his chest. Hoping the next sound was not a bullet being fired at him as he lay there.

The police officer's voice rang out from the other side of the yard. "Freeze! Police! Put the gun down and turn around with your hands on your…"

Before he could finish, Sam saw the agent spin on his heel, his gun already drawn. A hail of bullets erupted from the agent's weapon. Sam's breath hitched as he scrambled to sit up, but his legs were tangled in the bush. Through the haze of his own panic, he saw the agent sprint forward, grabbing the drive off the grass without missing a beat. The agent's gun fired again, rounds exploding in the air as he made a mad dash for the house.

"Dammit!" Sam hissed, struggling to free himself from the bush. His mind raced. He had to stop him, had to do something, but his body felt heavy, his movements sluggish as if the adrenaline had turned to lead in his veins.

The sound of the back door of the house reached him. But that was drowned out by the sound of more gun fire, which now seemed to be coming from the front of the house also, mingled with shouts from inside and outside the house. Sam managed to pull himself to his feet, staring at the shattered fence, his heart thudding in his chest. The drive was gone. The agent was gone. And Sam was left standing in the wreckage, unsure of what to do next.

51

Agent Thompson gripped the wheel. White-knuckled. The battered hatchback screamed down the narrow city streets. Bullets had turned the small car into a sieve, but the car seemed to still be pointing in the right direction, the engine still good. She dared not think about what it looked like from the outside.

In the passenger seat, Emily had righted herself, still clutching the flash drive she had retrieved from the bank, eyes wide with fear. Behind her, the police officer was also righting himself on the seat.

"Keep your heads down!" Agent Thompson yelled over the roar of the engine and the crack of gunfire. "Officer, can you see where they are?"

"It's Gomez, and yes, they are right on us!" he shouted back, his voice strained.

Agent Thompson's mind raced. She had to get them to the FBI office. The drive Emily carried was too important to fall into the wrong hands. She dared a quick look in the rear vision mirror. The sedan behind them, a sleek, powerful beast, was gaining quickly, its engine a low, menacing growl, headlights the eyes of a predator who had its prey in its sights.

She couldn't outrun them. The hatchback was never designed for this kind of chase. She had to rely on skill and sheer luck.

She took a sharp left, tires screeching, the car skidding dangerously close to the sidewalk. Emily yelped, gripping the seat with one hand and the drive with the other. Agent Thompson's eyes flicked to the rearview mirror once again. The sedan followed, effortlessly making the turn, closing the gap with ease.

A deafening crash erupted as the back window shattered, shards of glass spraying into the car. Agent Thompson instinctively ducked, her heart hammering in her chest. Emily screamed, curling into a tight ball, the flash drive clutched protectively. Bullets whizzed past them, dangerously close.

Every second stretched into an eternity. She gritted her teeth, gripping the steering wheel tighter, her eyes flicking to the rearview mirror. The performance sedan was relentless, its occupants determined to bring them down.

Gomez didn't hesitate. He sprung back up, gun in hand, and returned fire through the shattered window. His shots rang out, sharp and precise, forcing the pursuing agents to take evasive action. Agent Thompson, once frustrated with Gomez's audacious move to join them, now felt a surge of gratitude. His quick reflexes and steady aim were keeping them alive. Without his presence, their chances of survival would have plummeted.

She weaved the hatchback through the narrow streets, her mind laser-focused on getting them to safety. Gomez crashed to each side of the car as she did. He did not seem to mind though, as he continued to get back up and fire, taking out one of the sedan's headlights. The urgency of their mission burned in her veins, pushing her to drive faster, smarter, to outwit their pursuers at every turn.

She swerved to avoid a pedestrian, the car bumping and jolting as it hit the curb and bounced back onto the road. Her mind was a whirlwind of calculations. The FBI office was still miles away. She needed to shake the tail, even momentarily, to buy some time.

"Emily, look out for a place that we can hide," Agent Thompson commanded, her voice tight.

Emily shook her head. "Hide! How are we going to be able to hide with them on our tail?"

Agent Thompson cursed under her breath. She was probably right. She cut into an alleyway, the narrow passage barely wide enough for the hatchback. Trash cans and debris clattered as the car sped through, the sedan right behind them.

"They're still on us!" Gomez shouted, sitting down deep into the back seat, his gun empty now. He scrambled to reload, hands shaking.

Agent Thompson's eyes darted to the rearview mirror again. She saw the driver of the sedan, his face a mask of cold determination. She needed to do something drastic. Ahead, the road split into two. With the sedan much wider and longer than her car, it would be harder for it to make the turn.

At the same time, Gomez popped back up and fired another volley of bullets. She saw one of the bullets hit the driver in the arm. The distraction almost caused her to miss her mark. Aiming for the left, at the last second, she jerked the wheel to the right. The hatchback lurched, tires squealing, as it barely made the turn. Gomez went flying across the back seat, crashing into the door.

The last-minute turn, the size of the sedan, and the injury to the driver, all worked in their favour. He tried to make the turn, but it was all too much. The car hit the median, bouncing over it, fishtailed, skidded, spun, and slammed into a wall, rear end first. The impact was brutal, metal crumpling, glass shattering, as the car came to a violent stop.

"Yes!" Gomez shouted triumphantly, but Agent Thompson's mind was still racing. They couldn't stop. A rear impact would not be enough to stop the car from driving. She had to assume the pursuit was still on.

"Hold on!" Agent Thompson yelled, flooring the gas pedal. The hatchback squealed as much as it could, and sped away from the scene. Her thoughts were a tangled mess of relief and urgency. She glanced at Emily, who was still clutching the drive like a lifeline. "We're not out of the woods yet," she said, her voice softer now but no less intense. "We still need to get to the office, and I doubt that would have completely disabled their car."

Emily nodded, her face pale but resolute.

The roads ahead seemed endless, but Thompson focused on each turn, each stretch of asphalt. She couldn't afford to let her guard down. The office was their only sanctuary now, the only place where the drive—and Emily—would be safe.

"No sign of them. For now," Gomez said. "Which is a good thing, because I am down to my last clip."

Agent Thompson nodded, not daring to relax just yet. The FBI office was still a few miles away, but they had a chance now, a fighting chance. And she was determined to take it, no matter what.

As they drove on, the city blurring past them, Agent Thompson's thoughts sharpened. She had made it this far, and she would see this through to the end. The drive was too important. She would get them to the office, one way or another. The battered hatchback, though limping and riddled with bullets, continued its path, albeit a bit shakier than when they first began, carrying them towards what they hoped would be safety.

"Emily, use my phone. Call the Bureau," Agent Thompson instructed, reaching into her jacket pocket and pulling out her phone, then handing it to Emily, her voice steady despite the adrenaline coursing through her veins. "The number is (555) 7190926. Tell them you're with me. My number is 2619. Tell them what's happening," Agent Thompson instructed, eyes darting between the road ahead and the rearview mirror.

In the back seat, Gomez sat trying to recover his breathing, hand still clutching his service revolver, in case it was needed again. His face a mask of grim determination and confusion.

Emily relayed Thompson's words, her voice rising with anxiety. "This is Emily, I am with Agent Thompson and Officer Gomez… sorry, you won't know Officer Gomez, but he…"

"Emily, just give them my number, tell them we are heading to the office, pursued by CIA agents. And that we need assistance," Agent Thompson said, cutting in. "They just need the hard facts, don't embellish."

Emily looked at Agent Thompson, anguish on her face. She knew Emily was not experienced at this, so could understand, but there was no time to give a lesson. "Tell them," she mouthed the words, urging her on.

Emily nodded. "Sorry," she apologised into the receiver. "We are being chased by CIA agents, who have crashed, but we think they might still be behind us. We need assistance."

Thompson could hear the faint voice of the FBI agent on the other end, indistinct but calm. Emily's face reflected the urgency of the conversation, her eyes wide.

"Oh, Agent Thompson's number is 2619," Emily said.

There was more silence before Emily said, turning to Agent Thompson, "They want us through the gate, around back. Underground lot. Officer will be waiting."

Agent Thompson nodded, her jaw set. "Got it. Tell them we're about five miles out. We'll be there soon."

Emily conveyed the message, and the call ended. Agent Thompson took a deep breath, focusing on the road. The city streets blurred past them as she navigated through traffic, her mind racing with contingency plans. She knew the CIA agents wouldn't give up easily, and every second counted.

"Gomez, keep an eye out," she said, her tone brooking no argument. "If you see anything suspicious, let me know immediately."

Gomez nodded, his eyes scanning their surroundings. Agent Thompson's heart pounded in her chest, a steady rhythm that matched the thrum of the engine.

52

Sam's heart raced as he sprinted over to the officer who was slumped against the backyard shed. He looked to have been shot in the leg and side. Gunfire echoed from Harper's house, making him flinch with every shot, but his focus stayed on the officer.

"You okay?" Sam asked, breathless, crouching beside him.

The cop grunted, wincing as he pressed a hand against the bloody wound on his side. "Yeah, it's just a graze. Hurts like hell, though." He blinked, recognising Sam. "What the fuck is going on?" he demanded.

Sam glanced at the house, his voice tight. "What are you doing here?"

"Came looking for a flash drive," the cop replied, grimacing as he shifted. "We got word Gloria and Vince might be held somewhere, and the drive was the best chance we had to get them out."

Sam's stomach twisted. "They are," he said. "They are being held at the CIA black site, on Whispering Willow Lane," he said, with a heavy heart. "They have been tortured by the two agents that are inside. You need to hurry and get someone there. I saw a picture of them, and honestly, I couldn't tell if they were alive or not, but they are in a bad way," he said, anger finding its way easily into his tone.

"What?" the cop said in shock, immediately followed by a wince of pain.

Sam clenched his jaw. "I need a gun."

The cop shook his head, gripping his side tighter. "Not gonna happen. If they come out here again, I want to be ready."

"I can't just stand here!" Sam hissed. "He's got the drive, and now Gloria—"

The cop cut him off, shoving something small into Sam's hand. "Take the taser. It's all I will give you."

Sam stared at it, his frustration rising. "A taser?"

"Better than nothing," the cop muttered, leaning back against the shed wall, clearly out of the fight.

Without another word, he ran towards the back door of the house, heart hammering in his chest as he charged into the chaos. As he approached, he heard the officer behind him call the situation through to dispatch.

"Dispatch, this is Detective Winson. I've got shots fired, officer down at 25 Meadowbrook Drive. Request immediate backup and EMS. Be advised, two detectives—Lawson and Marshall—are reported in critical condition at a CIA facility on Whispering Willow Lane. Situation is urgent. Repeat—officer down, shots fired."

Sam crept through the open front door, the sounds of shouting and gun fire all around. There may only be three people involved, but it sounded like many more. He heard the two CIA agents shouting instructions to each other from inside, while the cop at the front of the house called for them to put their guns down and come out peacefully. But there would be no peace here. They did not offer Gloria and Vince any peace. Sam was determined to return the compliment. Besides, Sam wasn't going to let them leave with that drive—not without a fight.

He moved deeper into the house, his breathing ragged, heart pounding in his chest. The air was thick, every shadow feeling like a threat. He tightened his grip on the taser, knuckles white, scanning the hallway for movement.

Sam reached the kitchen. The burly agent stepped in, eyes scanning the room. Sam reacted without thinking, his thumb pressing the taser's trigger as he fired it straight into the agent's chest. The prongs hit home, and the agent's face contorted in shock, muscles locking up as electricity surged through him.

Sam didn't waste a second. As the agent's body jerked and spasmed from the taser, Sam lowered his shoulder and barrelled into him with all the force he could muster. The agent crashed into the wall with a thud, his head smacking against the plaster. He slid to the ground, limbs still twitching from the shock.

Sam stood over him for a brief moment, relishing in seeing the agent lying on the ground. He reached down to retrieve the drive. As he did, a bullet whizzed by him, crashing into the kitchen wall. Tiles shattered and sprayed everywhere. Sam dove behind the kitchen island, chest heaving as more bullets tore into the room.

His mind raced.

He heard the sound of a gun being reloaded. He peeked out from behind the island just in time to see the tall agent, crouched next to the burly agent sprawled on the floor.

Sam's pulse quickened. He couldn't take them head-on. He did not even have his taser anymore, having let it go when he dived behind the kitchen counter. His eyes darted around the kitchen, searching for something, anything, that might give him an edge. His gaze landed on the knife block next to the stove. Too far away.

Sam noticed the second agent take aim again just in time to duck, as another burst of gunfire tore through the air, splintering the wood of the island's counter. He ducked low, heart pounding like a jackhammer. He needed a plan—now.

From the front of the house, the officer's voice rang out again, louder now. "We've got this house surrounded! Drop your weapons and come out now!"

The agent wasn't listening.

Sam stole another glance, around the island bench. The tall agent kicked the burly agent. "Get up!" he yelled.

The burly agent stirred, helped by the tall agent. This was Sam's opportunity. He needed to be quick. He stood to a crouch and ran to where the knife block was. He grabbed a handful of knives and started hurling them towards the agent. To his surprise, the fear of being hit by a knife, despite how badly they were being hurled, was enough for the agents to cower and move out of the kitchen. Not before blindly returning some gun fire.

Sam crouched behind the kitchen island once again, his heart thundering in his chest, every muscle tense as he listened for the next move. His fingers gripped the last knife he took from the block. Then, he heard their voices, muffled but clear enough.

"We're coming out! Don't shoot!"

The sound of the front door swinging open was followed by the crack of further gunfire. Sam's pulse spiked, and he bolted towards the living room, his body moving before his mind could fully catch up. He caught the scene outside.

The two agents were already in the yard, sprinting across the grass, firing at the officer who'd called for their surrender. Bullets cut through the air, and Sam's heart dropped. The cop had no chance against their assault.

"Damn it," Sam cursed under his breath. Without thinking, he charged through the front door, bursting onto the porch.

By the time he reached the yard, the agents were diving into their car, the engine revving to life.

Sam shouted, but his words were drowned by the screech of tires. The car peeled away, disappearing down the road.

Sam stopped, panting, his shoulder slumped as he watched the car grow smaller. For a second, hopelessness clawed at him. They'd gotten away.

But he straightened up, his eyes narrowing as determination surged back into him.

He knew where they were going.

"You're not getting away from me," Sam muttered to himself, his gaze locked on the road where the car had vanished. He clenched his fists, breathing hard, adrenaline still coursing through his veins. This wasn't over. Not by a long shot.

By this time, the second officer had reached him. Sam turned to him, his eyes blazing, "I know where they are going, Whispering Willow Lane."

"I know," the officer said to Sam's surprise. "I'm Detective Harding. My partner has already called it through. Officers and an ambulance are already on their way here. There are also officers on their way to Whispering Willow Lane."

53

❦

As they neared the FBI office, Thompson's focus sharpened. The familiar building loomed into view. Her eyes were locked on the gate ahead, where an FBI agent stood waving them in. Her mind raced through the manoeuvres needed to swing the car safely into the facility.

A sudden, jarring impact slammed into the side of their car.

The world spun violently. Metal screeched as the side of the car buckled inward. Thompson felt a sickening lurch in her stomach as the car was lifted off the ground, flipping and rolling. Her vision blurred, the world outside a chaotic whirl of sky and asphalt.

She slammed into her seatbelt, painfully biting into her shoulder and chest. Emily's terrified scream pierced the air, mingling with the cacophony of shattering glass and crunching metal. Gomez's grunts of pain were barely audible over the noise.

For a split second, everything slowed. Thompson saw the dashboard crumple inward, airbags deploying with explosive force. The roof caved slightly as the car continued its deadly roll. Her thoughts were a disjointed mess of survival instincts and flashes of training.

Finally, the car came to a jarring stop, upside down on the sidewalk. The world was eerily silent, the only sounds her head throbbing, her heart beating. Blood trickled down her forehead. Pain radiated from her shoulder and side where the seatbelt had held her in place.

Disoriented, she looked around. The car's interior was a disarray of broken glass and twisted metal. Emily was upside down in her seat, her eyes wide with shock but seemingly unharmed, save from a few scratches. She could not hear Gomez in the back. She could not see him either, because the rear mirror was no longer attached to the car.

Thompson's world became a blur, suspended in a twilight state between consciousness and darkness. The throbbing in her ears muted every sound, creating an eerie silence that enveloped her. She hung upside down, disoriented and unable to piece together what had just happened. Her mind was a foggy void, refusing to form coherent thoughts.

In the distance, she thought she heard gunshots—sharp cracks that seemed both distant and impossibly close. Metallic thuds reverberating through the twisted frame where the car was being hit by bullets. It all felt like a dream, indistinct and unreal. She turned her head again to the side, the motion sluggish and heavy. Emily was beside her. Had she noted that previously? Emily's mouth moved rapidly, shouting something. But the words were lost in the haze, a silent film playing before her eyes.

Time lost all meaning. Thompson couldn't tell how long she had been hanging there before she saw a pair of dress shoes appear just outside her shattered window. The shoes were polished, incongruous against the wreckage. Suit pants disappeared into the wreckage that was the side of her car. A man bent down, his face obscured by the shadows and her dazed vision. She felt herself being dragged out of the car.

She didn't recognise the man, but she couldn't muster the strength to resist. Her body was a dead weight, muscles unresponsive. She was pulled from the wreckage, the transition from upside down to upright a jarring shift that made her head spin. She managed to stand, swaying unsteadily, supported on either side by the man and someone else. In her haze, she realised the other person was Emily, her grip firm but urgent. How did she get there? Wasn't she in the car still?

Thompson's gaze drifted back towards the car, her vision blurred and unfocused. She saw three figures lying on the ground, motionless, one dressed in a police uniform. Her mind struggled to process the scene, each detail slipping away as quickly as it appeared. The throbbing in her head intensified, and the world around her seemed to dim, the edges of her vision darkening.

She took a stumbling step forward, leaning heavily on Emily and the unknown man, her senses a chaotic mess of pain and confusion. All she knew was that they had to keep moving, but to where, she couldn't remember.

Sluggishly stumbling towards the front gate of the FBI complex, her legs were heavy and unsteady. Each step was a struggle, but with every forward motion, she felt her mind becoming clearer. The fog of disorientation slowly lifted, replaced by the sharp sting of reality.

By the time they reached the gate, Thompson's senses had mostly returned. The pain was now a vivid reminder of what had just happened. She could feel every bruise, every cut, but her mind was sharp again. She knew where she was and what had happened. She began to replay the events leading up to the crash in her mind, then the crash.

As they approached the front door of the building, Thompson's thoughts landed on the three bodies she remembered seeing lying on the ground. She stopped, turning to Emily. "Where's Gomez?" she asked, her voice rough.

Emily's face was pale, eyes wide with concern. "The question is not where he is, but how he is. He was thrown from the car. I don't know how he is," she replied, her voice trembling.

Thompson's heart sank, a knot of worry tightening in her chest. She took a deep breath, focusing on the immediate task. "Do you still have the drive?" she asked.

Emily nodded, "Yes, I have it."

Relief washed over Thompson, mingled with the pain and exhaustion.

They had made it.

How had they made it?

54

Harper sat in the sombrely lit FBI boardroom, the atmosphere heavy with urgency. Around the long, polished table sat eight senior members of the FBI, including the head of the investigation, and Director Shaw, whose stern expression betrayed the gravity of the situation. Agent Miller and Chief Brennan, with a nervous computer scientist next to them, their unease apparent amid the quiet hum of the room, rounded out the people at the table. The only other person in the room was a second scientist who stood at the head of the table.

The boardroom itself was expansive yet austere, decorated with the solemn trappings of federal authority—dark wood panelling, muted paintings on the walls, and an imposing American flag in one corner. The air conditioning hummed softly, a stark contrast to the nervous energy emanating from those present.

The scientists looked like they would rather be anywhere else. One nervously adjusted his glasses, his eyes darting around as if searching for an escape. The other, seated at the table with a laptop open before him, tapped his fingers anxiously on the keys, his brow furrowed in concentration.

One of the executives cleared his throat, drawing everyone's attention. His voice was steady, commanding respect, his gaze sweeping across the room—though clearly addressing Director Shaw.

"We believe we are facing a dire threat. A faction within the CIA has developed a device, a weapon if you will, capable of unprecedented espionage—something that could potentially destabilise global security. We also believe the weapon has been used on the First Lady, and Victor Langford. What we do not know is what caused the First Lady to act like she did, after being hit with the device."

There were collective gasps around the room. He paused, allowing the weight of his words to settle.

"Dr. Johnson is here to try and explain what he believes the device does," Mr. Walker said, lifting his arm in the direction of Dr. Johnson.

Dr. Johnson was in his late thirties, with dishevelled dark hair that appeared hastily combed. His glasses sat slightly askew on his nose, magnifying his anxious, darting eyes that constantly scanned the room. In a wrinkled dress shirt and khakis, the shirt collar open and his tie loosened as if he had been tugging at it, he was not dressed for a meeting like this one.

He shifted uncomfortably as he looked to the image that was being projected onto a screen hanging down from the ceiling.

"From what Harper has shown us," he started, gesturing towards her, "this weapon operates like a camera, but instead of capturing images, it captures data from individuals."

"What the hell does that mean, 'captures data from individuals'?" one of the people at the table asked.

Dr. Johnson swallowed nervously, adjusting his tie. "Uh, yes, well," he began tentatively. "Imagine this device as a sort of...digital lens. When fired on a person, the camera takes a digital snapshot of the person's DNA, for want of a better term."

A murmur of confusion rippled around the table. "So, why would taking a photo of someone's DNA cause that person to act like the First Lady?" another person asked.

Harper could see Dr. Johnson shifting his weight and looking back at the screen. He clearly did not have a good explanation for what this device did. He obviously had not understood what Harper had thought she clearly outlined when speaking with him.

"The device extracts a person's consciousness. That is why the First Lady acted the way she acted. Because she was simply an empty shell of neurons and nerve endings," Harper interjected, speaking as straight to the point and plainly as she could.

Every eye in the place turned to look at her. Her burst of confidence fleeing like a scared child deep inside her, leaving only her self-consciousness exposed. All she could do was just stare. She could have kissed Chief Brennan, who was the next person to speak.

"Harper, you probably know more about this thing than any person in this room," he said, staring directly at her. His eyes did not leave hers as he spoke. There was something in his stare that did not scare her. On the contrary, it began to restore her fading confidence.

"From what you have told me," he continued, "there is more on the drive, which we hope makes it to us, that can help explain what this device does than we can possibly understand from a picture. What we need here is for you to tell it to us, like it is. If no-one here understands, that is because they do not understand, not because it is untrue."

He believed her. He believed the impossible was possible.

She felt herself becoming more confident again. "I know it is hard to believe, but it is true," she said, looking to the people in the room. "A scientist, Dr. Taylor, has been able to prove we have a consciousness, and has been able to isolate it. Dr. Taylor has also been able to create a device that can extract a person's consciousness from their body and load it into a database. But what is more shocking than that, is this technology has been kept hidden by the CIA for the purpose of who knows what. For leverage? To be bought and sold? They are playing God. We are on the verge of the essence of what we are, being stolen, reduced to a commodity."

Harper leaned back in her chair. She found herself breathing hard. Had she been talking aggressively? She didn't know. She did not mean to rant, but that was what it turned into. She turned her gaze back to Chief Brennan. He was smiling at her, the widest smile she had ever seen him make. She smiled back.

The room fell into a tense silence at the implications of what Harper was saying. Dr. Johnson walked back to his chair and sat down. The look on his face was doom. "How can this even be possible. How…when…who…" Dr. Johnson stammered, trying to comprehend what Harper had just said. Confusion was evident all over his face. At least he seemed to understand the point she was trying to make.

The pregnant pause that now filled the room sat heavily in the face of such a profound truth. Harper's hands rested on the cool surface of the long conference table, but she barely registered the sensation. She could feel their eyes on her, their minds grappling with the weight of what she had just revealed.

Suddenly, the shrill ring of a phone pierced the stillness. Everyone flinched, the collective introspection shattered by the harsh sound. Harper's gaze shifted to Chief Brennan as he answered his phone, his face hardening as he listened to whoever was on the other end. His jaw tightened.

"I'll meet you there," he said, his voice low and firm.

He stood up, the chair scraping loudly across the floor in the quiet room. All eyes were on him. He cleared his throat, his gaze sweeping the room as he addressed the assembled officials. "Two of my detectives have been captured by the CIA. They're being tortured for information. I'm going to get them out."

Director Shaw, seated at the head of the table, leaned forward. "Chief Brennan, I understand your concern, but this is a federal matter now. You need to let us handle it. The FBI has resources—"

"I don't need the FBI to protect my officers," Brennan interrupted, his tone polite but resolute. He did not look at Director Shaw or slow the speed of his exit. Harper could sense the tension rising again, a subtle shift in the power dynamic of the room.

Director Shaw narrowed her eyes, her voice firm but controlled. "Agent Miller will go with you, Chief Brennan." Director Shaw turned to one of the other executives. "Find out where he is going and get SWAT there. This can't turn into some type of state versus federal vigilante justice shit show. We're not leaving this to chance."

Harper glanced at Agent Miller, who gave a stiff nod, already standing up. The tension in the room was palpable again, but this time it was charged with purpose. Chief Brennan didn't argue further. He gave a single nod of acknowledgment, then strode out of the room, determined.

As the door closed behind Chief Brennan, Agent Miller, and the departing FBI executive, Harper sat still, trying to read the room. Tension hung in the air, but it had shifted, redirected towards the urgent rescue mission. The discussion about the flash drive, so critical moments before, now felt secondary.

Harper scanned the faces around the table—tight lips, furrowed brows, eyes flickering with thoughts that had nothing to do with her revelation about consciousness. She felt a twinge of unease creeping in. Had she lost the room? Had Brennan's crisis taken the edge away from her groundbreaking discovery? Her pulse quickened. This meeting had been her chance to make them see how important this was—but now, it felt like the focus had slipped through her fingers.

Harper's heart raced as the silence stretched on, but then Director Shaw spoke, her voice cutting through the lingering tension.

"To acknowledge what just happened—it's serious, and it will be handled. For now, however, let's get back to Harper's fanciful story," she said.

Harper looked at her, as did everyone else.

"I mean, can we really be expected to believe that someone has discovered the human consciousness, and that information has not been made public? If that were true, that would be the biggest discovery in human history. Something like that couldn't possibly be kept secret," she added.

Director Shaw's words seemed to bring the room out of the sense of wonder it had fallen into from Harper's rant. People began to nervously murmur, laughing at their own stupidity for even contemplating what Harper had said. Everyone but Dr. Johnson, who had not reacted to Director Shaw's words.

"What's more," Director Shaw continued, feeding on the energy in the room. "You expect us to believe that not only has that information been kept secret but is being used for the purpose of profit?" she added. "Tell us, Harper, who could even pull that off?" Each word an attack on Harper's character.

Harper barely flinched. The blow landed, but she just rolled with it, reducing its impact. She stood her ground, her heart pounding with a mix of anger and resolve. The person attacking her convictions—a high-ranking official entrenched in the very conspiracy she was determined to expose—loomed over her, her voice dripping with condescension and authority. She had the power to command the people around her to crush her efforts, to silence her once and for all. But Harper wasn't a pushover. She met her gaze with steely determination, her mind racing with strategies to turn the tables. She was ready to show her that her resolve was unbreakable, and that no position of power could intimidate her into submission.

"Who could pull this off, Director Shaw? People in power. The ones running the show. The kind of folks who bury the truth for a living," she said, staring Director Shaw down. She had an ace up her sleeve. She hoped Director Shaw, a person whose daily life operated between the lines of policy, understood the point she was making.

Harper's words put a halt to the murmurings. All the faces were looking at her once again. This time, however, Harper was not going to shrink back into herself. The fight was on. If the Director wanted to spar with her, she was ready.

Before anything else could happen, the room was interrupted by the door opening. Harper smiled as she saw Agent Thompson and Emily walk in, flanked by two other FBI agents. Her smile was instantly replaced with concern when she saw the state of them both.

They looked a mess but were miraculously still on their feet. Their clothes were torn, their hair dishevelled, matted with sweat and traces of blood. A large bruise was forming on Emily's forehead, but that paled in comparison to what Agent Thompson looked like. Her face looked to be covered in bruises that were starting to form, and large cuts. From the look of the blood-soaked cloth she was carrying, the cuts had been deep. Despite the look of the two women, the determination on each of their faces meant their appearance was unimportant.

"Sorry to interrupt," one of the agents said, addressing the room. "I have Agent Thompson and a civilian Emily, who say they have something important to share."

"Thank you, agents. We have been expecting them. You are dismissed," the head of the investigation said. When the agents had left the room, the head of the investigation said, "Welcome Agent Thompson, and Emily." He smiled at them. "It appears things did not go smoothly on your way here. We are all glad you made it. And we will be even happier if you have managed to bring us the drive."

Thompson smiled, which seemed to Harper to be extremely painful, as it was immediately followed by a grimace. "Thank you, Sir," Thompson said. "Yes, the journey here did not go to plan. But the good news is Emily managed to keep hold of the drive." Thompson turned to Emily and instructed her to give the drive to the person with the computer.

Emily walked to the man sitting at the computer and handed him the drive. The scientist plugged it into the computer, and all eyes turned to the screen. The first things that came up were the myriads of folders and picture thumbnails. Before the scientist could begin accessing anything on the drive, he was interrupted by Director Shaw.

"What is on this drive that we do not already know?" Director Shaw asked.

All eyes turned to Harper, who seemed to have become the senior analyst in the room. And she was fine with that. "Well, the files on this drive are what seem to run the whole system, outside of simply operating the device. You see, when the device extracts a person's consciousness, it is stored inside a canister, like the one sitting on the table there." Harper pointed at the canister that they had found at the warehouse. The canister that had the initials "JT" on it. It was the first time anyone had acknowledged the canister.

"After that happens, you need to able to access the database to load the consciousness into it. This drive has that program, acting like a key. There is a program that allows the drive and the database to talk to each other, allowing the load process to happen. Once the consciousness is uploaded, you also need a program to allow you to access and talk to the consciousness. The drive is essential for both."

Harper turned to look at the Director, staring her dead in the eyes. "Believe me or don't—but answer me this. Where is the scientist who discovered and developed the technology? Where is Dr. Jonathon Taylor?"

"Well, our intel on that is sketchy," the head of the investigation said. "But our understanding is he died in a fire, after some type of failed experiment."

"Did he? And what about his second-in-charge, Isabella Gray?" Harper asked.

"Well, we all know about her tragic case," the head of the investigation said.

"Or is it possible, perhaps, that they found out what was being planned for this technology and had decided to expose it, which included stealing the only drive that could make the system work, and…well…"

Harper stood up and leaned over the table to where the canister lay. She turned the canister to face the Director, where the initials, "JT" could be clearly seen, then sat back down again.

Those present were struggling to believe what they were hearing, turning to each other in confused conversation.

"Give us the room," Director Shaw said, her voice low, but commanding. The conversations instantly stopped, and everyone turned to look at her. She did not move or say another word. She simply continued to look at Harper.

With everyone out of the room, Harper watched as Director Shaw stood up and walked over to the window, her back to her. She stood there for a long time, her silhouette framed by the dim light filtering through the glass. She could see the tension in her shoulders, the weight of unspoken words hanging heavily in the room. Had her challenge struck a nerve? Was she about to confess her involvement in the conspiracy, or would she attempt to dismiss her accusations with calculated deflection? Harper's heart pounded in her chest as she waited, bracing herself for whatever truth—or lie—she was about to unveil.

"Harper," Director Shaw finally started to say, "in my position, I'm often burdened with truths I wish I didn't know and forced to make decisions that, as a friend, a wife, a daughter, and a mother, I wish I could avoid. The weight of these decisions sometimes makes me question if humanity is even ready for the consequences of the choices we face. I knew about what was being developed, and I can assume that you're already aware of this. The list you've inevitably seen, and are likely holding onto as leverage, was initially nothing more than a group of people with knowledge of a speculative exercise. A hypothetical. But then, things spiralled out of control, and we lost our grip on the situation entirely."

She paused, turning to look at her, her eyes locking onto hers, the weight of her words hanging heavily in the air.

"None of us really believed in it. We certainly did not think it would go this far, Harper. But here we are, dealing with the fallout of our own creations. I'm laying all this out to you because I need to know—what do you want? How do you intend to move forward with this knowledge, and what can I do to prevent further catastrophe?"

55

Sam sat in the passenger seat, gripping the edge of the door as the police car weaved through traffic. His pulse matched the rhythm of the sirens, the noise almost drowning out his thoughts. Detective Harding beside him, face set with grim determination, accelerated again, cutting through another red light.

"Those motherfuckers!" he yelled, banging his hand on the steering wheel.

"I am telling you, they tortured them," Sam said, his voice trembling. "They had shot them both in the leg. Strapped them to a chair, then beat the shit out of them. They just left them lying on the floor. I don't know if they're alive. Those CIA agents—they enjoyed it."

Harding's jaw clenched, knuckles white on the wheel. "Bastards."

Sam glanced at him, seeing the fury simmering just below the surface. "We need to catch up with them before they disappear into the building."

Harding growled under his breath. "I swear, they're not getting away with this."

Sam hesitated for a second, but then asked, "Listen, I barely got out of the house back there. If it wasn't for some knives, I was able to get, I would be dead. If we are going to stop these guys, I need a gun."

Harding didn't even blink. "Spares are in the trunk. We can get them when we stop."

Sam's heart pounded in his chest as they raced towards the warehouse district. The sound of the siren blared in his ears, but all he could think about was Gloria and Vince—what they'd endured at the hands of those agents. He kept replaying their screams, their agony. His hands clenched into fists as the anger rose again.

Suddenly, the crackle of the police radio broke through his thoughts. "Unit 12, we have a visual on a black sedan pulling into the CIA warehouse driveway. The car is currently stopped in front of a large roller door, which is starting to go up."

Sam's eyes snapped to Harding, whose grip on the wheel tightened even more. Without hesitation, Harding grabbed the radio, his voice steady but seething. "This is Detective Harding. That car was just involved in a shooting, wounding an officer. Do not—repeat, do not—let the roller door close behind them."

"Copy that," the officer on the other end replied. "We'll block them in."

Sam turned his head towards the warehouse district coming into view through the windshield. Dark, hulking buildings loomed, the streets now eerily quiet, save for the wail of the sirens behind them. They were close.

"We can't let them disappear into that warehouse. They'll finish what they started." Sam's worry was genuine.

"They won't," Harding grunted, eyes focused on the road ahead. "They messed with the wrong people today."

The warehouse driveway came into view. Sam could see the back of a police patrol car sticking out from a very bent metal roller door. It looked like Unit 12 had just managed to get the hood of their cruiser under the door before crashing into it. Sam smiled and gave out a yell of triumph despite the situation. "You fucking legends!" he shouted.

Harding pulled the car into the driveway, almost losing control before stopping just behind the crashed Unit 12 and popping the trunk. The two officers were just getting out of the car as they pulled up. "Ready?" Harding asked, his voice dark and steady.

Sam nodded, adrenaline rushing through him as he grabbed a spare gun. There was no going back. They were going to stop those agents.

Sam ran under the bent roller door without having to duck down all that much. He was quickly followed by Harding and the officers from Unit 12.

"Listen, Harding, the Chief told us not to do anything rash until he arrived," one of the officers said.

Sam stopped and turned to the officer, his eyes ablaze. "You listen to me. Those agents tortured your colleagues almost to death. If we don't stop them, I am convinced they will finish the job. You know why?"

"Why?" the officer said.

"Because they don't need them anymore. They have what they want!" Sam urged, pointing to the sound of a car's wheels screeching. "The fuckers are cop killers. Now, stop wasting time, and let's go. Spread out—don't let them slip!"

He turned and began running without worrying what the officers had to say against his words.

The words burned as they left his throat. The image of Gloria, strapped to that chair, blood pooling from her leg, flashed through his mind, fuelling his rage. Vince's bruised face came next. Then the thought of Harding's wounded partner waiting back at Harper's house. It was all too much. These agents needed to be stopped— here, now.

From somewhere down in the warehouse, he could still hear the screeching of tires. His pulse quickened. The agents had pulled into the car park. He rounded a corner just in time to see the black sedan swing into a space and the two agents, dark figures in the dim light, scramble out of the car.

"Freeze!" Sam shouted, his gun raised. "Get down on the ground!"

But they didn't. Sam could see it in their eyes: defiance, a challenge. Instead of complying, the agents turned and opened fire.

The gunfight erupted inside the parking lot. Bullets whizzed through the air, smashing into concrete pillars and ricocheting off metal beams. Sparks flew as rounds clanged against parked cars. Sam ducked behind the nearest vehicle as glass shattered overhead, spraying him with shards. He could hear Harding and the other officers shouting as they fired back, but the agents kept moving, ducking and weaving between cars.

Sam peered over the hood of the car he'd taken cover behind. The agents were also using the parked vehicles as shields, their movements quick and calculated. The tall agent seemed to be leading the charge. The burly agent, true to form, was more erratic, firing wildly but with purpose.

"Don't let them reach the exit!" Sam yelled, desperation creeping into his voice.

He could see it now: the agents were making a beeline for the doorway at the far end of the parking lot, near the lift-well. If they reached it, they'd vanish into the night, slipping through the cracks like they had so many times before. He couldn't let that happen.

He gritted his teeth and made a decision.

Leaving cover, he sprinted along the car line, exposed. Bullets whizzed past. Glass shattered. Metal buckled. But he didn't stop. His focus was locked on the two fleeing agents.

As the agents neared the exit, Sam saw the tall one reach for the door, his hand outstretched. They would need to slow down to get through the door, which they would have to take one at a time.

This was his chance.

Sam slid to a stop, raising his gun in one fluid motion. He aimed carefully, heart pounding in his ears, and squeezed the trigger twice.

Bang. Bang.

The first bullet hit the burly agent in the back. This caused him to lurch forward, stumbling into the tall agent, pushing him into the now-opening doorway. The second shot, where the tall agent had been just moments before, tore through the back of the burly agent's head, the result causing his body to become instantly stiff and fall. Sam's plan was to hit both the agents, but luck—or perhaps sheer desperation—was on his side in a different way. The burly agent's body fell into the doorway preventing the door from closing.

The other agent, now just inside the door, hesitated for a split second, glancing back at his fallen comrade. It was all Sam needed.

"Get down! Now!" Sam roared, his voice raw with fury.

He was running again. When had he decided to start running again?

The tall agent's eyes flicked between Sam and the door. There was no way he was going to be able to close the door in time. But there was something else in that look—fear, worry, regret, sadness for a fallen friend? The look caused Sam to slow his running slightly. The agent lifted his gun and fired through the doorway back at Sam.

A sudden wave of bullets came from Harding and the other officers. The doorframe and wall where the agent had stood were shredded. Sam had forgotten, in the adrenaline rush, that he wasn't alone.

He could not shake the look in the agent's eyes, however. Even in the chaos, his thoughts drifted—Emily. His heart clenched. He remembered how it all started. The irony of him trying to protect her from the darker side of his work by keeping her in the dark. But in doing so, he had disrespected her—and their relationship. She was his partner, in every sense. She didn't need every detail, but she needed to know when danger crept close to their lives. He hadn't warned her. He hadn't trusted her. And now everything had spiralled out of control.

Sam's reverie was broken by a forceful tug on his clothes, followed by a man saying, "Hey, snap out of it!"

Sam turned to see Officer Harding standing next to him.

Sam burst through the door after the tall agent, heart racing as his boots pounded down the narrow, dimly lit staircase. The air in the stairwell was thick with dust. He could hear the agent ahead of him, footsteps echoing sharply, each one driving Sam forward. His mind raced.

He had to stop him before he reached Gloria and Vince.

As Sam turned a corner, he heard a shot ring out, the sound reverberating loudly against the concrete walls of the corridor. Pain exploded in Sam's shoulder. He staggered, gritting his teeth as he fell hard, sprawled on the floor, his body slamming into the cold concrete. His vision blurred with the sudden shock of the hit, but through the haze, he heard the agent, laughing—a cruel, mocking sound.

Sam looked up, trying his best to ignore the searing pain in his shoulder. The agent was looking at him with his gun raised, aiming directly at him. The agent chuckled before his face went serious again. "This is for my partner," he sneered, pulling the trigger.

Click. Empty.

The agent looked at his gun, as if that was going to make a difference. He pointed the gun at Sam again.

Click. Click.

The agent laughed at the absurdity.

But his laughter died the moment Harding appeared behind Sam, gun already up. He fired two shots, forcing the agent to dive into a cell he had been unlocking.

Sam's body screamed in pain, but Harding hauled him to his feet. "Come on!" he urged, his grip tight as Sam leaned on him.

They reached the door, but it was too late. The agent had locked it from the inside. Sam grabbed the bars, shaking them with all the strength he could muster, but they didn't budge. He could see the agent through the narrow window, a dark silhouette retreating deeper into the cell block.

Sam's chest heaved as anguish swelled inside him. This was the cell where Gloria and Vince were held. He could feel it. "No!" he roared, slamming his fist against the cold metal bars. "Gloria! Vince!"

The response to his shouts was barely audible, but unmistakenly Gloria's. "Hey, Sam. If you get the chance, shoot this asshole," she yelled.

Sam's heart surged. "Hey, hang in there, Gloria," he said back to her.

56

Chief Brennan stepped out of his car, eyes narrowing at the sight before him. A line of squad cars and a few plain sedans cluttered the street in front of the warehouse. His officers were scattered around, some already taking notes or talking quietly in clusters. The Chief noted the garage door—a now disjointed hunk of metal stuck slightly open—and the back of the car hanging out of it. Agent Miller was by his side, his presence was a damn annoyance. To him, this was a local matter, for local cops to sort out. He did not need big brother watching over him.

He didn't hesitate.

"Alright, you three," he barked at some nearby officers, "get into the parking lot and give me a status update. But before you do, get me a radio and a fucking gun." He did not wait for a yes before continuing. "The rest of you gather around and listen up. The plan is simple. We are going to walk in the front door," he pointed at the warehouse, "and arrest every single person in there until someone tells us where they are keeping Gloria and Vince. If they resist, then you make them. I'll take the heat for this, so act fast and be clear. Give them one chance, then act."

He turned to look at the warehouse. Without waiting, he began walking.

The group marched behind him towards the main entrance. They didn't run or execute any kind of tactical manoeuvre—they simply walked straight up to the front door.

Brennan's frustration simmered under the surface—and with every step, it burned hotter. He was angry at the Feds, but not as much as he was with Gloria and Vince. They had the gall to investigate this mess after he'd told them, in no uncertain terms, to stay out of it. Now, here he was, having to rescue them.

In the lobby, Brennan's jaw clenched. He could already hear the chatter from inside—behind the locked sliding door. His fists tightened, but he pressed on. He was done being sidelined. This was his turf, his officers. If Gloria and Vince were still breathing, he was gonna kill them himself—for putting him in this damn mess. He turned to Agent Miller.

Agent Miller took a quick, sweeping glance around the reception room, trying to size it up while keeping his expression neutral. At first glance, it looked like any ordinary warehouse front. A small counter, manned by a lone receptionist, sat beneath a flickering fluorescent light that cast a pale glow over the room. The walls were bare concrete, giving off a cold, industrial vibe, with faded posters promoting workplace safety and generic shipping schedules— exactly what you'd expect in a warehouse. Behind the receptionist, rows of grey filing cabinets lined the back wall, though none were marked or labelled.

But Agent Miller could sense the deception. There was something off about how tidy everything was, like it had been deliberately staged to appear inconspicuous. The air smelled too clean for a place that should have been dealing with freight. A dingy sliding door, locked and slightly scuffed, separated the reception from the rest of the warehouse. It was intentionally unassuming, a front for something far more sophisticated. There were no scuff marks on the other walls, however, no signs of real activity. His eyes flicked to the corner, where a security camera blinked—standard, but a little too polished for a simple warehouse. Even the placement of the cheap, faux-leather chairs in the waiting area seemed calculated.

Agent Miller stood a few paces behind Chief Brennan, who turned to him and said, "If you have to be here, you might as well make yourself useful. Get us behind that sliding door."

Agent Miller's gut clenched slightly, but he stepped forward without hesitation. This wasn't the first time he'd had to navigate a delicate standoff between local law enforcement and federal agencies, but today felt different. Too many lines had already been crossed.

Approaching the receptionist, his badge glinting under the harsh warehouse lighting, he introduced himself calmly, "FBI, Agent Miller. We know this warehouse is being run by the CIA, and we also know you've got two local detectives, Detective Lawson and Detective Marshall, held here—against their will and without charge."

The receptionist barely blinked, but Agent Miller saw her eyes flicker with hesitation. Before she could respond, he leaned in, voice firm but controlled.

"Now, you can ask me for a warrant," he said, "or you can look at the expressions on the faces of the officers behind me."

He nodded towards the foyer, where Brennan's men were now crowding the room, faces hard with barely contained anger. The situation was like a powder keg ready to explode.

"I don't know how long you have been working for the CIA, but I would suggest it isn't long. They don't give receptionist roles to seasoned agents. You tell me if it's worth your while to wait and find out how this goes."

For a tense second, the air seemed to freeze.

Then, without a word, the receptionist's hand moved to the panel beside her, and the sliding door hissed open. Miller gave a quick nod of acknowledgment, his pulse steady. They were one step closer.

Agent Miller stood a few feet back, his eyes tracking Chief Brennan as he walked through the sliding door, shoulders squared with the kind of determination he had come to expect from him. Brennan didn't hesitate, not for a second. The other officers followed suit, filing in with the same steely resolve, their expressions hard as stone.

From the other side of the door, Agent Miller heard Brennan's gravelly voice cut through the room.

"Stop what you're doing and put your hands on your desks. No one moves."

His tone left no room for negotiation, commanding authority in the way only Brennan could.

There was a beat of silence, an almost unnatural pause as the room seemed to hold its breath, waiting for the next move.

As Agent Miller waited, the scene unfolded in his mind with sharp clarity. He imagined a room filled with rows of desks, each occupied by startled computer scientists, their fingers hovering over keyboards mid-task. Men and women in bland, buttoned-up attire, frozen in place as Brennan's commanding voice echoed through the space. They weren't soldiers or trained operatives—just tech people, code jockeys who probably hadn't faced a real confrontation in their lives.

Their wide eyes would be darting towards one another, panic starting to creep in. He could see a few trying to hide their fear behind blank stares, while others might instinctively reach for their phones, hoping to call for help. In Agent Miller's mind, the room was bathed in a thick, oppressive silence, a nervous tension running through the air as the scientists sat stiffly at their desks, praying this would all pass without them getting hurt. No one would be moving. No one daring to. But beneath it all, he could sense the potential for chaos—because even unarmed, fear could make people unpredictable.

He readied himself. There was something about the stillness that hung just beyond the door that kept him alert, like the calm before a storm.

The storm came.

What started it, Agent Miller couldn't tell, but the warehouse exploded into chaos. The unmistakable crack of gunfire echoed through the doorway, followed by the sound of shouts and the sharp ring of bullets ricocheting off metal. Agent Miller instinctively ducked back against the wall, his hand flying to his weapon. Screams pierced the air, blending with the deafening bursts of gunfire, turning the once sterile, silent warehouse into a battleground. His mind raced, his instincts firing on all cylinders.

Brennan and his officers were in the thick of it now, and there was no turning back.

Agent Miller stepped through the sliding door, into the chaos erupting around him. The noise was deafening. The air was thick with the acrid smell of gunpowder, punctuated by the harsh cries of startled voices. A flurry of bodies scrambled away from their desks, some diving for cover while others sat frozen, wide-eyed and paralysed by shock. Papers fluttered through the air, and monitors flickered, casting eerie glows on the faces of terrified scientists. The shriek of alarms blared in the background, drowning out the panicked shouts as Brennan's officers pushed their way into the fray, their weapons drawn, a stark contrast to the bewildered faces surrounding them.

Agent Miller's pulse quickened as he took in the scene—an intricate network of cubicles now transformed into a war zone. He spotted one scientist crouched beneath a desk, hands clasped over his head, trembling visibly, while another stumbled over a fallen chair, eyes darting as if seeking an escape. In one corner, a group of agents shouted orders, urging the frightened desk jockeys to remain calm, but the hail of gunfire drowned out their words. Agent Miller's instincts kicked into high gear.

This had turned into a full-blown shitshow.

A ticking clock with lives on the line.

As he moved deeper into the chaos, he prepared himself for the worst, his mind racing through every possible outcome, each grimmer than the last.

Agent Miller's gaze swept the room, eyes catching movement near the far corner. A man, dressed in nondescript clothing, was slipping out of one of the offices, lugging a large case in his hand. Something about the way he moved—the hurried, almost desperate steps—set off alarms in Agent Miller's head. Without hesitation, he yelled, "You with the case! Stop! FBI!"

But the man didn't even flinch. Instead, he quickened his pace towards the back exit, his grip tightening on the case. Agent Miller felt the tension coil in his gut as the man reached into his jacket. Before he could shout another warning, the man spun around, his arm raising, and began to fire. Bullets flew in his direction, bouncing off the walls—one brushing the hair on the side of his head. He ducked, adrenaline flooding his veins as the crack of gunfire filled the air.

Instinct took over. Agent Miller fired his weapon, his hand steady despite the chaos. His shot was clean, honed by years of training. The bullet struck the man in the side of the head, just above the ear. The man crumpled instantly, the case falling from his hand and hitting the floor with a dull thud.

He navigated through the chaos, ducking and weaving around overturned chairs and panicked bodies. The sound of shouts and gunfire buzzed in his ears, but he kept his focus on the man who had dropped to the floor, a sense of urgency propelling him forward. He reached the fallen figure, adrenaline surging as he snatched the case from the ground. The weight felt significant in his hands, a tangible reminder of the stakes at play. Just as he began to assess the situation, he looked up and froze. A man stood a few feet away, gun raised and pointed directly at him, eyes wide with a mixture of fear and aggression.

Before Agent Miller or the man could react, the air erupted again, but this time it wasn't just a few erratic shots. Bullets rained down, a deafening barrage that sounded as if someone had wheeled in a minigun.

He ducked instinctively, bracing against the nearest table, heart racing as plaster and debris exploded around him, ricocheting off walls and ceilings. The sheer noise paralysed the room, freezing everyone in place, caught between fear and confusion as bullets whizzed overhead without finding their mark. Agent Miller's mind raced, trying to comprehend the sudden escalation.

Then, as abruptly as it had started, the chaos ceased. A commanding voice cut through the silence, clear and authoritative.

"SWAT! Drop your weapons! Hands where we can see them! We're here to secure the situation. Engage, and we will return fire!"

Agent Miller felt a wave of relief wash over him, but it was tempered by the reality of the situation. SWAT's intervention could either restore order or escalate the conflict further. He watched the man standing over him kneel down onto one knee, then toss his gun under one of the desks. He did not turn his eyes from Agent Miller, however. He glanced around, searching for the nearest officer, ready to make sure they were all on the same page.

57

Sam stood by the cell door, terror eating at him, when he heard the sound of heavy footsteps approaching from behind. He turned, momentarily forgetting the throbbing pain in his shoulder. The other two cops joined him, and Harding, their expressions a mix of confusion and concern. But as Sam's gaze drifted past them, he saw a team of people dressed in full SWAT gear rounding the corner, moving with purpose.

"SWAT! Hands up! Now!" one barked.

Without hesitation, Sam and the officers around him raised their hands. Sam winced from the pain in his shoulder. What the hell was SWAT doing here?

"Is anyone here Sam Caldwell?" the SWAT commander called out, eyes scanning the group.

The words hit Sam like a cold wave. "That's me," he replied, his voice steadier than he felt.

The commander gestured to the other officers. "Everyone else, step out. Now!"

Once the corridor cleared, Sam felt a mix of relief and desperation. The SWAT commander stepped closer, his expression serious. "We've been briefed. Give us a rundown on the current situation."

All Sam could do at first was to just stare at the SWAT commander, his mouth pursed, about to ask a question. After a moment, he took a deep breath, trying to focus despite the chaos still pulsing in his mind and veins.

"There's a rogue CIA agent in the cell," he began, urgency seeping into his voice. "He's holding two police detectives hostage—Detective Gloria Lawson and Detective Vince Marshall. He was torturing them for information. He is unstable and dangerous. We need to get them out of there now!"

The commander's expression tightened as he confirmed with Sam, "Detective Lawson and Detective Marshall?"

"Yes!" Sam nodded, feeling the weight of the situation pressing down on him.

"Back away from the door," the SWAT commander ordered.

Sam stepped aside, a mix of frustration and hope swirling in his gut. He could feel the tension in the air as the SWAT team moved in.

One of the team members pulled out a spray canister, aiming it at the locking mechanism. The sound of the nozzle hissed as some type of chemical mixture was sprayed around the lock, which foamed up. Sam watched, holding his breath, as the SWAT officer ignited the sprayed substance.

The chemical caught fire instantly, the heat radiating towards Sam's face. The substance hissed and sizzled, and the locking mechanism glowed ominously as it began to weaken under the heat.

With a final push from the team, the lock fell away, clattering to the ground. The cell door swung open with a creak, revealing the darkness inside.

Sam stood just outside the cell, his heart pounding as the SWAT team swept in. One of the officers flicked on the light, casting a harsh glow over the horrific space. The air reeked of stale blood, sweat, and piss, the sharp stench burning Sam's nose. His stomach churned as he stepped closer.

A voice cut through the tense silence.

"I want to make a deal!" the CIA agent barked from his position near the back of the room.

Sam's eyes zeroed in on him, crouched behind Gloria and Vince like a coward, using them as shields. The agent's hands hovered near their bound bodies.

Gloria and Vince were slumped in their chairs, barely holding their heads up. Their faces were pale, and they looked disoriented, their eyes half-open, struggling to stay awake. Seeing them like that—weak, broken—fuelled Sam's rage even more.

The SWAT team had their guns trained on the agent, unwavering in their aim.

"Not our call. We're just here to bring you in. If you've got something to say, save it for the Feds," the SWAT commander said calmly, keeping his team steady.

Sam's blood boiled as he stared at the man who had done this. The agent slowly stood up, raising his hands in surrender, a smug grin spread across his face as if he'd already won. Rage took over. This man, this monster, had tortured these good people whom Sam had come to admire. The thought of what they must have endured made something snap inside him.

Without thinking, without hesitation, Sam raised his gun, his finger tightening on the trigger. The shot rang out before anyone had time to react. The bullet hit the agent square in the forehead, and his body dropped instantly, collapsing onto the blood-stained floor with a sickening thud.

Every SWAT agent suddenly turned and locked in on him—weapons drawn. Sam stood frozen, his chest heaving, pain pulsing through his wounded shoulder, rage still coursing through him.

Slowly, he lowered himself onto one knee. He let the gun fall from his hand; it clattered to the floor.

Raising his one good arm in surrender, he didn't say a word. His eyes met Gloria's. Despite her bruises, despite the exhaustion in her expression, she smiled.

58

Landon sat behind his large mahogany desk. His office was usually a place where he felt in control. Looking at FBI Director Shaw sitting across from him, her face a mask of stern resolve, he no longer had that feeling. It felt more like a cage, the walls closing in as the conversation unfolded.

"I am not sure what it was like for you, Landon, but I can still remember what it was like when I first heard about the possibility of human consciousness being found. At first, I was cynical. I did not believe it, commenting that if that were true then goodbye to any semblance of the world we live in. But then I became scared by it. I mean, what would it mean, and what would happen if it could be weaponised? Because, well, that's what we do as humans, who crave power over others," Director Shaw said.

Landon's heart pounded in his chest, but he kept his expression neutral. He had been preparing for this moment, yet the reality of it was suffocating. He and Director Barrett had been working in the shadows, developing a weapon so powerful it could bring nations to their knees. Their plan had been to steal it, use it to blackmail governments, and manipulate global events to their advantage.

But now, it seemed, the jig was up. Director Shaw had never set foot in this room without a formal invitation or a critical need, and her unannounced presence now could only mean one thing: they had finally connected the dots. The weight of his clandestine activities, the secretive development of the weapon, and the intricate web of deceit he had woven were about to unravel. The Director's stern gaze and deliberate silence spoke volumes.

Landon's mind raced, the façade of control slipping away as he realised there was no escape from the reckoning that had finally arrived. He stayed silent, however; he was not one to give up information easily.

Director Shaw leaned forward, staring him down. "The decision seemed simple. If it was true, and technology was going to be built to isolate it, then that needed to be done in house, with only very few people knowing about it. Then we could control the exposure to the concept."

Another pause. Landon continued to stay silent. He was not about to say anything until a point was made.

"What I never imagined was this level of treachery from within the system. I mean, it is one thing to not let other agencies be involved, but to pretend something has gone missing, and pretend to be investigating it, while all along planning how to use the technology to manipulate world events for your own financial benefit? That is a whole other level, don't you think, Landon?"

There it was.

"It is a very dangerous game you and Director Barrett have been playing," Director Shaw added.

"I don't know what you're talking about," Landon said, his voice steady, betraying none of the turmoil inside him.

"I do admire your audacity," Director Shaw continued, ignoring Landon's denial. "I mean, when you found out that Dr. Taylor and Dr. Gray were planning to steal what you had stolen, and expose it, that must have sent shockwaves through your plans. But you didn't let that bother you, did you, Landon? You figured you might as well keep going with the plan and start using the machine even though you didn't have access to the database. That showed absolute faith that you would get the drive back."

Landon stayed silent, his mind racing as he tried to work out how he could make a deal. He knew he had to tread carefully, weighing his options while Director Shaw's piercing gaze bore into him. Every second of silence felt like an eternity as he assessed the situation, considering what information he could leverage. He thought about the key players he could sacrifice, the secrets he could divulge, and the strings he could pull to secure some semblance of safety for himself. His career, his freedom, his very life was on the line, and he needed to navigate this conversation with the utmost care.

The Director didn't blink.

"Staying silent will do nothing for you. We have witnesses, Landon. We have documents. We have enough to bring you down."

Landon was rocked by Director Shaw's claims: witnesses, documents, what could she have against him? The realisation hit Landon like a slap in the face—the FBI had the drive.

All he could do was stare at her. His face must have been readable, because the Director spoke again.

"But I'm giving you a choice. You can make a deal with me. Give up everyone involved in this, including the locations of everything, in return for saving yourself and your career. Your other option is going to prison, and we will continue on with our investigation."

Landon's mind raced. He thought of Director Barrett, the mastermind behind their plan. He thought of the years they had spent developing the weapon, the risks they had taken, and the people they had manipulated. He thought of his own career, his reputation, everything he had worked for. He thought about the fact he knew that in his position, Director Barrett would throw them all to the wolves in a heartbeat.

"Why are you offering me this deal?" Landon asked, buying time as he weighed his options.

Director Shaw's expression softened slightly, a hint of the personal stakes in this matter showing through. "Because despite everything, I actually believe you could still be useful. You are a very smart man, Landon, and you know how to work inside the intelligence community. I believe you can make the right choice. And frankly, because we need this to end without causing a scandal that could shake the very foundations of our intelligence community. This is bigger than you or me, Landon. This technology is going to get exposed. When it does, those people who are part of this thing are never going to see the light of day again."

Landon leaned back in his chair, his eyes drifting to the window where the city sprawled out beneath them. He had always prided himself on his loyalty to his country, his willingness to do whatever it took to protect it. But somewhere along the way, he had lost sight of that, seduced by power and ambition.

He turned back to Director Shaw. "If I make this deal, I need assurances. I need to know that my family will be safe, that my career won't be completely destroyed. I need to know that I won't be left out to dry."

Director Shaw nodded. "You have my word on that. You'll be protected, and we'll handle this quietly. But you need to give me everything. Names, dates, locations. Everything."

Landon took a deep breath, feeling the weight of his decision. Strangely, he felt like a fog had been lifted from his mind. He thought of the device, the destruction it could cause in the wrong hands. His had become the wrong hands—from what he'd become.

"Alright," he said finally, his voice barely above a whisper. "I'll make the deal."

Director Shaw stood and extended her hand. Landon followed suit, sealing his fate with a firm shake. As their hands clasped, Landon felt a mix of relief and resignation.

"I'll have my team contact you with the details. Thank you, Landon. You're doing the right thing."

Landon watched Director Shaw, walk to the door of his office, while he sat back down on his chair. When she opened the door, two agents walked in to take him away. He had made his choice, but the path ahead was uncertain. He could only hope that, in the end, he could find a way to make amends for the mistakes he had made.

59

Harper sat in the middle of a row of seats, three rows back from the podium where CIA Director Chris Barrett was delivering his speech about integrity in the security sector. The conference hall was filled with an attentive audience, their faces reflecting varying degrees of interest and scepticism. Harper had only ever seen Director Barrett in action on TV before, but even then, she had recognised his charisma—his ability to command a room. Today, though, she watched him with particular intensity. She had reason to scrutinise every word, every nuance.

He began with the usual platitudes, acknowledging the growing call for more transparency within the security sector. His voice was measured, calm, and persuasive.

"Transparency is crucial," he stated, pausing to let the words sink in. "It builds trust between the agencies and the public, and I wholeheartedly support it. That's why we are in the process of implementing new measures within the CIA to ensure greater transparency."

Harper noted the murmurs of approval from the crowd. The Director's words were carefully chosen, designed to appeal to the audience's desire for openness and honesty. He spoke of new protocols, reviews, and audits that would ostensibly make the CIA more accountable.

But Harper knew better.

She had seen the darker side of this business, the secrets and lies that lay beneath the surface.

Then his tone shifted subtly, taking on a more serious note.

"However," he continued, "it must be acknowledged, even from those calling for change, that there are certain aspects of our work that, if made public without context, could result in misunderstanding and potentially jeopardise national security. It is vital that some matters be managed internally within security agencies to ensure that when the information is released it is done so in the most appropriate manner."

Harper felt a chill run down her spine. This was the crux of his speech, the underlying message masked by his earlier promises of transparency. The Director was laying the groundwork for selective disclosure, for controlling the narrative under the guise of protecting the public. His words were a carefully crafted mix of reassurance and veiled warning.

"The safety of Americans," he went on, "must always be our top priority. Sometimes, this means withholding certain information until it can be presented in a way that is clear and does not incite unnecessary fear or confusion. This is not about hiding the truth; it's about ensuring that the truth is understood correctly and that it serves the greater good."

Harper clenched her jaw, her mind racing. She knew all too well what "managing internally" meant. It meant secrets, cover-ups, and a selective truth that served the interests of those in power. In other words, nothing was going to change. She watched the audience, seeing nods of agreement, expressions of trust. They were buying it, just as Director Barrett intended.

As he wrapped up his speech, Harper couldn't help but feel a surge of determination. She had pieces of the puzzle the Director would kill to keep buried. Director Barrett did not know the FBI had set up the question-and-answer to start with her, for as long as she needed. In fact, one of the microphones being used for the questions was already sitting in her lap.

Director Barrett finished to a round of applause, staying at the podium, his smile a polished mask of confidence that covered over his true self. It was now time for the questions portion of the evening. The time when he would be caught in his own web of lies.

An announcer, smartly dressed in a navy suit, walked onto the stage, his presence commanding attention. He cleared his throat, his voice resonating through the hall's sound system.

"Ladies and gentlemen, we will now take questions from the audience," he announced, a warm smile spreading across his face. "To start us off, the first question will come from the young lady sitting there, in the middle of the third row," he said, pointing to Harper.

All eyes turned to Harper, who stood up, her heart pounding with a mix of nerves and determination. She felt the weight of the moment as she prepared to challenge Director Barrett, ready to cut through the carefully crafted facade of his earlier remarks. Time to stir the hornet's nest.

"Hello, Director Barrett. Is it true that a scientist by the name of Dr. Jonathan Taylor discovered human consciousness—and was able to successfully isolate it?" she asked directly, her voice loud and confident.

Shock and awe ran through the audience, followed by murmurs and conversation, questions and non-answers.

Director Barrett took a measured breath, his expression neutral, like a rock, despite the gravity of the question, yet his eyes were that of a deer caught in the headlights. Harper knew that he would have to have an answer if his plan came out in some way. That is what the Director of the CIA was good at. Not answering direct questions about operations.

"Well, damn, that's a hell of a question," Director Barrett said, holding his hands up in mock surprise.

As he looked around the room, Harper could feel the gravity of the question she had just asked slipping away. As people began questioning their own reaction.

"It sounds to me like you have been watching too many science fiction movies," he said with a smile. A warm, friendly, slightly patronising smile.

Harper's question could not have been answered any better, or worse, depending on which side of the fence you sat. As the soft chuckle from people in the crowd was beginning to build into more global laughter, Harper knew she had to move on quickly.

"And isn't it true that you have been creating the technology to strip a person's consciousness from their bodies, and store that consciousness on a database, allowing that entity to be interacted with as if they were a living sentient consciousness?" Harper said, her mouth pressed firmly against the mic, so her words could be clearly heard.

The crowd fell instantly silent.

Director Barrett looked to his right, towards the side of the stage, at the announcer, and shook his head, lifting his arms up as to question what was happening. "Is this really going to be the nature of the questions here tonight?" he said. "I think we should move on to the next questioner," he added.

Harper continued. "And, Director, is it true that you have stolen this technology and created a rogue faction of the CIA, which has not only developed the device, but has successfully used it on the First Lady?"

The room erupted into chaos. Voices rose in a crescendo of outrage and disbelief, the audience's collective reaction to the startling allegation against the CIA Director. Some people stood, demanding answers, while others exchanged heated whispers, their faces etched with concern and suspicion. The announcer tried to restore order, but his voice was drowned out by the clamour. Reporters thrust their microphones forward, desperate to capture every word of the unfolding turmoil. Amid the uproar, Harper remained steadfast, her gaze locked on the Director, knowing this was just the beginning of a much deeper confrontation.

Director Barrett finally held up his hands in an attempt to quieten the crowd. "Please, ladies and gentlemen, can we have some semblance of order…please," his voice ringing through the speaker system with a command that showed him to be the formidable figure people thought.

"That's quite a significant question, or claim, shall we say," he began, his voice steady. "I am aware of Dr. Jonathan Taylor. He has been working in the field of human consciousness for many a decade. As you can imagine, the field of human consciousness is one of immense interest and complexity."

He paused, allowing the weight of his next words to sink in.

"I cannot comment on the questions you raise, because they… well, quite frankly, are too complex to fully digest here on this stage, tonight. I can, however, assure you that the United States is committed to advancing scientific knowledge in a manner that ensures both ethical standards and the safety of our citizens. The idea of isolating human consciousness is profound and, if true, would represent a monumental shift in our understanding of human identity and technology."

Director Barrett's eyes conveyed a mixture of authority and carefully measured openness. "Any developments in this area would be handled with the utmost caution and responsibility. It is crucial that such advancements are not misused or misunderstood. Our goal is always to protect the American people and maintain global stability."

Harper knew he would have to deflect, yet not deny outright. The truth, buried deep within layers of classified operations, would be too dangerous to reveal, especially if he was involved in clandestine operations.

"To directly address your question, while there is always ongoing research and development in various advanced scientific fields, any suggestion of weaponising such discoveries is purely speculative. Our focus remains on the well-being and security of our nation."

His tone softened slightly. "Transparency is important, but so is discretion, especially when dealing with matters that could have far-reaching consequences. Rest assured, we are always working in the best interests of the American people."

Director Barret smiled. He looked very happy with his answer to her questions.

If Harper had to guess, she would say that he answered her questions perfectly. She would have no angle with which to approach follow-up questions. Good thing she had other more compelling things to show the Director, and the audience, who were at this stage enthralled with the impromptu interrogation they were witnessing.

Behind the Director, the large screen that had been, to date, left unattended, came to life. Harper smiled, as she saw the image of Dr. Taylor appear. He was sitting in what looked to be a cozy living room. He was in his late sixties, sitting on a couch, a time-worn piece of furniture that had moulded perfectly to his frame over the years.

His hair, a mix of silver and white, framed a face lined with the marks of time and experience. Deep-set, kind eyes peered through a pair of round spectacles perched on his nose, reflecting the soft glow of the nearby lamp. He wore a well-loved cardigan over a button-down shirt, the sleeves slightly frayed, and comfortable trousers. His hands, slightly weathered and showing the faint tremor of age, rested on the armrests as he leaned back, sinking into the familiar comfort of the couch. Surrounding him were framed photographs and trinkets, mementos of a life rich with memories. He exuded an air of quiet contentment, finding solace in the familiar embrace of his favourite spot in the house. He was looking out of the screen, as if he was looking directly down the lens of a camera.

The audience went instantly silent.

"Your answer, Director Barrett, while extremely well crafted, was at its core, completely misleading," the image of Dr Taylor said.

The Director turned around to look at the screen, the shock of seeing the image showing on his face, as with everyone in the room.

"While it might be considered science-fiction fantasy, I am here to tell you that it is anything but," the image of Dr Taylor said.

"Good evening," he began, his voice resonating through the speakers. "I know many of you have been told that the idea of isolating human consciousness is mere science fiction. And then being able to extract it and store it inside a database to be totally laughable. But I am here to tell you otherwise. The technology is real, and I am the 'living' proof."

A collective gasp rippled through the audience. Dr. Taylor's eyes, filled with a mixture of determination and sorrow, scanned the room. "What you see before you is not a recording or a simulation. My consciousness has been transferred into this digital realm. Every thought, every memory, every aspect of my identity has been preserved within a database that I designed and implemented."

He paused, allowing the gravity of his words to sink in. "This technology, while groundbreaking, carries immense ethical implications. Transferring myself into this database, I did out of necessity. I implore you, however, to consider the consequences and the responsibilities that come with it. I am both a testament to its potential and a warning of its dangers."

Director Barrett turned to look back at the audience, then over to where the announcer was standing. "What the fuck is this!" he said, directed at the announcer.

"This, Chris Barrett, Director of the CIA, is your lead scientist, who you had develop the technology that I discovered, under threat of my family, only to discover that you were planning to kill me and my family anyway, and the rest of the development team, so you could steal it for yourself. Something that I could not let happen," Dr Taylor said, addressing him directly.

The crowd lost it. Total meltdown. People were yelling, crying, and praying. Some left the auditorium, unable to handle what they had just seen.

But Harper sat still, watching. For her, this was about justice. For Isabella, who gave her life. For the private detective who had refused to stop asking questions. For the officers who had believed. And for a world teetering on the edge of madness—but not quite fallen.

Harper watched as Director Barrett scanned the room with growing unease. The uproar from the audience had reached fever pitch, his position precarious. Seeking a discreet escape, he began to make his way to the nearest exit. Harper saw at the same time as he did, FBI agents, standing firm and blocking the doorway. She watched Director Barrett's eyes dart to the other exits, all blocked. Harper smiled, watching with pleasure as his carefully constructed facade cracked, realisation dawning that the net was closing in. He was trapped, the truth he had so meticulously concealed unravelling in the most public and damning way possible.

60

Sam leaned against the polished wooden bar, waiting for the bartender to finish pouring the last beer of his order. The bar was dimly lit, a cozy haven from the bustling streets outside. He was idly looking up at the television, mounted in the top corner framed by an array of colourful neon lights. A news report came on, featuring an image of the First Lady addressing the camera with a composed and solemn expression. The bartender placed the last drink of his order on the tray.

"Hey, mind turning that up a little?" Sam asked, his interest piqued.

The bartender grabbed the remote and pointed it towards the screen. The sound increased to a point where Sam could hear it, but it did not overpower the ambience of the room. "That good enough?" the bartender asked.

Sam nodded his approval.

The First Lady spoke about the development of technology that could transfer human consciousness back into a biological body, a claim that had sparked widespread ethical debates. Sam was caught by the seriousness of what she was saying, the implications of such technology resonating deeply with the recent events they had all been involved in. She spoke about the ethical concerns with a measured tone, emphasising the need for stringent safeguards and oversight. Sam shook his head slightly, contemplating the weight of the technology's potential and the ethical quagmire it presented.

Shaking off his thoughts, Sam grabbed the tray of drinks, a refreshing assortment for his group. He maneuvered through the people, his gaze fixed on his companions gathered at a corner table. The group included Emily, now his wife, who looked radiant, and Gloria, with her keen eyes observing the room. Next to her sat Vince, the grizzly old man who had taken the concept of human consciousness being discovered and extracted completely in his stride, who was absorbed in conversation with Harper. Thompson and Miller rounded out the group, their expressions relaxed but alert.

Sam approached the table, setting down the tray with a cheerful clink. He handed out drinks, making sure Emily got her lime and soda, which she accepted with a grateful, knowing smile. The ring that she had purchased years before proudly displayed for all to see on her finger. As he settled into his seat, the hum of conversation filled the air, mingling with the background music that played softly.

"Alright, everyone," Sam announced, raising his glass and capturing the group's attention. "I have some news to share." His voice was steady, but excitement tingled his words. "Emily and I are expecting our first child."

For a moment, silence.

Then cheers erupted followed by laughter and congratulations. Emily's eyes sparkled. Glasses were raised. Hugs were exchanged.

Emily's eyes sparkled with joy, and the group leaned in, eager to celebrate this new chapter in their lives.

And for a brief, perfect moment—after all the danger and loss, with the truth revealed—the weight of the world lifted.

They had made it.